Rites of Spring

Jonathan Reuvid

Published by New Generation Publishing in 2021

Copyright © Jonathan Reuvid 2021

First Edition

Paperback ISBN: 978-1-80369-047-6
Ebook ISBN: 978-1-80369-048-3

www.newgeneration-publishing.com

New Generation Publishing

Author's Note

This book is set in the context of an American multinational corporation with manufacturing subsidiaries in Europe and Latin America over three months in 1978. It was a very different business environment then; by today's standards communications were primitive. There was no worldwide web, no email and no search engines to access information. Written communication was confined to the telex - a kind of cumbersome self-originated telegram transmitted through international telephone lines – or by sending documents through Federal Express, American Express or other courier services. Facsimile telecopying did not come into common usage for several years yet. Consequently, the life of the international manager with line responsibilities working across many countries involved constant travel for face-to-face discussions and meetings including the dreaded 'corporate review' when teams of senior executives were jetted in across the Atlantic to cross-question local management on its performance. The glamour of living well out of a suitcase at the company's expense did not compensate for regular absences from home. I hope that a flavour of this false lifestyle is conveyed in the book.

The criminal events described in Germany and elsewhere are fictitious although not entirely implausible. The villages of Leuffen and Hohenleuffen where much of the action takes place do not exist; nor, to the best of my knowledge, do the private houses or factories anywhere. Other locations are real and were much as I have described them in 1978. References to events of World War II and terrorists in the 1970s are largely accurate. Any resemblance that the characters who inhabit these pages may have to persons living or dead are, of course, coincidental.

JR

CAST OF CHARACTERS

London

Tom Hardy	Director of European Operations, Allied Autoparts
Julian Radclive	European Director of Marketing, Allied Autoparts
Gaby Radclive	Julian's wife and a market research manager
Molly Fellows	Administrator and Secretary, Allied Autoparts London office
Stelios Patarkis	Proprietor of a Bayswater taverna

Tipton

Bernard Tompkins	Sales Director, Tipton Springs
Nora Tompkins	Bernard Tompkins' wife
Gladys Clegg	Their daughter
Arthur Tompkins	Their son
Alfred Clegg	A Wolverhampton solicitor and husband of Gladys
Cyril Snell	General Manager, Tipton Springs
Gerald Jarvis	Accounts Manager, Tipton Springs

Sussex

Bill Fentiman	A country solicitor and old friend of Julian Radclive
Barbara Fentiman	His wife
Max Salinger	A retired diplomat
Miranda Salinger	Barbara Fentiman's aunt and husband of Max Salinger
Baron Konrad von Richthaven	A steel magnate and racehorse owner
Magda von Richthaven	A celebrated hostess and wife of the Baron

Leuffen, Germany

Manfred Hartmann	Retired chairman of Hartmann & Holst GmbH,
Peter Hartmann	General Manager of Hartmann & Holst and his son
Dr. Heinrich Hoffmeyer	Technical Manager, Hartmann & Holst
Ethel Hoffmeyer	Heinrich Hoffman's wife
Dieter Trautman	Accounts Manager, Hartmann & Holst
Gottfried Klinger	Warehouse Manager, Hartmann & Holst
Johann Glock	Warehouseman and driver
Frau Päsche	Secretary to Peter Hartmann
Otto Krantz	Proprietor of Leuffen Gasthof
Brigitta Krantz	His voluptuous daughter

Stuttgart and Munich

Klaus Kramm	Polizeihauptmeister, Stuttgart
Kurt Vogel	Kommissar, Stuttgart Landespolizei
Ernst Bloch	Senior Purchasing Manager, Mercedes-Benz Research and Development, Sindelfingen
Wolfgang Kessler	President, Kamaradenwerke
Willi Schmitt	His Assistant

Campinas and Rio de Janeiro

Count Frederik von Falkenburg	General Manager of Grunwald Metallwerk, Amparo
Izabel	His companion
Luiz Otavio	His steward
Oskar Holst	Manager if the Amparo spring factory
Roderigo Morales	An import and export trader in coffee

Farmington, USA

Chester Case	Chairman of Allied Autoparts
Barry MacLennan	President of Allied Autoparts
Lloyd Parmentier Jr	Vice-President International
Erik Nielsen	Vice-President Finance
Loren Corley	Vice-President Engineering
Bennett Pullman	Director of Group Marketing

Shelley Frankel	Director of Procurement
Donna Fairweather	PA to the Chairman
Viktor Accona	Adviser to Carter Charles on Human Relations
Bill Banks	Pilot of Allied Autoparts Learjet

The Latin American Office, Mexico

Ronaldo Martini	Director of Latin American Operations
Oswaldo Carioca	Latin American Director of Marketing

Ribenda, Amsterdam

Jan van de Groot	General Manager
Bruin Brouwer	Sales Manager

AA Norrköpping

Ola Larsen	General Manager

The Prologue

USUALLY HE DIDN'T leave the factory early but today he wanted to telephone to Europe without risk of eavesdropping on the office switchboard or any tracing of the call later to his direct line. And so he was sitting comfortably in the high back desk chair in his study at the house in Amparo as he checked the local time in Baden Wurttemberg. It was 1930 there against 1430 here in Brazil's Campinas region, a good time to call the old man, before dinner and without interrupting his evening routine.

He dialled 0049 followed by the local ex-directory number. The call was picked up at the third ring; a familiar vice spoke: "The house of the family Hartmann. Good evening".

"This is the Oberst's friend from Brazil, Gunther. Please pass me to him," he said. A short interval and then the voice that he knew so well, a little frailer now but still strong and incisive.

"Frederik, I have been waiting for your news. Have the Americans arrived yet? We had our first encounter with their senior management team this week."

"Good evening, Manfred. Contracts were completed on Tuesday and the money paid into our notary's account for distribution to shareholders, but so far we have met only their legal counsel and the director of their technical centre has toured the factory. We have time to reorganize our next special shipment before their management team is parachuted upon us".

"That's good. The eagle has not yet landed here, as our English friends say, but the time is short," Manfred Hartmann replied in measured tones "We can handle just

one more shipment from Germany by the usual route. It will be dangerous but I am sure that I can count on Gottfried and his group to handle the procurement, packaging and despatch by container. After that the risk will be too great and you shall have to find another route. How confident are you, Frederik, of being able to receive our shipment and to complete the exchange?"

"I do not have the same reliable staff here as you, Manfred, but our customers are very efficient and we use their people to handle the receipt and all onward movements of your valuable cargo and return product. It is well known that not respecting their instructions is unwise and can be fatal. I shall be ready to work to your timing," he added.

"Very well, we set the schedule here and organize the logistics. It will be the biggest and last shipment we can manage. I will advise you of the arrangements in twenty days' time. Good night, Frederik".

"Gruss Gott, Manfred, und uber alles."

Von Falkenburg replaced his receiver and reflected. Probably three months before the shipment would be delivered to the factory beyond Amparo but time for him to make plans for his own future welfare and continued prosperity. Since his departure from Germany as a young man in 1945 by courtesy of the Vatican Ratline he had built himself a secure position here in Brazil with his shareholding in partnership with the Grunwald brothers in the metalworking factory which they had founded in the 1930s when they too had fled Germany with their families in the early days of the Third Reich. As general manager of Grunwald Metallwerk, a respected member of the local business community and with his house within its protected compound here in Amparo, von Falkenburg was as under cover and safe as he could hope to be from those who might seek his extradition. Now, following acquisition of the company by the US multinational Allied Autoparts Inc the foundations of his current way of life were shaken. As a part of the deal he remained general manager but who knew what complications working with the Americans would bring. Much food for thought, he considered, but no cause for hasty decisions which he would regret later.

Meantime, a little light entertainment was in order. Frederik picked up the house phone and buzzed his assistant who doubled as housekeeper and butler. "Luiz Otavio," he said "Have Izabel come to the house for dinner tonight and send the car to collect her at 8:00 p.m. Oh, and tell her to bring the clothes to change into later for our special party game."

---ooo0ooo---

Manfred Hartmann reflected rather more deeply when he had disconnected. Taking a bottle of ice-cold Mathusalem Belvedere Vodka from the refrigerator behind the fake panel of books in his library he poured himself a generous shot and took stock of his current position. For more than 30 years he had laboured hard to build the family business in partnership with his old friend Jurgen Holst who had served with him in the Wehrmacht from the Afrika Korps to the final days of the war here in Baden Wurttemberg when he was appointed Commandant of the Allied officers POW camp after injuries on the Russian front. Holst had been a highly qualified engineer before the war and rose happily to the challenge of starting a factory to manufacture critical metal parts for the recovering German motorcar industry. He, Hartmann, had negotiated the purchase of the POW camp in 1946 from the local government and planned its conversion into a factory, handling the bureaucratic and political complications with his customary people skills and mastery of detail. Holst had recruited from the ranks of their old regimental engineering corps the skilled workforce they needed for the toolroom, to operate the machines and to design the products and the factory under his management.

Over 30 years Hartmann & Holst Gmbh had prospered mightily in common with the many other family-owned companies of the Mittelstand, the dynamo of the German economic miracle. They had become a trusted supplier to Daimler Benz, Opel and most recently Volkswagen. Then, five years ago, there had been a surprise call from the local representative of the Kameradenwerk. Would Hartmann & Holst be interested in acquiring a factory in Brazil to supply the local plants of German motor manufacturers already installed there? That seemed an attractive proposition because it offered the opportunity to penetrate major customers further, particularly Volkswagen. So Manfred Hartmann had flown to Sao Paulo to see for himself and had negotiated with the owners of Grunwald Metallwerk. He'd known Count von Falkenburg in Berlin during the war and disliked the man, what he did and the organisation in which he had served. Hartmann was dimly aware that he had been registered as a war criminal and had fled to South America; he never expected to meet the man again.

Nevertheless, business was business and the opportunity too good to pass up. However, being a cautious man, Hartmann had put aside the option of an outright acquisition and negotiated instead a co-manufacturing joint venture between Grunwald Metallwerk for his company to exploit the Brazilian market to supply components to original equipment manufacturers. And for the first year the venture had proved productive with the highest specification parts supplied from Germany and some less technical parts manufactured at lower cost in Brazil shipped back to Germany for resale to Hartmann & Holst customers.

Then von Falkenburg had introduced his hidden agenda for shipments to Campinas of valuable contraband and onward disposal. The profits from this illegal traffic were so high that Hartmann had buried his scruples and gone along with the plan. He had been able to delude himself that he was engaged in a harmless form of money laundering until quite recently when von Falkenburg had revealed that there was no possibility of applying whitewash since the proceeds in Brazil were "laundered" through the local drug trade. Of course, the disclosure was deliberate; as von Falkenburg had reminded him with satisfaction, Hartmann & Holst were too deeply involved to escape.

Shortly after the extent of their entanglement became clear Otto Holst suffered a series of increasingly severe strokes and had died aged 69. Whether this was the result of an elderly man overworking or the additional stress of carrying the burden of criminal activity Hartmann would never know, but he suspected the latter. Whatever the cause, it had been time for a radical re-think. Now 72 himself, he had no appetite for pursuing the adventure although there was a natural succession with his son Peter now working in the business. The solution was to sell the company which would force von Falkenburg to suspend his present trafficking. Therefore, Hartmann approached Allied Autoparts with a proposal to expand their activities in Europe by securing a foothold in the lucrative German market. The plan had worked better than expected. Not only had the Americans purchased the shares of his company at a handsome price but had satisfied their territorial ambitions further by making an offer to purchase Grunwald Metallwerk, an offer that was gratefully accepted by the Grunwald brothers albeit with less enthusiasm by von Falkenburg as a minority shareholder.

Well, escape was on the horizon, if not actually in sight. Manfred Hartmann walked on to the terrace outside his library and gazed with satisfaction from the only habitable wing of Hohenleuffen Castle on the rim of the Schwabian Jura with its spectacular view of the plain below. Far below through the clear evening air he could see the swimming pool of the health spa at Leuffen and beyond he could make out the roofs of the factory on the road to Nurtingen with the river Neckar winding its way in the distance. His *favourite panorama always afforded satisfaction. The evening was turning chilly; so he turned and refilled his glass with Methusalem Belvedere, adding this time a measure of tonic water. Vodka, he reflected, was the only good thing ever to come out of Poland.*

----ooo0ooo----

Part One

CHAPTER 1

2 May 1978, Germany

THE LUFTHANSA FLIGHT FROM HEATHROW touched down at Stuttgart Flughafen precisely on schedule at 1435, an immaculately smooth landing as the tyres rolled on concrete and the engines powered down. It was my first visit to Germany, except for attendance at a Frankfurt Trade Fair, since serving in the Rhine Army nearly 20 years before. At my side in the window seat Bernard Tomkins, ever impatient to get going, unlatched his seat belt while the bulkhead lights warning passengers to remain seated lit up.

I had expected the aircraft to complete a half turn off the runway to the left before taxiing towards one of the disembarkation points at the distant airport terminal but instead it turned right and trundled towards the airfield perimeter. At the same time a crackle of automatic gunfire broke out from the direction of the buildings and, by peering across Bernard through his window, I could see a mass of blue and white police cars with flashing roof lights to the the left. To the right, among a cluster of small, private aircraft on the other side of the main building, I detected movement from a handful of people as their return fire erupted. We were witnesses to an unscheduled gun battle.

"Keep your seat belts on," intoned the pilot on his intercom "There will be a short delay while order is restored." The flight attendants moving up and down the aisle tried to maintain composure but could not match their pilot's studied calm. The flight was not full and those of us on the left-hand side had a grandstand view of proceedings. It took almost an hour before gunfire ceased and a detachment of heavily armed police who had circled the terminal subdued the gunmen and led them to waiting police cars. Our pilot restarted the engines and taxied us to the terminal. There was no comment from him as we retrieved our hand luggage from the racks above us and disembarked other than the customary "Thank you for flying Lufthansa. We look forward to you flying with us again soon."

Only while we were in the baggage hall waiting for our heavy luggage to come up on the carousel was an explanation forthcoming when Bernard buttonholed a customs official. "Surviving members of the Baader Meinhof Gang or Red Army Faction," we were told "trying to escape by stealing a plane."

"That sort of thing would never happen in England," was Bernard's verdict as we drove down the autobahn in the VW Golf hired on my Hertz card at the terminal. We were finally able to depart for Leuffen close to 1600 hours. In the few weeks that I had known him, Bernard's stalwart Britishness was a constant source of amusement. However, his mindset in no way detracted from his effectiveness as a salesman. A small rotund figure with the birdlike mannerisms of a robin redbreast, Bernard was sales director of Tipton Springs, the Midlands Black Country subsidiary that Associated Autoparts had acquired some five years previously to gain its foothold in the UK market. Similar acquisitions in Sweden and the Netherlands in pursuit of its international growth strategy had been followed by the recent purchase of the German factory that we were now visiting. Bernard's sales technique was based on a complete mastery of the products he was selling supplemented by a detailed knowledge of the buyer and his family's habits, likes and dislikes, children's schooling and pastimes down to the details of family holidays. Armed with this encyclopaedic body of knowledge, he was able to build strong personal relationships which helped him to gain trust and consequent orders. Rather unkindly perhaps, I had characterised his technique as "mastery of the controlled grovel." The strategy was not as mercenary as it sounded; Bernard genuinely liked people and making friends.

Quite soon we turned off the autobahn at the exit signposted Kircheim unter Teck which was where our route lay and then dropped down to the outskirts of Nürtingen. As we joined the main road entering the town we were overtaken at speed by a large white Mercedes Benz which had to brake sharply to avoid oncoming traffic, causing me to jam on our brakes too . "Typical selfish Mercedes road hog," snorted Bernard "I'll give him a piece of my mind if we ever catch up with him."

"There's a long queue of road hogs before him in my little black book," I replied. "Sadly, one never meets and seldom sees them again." We crossed the river Neckar flowing sluggishly as we entered the town and then exited by a secondary road with Leuffen signposted as some 20 km distant. "Apparently the factory is on the right shortly before we reach the village."

And so it proved to be. With a billboard at the open gateway proclaiming that this was the home of Hartmann & Holst GmbH, the factory presented itself as a sprawling campus of single storey wooden buildings in the foreground with several larger brick and concrete buildings at the rear. The factory's origins as a military camp were apparent at first glance. Close to the entrance and tethered firmly to the ground was an unusual inflated grey structure resembling a blimp or World War I zeppelin. I drove in and parked at one of the visitor slots outside the timber framed main office building. There were half a dozen other cars alongside including one large white Mercedes Benz. Before mounting the steps to reception I confirmed that its bonnet was still warm. "Julian Radclive and Bernard Tompkins from London," I announced to the middle-aged receptionist who greeted us. "Herr Hartmann is expecting us".

The large room into which we were ushered doubled as boardroom and general manager's office with matching teak furniture. Poor natural light was supplemented by electric light from wall-mounted sconces and a handsome brass desk lamp. The two men who rose to greet us from the nearer end of the long boardroom table contrasted sharply. The tall, heavily built figure of Tom Hardy, Director of European Operations, dominated any room in which he was standing. The other, whom I took to be Peter Hartmann, of lesser height and prematurely balding was wearing a green tweed suit of a definitely non-British cut. Tom had sat in at one of the interviews for my appointment six weeks earlier, giving the misleading impression then of an amiable Norfolk farmer judging livestock at a county fair. He came forward now to greet us with crushing handshakes.

"Glad to see you both," he said. "You're late, of course, but we heard of the little excitement at the Flughafen; so not unexpected. This is Peter Hartmann who has only just arrived and these, Peter, are Julian Radclive from our London office," he continued "and Bernard Tompkins, Sales Director from your UK sister factory at Tipton."

Hartmann's comparatively limp handshake was accompanied by a formal declaration.

"Welcome to Leuffen and the home of German quality springmaking," he asserted with more than a hint of arrogance "Tomorrow, we shall show you how it is done."

Ignoring the challenge I replied "Hello, Peter, we nearly met you just now on the road into Nürtingen. Bernard was full of admiration for your car's acceleration." Bernard cast me an old-fashioned look but did not rise to the bait, while Tom looked amused sensing the implied criticism. A hooter sounded from the direction of the factory forestalling any comment that Bernard might have made about the Mercedes or its driver.

"Well that signals the end of the production working day," confirmed Tom picking up the papers he had been studying when we arrived. "I spent the afternoon with Dr. Hoffmeyer in the factory discussing the capital equipment that he proposes for next year's budget and I'll want your comments on it in the morning, Peter." Then, turning to

Bernard and me "I'll check you both into the Gasthof, and we can take an early dinner together."

---oooOooo---

While Peter Hartmann sped off in his white Mercedes, Tom preceded us in his car to the centre of the village where we parked in a small square opposite the Leuffener Gasthof, an ancient oak-beamed building with its four upper storeys bulging out in successive tiers. "Like a stage set from the Student Prince," commented Bernard. "But solid as well as picturesque," added Tom.

We were met in the entrance hall of the inn by a flamboyant figure in a red jumpsuit, a large girl with ginger hair, which clashed with the colour of her clothes; the gold sandals that adorned her feet were encrusted with rhinestones.

"This is Brigitta," said Tom introducing us "Herr Kranz's daughter and mistress of all she surveys." Brigitta seemed doubtful whether this was a compliment or joke but chose to respond with dignity

"Herren Hardy, Radclive and Tompkins, your rooms are ready. I will show the way".

And with that she picked up a heavy suitcase in each hand and bounded up the stairs. Although Tom still towered over her, Brigitta matched me in height at over six feet and I found it difficult to keep pace as she galloped ahead. Bernard struggled noisily to keep up in the rear. As a regular guest, Tom was housed on the second floor with Bernard and myself on the floor above.

Our rooms were sparsely furnished but immaculately clean and with large beds and voluminous duvets. We each had our own shoebox of a bathroom. Forty-five minutes later, showered and more casually clothed, I descended to explore the main living area, a bar and dining room combined. Tom was already there chatting to another large figure behind the bar. "Ah, Julian, Come and meet our host, Otto Kranz."

"Willkommen, Herr Radclive. I hope my daughter Brigitta has looked after you." His English was guttural but fluent; Otto Kranz wiped enormous hands on his apron and extended a bunch of banana-like fingers across his bar which I grasped as firmly as I could in mine.

Looking at him directly, I stifled any reaction. His face bore a deep scar from above his left eyebrow across the bridge of his nose and down his cheek to the right hand corner of his mouth. Plastic surgery had done little to mellow this fearsome countenance, particularly when he smiled, as he was doing now.

"Thank you, Herr Krantz, I'm sure that I shall be very comfortable," was the best I could manage noting that while his right eye flickered towards the door where Bernard had just appeared, its its mate stayed fixed upon me.

Having supplied Bernard with a beer, Tom led the three of us to a table against the wall at the back of the room where we settled down. "What happened to him?" queried Bernard nodding in the direction of the bar.

"A somewhat unusual story," Tom explained "In the final stages of the war, when the Americans were closing in, Otto was a despatch rider delivering orders one night from German headquarters across US Army front lines to the Kommandant of the camp here at Leuffen. Speeding through the woods he encountered a wire set across the road by an American forward patrol which caught him across the face and unseated him. He finished up in an American military field hospital which did their best for him."

"What happened to him then? Did he finish up as a POW?" I queried.

"Well, he was classified as a POW but he had served here as a lad at this inn which his father owned before the war. So, an American colonel, who was careful of his creature comforts in wartime, sent him to the old Kaserne Barracks at Stuttgart which they had taken over to serve as a steward in the officers' mess. After the war, of course, he returned here without difficulty."

"Was he not bitter afterwards about his military experiences."

"Quite the contrary. He regarded it as more of a road accident than enemy action. And the irony is that the despatch he was carrying was an instruction to the Kommandant to hand the allied officers housed here in the camp over to the Americans at the earliest possible opportunity."

"And how did the camp become a factory after the war "It's hardly purpose-built for manufacturing."

"That was an almost natural change of use," explained Tom finishing the story "You see, the Kommandant was Peter's father, Manfred Hartmann. He finished his war with a blameless reputation and in good standing with the occupying force. There was a shortage of undamaged factories locally; the camp buildings were in good condition and could be converted quickly. With the emphasis on getting German manufacturing up and running quickly Manfred's offer to take over the camp and convert it into a manufacturing plant was welcomed by the civilian authorities with open arms."

"And so they all lived happily after?" I concluded.

"That remains to be seen," Tom responded. "It's currently a loss-making business and that's why we are all here".

Further discussion was interrupted by Otto Krantz looming over us to take our orders for dinner. The main offering of the day, which we all ordered, was *sauerbraten*, which Tom identified as beef marinated in vinegar before cooking, with *spätzle*, soft egg noodles, and *filderkraut*, fermented white cabbage, all identified as local specialties by our host. To drink, Tom ordered a *riesling spatlese* while Bernard preferred to stay with beer. I started with the riesling which I found insipid, like most German white wine, and then switched at Otto's recommendation to try the local red wine, *lemberger*, akin to a pleasant but anaemic burgundy.

Over the food, which was excellent but heavy, our conversation resumed. "Did we know that the company was losing money when we bought it?" I asked. Tom considered the question carefully before replying.

"I'm told that the corporate office in Farmington was aware that it wasn't actually making money but thought that it was close to breakeven. The price paid for Hartmann & Holtz GmbH was based on the audited balance sheet and previous year's trading which were strong. But the incentive was that Allied Autoparts wanted a foothold in Germany and family-owned quality springmakers are very seldom offered for sale."

"So, how does AA think that it can be converted to profit quickly?"

"Well, that's where it gets a bit hazy. We have to hope that it doesn't actually become foggy. "The Americans think that German designs and production processes are over-engineered and that they can take cost out with 'good 'ole US of A' manufacturing methods. They also think that there is scope for more aggressive pricing and new business development. That's the real challenge for us, particularly you and I, Julian."

Bernard who had been listening intently and was unused to being exposed to head office thinking, intervened.

"Be careful of the quality issues," he cautioned. "My job tomorrow is to visit the buyer at Sindelfingen with Heinrich Hoffmeyer to reassure them that valve springs made by us in England are reliable enough for the engines they are building for the German entry at next year's Le Mans twenty-four hour race. Normally, we wouldn't get within shouting distance except that this engine is of British design with other powertrain components manufactured in England. In fact, Dr. Hoffmeyer has arranged to meet me in his office tonight at eight-thirty to plan our tactics and what each of us will say at the meeting tomorrow morning."

By now the bar was filling up with a dozen or more newcomers including couples in the restaurant part where we were, either preparing to place their orders or already eating.

Glancing at his watch, Tom asked "In that case, why don't we come with you and, while we are there, Julian can have a first look at the factory." The question was more of a decision rather than a suggestion; so we drained our glasses. "Let's go" said Tom. And we went.

---ooo0ooo---

CHAPTER 2

SINCE THE DISTANCE WAS SHORT we travelled in the Golf with Tom's long legs folded uncomfortably in the front passenger seat and Bernard with his bulging briefcase in the back. This time the factory gates were shut and locked; we gained access to the floodlit compound when Tom entered a six figure code on the keypad at the side of the gate. I parked opposite the offices outside a larger wooden building with several lighted windows.

Standing outside the inflated rubber envelope as we passed was a large black van with open rear doors from which two men were unloading wooden boxes, plainly heavy, which they were manhandling together and carrying into the blimp. As we watched, we could see that the task was laborious; the shorter of the two had to open an airlock in the side of the blimp to gain entry releasing a hiss of air. They were careful to close the airlock each time before emerging to repeat the process for the next load.

"The man in charge is Gottfried Klinger, the warehouse manager," Tom informed us "and that must be the driver in overalls who is making a delivery."

"Isn't it a bit late for deliveries; what do they store in the blimp?" 1 asked.

"Raw materials, mainly spring wire, and finished goods ready for shipment as well as tools, components and other production supplies. With components and sub-assemblies from other factories arriving from all over Germany and further afield, they often have to work late."

My curiosity satisfied, we turned towards the lighted offices in search of Dr Ing Hoffmeyer. Tom gave a cheerful wave towards the two struggling with another box and received a gruff acknowledgment in return. The one in overalls, a massive fellow with beetling black eyebrows cast a brief glance over his shoulder before turning away.

We found Heinrich Hoffmeyer in shirtsleeves at his office desk poring over a set of drawings held down at the corners by glass paperweights. He was fit-looking and in late middle age, of medium height and round-headed with carefully groomed grey hair and very blue eyes twinkling brightly behind rimless spectacles. On the way down from the inn Tom had briefed us that he was a doyen of the industry with a doctorate from the Technical University of Munich and a committee member of the German Institute of Spring Technology (IST). The walls of his office were covered with open-fronted filing cabinets to which he pointed as he rose from his desk.

"One file for the case history of each part that we have designed, tested and manufactured in the past five years," he explained as Tom introduced us.

"Heinrich, do you mind if Julian and I sit in on your briefing for tomorrow with Bernard?" Tom asked politely.

"Willingly, as you say in English 'two heads are better than one'; so, perhaps four heads may be twice as good."

"We also say that three's a crowd," replied Tom. "So the extra two of us will listen and speak only when we are spoken to."

The briefing didn't take long. It was agreed that Bernard should lead on matters of pricing and logistics and Heinrich on all questions of specification and technical detail. Pricing might not be too difficult to agree since quantities of the valve springs were small but quality would be a tricky issue, since the Tipton factory could not offer quality assurance procedures and testing equipment to German industry standards. Heinrich came up with the solution; he would personally install the procedures at Tipton and testing of the finished products would take place and be monitored at Leuffen on Hartmann & Holst's advanced equipment.

"And now," suggested Heinrich "I will show you our test bay where the quality of each new compression spring we design is fatigue tested."

"Thank you. And a very quick tour of the production lines for Julian's benefit, please," requested Tom.

Dr Hoffmeyer led us through the production planning department adjacent to his office where the detailed activity of the factory was recorded. Here the progress of each batch, process by process and machine by machine, was plotted on wallcharts for the coming week. Down a short passage where we were taken next we could hear the sound of an engine running at speed and, behind a glass-panelled door, its source. In a small room on blocks was mounted a six cylinder engine with a rev counter and an assortment of sensors and wires attached. The equipment was unattended.

"Tonight we are testing the trial production run of a new fuel injector nozzle spring," explained our guide. "The engine will perform two million revolutions and the performance of each spring will be recorded on this computer tape which will reveal any aberrations as the engine speed is varied at intervals from 2,000 to 7,000 revs per minute".

"What happens then," I asked.

"Assuming that no faults or weaknesses are detected, this is the final step in our quality assurance programme. The test results are presented to the customer and we request a first order at the agreed price."

"And the price is negotiated in advance?"

"Yes, but like everything in business, nothing is certain until we receive the first order."

From the test bed we moved into the main area of the otherwise silent factory in a connected building subdivided into a series of numbered *Hallen*: Halle 1 for the ranks of coiling machines, silent now under their dust covers, Halle 2 for grinding machines, Halle 3 for the heat-set furnaces and so on. There were separate areas for the toolroom and work in progress. With pilot lights only the factory was eerily silent, as if asleep waiting to be roused in the morning.

"And now, there is more to see," said Heinrich; then, as if sensing my thoughts, "Other parts of the factory that never sleep – Halle 9 for shot peening and acid passivation and Halle 10, the warehouse".

At this point in the tour Bernard announced that he would go back to the hotel to catch up on his notes for the following day's meeting. "A quick walk, no more than twenty minutes will clear my head and prepare me for bed," he asserted.

Tom and I continued to accompany Heinrich who led us to another brick building at the rear of the site from which a rumbling metallic sound emanated. "And here," he informed us entering Halle 9 "is our own shotpeening process, the only one in commercial use outside the Institute of Springmaking Technology."

The machine to which he proudly pointed was a large round metal drum rotating noisily on its axis and bolted firmly to the concrete floor. Heavy Perspex panels in the dome allowed a view of what was happening inside. Springs hurled about by rotation of the drum and the discharge of air were being bombarded by a stream of spherical shot particles propelled at their surface by centrifugal force from an impellor wheel.

"As the shots strike, they cause the surface of each spring to deform with hammer head like impressions into the surface," Heinrich Hoffman explained. "That removes burrs, metal flashing and scale, reduces the risk of surface cracks and improves the life of the spring."

"And what kinds of spring do you shot peen?" I asked.

"Particularly injector nozzle springs like the ones you saw being tested tonight. They have the highest specification and shot peening polishes them at the same time," and pointing to a wall-mounted control panel "Here we can pre-set the timing, the rotation speed and the air speed propulsion of the shot particles," and pointing to an adjacent room "That is where we keep under key the vats for acid dip and passivation of stainless steel springs."

We left Halle 9 which Heinrich locked behind us and strolled down towards the gate. There was no sign now of the black delivery van outside the warehouse blimp, nor of Klinger its manager. "Let me show you Halle 10 as the final part of the tour," said Heinrich. "To keep the envelope inflated and the air inside fresh, we inject clean air continually by means of an electric pump and extract stale air at the same time. But to maintain pressure it is important not to leave the entrance portal open. And so, when the airlock has been opened to gain entry it relocks automatically after precisely three minutes and can only be opened again by entering the correct code on the keypad."

Suddenly, as Heinrich was about to key in the code the floodlights went off and the sounds of machinery from Halle 9 and the test bed were stilled. He uttered an expletive in German, which sounded like *scheissel* , before pulling a torch from his pocket. "Don't worry about the shot-peening or the fatigue test," he said. "It can be resumed in the morning."

"But what about loss of pressure here in the warehouse envelope?"

"*Kein problem*. There is a petrol driven generator with a pump in that small building there which will now activate." And as he spoke we could hear the generator start up in a wooden shed at the side of the blimp.

"Time to call it a day, Heinrich," said Tom turning to the Golf "we've kept you up long enough. We'll leave you to shut up shop, if you will let us out."

"And thank you for showing us round," I added.

---ooo0ooo---

All the street lamps remained out as we drove back to the inn; there was no light other than that cast from oil lamps and flickering candles in the windows of some of the houses we passed. The Leuffener Gasthof was likewise unlit. However, there were four paraffin lamps, three unlit, on the hall table with boxes of matches at their side. Tom and I each helped ourselves and having lit our lamps mounted the stairs. I bade Tom goodnight at the second floor and ascended the third flight to enter my room. As I fumbled with the key the light from a torch was directed upon me. I turned, expecting to see Bernard, but was confronted instead by an apparition smelling strongly of palma violets. I raised my lamp to reveal Brigitta looming and resplendent in a peach coloured negligée trimmed with an abundance of frothy lace.

"Guten Abend, Herr Radclive, is there anything I can do for you?"

"No thank you, Fraulein Krantz, Gute Nacht," I replied firmly managing to gain entry and shutting the bedroom door firmly behind me. It was still not yet 10:30 as I climbed into bed and turned down my lamp. A potential fate worse than death had been avoided.

---ooo0ooo---

"I don't like German breakfasts," Tom announced beating a boiled egg into submission with a teaspoon as I joined him downstairs the following morning. "They are incapable of serving a soft boiled egg and scrambled eggs are out of the question. Nor can you get a decent pot of tea. They only have teabags labelled 'Liptons', a brand that went off the British market more than twenty year ago."

"Good morning, Tom," I ventured. Tom continued his litany.

"You can get toast if you ask nicely," pointing at a plate on the table "but marmalade is another unknown. Only little pots of jam or jelly."

"Well, they do serve cheese and salami slices with the bread rolls."

"Bah. That's not proper breakfast food. Besides, they do that sort of thing better in Holland." He poured himself another cup of the offending tea from the metal teapot in front of him and changed the subject. "You haven't told me yet how you got on in Farmington last week. How was your briefing?"

"As you know, I was there for the first time on a ten day visit, partly an orientation course and an opportunity to meet the corporate office people, but also to discuss the consolidation of the European operations and expansion policy. It was also the first time I had visited Connecticut. Everyone was very friendly and went out of their way to make me feel part of the home team."

I had been head-hunted in London less than two months ago and appointed as European Director of Marketing Services by Bennett Pullman, AA's corporate Marketing Director. I reported to him in Farmington overall but for practical purposes in Europe answered to Tom.

"What is your understanding of European policy having talked to Bennett and the corporate office people?" Tom asked. His management technique included penetrating questioning and probes at all times of all those he worked with, often more to monitor how they were thinking rather than extract information he already had. Some people found the technique irritating but I had already noted its effectiveness in his dealings with UK managers.

"The strategy is certainly bold. In the States each plant has its own specialty product lines in helical springs, flat springs or pressings which they sell throughout the USA, such as the valve springs manufactured in Detroit for the motor car industry, which they also sell to the newer automotive plants of German and Japanese manufacturers in the southern states. And the same for seat belt retractor springs manufactured in Farmington which they sell to General Motors and Ford in Michigan. They think that the same strategy will work in Europe where the specialty of one factory can be sold to original equipment manufacturers in another country, particularly to customers which are subsidiaries of American corporations. And that goes for increasing penetration in home markets too, such as selling valve springs made here in Leuffen to Ford Cologne, or to Opel."

"And how successful do you think that policy can be?" Tom asked.

"I don't know yet. The logic is clear, but has to be tested in practice. My first task here is to start talking today to Peter Hartmann and Heinrich when he gets back from Sindelfingen this afternoon."

"I'll be interested to hear how you get on with Peter. I am trying to tell him how AA expects him to develop his management team."

Having both finished breakfast without any sign of Bernard and collecting papers from our rooms we prepared to leave for the factory. I knocked on Bernard's bedroom door in case he had overslept and then realised that he must have walked down to meet Heinrich for an earlier start.

---ooo0ooo---

At the factory gates we could see immediately that something untoward had occurred. There was a knot of people clustered around the area of Halle 10 where the warehouse blimp had stood last night. But this morning the envelope had collapsed, like a beached whale, into an untidy heap of rubber draped over whatever inventory of goods were housed beneath. Factory workers were tugging at the guy ropes which secured it to the ground while several more were assisting Herr Klinger to re-start the air pump which would breathe fresh life into the blimp as it reflated. Overseeing operations and shouting instructions in all directions was Peter Hartmann, a gesticulating figure; no-one appeared to take the slightest notice of him.

We parked again next to the white Mercedes and walked over to investigate. Heinrich Hoffmeyer bustled out from his office to greet us. "Do you have Bernard with you? I was waiting for him here over an hour ago since 7:30 when we agreed to meet."

"No, we assumed he was with you," I answered "What shall you do about the meeting?"

"I must telephone Sindelfingen to advise them. If you will come with me in Bernard's place, I can arrange for us to be late. If not, I shall have to postpone the meeting until another day."

"Why don't we go together now. I picked up enough from last night to stand in for Bernard and say what he would have said."

While Heinrich went off to telephone, I turned my attention back to the attempts to reflate the blimp and rejoined Tom. An uneasy thought stirred as I addressed him. "Tom, do you remember that last night when we returned to the Gast Hof there were three unlit lamps and boxes of matches waiting for us. One must have been intended for Bernard. You know what that means?"

"It means that Bernard never arrived back at the Leuffener and ….."

"May never have left the factory last night after he said goodnight to us," I finished.

We looked again at the stricken Halle 10 and turned to each other. Our eyes met. The uneasy thought had become an unpleasant likelihood.

---ooo0ooo---

CHAPTER 3

ANY IMPRESSION OF an amiable Norfolk farmer had dissipated as a grim-faced Tom Hardy took control of the situation. In what sounded to me like passable German he directed Gottfried Klinger to redouble efforts to reflate the blimp and instructed Peter Hartmann to return to his office for their planned meeting. Turning to me and Heinrich, who had returned from his call to report that the buyer at Sindelfingen would see us at midday, Tom said.

"There is nothing that can be done here until the warehouse is up and running. Klinger estimates that reflation will take at least two hours with another hour to check that there are no punctures. If you go now, you should be back by mid-afternoon to take part in a full review of what happened here last night."

Heinrich confirmed that allowing for a ninety minute meeting and the return journey time he would expect us to make it back by 3:00 p.m. and we set off for Sindelfingen in his dark green turbocharged Audi A8. Eschewing the autobahn as we left Nürtingen, Heinrich drove fast but not furiously on secondary roads and by 11:30 we were approaching thw building topped by the famous three-pointed Mercedes star, where their research and development centre was located. Checking in at the security guard post it was apparent that every vehicle in the car park was a Mercedes Benz so that the guard's expression of disapproval as he handed a pass to Heinrich was hardly surprising. Indeed, the green Audi stood out like the proverbial sore thumb.

On the way there we had discussed Bernard's disappearance and agreed that it was unaccountable. "You and Tom Hardy think that he is under the warehouse envelope, don't you?" asked Heinrich.

"He certainly never reached the Leuffener Gasthof last night," I replied "and unless he was kidnapped on the way while walking back, he must still be on site somewhere."

"And the envelope is an obvious place where he could have become trapped?"

"Well, Heinrich, you know the factory intimately. Is there anywhere else that springs (no pun intended) to your mind?"

"No, but how could he have entered the warehouse without the keypad code? And he could have left the factory without a problem. There is a pad on the inside of the gate matching the keypad on the outside activated by a simple green pressure button."

"Perhaps he didn't see the green button?"

"Impossible, Julian. Above the button at the right hand side of the gate is a large sign saying 'Ausfahrt'." I had to agree; after our brief autobahn journey the previous afternoon that even Bernard would have recognised the German for "Exit."

----ooo0ooo----

Ernst Bloch, senior purchasing manager at the Sindelfingen research and development unit, met us as we stepped from the lift on the third floor. Dressed in a clinical white coat, he was a short man with an almost bald head framed by horn-rimmed spectacles and wearing thick rubber soled shoes to compensate for his lack of inches. His voice was surprisingly deep with a limited command of English so that our meeting was conducted mostly in German with Heinrich Hoffmeyer translating for me. Bloch led us to his sparsely furnished functional office down a long corridor; his rubber soles squeaking on the composite surface of the floor substituted for conversation. Once perched behind his grey metal desk on a padded desk chair with his visitors installed on lower, less comfortable grey metal chairs before him, his authority was more firmly established. We accepted the ritual mugs of instant coffee offered by an unsmiling secretary.

"And so, Dr. Hoffmeyer," Bloch began "we know that Hartmann & Holst manufacture the springs for the fuel injection systems that Messrs. Robert Bosch supply for Mercedes-Benz production models, but you are not a direct supplier. Please explain what is your role in the new Mercedes performance engines that will be modified in England for our entry in the 1979 Le Mans race."

Heinrich replied that we were there on behalf of Tipton Springs to make their proposal for the valve springs which they had been commissioned to manufacture for their performance engines' He explained that I was there in Bernard Tomkins' place and my role in Associated Autoparts, the international parent group of both our companies.

Following this introduction I explained my position in Allied Autoparts and that we understood the need for Tipton Springs to satisfy quality standards as supplier of such a critical component to Mercedes' English sub-contractor. For that reason, I continued, we had invited Hartmann & Holst, as a qualified German supplier to provide the necessary quality assurance. As we had rehearsed, Heinrich then presented our proposal confidently and in great detail, producing a copy of the Hartmann & Holst quality manual "for Herr Bloch to study at his leisure." The presentation was received without interruption but his nodding at intervals indicated a measure of acceptance by Bloch. There followed a short silence while he maintained a deadpan expression. Then, as we had anticipated "One question for you, Mr. Radclive. What is the price you will be charging for the valve springs in England?"

I quoted the price that Bernard had mentioned the previous evening adding ten per cent "Of course, this price relates to the cost of designing the spring, its performance in the prototype engine and a limited production run of only 500 pieces".

"That is a much higher price than we could consider paying in Germany. You should take into account that this engine, if we are successful at Le Mans, may become a production engine after next year. You should reduce the price."

"We are not gamblers, Herr Bloch," I responded, with an insincere smile "but you can be sure that if we are asked to quote for a production quantity in the future the price will be lower because the development cost is already amortised."

This retort earned the flicker of a return smile on the otherwise expressionless face. "Thank you, Herr Radclive, we shall see when that happens."

The meeting seemed to have come to a natural conclusion with an understanding that the Tipton valve springs would be tested at Leuffen to Ernst Bloch's approval for inclusion in the performance engine. We were dismissed by Herr Bloch and led back to the lift in silence by his expressionless secretary. We seemed to have been successful but it didn't feel like much of a victory.

---ooo0ooo---

"Why did you decide to add ten per cent to the price?" was Heinrich's immediate question as we left the car park.

"Two reasons," I replied "First, I have learnt never to bid your final price as the opening offer in any negotiation and, in this case, we need to provide a margin to cover the cost of Hartmann & Holst's quality assurance testing. If the AA European factories are going to work together, it has to be profitable for us all." Heinrich nodded his approval.

"Ah, like the Marshall Plan after the war. America's acts of charity to Europe have also been profitable for American business." The eyes behind his rimless spectacles twinkled as he accelerated sharply.

On the drive back to Leuffen we stopped off at a private house which served lunches only on weekdays to a regular clientele, in effect a small private restaurant of a kind not uncommon in Baden Wurttemburg. Some of the dozen or so men seated at simple tables in the large open plan kitchen recognised Heinrich and welcomed us with *"Mahlzeit"* which he repeated in return. As we sat down, he explained that this was the traditional Schwabian lunchtime greeting among people who met for the first time, as well as colleagues.

Our hostess, a rosy-cheeked, middle-aged woman wiping her hands on her over-size apron came forward to take our order. Heinrich studied the handwritten menu and ordered *Matjesfilet nach Hausfrauenart* for us both. Helpings of the dish consisting of herring fillets with sour cream sauce garnished with dill, slices of apple, onions and gherkins and served with boiled potatoes appeared at our table within five minutes. Washed down with *apfelsaft* we enjoyed the meal in companionable near silence. Twenty-five minutes later we were back on the road.

For the rest of the journey I took the opportunity to expand my scanty knowledge of the spring industry. "When I was in the States two weeks ago they impressed on me that they regard valve spring manufacture as the pinnacle of their technical capability. Why valve springs and is that the same in Germany?"

"During the war valve springs were the top priority on both sides of the Atlantic; in Germany because they were vital to the Luftwaffe," Heinrich explained. "If a valve spring breaks in an airplane engine, it is *kaput*; it falls out of the sky and that is *schrecklich*. You lose one good aircraft and also, of course, a pilot." As Heinrich became excited, his vocabulary relapsed into German.

"Of course, valve springs were also important in tanks and motorcars, but they could be replaced easily. Now they are still used in vehicles and American autos with their big engines use more than smaller European or Japanese cars.

But most airplanes now have jet engines so that there is no longer a high demand from the aircraft industry. Also, here in Germany we have developed fuel injection systems for motor cars, which are a new market for springmakers, and injector nozzle springs are a quality challenge."

"Surely, injector springs are much the same as valve springs, only smaller?"

"Not so," admonished Heinrich, taking one hand off the steering wheel to wag a finger at me. "The injector nozzle spring has closer tolerances and is harder to make. Each spring has to be cut off after coiling and ground so that the ends are flat and the spring perfectly perpendicular. The valve spring is crude by comparison and can be made by many springmakers." Heinrich's English had recovered its normal fluency as his excitement abated.

That comment would go down a storm, I thought, in Farmington.

---ooo0ooo---

We drew into the factory at shortly before three o'clock to find two police cars and an ambulance parked outside the warehouse envelope; largely but not fully inflated, it still resembled a beached whale rather than a deflated zeppelin. As we parked, a trolley was wheeled out of the blimp bearing a black body bag on a stretcher. Two attendants lifted the stretcher carefully into the back of the ambulance which was driven off followed by one blue and white police car. The two occupants of the second car, one in uniform and one in plainclothes were engaged in conversation with Gottfried Klinger.

Reporting back to Tom Hardy, Heinrich and I found him in the boardroom with Peter Hartmann. Grim-faced, Tom was seated opposite Peter who had installed himself defensively behind his leather-topped teak desk and was clearly ill at ease.

"The immediate priority is to take care of Bernard by ensuring that his body is released and sent back to his family as soon as possible" Tom was saying "The London office will pay for him to be returned by air but I require you to make all the arrangements. When that is done, I shall need to understand precisely how he was locked into the warehouse and died, and why the generator failed during the power cut."

"This is all very inconvenient," replied Peter looking sullen. "To have the police in the factory in these circumstances is very bad for our local reputation and the arrangements will take up much of Frau Päsche's time for the next few days."

"Not your secretary's time. I expect you to make the arrangements personally. This is a human tragedy involving a guest visitor to your factory and he deserves your respect and attention." Tom's tone was icy, but I could see that he was furious from the reddening of his neck.

"The responsibility for this unfortunate accident is Klinger's as warehouse manager and he must be disciplined firmly," Peter persisted, ignoring the direct instruction and misreading Tom's apparent calm. "I will send for him tomorrow morning."

"When the police have finished with him, send for him and we'll hear his explanation." The police were still interrogating Gottfried Klinger; instead we gave our report of the meeting with Ernst Bloch. "At least, some of us had a good morning," commented Tom.

Looking self-satisfied and without giving a single word of credit to Heinrich, Peter added his own triumphant conclusion. "And so you can see that Hartmann & Holst are able to gain entry to the German market even for an English springmaker."

Tom glanced at his watch and turned to me "In your absence, Julian, I have changed my flight back to this evening instead of tomorrow so that I can visit Bernard's family in the morning and support them in making the funeral arrangements. I 've checked out with Otto Krantz but left your room reservation for tonight. I'm driving to the airport now; perhaps you would come with me to the car so that I can have another word with you."

As we reached his Hertz car, Tom gave me his instructions: "There's a mystery here which we need to clear up to avoid any lengthy discussions with Farmingon or inadequate explanations. I would like you to stand in for me with the Landespolizei, to investigate a bit for yourself and report to me in the London office the day after tomorrow. Above all, I would like you to interview Gottfried Klinger in Peter Hartmann's presence and form your own conclusions. I'm not altogether sure that I understand his role at the factory. It seems to be rather more than warehouse manager."

With that Tom folded his six feet six inches into the Opel and departed leaving me to join the group in front of the blimp.

---ooo0ooo---

CHAPTER 4

THE PLAINCLOTHES OFFICER introduced himself as Kommisar Kurt Vogel. A younger man than I had expected with an air of quiet authority, he had accepted Tom Hardy's departure without objection having heard that the two of us were together throughout our visit to the factory the previous evening. He was preparing to enter the warehouse, now fully inflated, with his sergeant and Gottfried Klinger and invited me and Peter Hartmann to accompany them.

Klinger punched numbers into the keypad; there was a faint hiss of escaping air as he unlocked the door, stood aside for us to enter and closed it firmly behind us. The interior of the blimp seemed surprisingly large. About fifteen feet to the topmost point of its domed roof, the structure was supported by flexible ribs within the heavy rubber envelope. The sounds of clean air pumping in and stale air escaping from the ventilator prompted me for a moment to imagine that, Jonah-like, we were in the mouth of some leviathan. The strong smell of rubber told me otherwise.

The contents of the warehouse were in disarray following its overnight collapse. On either side in frames like bicycle racks stood giant coils of wire, raw material for the spring coilers, each bearing a label to identify its specification and date of delivery. While the racks had been sufficiently heavy to remain upright, the stores of machine parts and maintenance supplies stacked in the centre and at the far wall of the building were strewn about. Tiers of metal racking had toppled over and shelves had disgorged the open bins and trays which they normally housed. Untidy heaps of boxes at the further end, previously arranged on wooden pallets and in stacks bore witness to the weight of the rubber envelope as it had slowly subsided. Among these were wooden boxes similar to those delivered the night before; one had split open as it fell revealing their contents which Klinger identified as grinding wheels. A chalk outline on the floor showed where Bernard's body had been found.

"Now Mr. Radclive," the Kommissar asked taking a notepad and ballpoint from his pocket. "May I have your account of the visit to this factory last night?"

"Certainly. Mr. Hardy and I arrived shortly before 8:30 p.m. with Mr. Tompkins to attend a meeting with Dr Hoffmeyer in his office. The meeting lasted less than an hour; then at our request Dr Hoffmeyer gave us a guided tour of the factory starting with the test facility and then moving though the production halls. Before we left the main building Mr. Tompkins decided to have an early night and to walk back to the Leuffener Gast Hof. The rest of us then visited Halle 9 where a production run was in process for about five minutes before walking back down to the warehouse for the final visit on our tour. Before Dr Hoffmeyer could open the door, all the lights went out and we realised that there was a power cut since we could no longer hear the quality test run in the main factory. Almost immediately we heard the generator start up and Dr Hoffmeyer explained how it maintained air pressure in the envelope."

"And so, what happened then?"

"There was nothing more to be seen. So, we said our goodnights and drove back to the Gasthof."

"What time would that have been?" Vogel asked.

"I didn't look at my watch then, not until I was back in my room when I took it off before getting into bed. It was not quite 10:30 then; so we must have left the factory at around 10:00. Of course, you can verify that by checking the recorded time of the power cut."

"Thank you for telling me how to corroborate your story." Kommissar Vogel's deadpan expression concealed any hint of sarcasm.

After asking me for some personal details about Bernard Tompkins and confirming that I would be available the next morning for further questioning, he declared himself satisfied for the time being. Peter and I left him with Klinger from whom he was no doubt hoping to extract more information. I found it impossible to judge from his taciturn manner and lack of expression to judge whether the Kommissar was treating the incident so far as a routine accident enquiry or something more challenging.

---ooo0ooo---

As we crossed the yard back to the offices, the end of day hooter sounded and, after a cursory glance at his desktop to confirm that there were no urgent messages, Peter escaped as before in his large white Mercedes and I decided it was time to call home from his office. I telephoned the flat in Porchester Terrace which I shared with my better half when we were rather infrequently together. It was good timing as Gaby had just returned to London from the North where she had been conducting group discussions for the market research agency which she ran.

After the preliminaries "How are you doing, my sweet, in the land of lederhosen?" Gaby asked.

"More like Stalag 17. The factory is a converted prisoner of war camp and there was an unexplained death here last night when Tom and I were around. I'll give you the full story tomorrow night when I'm back."

"What an exciting life you high flying executives lead. Sounds dangerous. Are you in trouble?"

"No, not personally but we were probably in the factory when it happened. I may know more tomorrow before leaving. How were the denizens of Rochdale or whoever else you were soliciting?"

"Bolton housewives this time and I don't solicit. Just penetrating questions about washing machine performance and new products. Twin tubs versus separate washers and dryers. I can bore you with the inside story anytime."

"Gaby, I'll be on the Lufthansa flight tomorrow afternoon arriving Terminal 2 at six-thirty. I should be in the flat by eight o'clock. Let's eat out, shall we?"

"I'm off to the Harrods Spring sale tomorrow." Gaby replied "Anything for you other than the usual?"

"You know me too well, my love. Just pyjamas, socks and the perennial boxer shorts. I'll have to close now. There's someone waiting to see me."

"You too." Gabi acknowledged. Kissing noises and she rang off.

I had seen Heinrich Hoffmeyer at the door and he advanced now into the room. "Herr Radclive," he said "There is something I would like to show you. Come with me."

"I'm at your disposal." I replied, noting that we were not yet on first name terms, and followed him out of the offices and across the yard to the rear of the little brick shed that housed the relief generator for the warehouse envelope. Heinrich pointed to the fuel pipe running from the back of the building to a small tank which I judged to have a capacity of no more than 500 litres. The fuel gauge registered about one quarter full.

"It was empty this morning," he explained "and they put some kerosene in while we were visiting Singelfinden. "But this is what I wanted to show you," he added handing me a metal rod. "Just prod it into the ground here under the fuel line".

I took the rod and poked it several times through the loose shale around the fuel line and into the earth underneath. The ground was quite soft and little effort was required to push it down to a depth of four to six inches. The end of the rod when extracted was wet and smelt strongly of kerosene when passed under the nose.

"*Alles klar,*" exclaimed Heinrich "The generator did not run out of fuel on its own account. There was a leakage in the fuel line or....,"

"...the fuel line was dislocated deliberately." I added for him. We looked at each other and Heinrich raised a quizzical eyebrow.

"And that raises many questions." He completed the sentence for me. Somehow, I didn't think he looked altogether surprised.

---ooo0ooo---

Having left my Hertz car at the inn that morning, I needed to walk back to the Leuffener Gasthof or cadge a lift. I could have asked Heinrich to drive me but didn't want to discuss our findings further and we agreed not to reveal our discovery to anyone else until we had thought through the implications. I decided that the exercise would do me good anyway. As I approached the factory gates I remembered the conversation with Heinrich earlier and looked for the *Ausfahrt* sign above the green pressure pad. The pad was there but of the notice there was no sign. This was further food for thought on my walk back. I now had two questions to add to the primary questions of why and how Bernard had entered the blimp: who had severed or disconnected the fuel pipe and who had removed the exit sign at the gate, assuming that it had been there in the first place. I had no recollection of noticing it when Tom and I had left the factory the previous night, perhaps because Heinrich had pressed the pad when ushering us out and the open gate would have obscured the sign had it been there. And that posed two further related questions: when had the fuel pipe become disconnected and when had the sign been removed? Consideration of all these questions occupied my attention throughout my walk up the hill to the village square and the Leuffener Gasthof.

I enjoyed a relaxing shower and change of clothes before descending to the restaurant for a restful evening. Otto Krantz greeted me with a friendly nod and Brigitta, dressed this evening in traditional *dirndl* skirt and low-slung blouse, simpered from behind the bar. Tonight, without hesitation, I ordered Lemberger to drink and sat down at the same table as the previous evening. The wine came in a large green stemmed glass, the shape of a fruit salad bowl, described as a *viertel* or quarter bottle by the landlord, the measure for serious wine drinkers I was assured. I decided to eat simply and ordered *Schwäbische Spätzle*, the local equivalent of macaroni cheese with shredded Emmentaler, caramelized onions and homemade spätzle and a green salad. I settled down to enjoy my meal with a paperback novel.

However, my evening was not quite over. As I finished eating and was enjoying my second viertel of Lemberger, I became conscious that someone else had sat down at the next table and was inching himself alongside on the bench seat that we shared. A rat-faced sallow fellow with dyed black hair plastered to his skull, he looked furtively around the room before asking:

"You are British?" "Yes." I replied.

"And your royal family is German?"

"Ye-es." He inched himself closer and addressed me in an even more confidential tone. "If you had been with us in 1940, we would have ruled the world."

After pausing for thought "Well, you know, we already had an Empire and we really didn't want to rule anywhere more".

It seemed best to answer my interrogator conversationally in terms he would understand but I have no idea how long this somewhat surreal discussion would have continued had Otto Krantz not come to the rescue. Otto addressed him sharply in German as "Wolfgang" and waved him away, then sat down opposite me apologising for the incident.

"I am sorry for that, Herr Radclive. Wolfgang is quite harmless but there are still people here in this part of

Germany who look back on the Third Reich with fondness. Most of us are happy to have moved on and prefer not to look back," A grotesque smile, intended to reassure, crinkled his scarred face but was more threatening in its effect than anything further that Wolfgang might have said.

"But there are right wing terrorists around today," he continued "such as the Red Army Faction who interrupted your arrival at the Flughafen yesterday. Wherever they are active we all need to be careful, Herr Radclive, particularly visitors from England and America, in case they want to fight yesterday's battles today."

"Thank you, Herr Krantz, for rescuing me. We have reactionaries in England too, many of whom think we should not have joined the EEC five years ago and old war films where Germans are the enemy are still popular. One day, perhaps, we shall all get used to living together but it could take quite a long time."

---ooo0ooo---

CHAPTER 5

THE FOLLOWING DAY I awoke to another clear Spring morning, breakfasted and checked out from the Gasthof, then drove down to the factory and parked the Golf outside the office alongside Peter Hartmann's white Mercedes. Kommissar Vogel was already there and I joined him in Peter's office.

He greeted me formally with the same impassive face as before. "Good morning, Herr Radclive, I was just informing Herr Hartmann that, on the basis of Herr Klinger's testimony, I am satisfied – at least for the time being – that your friend Mr. Tompkins' death was a tragic accident. Of course, having become locked in the warehouse, he was unlucky that the electric power was cut and even more unfortunate that the relief generator also failed due to lack of fuel."

I wasn't sure that his impeccable English was an accurate expression of what he really thought or if he had chosen his words carefully as an alternative to the familiar statement which a British investigating officer might have used – *we are following various lines of inquiry.*

Taking the Kommissar's statement at its face value, and without referring to the fuel leak discovery of the previous evening, I thought that one question at least was called for. "Was the electricity supply outage just a normal power cut affecting the area?"

"Only the Leuffen area was affected." Then after a pause "But I can say that the local substation close to here was sabotaged." Then, after another pause to consider how much more to say "We believe that the substation may have been attacked by the members of the Baader Meinhof gang who were arrested at the Flughafen two days ago. Two of them, Agatha Speitel and Michel Kroll, escaped yesterday from Stuttgart prison and were seen heading in this direction."

"We shall be hearing Klinger's report ourselves this morning," Peter Hartmann intervened "and there is nothing more, I think, we can usefully add until we have spoken to him ourselves."

"In that case, Kommissar, if you have no more questions for me I am planning to return to London this evening. Am I free to leave?"

"Yes, Herr Radclive. We may have further questions for you in the future. Leave your contact details with my sergeant. Oh, and let us know, please, before you next leave England." We exchanged business cards and Vogel left the room ushering in the sergeant who took down my home address and telephone number.

As soon as we were alone, Hartmann lifted his telephone and instructed Frau Päscher to call for Gottfried Klinger to join us in fifteen minutes.

"Before he arrives, Julian," I was pleased that he had relaxed his somewhat pompous formality by several notches "I would like to give you a message from my father who is very distressed by the accident to Herr Tompkins – er, Bernard – and would like you to join him at Schloss Hohenleuffen at lunchtime to express his regrets in person."

"That's nice of him, Peter, but really not necessary. However, I would very much like to meet your father. So, please say thank you." Taking advantage of the more friendly atmosphere, I tried to prepare myself for the encounter with Klinger. "Tell me, Peter, something about Gottfried Klinger, if we have time before he arrives."

"Klinger is a long-serving employee of the company. In fact, he was here as a young man when this was a camp for Allied officers in 1944/45 and it was natural for him to stay with father when Hartmann & Holst was formed after the war."

"That's a fine example of loyalty. What was his function in the camp when the war ended?"

"I think you could say that he acted as adjutant to my father," Peter answered hesitantly "or, in civilian terms, as a kind of personnel manager."

"And today, he is simply Warehouse Manager?" Peter's manner which had been warmer started to cool again. He was plainly uncomfortable.

"No, he has other responsibilities. You see, thanks to your Ernest Bevin, we have very strong trade unions here in Germany since 1946 and Gottfried Klinger is also the IG Metall trade union representative, I think you would say shop steward, for the employees of Hartmann & Holst. It is good that we have a union representative who is also a friend of the management, don't you think?"

I was spared from commenting on the appointment of what sounded like a former Waffen SS officer as a union representative collaborating with management by a discreet knock on the door and the entry of Gottfried Klinger. This time I was able to study him more closely as he took a seat, uninvited and alongside me, in front of Peter Hartmann's desk. My first impression the night before had been of quite a short man but I could see now that he was only a little under six foot; the van driver with whom he had been unloading and carrying heavy loads into the blimp must be exceptionally tall. Klinger himself was broad shouldered and bulky, heavily muscled rather than fat, blond hair cut *en brosse* with a square head, wearing a bland expression of barely disguised superiority. Heavy-lidded black eyes and small ears laid back to his head completed the picture.

Adopting an air of authority Peter opened the conversation. "Klinger, you met Herr Radclive earlier when you were questioned by Kommisar Vogel. He is compiling a report on the unfortunate Tompkins accident for his superiors at our parent company. He would like to ask some more questions about the circumstances."

"Of course, Herr Hartmann. As always, I will do my best to help." Klinger's voice had that nasal twang, familiar to the characterisation of German baddies in British war films, although the response seemed genuine.

"I think you know that I was here in the factory yesterday evening with Dr. Hoffmeyer and Mr. Tompkins before he left us?" I carried on "When we arrived you were busy unloading boxes from a delivery van with the driver and carrying them together into the warehouse. We noticed that each time you entered and left the blimp you closed the door and reopened before carrying in the next load. That was at about 8:30 p.m. When did you finish unloading and what happened then?"

Klinger eyed me carefully. "There were twenty-two boxes to unload and we were perhaps half way through when you saw us. Some of the time we were able to open and close the door without punching in the code because the airlock operates automatically only after three minutes giving us time to fetch another lighter load. But for the heavy crates we had to open up with the keypad each time. You will understand, Herr Radclive, that we did not keep a detailed record of our progress but I would estimate that we completed the unloading by 2100 hours." His English was impeccable and delivered without hesitation.

"And after that?" I asked. "When did you leave the warehouse?"

"Again, I have no timesheet. I wanted to unpack the smaller items, tools and what I think you would call consumables – the small machine components used in production – and store them in their bins, logging the details on the bin cards. Our driver Johann had agreed to help me and we left together soon after 2200 hours."

"Did you unpack all the boxes?"

"*Nicht alles.*" My further question seemed to unsettle him. "Some of the larger boxes or crates contain heavier items, such as grinding wheels ordered for the Campinas factory, will be despatched to Brazil in the coming days and these we left untouched with their shipping documents for reloading into a container. But surely that is not important for your enquiry?"

"Probably not," I conceded and decided to move on. "And during that time until you and Johann finally left the warehouse you did not see Mr. Tomkins?"

"Obviously not." This time Klinger did not disguise his irritation.

"How then do you think that he could have gained entry and why did he stay there?" My question hung uncomfortably in the air. It was answered for him by Peter Hartmann who seemed anxious to avoid embarrassment and, at the same time, bring the discussion to an end.

"It follows from what Klinger has told us and told the police that Mr, Tompkins - er, Bernard – must have opened the door during the three minutes after he and Johann Glock left. Then he could not leave when the airlock was activated automatically. This is our security system." Gottfried Klinger nodded his assent, exchanging glances with Peter, and made as if to rise.

"One moment, Herr Klinger," I said "A further question before you go. Apparently the fuel tank of the generator which powers the air pump for the blimp was left almost empty at the time. Who is responsible for keeping it topped up?"

"That is the responsibility of young Alberich Schiessel of the maintenance department which reports to Herr Hartmann" replied Klinger blandly passing the parcel to Peter. "Is that everything you wish to ask me?"

"Thank you, Klinger, for your assistance" responded Peter hurriedly. "I will discipline Schiessel myself later." This time, I made no move to halt Klinger as he stood up, smiled thinly and turned to leave the room.

Peter waited until he had left and resumed "This is a bad business. Normally Bernard would have spent an uncomfortable night but would have been released in the morning in good health. Do you wish to interview Schiessel now yourself? His negligence, it seems, is the cause of death." I had no intention of revealing to him Heinrich's discovery that the fuel tank had been drained off deliberately, at least not yet, and declined the offer. "I don't think that anything he says would add to our understanding of how Bernard died. I'll leave it to you as his manager to deal with him later.

Later events showed just how mistaken my judgement had been that day and that my poor decision was the indirect cause of two more deaths.

---ooo0ooo---

The lunchtime bell rang as Peter and I left his office for the meeting with his father at Schloss Hohenleuffen. Amid the customary *'Mahlzeit'* greetings as factory staff drifted from their workplaces to the factory canteen or home in the village we prepared to set off in the white Mercedes. In front of us two slim figures in matching motorcycle leathers and black helmets astride a racy looking machine sped away in the same direction. "That's young Schiessel and his girlfriend," commented Peter. "They live in Hohenleuffen village in his mother's house."

---ooo0ooo---

CHAPTER 6

4 May, Hohenleuffen

OUR ROUTE TOOK US through the village and on to the secondary road winding steeply up the right hand side of the Schwäbische alp. Peter drove more carefully than I had expected, perhaps for my benefit, and giving me time to admire the scenery. On the left hand side the thickly wooded slopes displayed their early summer foliage: a mixture of mainly deciduous beech and oak trees down to the road side with spruce and sapin firs in the darker interior. To the right the ground fell away precipitously. Here the trees clung to outcrops of rock descending to a stream far below at the bottom of a steep gorge. To begin with, the road climbed in a leisurely manner through shallow bends but soon the corners became tighter with a series of hairpins. In winter driving conditions, with only a slender metal barrier to impede skidding vehicles from sliding over the edge into the void, travel up and down was clearly hazardous.

Conversation during the short journey was limited. Not wishing to discuss further the Klinger interview or Peter's apparently logical conclusion, I asked Peter to tell me more about the business relationship between the Leuffen and Campinas factories.

"It is one of mutual benefit, you might say reciprocal trading," explained Peter "based on cost or quality advantage. For example, good quality grinding wheels cannot be found in Brazil and new spring coiling machines cost thirty per cent or more there than in Germany. And so we buy those items here and export to our friends in Campinas."

"And how does it work the other way round?"

"That is more complicated and relates to the lower cost of labour in Brazil. Certain products such as valve springs are made on similar machines with a number of operations and with wire from the same suppliers for the same customers in both countries, for example the Volkswagen Golf model. The manufacturing cost in Campinas is much lower than here in Leuffen; therefore, we purchase Golf valve sprigs from Campinas and sell to Volkswagen AG in Wolfsburg."

"And how do you pay each other?"

"Of course, we keep a careful account of each shipment and offset the invoice values against each other with settlement of the balance every three months. That is a simple matter for our accountants."

At this point, as we rounded yet another lefthand bed, Peter pointed across me at a track running through the trees with a barrier in front of the entrance, "That is our hunting lodge," he declared proudly "We have jolly evenings there in the winter after our weekend shooting parties. You must join us when the season starts in October."

Shortly afterwards we reached the village of Hohenleuffen, no more than a hamlet of a few houses grouped around a small open-sided square with a half-timbered Gasthof, a minor version of the larger Krantz hostelry below. "They serve good food," commented Peter "but have only a few rooms for visitors." With its bright red geranium-filled window boxes, colourful in the Spring sunshine, the Gasthof looked cheerful and welcoming.

By contrast, the narrow road on to which Peter now turned at the back of the square was darker and overcast by the trees clustered on either side with their branches meeting overhead. This road soon became little more than a track as it wound steeply ever upwards. After about a kilometre our road opened up and we passed through an open stone gateway on which a notice proclaiming 'Schloss Hohenleuffen' was posted. A further five hundred meters brought us to the castle entrance. Flanked by two sturdy towers beyond which battlemented walls stretched in either direction, the entrance itself was a tunnel through which the Mercedes was only just able to pass to gain entry to the open space beyond. Emerging into sunlight I could see that Schloss Hohenleuffen had been a genuine medieval castle, but not of the concentric type with a series of three walls and ramparts. Instead, there was the one open courtyard in which we found ourselves with the traditional tall keep in the far righthand corner. Now largely in ruins, I judged its present construction to be of the 15th or 16th century; only the righthand side of the keep seemed to in reasonable repair with glazed windows rather than gaping embrasures and it was in front of this that Peter now parked.

----ooo0ooo----

Peter rang a cast iron bell at the heavily studded door of the keep which was answered after an interval by a strikingly tall and heavily built man whom I recognized immediately as Gottfried Klinger's companion of two nights before. There was no hint of recognition on his part as we were admitted. Instead of a long breathtaking climb up the spiral staircase in front of us, Peter led me to a modern electric lift in a far corner of the lofty hall. "My father is no longer of an age when a steep climb several times a day is pleasant exercise," he explained.

"When he took over this part of the castle, he installed the elevator as well as modern bathrooms and a kitchen."

The lift control panel showed that there were nine floors to the roof of the keep; Peter programmed us to stop at the sixth. The lift door opened on to an unusually large room, part sitting and dining area and part study, lined with bookshelves floor to ceiling. The elderly man who greeted us was a spare upright figure in a sober dark suit and tie who gave an immediate impression of authority.

"Welcome Mr. Radclive to my simple dwelling. I am Manfred Hartmann."

"What a splendid location," I replied shaking the outstretched hand. "How kind of you to invite me here."

"Yes. It is a commanding position. Let me show you the view." A slight emphasis on 'commanding', I thought, in his formal, lightly accented English.

Our host led us to French widows on the far side of the study area which gave on to a large terrace overlooking the valley below. "A truly magnificent view," I commented surveying the details of Leuffen village laid out below, the swimming pool and buildings of the leisure centre in the foreground with the factory a short distance beyond and, to the right, the village square and Gasthof.

"Still a little too cool for us to take our lunch out here," Manfred Hartmann proclaimed after we had lingered for a minute or so and turned to lead us back inside. As I turned to follow, I noticed for the first time a metal platform cantilevered from the battlements on the left-hand side of his residence three floors above us.

"What is that for," I asked pointing.

"Ah, our skydivers launch pad. In the summer months we have many intrepid young people who take up this sport and throw themselves from there to hover over the valley."

"Isn't that dangerous. Are there many accidents?"

"Not really if they are properly equipped in skydiving bat suits. In the evening as it cools and hot air rises from the plain below they are able to hang over the valley for half an hour or longer or to travel some distance into the countryside."

"Now there is a skydivers' club based in Nürtingen," interjected Peter. "It is registered as a sports club with the state authorities and inspected regularly."

"I am sure you could join." The raising of one eyebrow suggested that the challenge was not entirely serious.

"Pass on that one," I replied in the same vein. "I'll check but probably beyond the scope of the company's accident insurance cover."

On re-entering the study we found an elderly retainer setting our table for lunch in the body of the room. Our host invited us to sit as the servant left through a door set between two of the bookcases backed by a full length mirror and filled Peter's and my wine glasses from a chilled bottle of Niersteiner. He did not pour any of the excellent hock into his own glass, remarking "I don't drink – wine." His emphasis on the word 'wine' delivered in measured and accented tones reminded me irresistibly of Bela Lugosi's Count Dracula in the original movie. I was almost relieved to see that he cast a reflection in the mirrored door as he passed by to take his seat at the table and pour himself a glass of water.

"Well now," Manfred Hartmann resumed "The news of your colleague's accident at the factory two nights ago is very sad. I hope that you will send a wreath, Peter, from us both for the funeral and a message of sympathy to his family. You will tell me, Mr. Radclive, if there is anything more we might do."

"Bernard's family will want some assurance about how the accident happened," I replied. "Of course, if they are advised that there was negligence on the part of Hartmann & Holst they could make a claim for financial compensation."

"And are you clear about the circumstances of the accident?"

This was my cue to relate our movements since Bernard and I arrived three days ago up to point that he had left Tom, Heinrich and myself in the factory on the evening of our arrival. While I was talking Manfred's butler served us silently with our meal, fillets of some flatfish, sole or plaice, grilled lightly in butter with fresh carrots and beans.

As I completed my account, Peter interjected with his conclusions from the Klinger interview including the possible failure of Alberich Schiessel to top the fuel tank for the auxiliary pump to maintain pressure within the warehouse. While he was talking I was able to study the interaction between father and son. There was a contrast between the measured urbanity of Manfred and Peter's over-emphasis of speech and unease of manner. There was also a marked physical difference between the two men. With his Roman nose, lean face and piercing black eyes Manfred Hartmann was a handsome man, elderly but still in full command of his faculties. By contrast, Peter's flaccid features were a coarser version of his father's without distinction or air of authority. Definitely not a 'chip off the old block' I concluded.

Our fish was excellent and was followed by a selection of fresh fruit and Bergkäse cheese. While we were helping ourselves, our host reopened the conversation. He had been listening intently as Peter trotted out his explanation, like a tutor checking that a pupil had learnt his lines. I sensed that he had heard it before.

"That seems the only possible explanation in the circumstances, don't you think?" he asked me.

"Well, it offers a logical account of what could have happened," I agreed "but there are coincidences in timing which make me feel uneasy."

"How do you mean?"

"Two in particular strike me. First, that the electricity outage occurred after Klinger left and as Tom Hady and I were leaving; second, that the air pump keeping the warehouse inflated ran out of fuel and failed after we and later Heinrich Hoffman had also left."

It had become clear to me by then that the reason for my invitation might have been to sound out how satisfied I was that Bernard's death was accidental. Again, I decided to keep quiet about the tampered fuel line.

Fixing me with his piercing gaze Hartmann persisted with his questioning. "Surely you are not suggesting that the Bader Meinhoff raid on the power station was timed deliberately for the period of Mr.Tomkin's incarceration? And is it likely that someone could have planned for the air pump to run out of fuel at the same time? In any case what motive could anyone have for making these elaborate arrangements?"

Peter hastened to add his unnecessary support. "The second question will be answered when I question Alberich Schiessel about his routine checking of the fuel tank. If there was negligence on his part, he will of course be punished." "Assuming he acknowledges any omission," I added.

"I understand that the police are still studying the case," Manfred resumed. "And that Kommissar Kurt Vogel is the investigating officer. From experience, he is a good man and I am sure that he will be very diligent."

"In that case," I concluded insincerely. "We shall await his report and I must not speculate further."

"Patience in such matters is always advisable."

I couldn't tell whether or not Manfred Hartmann was reassured although he appeared to relax. He was probably a better poker player than me.

With this discussion apparently at an end our conversation petered out and, after thanking our host for his hospitality, I rose from the table; we took our leave with a formal invitation to visit Schloss Hohenleuffen again "in happier circumstances."

There was no sign of Johann Glock when we reached the ground floor and left the building. Peter drove us back downhill to Leuffen in near silence, negotiating the tight bends skilfully at uncomfortable speed. There was ample time for me to drive the Golf back to Stuttgart Flughafen, return it to Hertz and check in with Lufthansa for the flight home.

---ooo0ooo---

After his guests had left Manfred Hartmann returned to the terrace, this time with a glass of his favourite vodka, and considered carefully the options for further action. He was unconvinced that the British executive Radclive whom he'd just entertained was in any way satisfied with the account that Klinger had given him or with Peter's explanation of what had happened. How then could he forestall further investigation by him or more senior managers from Allied Autoparts when the incident was reported to the US head office? He was confident that Klinger would stick to his story but less certain that Peter would stand up under questioning. With a little encouragement, he thought it likely that Kommissar Vogel would close the case having taken statements from all witnesses at Hartmann & Holst with a routine 'death by accident' report that the coroner would endorse.

But that might not be the end of it. American companies were famously persistent in pursuing the interests of their employees and that included those working for overseas subsidiaries such as the late Bernard Tompkins. Inevitably, the contents of the warehouse would be inspected rigorously at the end of June financial year end stock check as a part of the annual audit and it was essential that there should be no trace then of the irregular shipments to and from Brazil. He considered telephoning Frederik von Falkenburg to alert him to the situation but that could compound the problem. Frederik was capable of precipitous action; he might not have time to accelerate a further shipment from Brazil to reach Leuffen before the end of June but he could activate the Kamaradenwerk to push through another illegal shipment from Germany before the deadline and that would generate a further series of unquantifiable risks.

On second thoughts, better to despatch to Campinas as soon as possible the contraband received by Klinger and Johann two nights ago without sharing information immediately. Manfred Hartmann re-entered the room and turned to the telex machine in one corner of his study. Setting down his glass he typed in a short message to von Falkenburg: ADVISE FINAL LEUFFEN CONSIGNMENT FROM TO BE SHIPPED FROM FACTORY FOR

CAMPINAS MAY 19 LATEST. HARTMANN and sent. It did not occur to him that the telex should be sent by Peter, nor to consult with him as General Manager before sending Johann to instruct Klinger to make arrangements.

----oOo0ooo----

CHAPTER 7

LUFTHANSA DELIVERED me safely and on time at Heathrow Terminal 2 arriving shortly after 6.00 p.m. I had spent the flight of just over two hours trying to put my thoughts in order. There were so many unanswered questions arising from the circumstances of Bernard's death. I had taken a line pad from my document case. I started with the question 'When did Bernard enter the blimp?' There seemed to be only two answers which I wrote down as headings for separate columns: 'Before Klinger and Johann left' or 'After Klinger and Glock departed'.

My second question was why Bernard had entered. I wrote down two answers under the first column: 'Curiosity – heard or saw something,' and 'Couldn't find way out.' I entered the latter answer under the second column but couldn't think of another.

The third question was less straightforward. 'What happened to Bernard after he entered?' In either case the answer was imponderable. I wrote down 'Don't know', then speculated. In the first case, if the time lock had not been activated he could have wandered in and then seen something that he was not supposed to see, possibly the contents of boxes that Klinger and Glock were unpacking. If the door was locked, he must have been attracted by the entry light and made himself heard from outside; then one of the two inside must have let him in. What happened then was guesswork. Either Klinger or Glock could have knocked him unconscious or killed him to prevent his leaving or, less likely, there had been an accident. Either way the two Hartmann & Holst employees had left without him. In the second case, Bernard could have gained entry only in the first three minutes after they departed and before the door self- locked. If so, he would have had a further three minutes in which to leave before the door was re-locked. What could have attracted his attention sufficiently to tarry? Presumably Klinger would have ensured that the unpacking was complete and all contents stowed way in the racks or stacked; so, the warehouse would have been in order and only a particularly nosey visitor would have given more than a cursory glance at the stock shelves. Another mystery which I noted in the second column.

Moving forward, the next question to present itself was whether the sabotage of the local power station that caused an outage as Tom and I left that night was only a coincidence. If Klinger and Glock had departed before Bernard entered, that seemed likely. On the other hand, if they had disabled or murdered him it was plausible that they had disabled the station before returning home. I entered these thoughts into the respective columns.

And that led to a further question. 'When was the fuel tank for the generator pump syphoned off and by whom?' If Bernard had been assaulted as I had begun to suspect, the answer was clear. In order to be certain that the air supply would be cut off and the blimp deflated the pair would have had to ensure that there was insufficient fuel in the tank for more than a few hours to cover the period before Tom, Heinrich and I left the factory, and that meant that they acted immediately after leaving the warehouse and before quitting the factory. But they would have had no motive for tampering with the fuel supply if they left before Bernard made his entrance, and that is where my musing had closed with a question mark in the second column. As a final thought, I wrote down at the bottom of my pad one final note. 'When had Heinrich left for home?'

Having reclaimed my baggage and passed through customs with my trolley, there was a pleasant surprise. Gaby was waiting to greet me with a big hug.

"Welcome back," she said. "I got back to London early and thought it would nice to collect you for a change rather than the other way round."

We hastened across the bridge to the second storey of the Terminal 2 carpark, found Gaby's Ford Capri 2.8S and drove back to London against the evening traffic.

---ooo0ooo---

On the drive back from Heathrow Gaby had regaled me with a hilarious account of her group discussions with Bolton housewives on the rival merits of competing washing machines. The variety of usages to which spin dryers could be put were a revelation which challenged the imagination. One problem for Gaby was that her client's brand had been poorly rated against major competitors and she would have to write a report with unwelcome findings. She had to hope that the client would not 'shoot the messenger' and terminate her assignment. By consent, we decided to defer the full account of my adventures until we were home; so, when we reached our flat in Bayswater and having put the Capri into its slot in the underground carpark, I took a quick shower and changed into chinos, denim shirt and pullover, while Gaby poured restorative drinks – Chardonnay from the fridge for her and a stiff scotch and soda for me. Sitting comfortably at the kitchen table, I gave her a detailed account of events as they had taken place from the moment when Bernard and I had arrived at Stuttgart three days earlier until I had returned to the Flughafen that afternoon.

Gaby looked thoughtful. "Having escaped intact from castle Dracula, what are your first impressions of the people you met at Leuffen, starting with the Hartmanns?".

"Overall, a mixed collection of characters. I would say that Peter Hartmann is arrogant, overconfident most of the time but strangely respectful of his warehouse manager, Klinger. He lives very much in the shadow of his father

Manfred, an imposing character of authority and intelligence with more than a hint of his military background, perfect for Hollywood central casting in a war movie."

"What about Heinrich Hoffmeyer?"

"A highly accredited and respected engineer in the German spring industry and also an entertaining companion. Probably a soldier as a young man in the latter period of the war but not with Manfred Hartmann, I think. Seems to consider himself an ally in investigating Bernard's death."

"And Gottfried Klinger. You seem to be suspicious of him."

"Yes. I'm pretty sure that he was the resident Gestapo officer in Manfred Hartmann's allied concentration camp. That doesn't mean he's guilty of anything now, but I certainly felt that he was sparring with me. Probably still answers to Manfred although nominally he is responsible to Peter. As for Johann, his sidekick, he is a looming presence and certainly works for Hartmann senior."

"Well, that leaves the policeman and the father and daughter who run the Gasthof. How important are they to the plot?" I thought for a moment before replying. "Otto with his sinister appearance and the flamboyant Brigitta, not at all. But Kommisar Vogel will be highly important in deciding whether or not there was an accident. He certainly impresses as the voice of authority and may be a competent investigating officer if he decides otherwise."

"Unless he is also under Manfred's thumb," Gaby added.

That completed our survey of the *dramatis personae* and seemed a good point to take a break in our discussion. We were also coming up to the time of the table reservation that Gaby had made for us. And so, two hours after my landing we were sitting in our favourite Greek taverna, off Queensway and a short walk from the flat in Porchester Terrace. We were both ravenous and ordered quickly: dolmades, keftaides and taramasalata with pita bread for starters, followed by lamb kftiki with a salad rich in black olives and feta cheese. Neither of us cared much for ouzo or retsina; so we drank Naousa, the taverna's house red. Munching dolmades contentedly I took from my pocket the notes that I had made and passed the sheet to Gaby who studied them carefully before brushing a strand of blonde hair from her eyes and forking taramasalata on to a piece of bread.

"The balance of your analysis seems to be that Bernard was bopped by Klinger or Glock after they were interrupted," she concluded. "But what do you think they were up to?"

"Yes. I believe that the coincidences on which the accident theory depends are just too great to be plausible. And I think that what Bernard saw were contents of the crates that they were unpacking but we can only guess what they were."

Our debate was interrupted by the arrival of Stelios, the taverna's owner touring the tables, who greeted us effusively as regular customers. Placing an arm around my shoulders and giving me an over-familiar squeeze while bowing formally to Gaby, he enquired how we were in the pigeon English that he had failed to tame in more than twenty years as a London resident. Grinning inanely at our friendly response and after a few indecipherable comments about the menu, he grasped the bazouki which hung around his neck and struck a few chords. Stelios was under the delusion that he had musical talent; whenever he started to play waiters and guests alike raised eyebrows to heaven or huddled closer over their tables. This evening, as usual, after a flurry of discordant strumming he moved off to lavish his attentions on the next table, a party of American tourists for whom this would be unexpected entertainment.

Our waiter served our main course and I passed the salad to Gaby. "You know," she volunteered. "Klinger might not be the villain of the piece. There is another candidate."

"Who might that be?"

"Your friend Heinrich, of course. Suppose Bernard had found his way into the blimp just after Klinger and Johann left and was there when you and Tom left. Without any lights he might have found a way to attract Heinrich's attention either as he returned to his office or when he finally left."

"Alright, let's suppose he did. What then?"

"Well, after realising that Bernard was in there and had probably seen what was in the crates, all that Heinrich needed to do was to drain off enough of the fuel tank to ensure that the air pump would fail during the night - "

"Leaving Bernard to an unpleasant death of slow asphyxiation," I finished for her.

"Yes, it means that Heinrich was the instigator or a conspirator in whatever dodgy business was going on."

"I admit that it's possible, but I don't buy it," I replied. "That's only because you like him."

While reflecting on Gaby's alternative theory and trying to make an honest appraisal, I drained my wine and refilled our glasses. After a pause, I was ready to respond.

"I do like Heinrich but it's more than that. Murdering in cold blood seems out of character and I don't see him as a co-conspirator of Klinger or, for that matter, with the Hartmanns if they were directing operations."

Further speculation seemed pointless for now; so our conversation turned to plans for the weekend while we finished our meal with fresh fruit and Turkish coffee. We strolled back to the flat hand in hand and Gaby decided to take a shower while I poured myself a nightcap and pondered further. The outstanding question for the Leuffen incident was what Bernard had seen in the warehouse and where it was now. That would be the focus of my review with Tom tomorrow.

"Come up and see me sometime," called Gaby from the shower giving her exaggerated imitation of Mae West.

"But I've already showered."

"This one might be different." There was no answer to that, so I did as I was told. A warm welcoming embrace with shower gel and hot water were irresistible. One thing led to another and it was midnight before we turned over in bed and fell soundly asleep.

----ooo0ooo----

CHAPTER 8

5 May 1978, London

THE NEXT DAY BEING FRIDAY we were due to drive down to Sussex after work for a weekend with friends. It was a beautiful Spring day and I decided to walk across Hyde Park, Green Park and St, James's Park to the offices in Buckingham Palace Gate leaving Gaby to load the Volvo with our weekend bags and collect me there later that afternoon. With the daffodils in full bloom under a cloudless sky, a few intrepid bathers splashing in the Serpentine and a detachment of Household Cavalry from Knightsbridge barracks exercising in Rotten Row as I passed by; this was picture postcard London at its best and I wondered briefly why anyone would choose to live in another city. The brisk walk which took me some forty-five minutes helped to clear my brain about the three previous days' events and prepared me for the catechism from Tom which I knew awaited me.

Allied Autoparts occupied the fourth floor of rather cramped offices in a converted Victorian building in Buckingham Gate. The upside was that the address was in central London and that AA had three spaces allocated in the underground car park accessed from the rear of the building. When our complete team of four were all in London there was a scramble for the remaining two spaces after the one reserved for Tom by right of seniority. Another good reason for walking when the weather was clement.

Today, Tom's door was open as he sat behind his desk peering over his half moon clerical spectacles. Although his office was more spacious than the others his bulky frame was shoehorned behind a desk which appeared too small for comfort.

"Come in Julian," he called "and close the door before you sit down." I did as I was told, lowering myself into the single chair in front of the desk.

"Now, I want your complete report of what happened after I left and throughout yesterday," Tom continued. "The facts in detail first and then we can come back to your impressions and conclusions."

My unembellished report took some twenty minutes to deliver. Tom listened to me carefully throughout, writing down only a few notes at key points in the tale as they occurred to him. At the end, there was lengthy period of silence, while he scanned my face carefully over his spectacles; the Norfolk farmer, I thought, assessing his livestock.

"You realise," he said at last "that there are a number of inconsistencies in the evidence on which we should focus."

"Of course." I repeated by rote the questions that I had summarised during my flight backthe previous evening.

"And which of the two hypotheses do you favour, young Julian; accident by misadventure or skullduggery by Klinger and his sidekick?"

"Well, the unfortunate accident theory is only plausible if you accept the coincidences of timing with a high degree of inquisitiveness by Bernard, and ignore the evidence of the leaking oil line to the air pump."

"Do you think Kommissar Vogel will get to the bottom of it?"

"I would hope so, but he might be inclined to go for the more comfortable explanation for the Hartmann family."

"And that raises the question of whether Hartmann father and son are involved," mused Tom.

"There is an alternative candidate," I interrupted advancing Gaby's theory. "Heinrich Hoffmeyer could have been the perpetrator given the timing, after Bernard's entry into the blimp."

"On the face of it an unlikely candidate but we can't dismiss the possibility altogether. He could have acted on the spur of the moment to drain the fuel tank if Bernard succeeded in attracting his attention after locking himself in unintentionally. But what was his motive since he would hardly have been acting under instruction?"

"It must have been something secret that the company was planning to ship to Brazil, probably a part of the consignment delivered to Leuffen that evening. And that something would have been the same motive for Klinger and Glock – although they certainly were following instructions."

"Whereas Heinrich would have been a principal player, if there was a plot, do you think?" Tom asked.

"I still don't see him as a conspirator in something shady," I replied. "On first impression, he seems far too extrovert and dedicated to maintaining his professional reputation than to engage in something illegal or dangerous. Also, I like him."

"I like him too but you would be wrong to think of him only as a boffin. He has a reputation as a man of action." Tom saw my expression of incredulity and continued. "Heinrich Hoffmeyer is another member of the cast at Leuffen with a colourful war record, in his case as a demolition expert."

"I can see that as consistent with his expertise and draining the fuel tank, but 'man of action' – surely that's pushing it a bit, Tom?"

"Not at all. No doubt he was fitter and thinner with better eyesight then, but as a young man in 1943 he parachuted on to the Corinth canal bridge at night, set demolition charges, abseiled down to a boat waiting for him below and then detonated the fuses as they sailed away."

"That's a remarkable story. What happened to him then?"

"He was captured two days later by Greek partisans who could have shot him out of hand, but fortunately for Heinrich they were impressed by his feat and regarded him as almost one of their own. They handed him over to us and he spent the rest of the war in a British concentration camp in Yorkshire." "Hence Heinrich the anglophile."

"So it would appear," concluded Tom "but as we both know appearances can be deceptive." There was a further pause for reflection as we both considered where the conversation had so far taken us. This time, I broke the silence. "What should we do now?" I questioned. "Probably very little for the time-being." Tom peered over his half-moon spectacles again.

"I'll draft a report for Farmington giving a short account of the facts and explaining that the Polizei are carrying out an investigation."

"Do you want me to write a report to you that you can draw on?" I volunteered.

"I think not. Let's avoid frightening the horses until we're sure that something more sinister than an accident is involved. An army of corporate US investigators at this stage with little or no experience of conditions in Germany or even Europe would be counter-productive and a nightmare for you and I to handle. Better to be parsimonious, if not economical with the facts."

As I stood up and prepared to leave Tom's office. "There are two other things we can do today," he added. "I will call Peter Hartmann to check when the consignment for Campinas is due to leave Leuffen and ask what young Schiessel had to say about filling the fuel tank." "Yes. If there was something dodgy in this week's inward consignment it will be intended for shipment to Brazil and it is possible that Kommisar Vogel and his team fail to inspect the warehouse thoroughly while it is still in there."

---ooo0ooo---

I spent the rest of the morning in my shoebox of an office down the corridor from Tom's and focused on the assignment I had been given to introduce into each of the European subsidiaries the same mail order catalogue and service offered to design engineers in the US for a range of nearly 1,000 standard specification spring components. Based on a behavioural analysis of how engineers designing machines, engines and pretty well anything with moving parts, this was less boring than it sounded. Apparently, the norm was for them was to configure designs for the shape, chassis and functional parts, such as pistons, valves, levers, rotor arms and so on first, leaving a hole or gap for the spring necessary to activate the machine; and then to pass the spring design and prototype manufacturing requirement to the springmaker. This was a time-consuming and costly exercise for the springmaker with no certainty that the machine or engine would ever see the light of day or that the contract to manufacture the spring would be awarded to them. The AA solution was to provide a comprehensive catalogue of springs offering the required functional performance in alternative dimensions from which the original equipment manufacturer could select at the outset of the design process and receive by return mail. Originated by the technical team at Farmington, the catalogue had gained rapid acceptance from automobile manufacturers in Detroit and was a big hit among office machine producers elsewhere. As usage flourished among a wider variety of industries the catalogue range expanded and the service was named DES, an acronym for Design Engineers Springs.

It was my job to work up a presentation of DES for each of the AA European subsidiaries and to sell the concept to the management at each location before developing the project with them. I was not at all sure of the reaction to the US mail order approach.

At lunchtime I munched on a salami and cheese toastie which Molly, our office administrator and shared secretary thoughtfully provided with a cup of coffee. By midafternoon having drafted my presentation I had identified a short list of potential catalogue printers with London offices and was working through them by telephone to invite proposals. Shortly after 3:00 p.m. Tom poked his head round the door and asked me to join him. I could tell from his expression that he had something serious to impart.

"I've spoken to Peter Hartmann and there's bad news," he announced without preamble. "Young Schiessel is dead; both he and his girlfriend. They were biking down to the factory from Hohen Leuffen this morning, when his motorcycle skidded off the road on one of the hairpin bends and crashed into the gorge below."

"How can that be? Was it raining?"

"No, another fine Spring morning. The police say that there was probably a patch of oil on the road."

"Let me guess," I said "That means Peter never had the opportunity to question him about the oil tank."

"Quite. And Peter did not seem too cut up about it. More of a tiresome inconvenience than anything else."

"That's in line with his reaction to sending Bernard's body back to England. Perhaps he's just habitually insensitive rather than callous. Did you ask Peter when the consignment for Campinas is scheduled to leave the factory?"

"Yes. He looked in his planner and said that the despatch date would be 18th May. That gives us time to make our own warehouse inspection the week after next before it leaves and when we shall be there anyway for a visit from Farmington top management for a first visit to Hartmann & Holst since the acquisition. There was a call from the corporate office earlier."

Changing the subject, Tom passed me a copy in longhand of his report to Farmington. "You might want to comment," he said. It was little more than a single page bulletin setting out the reason for Bernard's visit to Leuffen on Tuesday, the timeline of his and our movements until we parted in the factory that evening and the discovery of the flattened blimp and his body the following morning in the presence of the police. There was no mention of the discharge from the pump fuel tank which Heinrich Hoffmeyer had brought to my attention. Tom noted my raised eyebrow. "Plenty of time to go into it all later when we have the Kommisar's report."

"I don't suppose you'll add on the news of Alberich Schiessel's death?" I questioned.

"Just another coincidence. Besides, Molly has already typed up my report as a telex and sent it". Tom beamed blandly.

"Or a case of collateral damage if our suspicions are correct." We left it at that.

---ooo0ooo---

Gaby collected me at five o'clock having parked on a meter without paying and then coming up to the office where she and Molly enjoyed a few words together. There was a ticket on the windscreen of the Volvo when we descended – not a good start to the weekend – but we were ahead of the worst of the traffic and I took back doubles through Fulham and Chelsea avoiding Sloane Square so that it was barely 5:30 when we crossed Putney Bridge. There was no avoiding the Friday night exodus after that and we took nearly another hour to reach the Dorking bypass when the traffic began to thin out. I had plenty of time to update Gaby on the day's events and she shared my view that the motorbike accident between Hohenleuffen and Leuffen as reported beggared belief as a coincidence. "If we're right that the accident was rigged," she asked "does that support the Klinger and co. or the Heinrich theory best?"

"I don't really see Heinrich venturing up the road in the middle of the night to smear oil on the road although the tale of his wartime exploit does confirm that he would have the nerve."

"Either way, I don't like the sound of it. Leuffen begins to sound a very dangerous place in which to start asking questions and I don't like the idea of you rootling around there on your own."

"There's little risk of solo rootling," I replied defensively "Tom has ruled that we do nothing before the police complete their investigation and, in any case, when we do explore the warehouse, we'll be doing so together. Manufacturing another accident for the two us really seems unlikely."

"Don't be so cocky. You never know what might happen in another country," said Gaby darkly.

CHAPTER 9

5 May 1978, West Sussex

AS WE NEARED PULBOROUGH my thoughts turned to Bill and Barbara Fentiman, our hosts for the weekend. Bill was a close friend from Oxford days where he had read Law seriously while I had sauntered through Philosophy, Politics and Economics (PPE). We had both graduated, Bill with a solid Second and I with a casual Third having scored rather better in Economics than the other papers. Since then our paths had diverged, mine into the world of business and Bill's into a middle rank City law firm. We had kept in occasional touch until five years ago when he had married Barbara and I had attended the wedding with Gaby who was already my established partner. While Gaby was blonde, fine-boned with high cheek bones and slender, Barbara was brunette, fuller faced and heavier set. Where Barbara was extrovert and vivacious, Gaby was more reserved but they shared a similar overdeveloped sense of humour. Experience had taught me that the wives of male university and old school friends seldom got on well, but the two of them related immediately when Gaby dropped a canapé into the champagne glass of an over-attentive admirer as Barbara and Bill came across to talk to us after the reception line-up. While Bill and I contrived to kept straight faces, the girls collapsed in stitches.

After that we socialised regularly; dinner parties in our flats, evenings together at the theatre and even the occasional weekend in Cornwall. We talked about holidaying together in France or Greece but instinctively shied away from that level of commitment having seen how shared holidays abroad had become the graveyard of beautiful friendships among many of our acquaintances.

Then two years ago, Bill's father who was the senior partner in a firm of West Sussex solicitors, died suddenly of a massive heart attack and his mother decided to move to Northumbria to live with her widowed sister. Bill decided to replace his father as a partner at the Arundel law office and to take on his parent's house at the foot of the Downs. Barbara, who had never been a city girl, was delighted and adapted easily to a more relaxed country life plunging into the local village round of fetes, WI and church activities. With his experience as a corporate lawyer Bill brought a new dimension to the rather sleepy law office which had subsisted mainly on conveyancing and family affairs. Within six months he had added a number of local businesses to the firm's clientele.

Shortly after the Fentiman's move to Sussex, Gaby and I finally got married. We had been in no particular hurry to tie the knot as we had decided that we were probably too selfish to have children but my mother had been nagging us to marry for several years. She had done her best to accept our co-habitation although her friends no doubt considered it 'living in sin' and she saw an opportunity to push us to the altar when she and my father decided to take a long holiday in South Africa from which "we might never return if we are struck down." Bill was my best man and Barbara was enlisted as Gaby's maid of honour.

And so we became regular and always welcome visitors to Badgers, the stone Georgian former rectory which was now Bill and Barbara's home near Bury Gate off the main road between Pulborough and Arundel. This evening as we pulled up outside the wisteria clad stone frontage bathed in the glow of a setting sun the old house looked its mellow best.

Barbara and Bill had heard the scrunch of the Volvo's tyres on the gravel and were there to greet us before we had time to take our bags out of the car.

---ooo0ooo---

"Well done, you two," cried Barbara "Lovely to see you both. We thought you would be later; so it's a simple supper. Fish pie and a blackberry and apple crumble." "Perfect. I'm famished," replied Gaby linking arms as they marched into the house. Bill helped me with the bags and we followed them.

"You look tired Julian," Bill commented "Have you had a tough week?" "More unsettling than arduous. We'll tell all at dinner."

As usual when we had not been together for some time, conversation took the form of catchups on what we had been doing and then gossip about mutual friends. Fortified by fish pie and a robust Chilean cabernet sauvignon, Gaby entertained our hosts with a more elaborate account of her washing machine saga with Bolton housewives which they received with gales of laughter. Barbara countered with a series of vignettes of village life including the latest news on local feuds and rivalries among candidates for the forthcoming Parish Council elections.

"As you can see," Bill commented "we have all the ingredients for an Agatha Christie murder mystery."

"With Barbara as a young Miss Marple," I suggested.

Ever the discreet solicitor, Bill confined his contribution to the gently amusing tale of an unnamed elderly client who sought advice on changing her will so that her dogs were the sole beneficiaries and, more controversially, on the appointment of her most intelligent Labrador as an executor.

When it came to my turn I tried to maintain the mood with as jokey a report as I could muster of my week in Germany, focusing on encounters at the Leuffen Gasthof and my visit to Schloss Hohenleuffen which Gaby continued to call Castle Dracula. When Bill and I went through to their sitting room to turn on the ten o'clock TV news while the girls repaired to the kitchen, I realised that my attempt at levity had failed to convince him. "Your experience at Leuffen has more to it than you make out, hasn't it?" he asked.

"I fear that it might, whatever the conclusion that the Polizei reach about Bernard's death", I replied.

"In that case, you should start having a thought about your own safety."

"That's what Gaby says and I've promised her that I won't try to carry out any investigation by myself."

"I know you of old too well, Julian, to be satisfied by that assurance. You need to remain an observer rather than become a participant"

"Yes Bill, I know you're right," I replied meekly.

---ooo0ooo---

6 May 1978, Sussex

Plans for the weekend featured a visit to the Chichester Festival on the Saturday evening to see a new stage adaptation by Michael Redgrave of The Aspern Papers and then lunch on Sunday with Barbara's aunt Miranda and her second husband Max joining us from their home near Lewes.

On Saturday morning Barbara and Gaby drove into Arundel to shop while Bill and I played tennis. At Oxford we had played as doubles partners on the college team but Bill was the better singles player and had gained a Blue. On grass courts he outpaced me every time but on his slower hard court I stood a chance. Today I took two games off him in the first set and three in the second. In the third set I surprised us both by taking him to five all when we decided to call it a day. A sit-back in the garden after a late lunch and it was time to change for the theatre. It was another sunny evening and the girls had decided to wear long dresses, green floral for Barbara and a bold pink sleeveless shift for Gaby, but Bill and I were allowed to dress less formally in dark suits.

We had brought champagne and smoked salmon from London with us; so we drove into Chichester early and enjoyed drinks and canapes while strolling on the Festival Theatre lawn. In the theatre lobby we viewed the photographs of past productions and the studio portraits of former festival directors from Laurence Olivier to the present day; I placed an order for interval drinks at the bar and was allocated a numbered ticket with instructions where we would find them when the time came. The four of us had enjoyed Chichester productions for several years, driving down from London when we all lived there and more frequently since the Fentiman's move to Sussex. As always, entering the splendid auditorium and taking our seats around the open stage gave pleasurable anticipation of the performance to come. This production of *The Aspern Papers* was not a disappointment – well-directed and acted – but less entertaining, I thought, than others that season; so, I was ready for the interval.

Our drinks were waiting for us on a small waist-height round table near the entrance and I was handing them out with my back to the bar when a familiar voice hailed me from behind.

"Good evening, Mr. Radclive. What a pleasure to se you again so soon." I turned and found myself face to face with Manfred Hartmann, immaculate in a dove grey suit and a knitted pink silk tie.

"Herr Hartmann," I said and, recovering myself "A surprise indeed. I had no idea that you were an English theatregoer. Let me introduce you to my wife Gaby and our friends Barbara and Bill Fentiman. This is Manfred Hartmann who entertained me to lunch at his castle on Thursday." He bowed formally over each lady's hand while shaking them.

"Manfred please. Julian and I are good friends, I think. Yes, I have a particular interest in the Chichester Festival. If the Director agrees I am hoping that it may be possible to present two of the plays from this year's programme at Hohenleuffen next summer."

"That's a marvellous idea." replied Barbara "Have you decided on your choice yet?" "Certainly *A Woman of No Importance.* We have no equivalent to Oscar Wilde in Germany, in terms of wit you know. Our authors have no lightness in their humour. But I am undecided on the second play."

"What about *The Aspern Papers*?" Bill asked. "There is some following for Henry James's work because of its American origin, but I do not find stories of Boston society particularly interesting."

"We haven't seen the production yet, but is Noel Coward's *Look after Lulu* as a companion piece to Oscar Wilde under consideration?" Gaby suggested next. Manfred seemed irritated and cast her his piercing black-eyed stare.

"I think not," he responded coldly "We had sufficient experience of 1930's decadence in Berlin with Kurt Weill and Lottie Lenya before they abandoned Germany." It's at time like this that I admire Gaby's talent for provocation.

At this point the end of interval bell sounded and relieved the tension. "I must return to my own party," Hartmann concluded "I am staying with my old friends Konrad von Richthaven and the Baroness who are signalling to me." Across the lobby I observed a large good-looking man and tall woman of severe appearance observing us closely. He bowed again to the four of us: "Perhaps I shall hope to welcome you all to Hohenleuffen next year," then turned on his heel and threaded his way across the crowded lobby. Von Richthaven nodded in Bill's direction and Bill returned the acknowledgment.

"What a charming man," said Barbara brightly as we returned to our seats.

---ooo0ooo---

The second half of the play was more absorbing than the first and we descended to the lobby in the companionable afterglow of an enjoyable shared experience. As we reached the theatre exit a sleek black limousine drew up into which we could see Manfred Hartmann and his hosts enter before they were swept silently away. "How the other half lives," commented Bill as we returned to his modest Rover in the car park.

"Tell us about Konrad von Richthaven," I asked as Bill drove off. "He seemed to recognise you back there in the interval"

"Yes, we do have a nodding acquaintance," he confirmed. "Baron von Richthaven, to give him his title, is a steel magnate who restored his family's fortune after the war when the Allies encouraged the revival of the steel industry as a key player in the recovery of the German economy. He is semi-retired now and spends most of the year here in England; he is a keen owner and breeder of racehorses."

"And Baroness Magda is famous as a hostess at their estate the other side of Petworth, particularly the annual cocktail party on the Sunday in May before Goodwood week for the great and the good of the County and the racing world," added Barbara from the back seat. "Will Bill's nodding acquaintance earn you an invitation this year as one of the privileged few?" Gaby asked. "Not quite that sort of acquaintance," Bill laughed. " I came across the good Baron when acting for a client last year who had a dispute about stud fees with him and wanted to take him to Court. My client provided the sire to the Baron's mare but the union was unproductive."

"What happened?"

"In the event the matter was settled at the Court door. Neither party wanted the publicity of a hearing and the Baron agreed a rather generous settlement under pressure."

"Your pressure I imagine, Bill?"

"Just doing my best for the client. Actually, the Baron behaved like a gentleman but it was clear that he would not be joining my fan club."

Arriving back at Badgers we enjoyed the cold supper that Babara had left prepared and mulled over the evening's entertainment. We agreed that the play had been well performed with some enjoyable content but rather dry like the Chablis that Bill served with our meal and not one that any of us would go out of our way to see again. The conversation turned to our surprise encounter with Manfred Hartmann. Barbara characterised him as a 'smoothie' and Bill as a 'downy bird'.

"More of a bat than a bird," said Gaby and then, as we climbed the stairs to our bedrooms "He might be harmless but, just in case, better put garlic round your window frames tonight."

---ooo0ooo---

7 May 1978, Sussex

Gaby and I overslept and we were late down to breakfast the following morning. Barbara had already had hers and was busy in the kitchen preparing Sunday lunch. Bill looked up from the sports section of The Sunday Telegraph to wish us good morning. "Hello you two. You're too late for eggs and bacon but help yourselves to the rest." He waved vaguely towards the coffee pot and toast rack and carried on reading. While I stuffed slices of bread into the toaster Gaby poured herself a cup of coffee and Joined Barbara in her labours. I settled down with my toast and coffee to the main section of Bill's paper which I didn't read normally preferring the less politically slanted Sunday Times. The international news stories were focused on a pro-Russian military coup in Afghanistan and the French intervention in Chad earlier in the week. The financial pages forecast another oil crisis for 1979 but no immediate economic problems threatened in either Europe or America. Even the gossip columns held no eye-catching scandals to attract attention. It made last week's incident in Leuffen seem little more than a storm in a thimble-size teacup.

At 12:30 Miranda and Max Salinger arrived in their elderly Bentley. Miranda in a cashmere twinset with pearls and a tweed skirt was a much older version of Barbara, grey-haired and chunkier with a deaf aid and a loud parade ground voice to compensate. In his late sixties, Max was a distinguished figure with the wings of his carefully cut white hair brushed over his ears, dressed in immaculately tailored grey flannel with a regimental tie and suede brogues. A former very senior foreign office civil servant only recently retired, Barbara had briefed us, his accent and languid speech were unmistakably those of a mandarin giving the impression that perhaps he had not quite been put out to pasture. By contrast, in chinos and well-worn blazer I immediately felt scruffy.

To lighten any possible awkwardness Bill had chilled and now opened the two remaining bottles of duty-free Taittinger I had brought with us and Barbara served the rest of the smoked salmon. We took our drinks on the sun-drenched terrace and, by the time Barbara called us to table, we were all chatting amiably as if we had known each other for years. Miranda and Barbara exchanged family gossip being careful to keep Gaby involved. She quickly grasped that in order to keep conversation with Miranda flowing it was necessary to talk loudly into the deaf aid and then to sit back for a responding bellow.

Meantime, Bill, Max and I started to break the ice by exchanging banal comments about the economy, Westminster politics and the performance of the Sussex County cricket team.

Then, as Bill replehed our glasses, Max turned to me with a direct question. "Is Charles Radclive by any chance a relative of yours?"

"Yes, he's my father as ever was." I responded. "Do you know him?"

"Indeed, I probably owe my life to him, certainly my good health today. You see, when I was wounded in the Italian campaign in 1943 they patched me up and sent me home to one of your father's convalescence hospitals without much hope that I would ever have an active life again. But, as a skilled surgeon, your father had other ideas. He had me transferred to the general hospital where he practised and re-set my pelvis. During the long period of recovery when they taught me to walk again I got to know him quite well. I didn't realise he was still alive. How is he?"

"Very well. He's retired now, of course, living in Oxfordshire and still enjoying the shooting season."

"Do give him my regards when you next see him. Perhaps he would welcome a call from me?" "I'm sure he would," I replied warmly.

Lunch was relaxed and convivial as we enjoyed a rack of lamb followed by trifle. Bill opened a bottle of his good claret but Max and I, mindful of driving home later, drank sparingly while both Miranda and the girls became quite merry. We were asked how we had enjoyed the theatre the previous evening and Barbara mentioned the coincidence of our encounter with Manfred Hartmann. This led inevitably to my visit to Germany the previous week and to the schloss which Gaby continued to call Castle Dracula. Max looked up from his trifle with quickening interest.

"Where did you say you were staying, Julian?" he asked quite abruptly. "A small village at the foot of the Swabian Alp called Leuffen." I replied.

"In that case the castle was Hohenleuffen," he exclaimed and then, as if realising that he had shown more than a passing interest, "A very fine example of the medieval castle dating back to the 12th century and expanded into a fortress at the beginning of the 14th century by Duke Ulrich of Wurtemburg. It actually held out under siege for more than a year during the Thirty Years War.......".

"Max," trumpeted Miranda from across the table "You mustn't bore everyone by riding your hobbyhorse through Barbara's splendid Sunday lunch."

"I'm suitably admonished," responded Max "I do tend to get carried away when discussing the history of medieval castles in Europe, particularly southern Germany."

"Oh, do go on," invited Gaby "I find European history fascinating."

"Of course, if you drive past Hohenleuffen and across the Swabian plateau towards Ulm," Max continued unabashed " you get good views from the road of one of mad Ludwig's more flamboyant castles – like an illustration for Grimm's fairy tales."

"Max, that's quite enough," bellowed Miranda and he subsided holding his hands up in mock surrender.

We took our coffee on the terrace enjoying the warm Spring sunshine and an uninterrupted distant view of Bury Hill beyond the garden and across meadows. Soon after 3:00 p.m Miranda showed signs of preparing to leave and started to make appropriate noises. "You mustn't go until you have seen my new flock of Favorelles hens. I've only had them a week and they are already laying." Drawing Miranda and Gaby to their feet she set off across the garden and through a wicket gate in the hedge while Bill gathered the coffee cups and took the tray back into the house. "Let's take a turn around the garden, Julian, shall we?" said Max strolling in the opposite direction. I guessed that he had something to ask or impart privately.

"You may have suspected that my interest in Leuffen and Hohenleuffen is more than casual?" he began as we moved away.

"The thought did cross my mind, but it was probably not so obvious to anyone else."

"I'm not usually quite so transparent," he continued "and I can't tell you too much now but I would like to offer some advice, if you find that you need it." He withdrew a business card from a pocket and passed it to me. The printed legend was simple: Maxim Salinger, MBE, and underneath *The Adnser, Special Operations Executive*, then an address in Knightsbridge and two telephone numbers.

"I thought that the SOE was disbanded soon after the War?" I questioned.

"Quite right, old boy." Max drawled. "Subsumed into MI6 at the end of 1946. But someone has to look after the archives and record news of the survivors who are still around. They offered me the job to keep me out of mischief when I retired."

"But why Leuffen? I thought that the SOE was never active in Germany itself."

"Not very successfully, but there were a few loose ends from operations in France and Austria which strayed into German territory at the end of the War and I am expected to record those too. All that I wanted to say to you today is that should you come across anything untoward in your sub-Swabian travels you might like to give me a call."

"And what kind of *untoward* did you have in mind."

"Nothing specific." Max was studiously vague now "Spoils of war and old soldiers who never die – that sort of thing, you know. Nothing more that I can tell you, Julian. I may have said too much already."

I studied the card again. "If I should want to get in touch, which number should I ring?"

"The first number is my direct line – there's an answer machine if I'm not there. Or if it's anything urgent the second number is manned day and night and you can speak freely." We had completed a circle of the house as Bill hailed us. "There you both are. Come and join the ladies. Barbara is very proud of her flock and likes to show it off to all visitors".

I had to admit that the Favorelles chicken were attractive with their distinctive beards, brown and pinkish white plumage and feathered feet, unusually five-toed. "They come from Normandy," explained Barbara "and are very friendly as well good layers."

"At least they're not German," cried Miranda laughing uproariously at her own joke.

---ooo0ooo---

Max and Miranda drove off in the Bentley soon afterwards having made Barbara and Bill promise to take us over to Lewes to lunch the next time we were down for the weekend. Gaby and I stayed a little longer; after packing our bags we took an early cup of tea and discussed when we would next spend time together – "Wimbledon, if not before" we promised ourselves.

Again we were ahead of the evening traffic, weekenders returning to London after rural rest and recuperation, and it was not until we were almost at Roehampton that Gaby picked up on our lunchtime conversation. "I liked Miranda and Max," she said. "She's right out of drawing room comedy, and Max is the archetypical diplomat but a bit of a smoothie. Strange how much he seemed interested in Leuffen. It wasn't just the castle was it?"

"So you picked up on that too." I hadn't meant to tell her about my opaque conversation with Max but handed her the business card. "What do you make of that? He buttonholed me to tell me about his part-time retirement occupation when Barbara dragged you off to inspect the chicken."

"That's curious," Gaby commented. "The address is somewhere behind Harrods but the second telephone number is certainly not Knightsbridge – somewhere south of the river, I'd say." The one that's manned day and night I reflected, but decided not to share the thought.

----ooo0ooo----

CHAPTER 10

THE GOOD WEATHER broke overnight and we woke to a grey London sky and rain. It was no day for walking; so I rose early and drove to the office hoping to secure a parking space. Gaby had a tedious day ahead commissioning freelance market researchers through her supervisors for a new client's national survey involving multiple telephone calls. I was in luck and was parking the Volvo when Tom's car swept into its slot. We travelled up to the office together in the lift and found ourselves the first to arrive. "Before we get started, you need to know about Bernard's funeral. I had a call from the family over the weekend and it's arranged for Thursday at 2:00 p.m. We need to be there. I'll brief you on it later."

As the seventh day after the previous month-end, 8th May was the due date for all AA subsidiaries to report their April financial results by telex via their regional directors to Farmington. And so our London office was fully occupied in receiving the numbers on long rolls of telex tape from Tipton, Amsterdam, Norkopping in Sweden and Leuffen which Tom then had to consolidate into a further report for Europe. To maintain security the headings were coded by line numbers which made the process even more cumbersome. The general managers also had to send short written reports of key management action under the heading 'Where do I stand' which had to be edited before being passed on with Tom's summary.

Since this was the first time that Hartmann & Holst had reported, some numbers were plainly incorrect and corrections had to be made by telephone and further exchanges of telex which taxed Tom's patience to the limit.

Peter Hartmann's report was threadbare of meaningful information and had to be supplemented by the information which Tom had gathered in person the previous week. By mid-afternoon the preparatory work was done and Molly was hunched over the telex machine typing in the final version for transmission.

I had spent the morning following up on the shortlist of possible printers for the DES catalogue. Some of them had sent me samples of catalogues which they already printed which helped to sort the sheep from the goats. Catalogues of tools and engineering consumables were relevant, some horticultural seed catalogues were of a similar complexity but illustrated mail order catalogues for women's lingerie were plainly unsuitable and had raised eyebrows when Molly had opened the post. It was something of a relief, therefore, when Tom called me into his office for a catch-up. He was in his shirtsleeves and the normally uncluttered desk was still strewn with paper from the incoming telex reports and his handwritten notes.

"We have an interesting ten days ahead," Tom announced. "The funeral on Thursday; then next week a visit from the Farmington corporate office top team to Leuffen which we are required to organize and attend. Their travel plan and the names of those who are coming will be revealed to us in the next day or so. But first the funeral."

"How did Bernard's family take the news when you were there last week?" I enquired.

"On the whole very well. His wife Nora was in a state of shock. She seemed a quiet, unemotional sort of woman but she may react more strongly when she comes out of her trauma. The daughter and son-in-law are another matter altogether."

"How do you mean?"

"Gladys the daughter takes it as a personal inconvenience that she has to look after her mother and her husband, a local solicitor has focused on claiming either against the company's travel insurance or against Hartmann

& Holst for damage due to negligence or both. He's a bumptious young man and bad news all round."

"Are there any other family?"

"Only a son working in Canada who is flying back today. Hopefully, he will be more supportive to Nora."

"What's to be done. Does AA have to consult its lawyers?"

"I've reported back to Farmington. AA has its own in-house attorney but they seem reluctant to defend a lawsuit. The first reaction is to treat it as a Human Relations issue; so they are sending someone to the funeral, the Chairman's personal management adviser called Viktor Accora. You'll meet him on Wednesday."

"That's a bit unusual, isn't it, for a US company to have an HR manager reporting direct to the Chairman?" I enquired.

"Viktor's an unusual kind of HR man," Tom continued. "To begin with he's not American. He's a Swiss national recruited from a well-known global security agency which advises on international staff terms and conditions and also workplace wrongdoing. Because he's Swiss he's also asked to assess European managers, their motivations and attitudes towards AA."

"So, we're all under scrutiny," I concluded. "From time to time," Tom conceded "but not quite Big Brother."

---ooo0ooo---

Tuesday was uneventful. Gaby was having problems recruiting researchers for her survey in the South West and decided to visit her Supervisor in Somerset driving down the next day and returning Friday. Tom received further instruction about the travel plans for the AA corporate office team in Europe the following week. They would fly over to Amsterdam on Sunday in the company Learjet where they would spend Monday in the Dutch factory before flying down to Stuttgart in the evening. We were asked to arrange transport and to book hotel rooms for seven for one night. On the Tuesday, the party would visit Hartmann & Holst for a business review and tour of the factory before returning to the airport mid-afternoon in order to fly up to Norrkoping for another review in the Swedish factory.

Since we wouldn't know the time of arrival until the Learjet flight plan was filed in Amsterdam we decided that the best plan of action was to book the AA flying circus into the Stuttgsrt Flughafen hotel for Monday night and to hire a minibus to drive them to Leuffen in the morning and return them to the airport in the afternoon. We agreed that we would take the first Monday morning flight to Stuttgart ourselves giving us time to conduct our inspection of the warehouse before I returned to the airport to meet the AA management team and stay with them overnight. Accordingly, we asked Molly to book eight rooms in the Flughaven, a minibus driver for Tuesday and our own return flights to Stuttgart and back later in the week.

During the afternoon each of us received a telephone call from Kommissar Vogel telling us that he needed to see us again before completing his investigation. We agreed to be interviewed in Leuffen on Wednesday 17th May. By the end of the day I had selected the three printers whom I considered most promising for the DES catalogue and had sent each of them a specification with an invitation to quote by the end of the following week.

I returned to the flat to find Gaby typing furiously in the study, having spent the day writing the questionnaire and instructions for her survey. She wanted to take copies with her in the morning for discussion in Bristol. I poured us both drinks and left her to it. After luxuriating in a hot bath with my whisky and soda I descended to the kitchen and started to prepare a spaghetti Bolognese, one of the few dishes in my limited culinary repertoire. I was pleased to find that we had all the ingredients including the parmesan cheese without which no pasta is complete. By the time

Gaby had finished and we had eaten it was time to watch the news on television, an episode of Dad's Army and so to bed.

Thursday dawned dark, miserable and threatening to rain. We left the flat at the same time, Gaby to drive to Bath and I by taxi to the office where Tom and I tossed a coin who should drive up to Wolverhampton where the funeral was to be held. Tom won the toss and elected to drive up there and we set off in his Jaguar in good time. As he drove Tom briefed me on members of the AA top management we would be meeting the following week. "Did you meet any of them when you were over there?" he asked.

"I was introduced to Barry MacLennan and Lloyd Parmentier but had only brief conversations with them individually. Barry was friendly and quite welcoming; Lloyd asked some questions about my experience including my time in the army which seemed curious. I didn't meet the others"

Tom smiled quietly to himself. "Barry is always a pleasure to meet. He likes to be underestimated but you do so at your peril. As President he has a relaxed management style and prefers to listen rather than talk unless someone says something really foolish. His comments are usually laconic and always to the point. Be sure to watch his expressions. What he doesn't say is often more important than the utterance." "And Lloyd?" I asked. "A very different character. While Barry came from a very modest background and worked his way up to Vice-President of an IBM division before joining AA, Lloyd is the younger son of an old Virginian family with a sense of entitlement. His father was a general in World War II and went on to found a leading Boston management consultancy. Lloyd never served in the army and that's probably why he may have a chip on his shoulder when he talks to you."

"But that's ridiculous," I protested. "My military career was no more than two years of National Service including less than six months in Germany."

"You know that and I know that, but you were commissioned in a well-known regiment and that is one up on Lloyd." "It only matters" Tom continued "because you'll be under his scrutiny and in contact with him more often than you might choose. You will soon realise that he's very ambitious and after Barry's job. So, both of us need to be careful not to be used as pawns in his game."

"And the others?" I asked again moving on to the other members of the party whom I had not yet met. "Erik Nielsen and Loren Corley," Tom mused.

"Erik is inscrutable. Another observer, he can maintain a poker-face and stay silent throughout a two hour management meeting. You'll probably only hear from him when he queries your monthly expenses report. Loren is a genuinely nice man with a keen intellect. He is the corporation's unchallenged authority on all things technical but always gives generous credit to those in the AA plants for their work. He is also married to Betsy, a member of the Case family, which gives him additional status."

"That leaves Viktor Accona, Chester Cases's bag carrier, and the man himself."

"You'll form your own opinion of Viktor for yourself this afternoon. Chester is the ultimate decision-maker. Although he is listed as a non-executive chairman and AA is a public-listed company, the Case family still hold more than thirty per cent of the shares; and so he involves himself in pretty well everything other than day to day operations. He's also a keen aviator," Tom continued "which is why there's only one professional pilot on the Learjet this trip. Chester likes to fly the plane much of the time when he is aboard except for difficult landings and take-offs. He is trying his hand at politics which could distract him from AA."

"What level of politics?" I enquired.

"He chairs the Democrat party organisation in Connecticut and because the family have a second home on the ocean at Hyannis and are chummy with the Kennedys the word is that he might seek nomination as a candidate for the State Governor's office."

"And that means AA has to be squeaky clean and avoid scandal." "You've got it." finished Tom.

We had sailed up the M1 with little traffic while the rain held off but the heavens broke again as we turned off the motorway to drive around Birmingham to the Gravely Hill spaghetti junction. All Tom's concentration was required to contend with windscreen washers and the spray thrown up by heavy vehicles and conversation was constrained. The rest of our journey to Wolverhampton passed in near silence as we drove through the sodden and depressing Black Country streets on our route to the crematorium. There were more cars than I had expected in the car park and a straggle of mourners, all of us in dark clothes and most with our umbrellas up against the rain, now an unrelenting drizzle. About thirty of us clustered under the overhang of the crematorium porch awaiting the arrival of the hearse and attendant family. One bespectacled figure in a black raincoat drew our attention when he signalled to Tom from the back of the group. There was no time for us to engage before the doors of the vestibule opened and uniformed attendants ushered us in. We congregated on the way into the chapel and took our seats together towards the rear with Tom between the newcomer and myself. "Good afternoon, Tom," our companion intoned in a heavily accented whisper. Then, leaning across Tom, "You must be Julian."

As I took Viktor Accona's proffered hand I could see that his tinted glasses were thick lensed making it doubly difficult to read his expression. With a sallow complexion, a carefully groomed thatch of glossy black hair, square face and letterbox mouth, Viktor gave a somewhat sinister first impression. An alternative greeting of "I've been expecting you, Mr. Bond" would not have surprised me. Introductions were interrupted by the arrival of Bernard's coffin to the accompaniment of canned organ music and followed by the family. As they passed to take up their places in the front pew we caught our first sight of each member. Nora, sombre but composed, came first leaning on the arm of what I assumed to be her son with a strong resemblance to Bernard. She was followed by a brassy blonde and a short tubby man with a toothbrush moustache, whom I took to be Gladys and her husband. All of them wore sober black albeit a rather unfortunate plastic trench coat in Gladys's case. The pallbearers were funeral directors' standard issue and a pair of senior undertakers with professionally mournful faces came last in the small procession.

The service was short but efficient: three prayers, two hymns, with one of St.Paul's despatches to the Corinthians read by Nora's son and a eulogy delivered by the clergyman, who had studiously compiled a catalogue of Bernard's life and achievements and highlights of his marriage to Nora with a generous account of his standing in the community. Finally, we came to that part of the cremation service which I like least: the committal prayer as the coffin slides automatically on its conveyor belt through the backlit red curtains into the unknown beyond usually accompanied by respectful piped music. It's the bleak finality which gets to me every time. On this occasion there was a surprise. As the coffin began its automated journey, in place of music there was a roar of accelerating high-powered cars; an acknowledgment of Bernard's passion for FI motor racing. It echoed aptly his sense of humour and Bernard would have enjoyed the moment.

The family and priest departed first through a side entrance; then the congregation of some fifty mourners filed out the way we had entered, signed the book of remembrance, inspected the wreaths recovered from the top of the coffin before incineration and looked lost.

Noticeable among the wreaths, now propped against a wall of the vestibule, were an ostentatious display of lilies with a card from Manfred and Peter Hartmann and a more conservative offering of roses from Allied Autoparts over the name of Barry Maclennan. as President.

The service sheet with a fine photograph of a younger Bernard grinning cheerfully informed us that we would all be welcome now for refreshments at the local Park View hotel. With Viktor carrying an overnight bag we walked back to the car and, after a decent interval to allow others to precede us set off for the station hotel to pay our respects. I have always quite liked funeral wakes, ever since the age of twelve when a friend of my father consoled me with the thought that he preferred them to christenings on the grounds that the teas afterwards were invariably better.

On the way there Viktor briefed us on how he intended to handle the compensation claim which he expected the Tompkins family to present. "Of course, Bernard was not an employee of AA or of Hartmann & Holst so that any claim against either would not succeed. The starting point could be a claim against Tipton Springs if it has no foreign travel insurance for staff."

"What about a claim for negligence against Hartmann & Holst?" I asked.

"They could do that," Viktor agreed. "And that might succeed if the company has third party cover for visitors. But the claim would take a long time to process. Like Swiss or even American insurance companies, German insurers will do everything they can to avoid paying out in this sort case. They would try to show that Bernard's death was not an accident in order to pass the claim on to someone else."

"So that Nora and the family would have to wait ages before receiving any cash," concluded Tom.

"It would be very expensive too. German lawyers charge even more than British solicitors and counsel, I believe; so I don't think the family would want to continue with a contested claim. Also, there is no widow's pension since Bernard had not reached pensionable age. Therefore, I have been authorized to offer a monthly pension for Mrs. Tompkins which AA will pay direct as compensation for her loss."

"That's a generous approach, I'm sure it will be appreciated," I remarked.

"Chester and the Board always like their employees to feel part of the family." Tom raised an eyebrow sardonically without commenting on Viktor's rather smug response.

Park View hotel, visible from the road, was approached by a sweeping gravel drive flanked by rhododendrons. The rain had lifted while we were at the crematorium but was sheeting now as Tom parked behind a row of cars rather nearer to the road than the hotel itself. We turned up the collars of our coats and made a dash for the entrance. The hotel was a solid late Victorian red brick building, probably built as the home for a prosperous Wolverhampton merchant or factory owner originally and converted in the 1920s or 1930s to its present use. The interior was dark and heavily panelled with a patterned Axminster carpet but a lighter wood reception desk with chromium fittings. The new stair carpeting and pine bannisters indicated that an attempt to modernize was in hand. Previously a resting place for commercial travellers or "gentlemen of the road" in pre- and post-war days, the hotel was in the process of adapting to the tastes of today's foreign visitors and Black Country tourists. We shed our coats and hung them up in the cloakroom, already heavily laden with damp-smelling raincoats and umbrellas, before proceeding to the spacious reception area where the wake was being held. The redecoration work had not yet reached what could have been a pleasant area. Instead, another Axminster carpet and flocked green wallpaper contributed to the solemnity of the occasion.

The Tompkins family were grouped at the farther end of the room holding cups of tea and looking rather lost. Most of the guests had already offered their perfunctory condolences and had descended on the buffet to load their plates with sandwiches, slices of egg and ham pie or quiches and cocktail sausages. Waitresses served tea or fruit juice from behind the tables.

There was a low burble of conversation and some covert glances were cast to the bar at the other end of the room which had not yet opened.

Tom led the three of us towards Nora who recognized him from his previous visit. "Nora" he greeted her in his best Norfolk farmer tones clasping her hand "A sad day but you did Bernard proud. A very moving service. These are my colleagues who have come to pay their respects. This is Viktor Accona from our head office in America and this is Julian Radclive who was with Bernard and me in Germany."

"Mrs Tompkins, I bring you the sympathy for your sad loss from our Chairman and the Board" said Viktor stepping forward and bowing stiffly. "We shall grieve with you and wish to assure you that we are ready to provide our support."

"Thank you, Mr. Hardy." Nora relied with the ghost of a smile "You've been very kind and you too Mr. Accona; thank you for coming all this long way. But I really don't know what I shall do now......."

My turn now to step forward and take her hand "I was with Bernard too, Mrs. Tompkins. I travelled out to Germany with him; I enjoyed working with him and he was a good travelling companion. I shall miss him" To add further expressions of sympathy after Tom and Viktor would have have sounded hollow.

Seldom at a loss for words and to avoid any embarrassing silence, Tom intervened offering his hand to Nora's son on her right "You must be Arthur. I'm glad you were able to come over in time." then turning to her left "You and I met last week, Mrs Clegg, when I visited your mother."

Arthur took Tom's hand in a firm grip "Thank you, Mr. Hardy, for making today's arrangements. My mother couldn't have managed on her own."

"Alfred and I could have helped her," interrupted Gladys sharply. "We're always here to look after her." Arthur gave her a brotherly scowl but kept his counsel. Little love there, I thought.

No longer wrapped in plastic, Gladys was now more conventionally dressed for a funeral and I thought that she could have been a pretty girl behind the heavy make-up but for her sullen expression.

The fourth member of Nora's group now thrust himself forward. "I'm Albert Clegg, Gladys's husband and the family's solicitor," and without further ceremony "I'm waiting to hear what Allied Autoparts is offering Mrs. Tompkins as compensation."

"We want my mother to have what is due to her." Gladys added superfluously.

Forewarned by Tom of what he might expect, Viktor was equal to the occasion. "This is neither the time nor the place for such discussion, Mr. Clegg. The company regards all members of its group as family and you may be sure that it will want to do the right thing." He regarded the whey-faced lawyer's unprepossessing appearance with polite disdain behind his horn-rimmed spectacles. Addressing Nora he added "Of course, Mrs. Tompkins, I would like to tell you tomorrow what I think the company can provide to help you. May I call on you in the morning at, say, 10:00?"

"I shall be free at 10:00 to see you in my office," the lawyer intervened.

"This is not a legal matter, Mr. Clegg. I'm sure your mother-in-law will be more comfortable talking about the future in her own home."

"And I'll be with you, mother," added Arthur. Nora looked gratefully at him and, addressing Albert, brought the discussion to a close. "I'm sure that will be nicer," she said.

A couple from the body of the room drifted over to talk to Nora giving us the cue to retreat. By now the bar had opened and I recognized several managers from the factory chatting together quietly with pint glasses in their hands. Nodding to them as we passed, Tom and I drifted towards the somewhat depleted buffet. We had not eaten lunch and needed to fortify ourselves for the return journey. Eschewing the anaemic-looking quiche we each loaded our plates with a wedge of Melton Mowbray pie, half scotch eggs and wilting cheese and chutney sandwiches which we washed down with cups of tea. Viktor who had briefly left the room re-joined us and confined himself to tea and a slice of madeira cake.

"I've booked myself in here for the night," he announced and asked Tom to introduce him to the Tipton Springs general manager. "I want to find out if there was any life insurance on Bernard which could be passed to the widow before I telephone Farmington for instruction on what we may offer her tomorrow."

Tom led him over to the group at the bar while I took Tom's car key and retrieved Viktor's overnight bag, leaving it for him at reception. Returning to the bar I heard Tom asking Viktor what his movements would be after meeting Nora the next morning.

"I'll fly from Birmingham to Zurich and spend the weekend there with my sister before joining Chester and the AA team in Amsterdam on Sunday evening," Viktor replied. "So you see we shall meet again in Germany on Monday evening."

This was something of a relief because I had feared that he might come down to London leaving Gaby and me to entertain him at the weekend.

"Time for us to return to London. Wagons roll, Julian; let's be on our way" said Tom, and when we reached the car "You have the keys and it's your turn to drive."

It had dried up while we were in the hotel and a watery sun raised hopes of a comparatively pleasant journey down the motorway. Having guided me back around Birmingham Tom adjusted the rake of the passenger seat, laid back and promptly went to sleep. The rain returned as we crossed the North Circular, the traffic flow into London increased and Tom awoke and cranked back his seat to its normal setting.

"Well, what did you think of our afternoon in Wolverhampton?"

"Pretty grim," I replied "but I thought Viktor handled the dreadful son-in-law rather well. It seems that AA will do the decent thing."

"More decently than it might do in normal circumstances." Tom raised an eyebrow and grinned cynically. "Don't forget that it's US election time again in November and Chester wouldn't want any bad publicity about treatment of staff dependents to get in the way of his run for the Governorship."

"Then they'll be hoping that the police come up with a clear verdict on Bernard of accidental death…."

"…. which means that we are expected to stifle any misgivings we may have when meeting with the Kommisar next week," Tom finished for me.

There seemed to be little more to say on the subject; so we finished the journey exchanging observations on the attendees at the wake. Tom dropped me off at the flat shortly after 7:00 p.m. I returned the call that Gaby had made on the answer 'phone, took a shower, ate a lonely boil in the bag curry, watched the news on television and so to bed.

---ooo0ooo---

Friday brought one surprise but was otherwise uneventful. The good weather had returned and I walked to the office to clear my head of Thursday's gloom. As I had requested there were three written quotations for the DES spring catalogue which I set aside in favour of a telex sent overnight from the AA head office in Farmington and addressed to me personally. Tom came into my office brandishing an identical personal telex. We were both summoned to attend a meeting of senior AA international managers in Rio de Janeiro for the week of 29 May, barely two weeks' time. The week in Brazil would include an overnight visit to the recently acquired Campinas factory of Grunwald Metallwerk. Although couched as invitations, they were signed off by Chester Case and we were in little doubt that refusals were hardly an option for those valuing their careers. In any case, we agreed that a week in Brazil as an all-paid business outing would be more of a holiday than serious work. We telexed back our formal acceptances and set Molly to investigate the flight options.

Turning my attention to the quotations I found that two were fixed price offerings similar in price and that the third quotation was much cheaper but made provisions for alternative choices of paper finish and four-colour rather than two colour print subject to further quotation. I mailed copies of all three quotations to Bennett Pullman with a note to explain that I was deferring my recommendation until I had a firmed up on the third quotation. I then telephoned the third firm of printers to confirm our specification for the paper and requirements for a four colour cover and two colour contents, requesting them for an amended quotation after the weekend. I also had to decide which of the four European subsidiaries of AA should become the major stockist of DES from which the other three could procure their top-ups. To that end I put a copy of the US catalogue in my briefcase for discussion with Heinrich the following week.

By mid-afternoon Molly had researched the travel options to Rio. The bad news was that there were no direct fights from Heathrow and that in order to arrive in good time we would have to fly first to Paris on Saturday 27 May and fly with Varig, Brazil's national airline, or Air France. We felt more comfortable flying with Air France but would still lose our weekends. On that note Tom decided to call it a day and we headed home.

----oooOooo----

CHAPTER 11

15 May, Leuffen

ON MONDAY MORNING Tom and I took the first flight to Stuttgart and arrived at the Leuffen factory shortly after midday. Peter Hartmann greeted us in his office and Tom wasted no time in coming to the point. "Tomorrow, Peter, when the AA management group arrive here they will want a complete tour of the factory before sitting down for a business review with you, Heinrich and Dieter Trautman, the financial manager. In particular, as the final location on their inspection they will want to visit the warehouse as the place where Bernard Tompkins died. We need to satisfy ourselves today that we are fully prepared."

"Heinrich, Dieter and Klinger are under my instructions to ensure that everything is perfect," Peter bridled adding "as it always is."

"In that case let's begin now with the warehouse before lunch and continue with the factory and offices when everyone is back at their place of work," said Tom heading towards the blimp with Peter and I in his wake. At the entrance he waited impatiently while Peter punched in six numbers on the keypad and the airlock hissed allowing him to open the door, switch on the lights and close the door behind us carefully. The interior of the rubber envelope was unnaturally quiet, silent except for our footfalls on the concrete floor and the circulation of air within. In sharp contract to our last visit, all was neat and tidy. The tall racks of wire were undisturbed, each with its bin card attached, as were the shelves, boxes and drawers of the eye-level racks at the rear and sides of the building. The aisles between the taller racks were free of loose crates or boxes allowing ready access for fork lift trucks to extract whatever coils of wire might be required for current production. There was no sign of the crates which had been unloaded by Klinger and Johann Glock on the evening of Bernard's death, some of which had spilled open when we were last there.

"When shall you be packing the consignment of material and finished product for shipment to Brazil?" Tom asked surveying the pristine condition of the warehouse.

"Everything was despatched in good time on 12th May." Peter replied blandly. "That's much earlier than you expected when we were last here," I chipped in.

"Yes indeed. There was an unexpected opportunity which Klinger found to take space in someone else's container and he was able to pack, load and arrange transport at short notice."

"That was very efficient, Peter," Tom commented returning Peter's unblinking gaze.

"Klinger is efficient," agreed Peter and with unconvincing modesty "but perhaps this time we were also a little lucky."

As we left the warehouse to return to the office hut Tom asked one further question: "How often do you change the code to the keypad?"

"To maintain first class security Klinger changes the code every weekend and informs me on each Monday morning." Peter answered smugly.

Frau Päsche had arranged lunch for us in Peter's office, a collation of buns filled with cheese or salami and apples or bananas to follow and to drink orange juice or the ubiquitous apfelsaft. Munching our way through I posed another question that had been at the back of my mind for some time. "Peter, do we keep a register logging the dates on which the fuel tank is scheduled for refill and when it last happened?"

"Of course, Julian. It was Alberich Schiessel's duty to keep it up to date." "Perhaps we could look at the log entries for the week up to, Bernard's death?"

"That is not possible," declared Peter "Kommissar Vogel has taken the register with him as evidence."

We resumed the tour rehearsal after lunch with Heinrich Hoffmeyer in attendance. Peter did most of the talking but was unable to answer many of the technical questions which Tom fired at him so that as we proceeded from the factory floor to the quality test area Heinrich gradually took over the role of tour guide summarising the functions of processes and machines fluently. Peter was more at home in describing the functions of office administration but it was a weak performance overall for a general manager. However, he seemed unaware of the poor impression he was making and at the end of the tour Tom took him back to his office for some personal coaching. That gave me time to discuss DES with Heinrich. He leafed through the US catalogue with interest and chuckled over the slogan on the back cover "Rush me my springs".

"Very American," he pronounced. "Useful for maintenance of standard products but very foreign to German design engineers who are our customers. They like to make big mysteries of their work and to claim that every new design is original. Selling springs from a catalogue will involve some education. *Dennoch*," he continued more cheerfully, twinkling with a touch of his usual humour "We too had standardisation in the war. The valve springs used for the Volkswagen were the same as those designed for the Messerschmitt aeroplane."

"How can the catalogue service be managed here at Hartmann & Holst?" I asked, taking his last remark as acceptance of the concept.

"The first task is to translate the catalogue into German amending all the dimensions to metric and, maybe, to add and subtract certain items. Then we must create a special store for the springs themselves and organize its management."

"In the warehouse?"

"Definitely no. This is not a responsibility for Klinger and the *dummkopf* Glock. We will keep the stock here in my department and one of my staff as DES manager will pick and pack the orders when they are received by the sales department."

"Thank you, Heinrich. I will organize a meeting for all European managers in a few weeks' time so that we can plan a launch for the service at the same time."

"And we will synchronize our watches!" joked Heinrich

At this point Frau Päsche appeared to tell me that Tom had received a 'phone call from Amsterdam to alert us that a flight plan had been filed for the Learjet to arrive at Stuttgart airport at 19:15 hours which meant that I should leave Leuffen within the hour to give myself comfortable time for meeting the AA team on their arrival.

I wandered over to Peter's office to find Tom in sole occupation. Peter, he explained, was giving last minute instructions to the staff in every department. "How is it going?" I asked.

"Well, I hope he has a better idea now of what to expect and he may just give a reasonable impression tomorrow on the tour, at least. The management review afterwards is another matter." Tom looked resigned if not content.

"I'll see you then in the morning," I said. "I'll drop your bag off at the Gasthof before driving back to Stuttgart."

"Good luck. It's your job to get them here in the morning, bright-eyed, bushy tailed and in as good a mood as possible.....I've every confidence." Tom added grinning broadly.

---ooo0ooo---

19:00 hours found me at the Flughafen by the door through which passengers from private aircraft were admitted. At 1915 precisely the Learjet with its distinctive blue and silver AA livery touched down and taxied to its designated slot. Two immigration and customs officials checked passports and luggage on the tarmac and soon the party appeared. Barry MacLennan led the team through followed closely by Lloyd Parmentier, then Loren Corley and Erik Nielsen, unmistakable from Tom's description. They were all clad alike in Burberry raincoats pulling their bags on wheels behind them.

"Good to see you, Julian" growled Barry. Are you our guard of honour this evening? "And where is Tom?" asked Lloyd.

"Drilling the troops in Leuffen," I replied in the same vein, treating his question lightly. Barry seemed amused.

Loren and Erik greeted me with handshakes; Loren seeming genuinely pleased to meet again while Erik displayed a deadpan expression upon introduction. In contrast to the first four, Viktor came next in his familiar black coat three steps behind a tall rangy figure in chinos and leather aviator jacket of the kind worn by US air force officers. This had to be Chester Case in pilot mode.

"Hello Julian," he hailed me in polished New England accents. "I'm sorry to have missed you when you were in Farmington last month. I was in Washington for a few days with the President's people. But plenty of time to catch up tomorrow on the drive down to Leuffen." His firm handshake, politician's smile and easy manner were those of the practised charmer. Max, hovering in the background, gave an approving nod and wished me good evening.

"I'll lead the way, shall I," I asked. "The hotel is less than three hundred yards from here and there are trolleys for your luggage if you need them."

"We're all good," said Chester who was without a bag. "Bill Banks is completing the landing formalities and will follow on with ours when he's through."

It had started to drizzle so that we were glad of the covered walkway as we progressed in single file over to the Flughafen hotel, a large concrete box set in a shallow hollow to the north of the airport itself. The hotel windows were heavily double-glazed so that no overhead flight traffic would disturb; despite the proximity, the bedrooms were relatively noise free. Almost without furniture, the lobby was devoid of any character. The floor was of composition tiling and the walls were painted an oyster colour with a hint of blue which Gaby would have called "Luftwaffe grey." Having registered, the group decided to meet for dinner in half an hour, except for Chester Case who announced that he would take room service as he had calls to make to the States.

"What time in the morning shall we take off?" he asked before entering the lift. "I've called the minibus for 8:00 a.m. to give us a good start," I replied.

Dinner was a fairly muted occasion. Viktor had arranged for tables in the hotel restaurant to be pushed together so that we dined with Barry MacLennan at one end and Lloyd Parmentier at the other end. I found myself between Loren Corley and Bill Banks on one side of the table opposite Viktor and Erik Nielsen. Conversation was desultory and confined to small talk mainly about the current baseball season and American politics to which neither Viktor nor I could contribute. We were the only two wearing jackets; the rest were in pullovers or cardigans without ties. The meal itself was unmemorable. The Flughafen hotel menu was limited and the food itself bland: an unappetizing grilled fish, possibly plaice, or chicken Kiev overfilled with garlic butter which spurted over the diner when attacked with purpose. Ice cream or apfelstrudel were the options for dessert. The dinner came to an end when Bill lit his corncob pipe which he was immediately ordered to extinguish by the restaurant manager. Barry declared that he was going to bed and the others followed suit except for Viktor who lingered behind and invited me for a nightcap in the *Fliegerin Bar* on the far side of the lobby.

We sat down on the leather banquette which ran around three sides of the room with a large wooden propeller attached to the wall above us to justify its name as a bar for aviators. We were the only customers and Viktor ordered schnapps for both of us before opening the conversation. "How are things at Leuffen?" he asked "Will the management make a good impression tomorrow?"

"Well, Tom has been preparing them as well as he can and the factory tour should go well, but there may be weaknesses in the business review," I replied. "When it comes to the numbers I've no idea how good the accounting system may be."

"What about the managers themselves and as a team?"

"This is only my second visit here and I haven't seen them in action together; so I can't really comment. I spent half a day with Heinrich Hoffmeyer visiting Mercedes Benz last time and he is clearly very knowledgeable and competent technically."

"And what is your opinion of Peter Hartmann?" asked Viktor to the point which I had sensed was coming. Mindful of Tom's caution, I replied carefully.

"It would be unfair to comment about him as a General Manager based on such slender acquaintance but he seems to have a grip on his staff."

Viktor realised that he was not going to get a firmer answer from me and changed the subject. Instead he told of the outcome of his meeting with Nora Tompkins. "She was very content with the AA offer to pay her a half share of Bernard's retirement pension starting immediately. There was accidental life assurance in the company's name which we can use to pay for the first few years' pension."

"A satisfactory outcome all round then." I concluded. Viktor finished drinking his schnapps and I drained mine. We agreed it was time for bed, wished each other "Gute Nacht" and retired, in my case 'not out'.

--ooo0ooo---

I rose early the following morning, checked that the minibus with driver would arrive promptly and descended for breakfast. Barry MacLennan was the only member of our party in the restaurant where he was toying balefully with a plate of overcooked scrambled eggs. He beckoned me to join him, then waited until I had placed my order and was pouring boiling water on a teabag for my first cup of the day. "What can we expect today?" he asked and I knew that I was in for a questioning similar to Max's.

"I can only give the same answer that I gave Max," repeating what I had said about Peter.

"Very diplomatic and quite the right answer for Viktor," Barry acknowledged. "But let me ask you a question on which you can surely give an opinion. If you were recruiting a General Manager for Hartmann & Holst, would you select Peter Hartman as a candidate having read his CV?" I realised that nothing short of a straight answer would do.

"That's a tough question," I hedged. "But I doubt that he would be on my shortlist."

We finished our breakfast together with a summary from me of the other Hartmann & Holst staff Barry was likely to meet and joined the rest of the AA team in the lobby where they were assembling. Chester Case, Viktor and I were wearing business suits and Bill was still dressed casually as he would not be coming with us but would take the bags across to the Learjet, refuel for the next flight and file the afternoon flight plan. The rest of the group were dressed alike in what I came to recognize as AA managers' uniform for foreign travel: blue blazers with brass buttons, grey trousers and tasselled loafers, all with pale blue button-down Brooks Brothers shirts and a variety of striped club or university ties. The individuality of the ties puzzled me. Some resembled school or regimental ties but were strangely different from their British equivalents. Width of stripe and colours were bolder but there was something more which I couldn't define.

The Volkswagen minibus arrived at 07:55 a,m. and we were loaded up and away on time. The driver chose to take the autobahn as far as Nürtingen, the faster route that Bernard and I had taken a fortnight before.

----oOo0oOo----

CHAPTER 12

TOM HARDY and Peter Hartmann were there to greet us as the minibus swung in through the factory gates. "*Willkommen,* gentlemen," exclaimed Peter as we disembarked. Viktor performed the introductions. "We shall begin with a tour of the factory starting from the receipt of an invitation to quote by a customer." He set off smartly for the offices on the right-hand side of the complex where the engineers were housed.

"Let's begin at the beginning," Floyd Parmentier called after him asserting his authority. "With the raw material store, please Peter." To his credit Peter simply turned and led the party to the blimp which he unlocked and ushered them in. After a cursory inspection Chester left the building and I followed him out with Viktor. "Is that where Bernard Tompkins died?" Chester asked.

"Yes, that's where we found him the following morning when the envelope had decompressed.".

"What a grim way to die. I'm glad we were able to look after his widow. Oh Tom," he called. "I shan't be sitting in on the meeting after the tour. Manfred Hartmann has invited me to lunch at his place to meet the Mayor of Nürtingen. I wonder if you would arrange for someone to take me up to Hohenleuffen at midday and bring me back afterwards."

The rest of the group emerged from the warehouse. Peter took the lead again and resumed the tour in the order which he had intended. We were joined by Heinrich Hoffmeyer after passing by his office where he was busy instructing one of his young assistants on the design of a new pump spring for a Robert Bosch fuel injector. We entered the factory as Tom and I had done on the evening of 1st May. In contrast to the previous visit most of the machines in the various Hallen were running with the operators fully engaged at their workstations and others moving wire to the coiling machines or semi-processed product from one workshop to the next. It was noisy and they had to raise their voices to be heard when they wished to ask questions. As the party circulated Heinrich provided most of the explanation on the various processes which served to cover any lack of knowledge on Peter's part. With increasing confidence Peter adopted some of his usual arrogance.

"As you can see," he proclaimed. "Every member of our workforce is dedicated to his machine and is fully concentrated on his work." Tom exchanged glances with me and I pondered that what Peter had claimed as studied concentration by the machine operators was more likely to be studied indifference in the face of visiting outsiders.

However, as we proceeded Heinrich was buttonholed with increasing frequency by Loren Corley who examined some machine operations minutely through wire-rimmed bifocals.

This was discomforting for Peter, bereft of Heinrich's expertise, who was unable to answer others posed by Barry MacLennan or Floyd. Tom covered for him some of the time but Peter's ignorance became apparent. When we reached Halle 8 Loren was even more interested in the test bed and entered into a long conversation with Heinrich on aspects of the quality assurance routine and reading of the data print outs. Consequently, we moved on to Halle 9 leaving Loren and Heinrich behind us so that Peter was left to demonstrate and answer queries about shot-peening and the tumbling of finished parts in another machine.

Fortunately, these were processes which did not differ materially from American practice and beyond identification of the product currently being treated as injector springs Peter was not challenged.

After brief visits to the sales order and accounts offices where we collected Dieter Trautman. Regathering in Peter's office, the boardroom table had been set out with notepads, ballpoint pens, glasses and bottled water in preparation for the business review. At Chester's request I had arranged with Peter for him to be driven up to Hohenleuffen by Johann Glock. Frau Päsche served coffee. Peter was positioned at the far end of the table flanked by Dieter on his left and Henrich on his right with Erik and Loren on opposite sides facing them. Tom was placed next to Erik and I sat opposite him and next to Loren. These arrangements left Lloyd in command of the meeting at the head of the other end facing Peter. Neither Barry nor Viktor sat at the table. Barry chose the role of observer relaxing in the more comfortable executive chair behind Peter's desk facing Lloyd's back but with a clear view of the three German managers, while Viktor took a ringside seat at Tom's shoulder. That the seating was significant became apparent as Lloyd, now without his blazer, squared up for confrontation with Peter. He had rolled up the sleeves of his shirt to the elbow revealing muscular footballer's arms which emphasised his adversarial approach to the forthcoming confrontation.

"Peter," he began "This is your first Hartmann & Holst business review as an AA company and I want to take you through the topics in our standard sequence. First is an overview of the German economy. What is the current outlook for GDP and inflation?"

Peter looked blank. "I did not expect that question. Why do we need to discuss the economy?"

Dieter Trautman came to Peter's rescue. "Chancellor Schmidt and the Bundesbank seem to have rebalanced the economy and the IPO Institute Munich now forecasts some recovery with growth for the rest of 1978 and next year of up to 2 per cent with inflation at 1.2 per cent."

I hadn't observed Dieter closely before but noted now that he was a young man with an open, cheerful face under a thatch of blond hair. Already he was making a good impression on the company around the table. Lloyd resumed his questioning.

"That suggests a positive sales outlook. What was the order book at the end of last month?" Dieter quoted a figure, while Peter looked blank.

"And what is your view Peter, as general manager, of opportunities for new business at increased prices?"

"In the past four weeks, I have visited the purchasing managers of our big customers all over Germany and they have accepted the acquisition of Hartmann & Holst by AA. I do not think we shall lose business as a result." Peter looked pleased with his report.

"That's not very positive." commented Lloyd grimly "Our investment in a loss-making supplier should be welcome. Do they understand that we need bigger orders at increased prices?" Although his tone was measured; a tightening of his jaw muscles and clenching of hands indicated that Lloyd was losing patience. Peter pressed on regardless.

"For big German manufacturers, the acquisition of a German supplier by an American company raises the risk that product quality will suffer. I've been very active in making more than 24 sales visits to important buyers and, of course, price rises are out of the question."

"Do not confuse activity with progress," remarked Barry laconically from the comfort of his reclining chair, easing some of the tension that had been accumulating.

"The situation with our customers is not quite so negative," contributed Heinrich. "In their technical engineering departments we have a high reputation for quality like most German springmakers and the arrival of Allied Autoparts suggests that we shall be able to make more capital expenditure into new machinery which will keep Hartmann & Holst competitive. You see," Heinrich continued "price increases are given in respect of the increased cost of raw materials but it is expected that other cost increases are recovered by the supplier from gains in productivity from more efficient machines."

The inquisition moved on to a review of the previous three months' financial accounts which showed a net loss at 7 per cent on sales. The first focus was on margins by verifying what costs were included in arriving at the gross margin of 5 per cent and it became clear that management accounting was rudimentary. Erik Nielsen joined in the interrogation of Peter and Dieter and it emerged that some indirect expenses and sales costs, which AA would have treated as fixed costs, had been included in calculating gross profit. Dieter had all the information at his fingertips while Peter could contribute little. Lloyd became increasingly impatient. "In a successful plant, gross margins should be not less than 20 per cent to cover sales and administration costs and hopefully a profit," he pronounced.

"The next issue is direct labour hours," he went on "You have a punched card system covering the number of springs manufactured on each machine in the factory. What do you do with it, Heinrich?" By now Lloyd had given up asking questions to Peter first. "Of course, we record the time spent on each spring part in each operation so that we can compare actual performance with the estimate when we quote and we pass the cards to Accounts to feed into the computer," Heinrich responded.

"And what do you do when the estimate is exceeded?"

"We identify which processes are over estimate and try to improve productivity, perhaps through multi-machine operations where one man operates two machines at the same time or by extending the production run where there are advance orders so that there is only one batch for machine setting."

"Nevertheless," interrupted Peter unhelpfully "Each production worker has his own machine and is dedicated to looking after it. So, we try to avoid multi-machine operations."

Lloyd ignored him. "And what do you do if those actions are not possible, Heinrich?"

"If we cannot improve the price, the final solution may be to buy a machine which operates faster while maintaining quality."

"We could think about sending over faster US machines such as Torin coilers instead of the close tolerances that German specifications require."

"Let's think about that, Loren. Food for thought" Lloyd continued.

"And you record the usage of raw material for each production run?" "*Ganz so*," from Heinrich while Dieter nodded.

"In that case you have all the data to construct the closed out job cost for each part number. Can Dieter do that through the computer, Erik?"

"I'll check that out now, while we pause for lunch," replied Erik looking at the sandwiches and drinks which Frau Päsche had placed on the desk behind Lloyd.

"Twenty minutes for lunch then," ruled Lloyd transferring the plates to the boardroom table.

While Erik and Dieter went into a huddle and Loren, engaged in an animated discussion with Heinrich about the comparative merits of spring-making machinery, Lloyd consulted with Barry in lowered tones and we all nibbled at the rolls which had the same fillings as the day before. Viktor took the time to write up the notes that he been taking throughout the meeting; Tom took an abashed Peter to the next room with me in attendance and told him firmly, but quite kindly, to keep silent if he could not agree with Lloyd's directions when the meeting resumed. After 20 minutes we took our same places around the table.

"Well Erik, can we produce closed out job costs in the same way as we would in the US?" "Can do." Erik and Ditte concurred.

"We're going to get Hartmann & Holst back in shape," Lloyd stated coldly. "Right now it's a bleeder and there are three actions on which you are going to focus, Peter, with Tom's support. Number one, I want to see the job cost history of the 100 top major parts for which you have orders when I come back here next month. Then you and I will visit those major customers and tell them that we have to raise prices where costs are higher. Number two, I want to hear your plans for increasing profitable orders and Heinrich's for increasing productivity. Number three, you will cut sales and administration fixed costs by 10 per cent within three months. And, finally you will produce a business plan for the next financial year with these improvements. Are there any questions?"

At the third point, Peter's jaw had dropped and he plainly wanted to speak but Tom forestalled him. "I'll start on the cost-cutting and the business plan with Peter tomorrow." His manner was that of a Norfolk farmer receiving a prescription from the vet for his cattle.

The meeting came to a close in sober mood as Chester Case rejoined us having returned from his lunch at Hohenleuffen. The final interchange came after he asked Heinrich how he had enjoyed his first AA business review.

"As the Führer said, if you survive you come out stronger," Heinrich quipped.

"Don't forget Stalingrad," Barry muttered as he picked up his document case preparing to leave the room.

---ooo0ooo---

We were in good time to follow the flight plan as we journeyed back to the Flughafen: this time Tom joined us at Barry's request. With Lloyd, Erik and Loren they congregated in the rear rows of the minibus for a post mortem on the meeting leaving Chester, Viktor and me to occupy the forward passenger seats.

"I always leave the wrap-up for this kind of meeting to the executive management," Chester opened the conversation. "Plenty of time for their conclusions on this evening's flight, but there is something I would like to discuss with you, Julian. Manfred Hartmann was talking to me about Bernard Tompkins' death. He believes it was an accident but he thinks that you are not convinced and might want to persuade the police to continue their investigation. You must have given him that impression when you were his guest the week before last."

"It's true that I am not entirely convinced," I replied. "There were so many coincidences in the timing that I was uneasy."

"I've read Tom's report but run me through the coincidences again."

"The first is that Bernard entered the warehouse blimp in the short interval after Gottfried Klinger and his Johann Glock left and before it self-locked; the second was the outage of the electricity supply shortly afterwards; the third was the failure of the auxiliary air pump which would have kept the blimp inflated; and the fourth was the fatal road accident within 48 hours of the young man responsible for keeping the pump fuel tank filled." I was careful not to mention the draining of the fuel tank which Heinrich had discovered but which was omitted from Tom's report."

"I hadn't picked all of that up." Chester looked surprised. "You and Tom are seeing the investigating police officer again in the morning. Perhaps he will have reached a conclusion."

"Maybe."

Chester reflected for several moments before continuing.

"Julian, I'm going to ask you to break the normal rules of AA internal communications that we follow. Tom will no doubt continue to report to Lloyd and Barry by telex, but I want to have your opinions more directly. If you are not satisfied with the conclusion which the Kommissar reaches, I want you to call Viktor direct by telephone. To avoid embarrassment any comment you may make will not be attributed to you."

"To tell you the truth," he went on flashing the sort of grin that Ivy League alumni share between themselves. "I'm not entirely comfortable with my visit to Hohenleuffen today and I didn't take to Glock who drove me there."

For the remainder of the journey we talked politics and compared our perceptions of what Jimmy Carter was achieving in America with the problems of the troubled Callaghan government in the UK. Chester was interested in my view that British government would not last more than another winter and that Britain's first woman Prime Minister might be elected next.

We delivered the AA group without further ado to the Flughafen where Bill Bates was waiting for them. Lloyd Parmentier had final words for me as we said our goodbyes:

"Julian, will you stay on with Tom for the rest of the week. I want a list of the top 100 part numbers with the customers names and where they are located by the weekend to plan my next trip here after the Brazil meeting." Taking this as a command, rather than a request, I acknowledged the instruction.

---ooo0ooo----

CHAPTER 13

WE WALKED BACK to the Hertz Golf in the hotel carpark where I had left my bag that morning and set off for Leuffen by the back route avoiding the autobahn while Tom relaxed in the passenger seat showing palpable relief that the day's ordeal was over.

"Normally," he reflected lazily after a few minutes "if it were not for our meeting with Vogel tomorrow, we would be travelling with them to Sweden on the quarterly review circuit but this time I'm glad not be part of the flying circus." "Hardly a happy day," I agreed.

"There's a lot of hard work to be done here and I'll need your help at the sharp end. How did you rate the home team's performance?" Tom asked.

"On a scale of nought to ten: Peter two; Heinrich eight; Dieter seven. On the upside Dieter was a welcome surprise. But what can be done with Peter?"

"That's not in our hands. I doubt that I shall be consulted but I expect that he'll be given a chance to show that he can adapt to AA management standards. He'll be skating on very thin ice from now on. As for Heinrich, I'm not sure that everyone enjoys his sense of humour and that last remark didn't go down well, however funny you and I may have found it. And Dieter – definitely the hero of the day. But what did you think of our friends from Farmington?" "Since you're not Viktor, would you like the unedited or the sanitized version?"

"I've always enjoyed *The Daily Mail* rather than *The Times*. Go on."

"Thanks to your rehearsal, the factory tour was alright; Peter's lack of knowledge was not too glaringly obvious.

The business review was another story – more of a brutal one-man inquisition really. Loren and Erik were supportive and Viktor played the part of the faithful scribe but Lloyd's grilling of Peter seemed unnecessarily inquisitorial. Is he always a bully at AA quarterly reviews?"

"Lloyd is one of nature's bullies but he is also a control freak and when he is running meetings the two character traits combine. But don't underestimate him. As you saw today, he is also effective in getting to the heart of a problem. When he abandons aggression and is polite, he's far more dangerous."

"I was fascinated by Barry's role as an inscrutable back seat passenger. Is that how he normally behaves at business reviews?"

"Nearly always. He likes the people who report to him to make the running when less senior managers are present. He takes the reins after the meeting when only his team are present.

That's what he'll be doing now on the Learjet as they fly up to Sweden. He was asking questions on the bus while I was there but the decision-making comes later. But what about you, Julian?," Tom asked. "You had Chester's attention on the way back to the Flughafen."

"I've been instructed to communicate with him direct via Viktor if I have lingering doubts about Bernard's death after our meeting with Kommissar Vogel tomorrow. Do I have any option?"

"No, of course you don't," Tom replied and then, more reflectively. "So long as you tip me the wink, you'll have no problem with me; nor with Barry. He and Chester update each other daily. However, you could have a problem with Lloyd if he finds out that he has been bypassed. He won't like the idea of you having an inside track. Conversely, Viktor will probably treat you as a trusted confidant and seek more from you about the line managers here in Europe. That will be uncomfortable if he expects you to play the school sneak."

Digesting these unsettling thoughts I concentrated on my driving and we relapsed into silence for the rest of the journey.

---ooo0ooo---

We arrived back in Leuffen just as the factory was closing. While Tom closeted himself with Peter, I found an empty office and called Gaby at the flat to tell her that I wouldn't be back the next day and might have to stay on through Friday. "So long as you're back Friday night," she admonished "I have a treat planned for us since you'll be rolling down to Rio the weekend following."

I stopped by Dieter's office to congratulate him on his performance at the meeting. "I couldn't answer all the questions," he said looking disappointed and concerned. "Perhaps not, but you kept calm and confident that you would be able to produce the answers. That was enough for the day," I encouraged him.

Confirming that he would make time the next day to help me identify the major parts with the highest value Dieter introduced me to his assistant, Hans Gruber, an older man of solid build with limited English. I joined Tom who was finishing his meeting with Peter to plan their work priorities for the rest of the week and we went on up to the Gasthof where Otto Krantz greeted me warmly and Brigitta simmered voluptuously behind the bar. A leisurely dinner with rather more *viertels* of Lemberger than were good for us brought a difficult day to a more satisfactory close.

---ooo0ooo---

At 10:00 a.m. the following morning Kommisar Vogel and his sergeant arrived at the factory. He had chosen to meet with us there rather than his Stuttgart police station but not for our convenience. He commandeered Peter Hartmann's office and told us that he also wanted to interview Heinrich and Gottfried Klinger individually before each of us in turn. As the last in line after Tom it was almost the lunch hour before I was summoned. Kurt Vogel motioned me to sit opposite him at the table with the sergeant at the far end to take notes.

"Herr Radclive," he asked "This time I shall need your written statement which you can give me before I leave. Is there anything you wish to add to what you told me last time?"

"One thing only. After you left that day, I inspected the fuel line and relief pump which should have pumped air into the warehouse when the electricity cut out and......," I began.

"....and you found that the ground under the fuel line soaked with oil, *nicht wahr*?" he interrupted.

"That's right. Dr. Hoffmeyer drew my attention to it."

"Dr Hoffmeyer has already reported this in his statement but you found no explanation?"

"No, but the release of kerosene seemed to have been deliberate. We found no leak in the pipeline or joints."

"I also inspected for myself the next day and have questioned the warehouse manager and Herr Hartmann thoroughly. There is an explanation which I can tell you and Mr. Hardy since you are not under investigation yourselves." The Kommissar looked at me unblinking, adopting the mask of a seasoned poker player. "Gottfried Klinger tells me that he regularly vents the fuel tank in order to remove any sludge which might block the fuel line and that he did so on 2nd May and informed Alberich Schiessel so that he would refill the tank."

"What evidence is there of that since Schiessel was killed in his motorbike accident on the morning of 5th May on his way to work?"

"Of course, there is no verbal confirmation and Klinger admits that he did not speak to Schussel. However, he wrote in the maintenance register that he had drained the tank as was his normal practice. It was Schiessel's duty to consult the log daily and he assumed that his request for a refill had been read. And before you ask me, here is the log for you to see."

His sergeant handed me the register and sure enough the last entry was dated 2nd May and initialled "GK". I leafed back through the register and found similar inscriptions at roughly four monthly intervals initialled "GK" and followed by entries of "*auf gefüllt. AS.*" I passed the log book back to Vogel without comment.

"Therefore," the Kommissar resumed "I have no evidence to say that Herr Tompkins' death was anything other than a tragic accident which is how I shall write my report. I understand that you may not be convinced that it was an accident. However, we have a similar verdict in Germany to your 'death by misadventure' which will be how the Coroner's verdict is recorded."

I decided to stick my neck out. "Kommissar, may I ask you if that is the decision you have been advised to reach?"

For a fleeting moment Kurt Vogel's impassive manner shattered and I realised that he was older than I had originally supposed. He responded with some asperity.

"Mr. Radclive, I need and take nobody's advice on how to do my job. There is no other recommendation I can make. Please just write your statement and give it to my sergeant." He could have added "and mind your own business" but instead stood up signalling that our discussion was at an end.

Then, having second thoughts, he faced me across the table and added "I do not believe in coincidences any more than you but in this case I have to accept them. Twenty-three years after the last war there are still sensitivities here in Germany when a British or American dies in unusual circumstances and it is best for everyone to reach a neutral conclusion quickly." He turned away and left the room.

---ooo0ooo---

I spent most of the afternoon with Heinrich discussing how to present the information which Lloyd Parmentier had demanded. We agreed that taking data from the current order book alone would be misleading and that we should focus on the top one hundred part numbers of those shipped during the past three months with an Appendix for high volume new parts on which Hartmann and Holst had quoted prices but not yet received orders. The part numbers in the main list would be grouped by customer name and plant with the location of relevant buying offices in third column. Heinrich's office would provide prices, direct labour hours and raw materials actually consumed in most recent production runs and, working with Dieter, I would be able to estimate actual direct costs. Working together through the files we managed to complete the basic data by mid evening and I lined up Dieter to work with me on the cost data the following morning.

While I was busy in Heinrich's office Tom had sat Peter down to discuss opportunities for cost-cutting in sales and administration. It was clear from Tom's expression when I joined him in the boardroom that the conversation had not been fruitful. He was making arrangements with Peter to meet in the morning with Klinger, as factory trade union representative, to discuss early retirements and redundancies. During the afternoon there had been a telephone call from Viktor in Sweden shortly before the Learjet took off at Norkopping for its homeward flight asking Tom to give Peter and Dieter advance information that there would be telex invitations for them to attend the gathering in Rio. Predictably, Peter had taken the invitation as no more than his right.

For a change, we decided to dine at the Gasthof in Hohenleuffen and I drove us there pointing out to Tom the entrance to the Hartmann family hunting lodge as we passed. Turning into the village square outside the Gasthof we noticed that there were two cars already parked: a small Opel and a dark red Porsche 911. We took a window table in the restaurant area which was separate from the bar and studied the menu having first ordered steins of beer. As the waitress brought our drinks through the swing doors from the bar area I caught a glimpse of three men sitting there. Two of them were middle-aged in unremarkable grey suits: one completely bald, facing us and flanking a third man with a familiar backview. The doors swung back before I could complete identification.

Having missed lunch we were both hungry; for our first course we ordered *schnecken*, the German equivalent of escargots, with garlic bread, to be followed by *kalbshaxen* - veal shanks. Tom opened the conversation.

"I suppose that Kommissar Vogel shared with you his decision to conclude the investigation and to file his report with the coroner as an accidental death. What do you make of it?" he asked.

"The Klinger explanation of how the fuel tank came to be empty seems too convenient and can't be corroborated. He showed me the maintenance register but Gottfried Klinger's last entry could easily have been added after the event. There are just too many coincidences in the circumstantial evidence for comfort."

"In other words, we both think it's fishy. But we have to consider it from an Allied Autoparts point of view. If the coroner delivers a verdict of death by misadventure it draws an oficial line under the incident and the company can move on undisturbed as Chester was hoping."

"Yes. Until it bites back. Also, I have to think what to say to Viktor, if anything."

We both switched our concentration to food, clamping shells and extracting snails before dipping them in garlic and consuming.

"If I were in your place," Tom advised "I would say nothing. There's no point in airing your misgivings and being labelled a scaremonger. It wouldn't help your career prospects. I shall simply telex Vogel's conclusions to Farmington in the morning and leave it at that."

As our plates were cleared we looked out of the window over the car park. The two men I had seen in the bar were climbing into the Porsche which then sped off up the hill. The third man unlocking the driver's door of the Opel facing us was Gottfried Klinger.

---ooo0ooo---

After dinner we drove back to Leuffen, downhill all the way. Directly opposite the track leading to the hunting lodge, now on our right, the headlights of the Golf focused on the crash barrier to our left and picked up a metal section that appeared to have been replaced recently. I slowed the car down and pointed.

"I suppose that's where Alberich Schiessel's motorbike crashed through," Tom remarked, then pointed to the right.

"Are you thinking what I'm thinking?" I asked.

"Yes, but we mustn't be paranoiac. Just another bloody coincidence."

---ooo0ooo---

I spent most of Thursday morning with Dieter Trautman and Hans Gruber, cross-checking data with Heinrich when in doubt. By early afternoon I had assembled a spreadsheet with details for each of the one hundred major part including cost of materials and direct labour hours for the most recent production runs in addition to the data developed with Heinrich the previous afternoon. I decided that there was more than enough to be telexed to Farmington and rang the airport to book myself on the evening flight to London. Molly could be enlisted to compose a monster telex with me the following morning.

Dieter consulted me on how he should reply to the invitation for Rio when it arrived. "There is so much work to be done here to set up the additional accounting system that Mr. Nielsen wants; I think I should say 'no'."

"It's not really a social invitation," I told him. "More of an instruction. And you can assume that Erik wants you to be there. Besides, I am sure that Hans can look after things very well for a week while you are away."

"I don't think Herr Hartmann wants me to attend. Should not Dr. Hoffman be invited instead of me?"

"No, Dieter. The conference is for General Managers, Sales Managers and Finance Managers only from each company together with the AA international management. Production managers and Technical Directors have to stay at home to keep the factories running. You may not want to go but this is an important opportunity for your future career. Take my advice and accept tomorrow when the telex arrives."

While discussing the conference in Brazil a further thought struck me and before leaving Dieter I asked him if I could have copies of the bill of lading and invoice for the recent shipment to Brazil – carriage and insurance paid to Rio de Janeiro I noted - which meant that Grunwald Metallwerk were responsible for unloadig and delivery to Campinas. "We might get a chance to track the documentation when we visit Grunwald Metallwerk," I explained. "Sooner or later we shall be asked to produce an audit trail." Dieter seemed satisfied with the explanation and decided that he would take copies too.

There was time for a quick catch-up with Tom before leaving for the Flughafen. Since he would need the rental car the following day, I rang for a taxi and while waiting told him what Dieter and I had achieved. Tom's morning had been less successful and he looked tired and irritable.

"Redundancy programmes in Germany are a nightmare," he declared. "Aside from the consultation process with staff and union officials which can take weeks, there are whole categories of employees who are protected by law against dismissal. War veterans, the disabled, widows and unmarried mothers have job security and, to cap it all, when it comes to deciding who among the rest can be made redundant, the rule is "last in – first out" which means that valued apprentices have to be laid off before those nearing retirement age. If you are a widowed unmarried mother with a wooden leg you can keep your job for life." On that happy thought I left Leuffen.

---ooo0ooo---

CHAPTER 14

FRIDAY WAS A DAY for administration. When I left for the office Gaby had not yet revealed any details of her treat for the weekend. "All will be revealed this evening," she promised. "You won't be disappointed. Good things come to him who waits."

Molly was not overjoyed with the challenge of my mammoth telex to Lloyd Parmentier but we sat side by side at the machine and I called out the numbers column by column for her to key in; we accomplished the task in a couple of hours. As a thank you I took her for lunch at the pizza parlour on the corner of Victoria Street. Early afternoon a telex acknowledgment of receipt came through with thanks for our labours. "At least someone has good manners," Molly commented, now restored to good humour.

The third printer quoting for the DES catalogues had revised their offer during the week on a fixed cost basis which was only marginally higher than the two quotations that I had previously favoured. I reasoned that there would be no grounds for claiming to have underestimated and that since this printer had a London office to service its printshop in Kent it would be easier to work with than the others from further afield. I put in a call to Bennett Pullman to report on the final position and we agreed that I should place the order with the third printer subject to a face to face meeting which I arranged for the week following.

During our conversation Bennett congratulated me on the data telexed several hours ago. "He won't tell you himself but you've impressed Lloyd," he said. "He's singing your praises all over the office."

"Beware of Greeks bearing gifts," I joked not believing for one moment that I had gained a permanent fan.

We talked a bit more about the marketing presentations that he, I and my opposite number Oswaldo Carioca, the market manager for Latin America, would be making in Rio. "Plenty of time to rehearse when we meet up on Sunday week," we agreed before ringing off. And that brought me to the end of my working week.

---ooo0ooo---

Saturday evening found us luxuriating in a four-poster bed at the Lygon Arms Broadway, the destination for Gaby's weekend treat. We had motored there in the morning driving West past Oxford, through Burford and up into the Cotswolds – a magical mystery tour since Gaby kept me in suspense until we reached Chipping Camden. After lunch in the hotel's bistro we spent an hour or so window shopping in the village's many antique shops whose prices were set at levels which would attract only well-heeled foreign tourists with dollars. We were tempted by a George III decanter but agreed that we could probably do better in the King's Road. To console ourselves we returned to the hotel and ordered a bottle of Bollinger from room service.

Since my return the previous evening we hadn't discussed developments in Leuffen at any length. But now Gaby's naturally enquiring mind returned to the circumstances surrounding Bernard's and my conversation with Kurt Vogel.

"Do you think that the Kommissar is on the take and doing what Manfred Hartmann or someone else tells him?" As usual, Gaby's question was direct and to the point.

"Well, I doubt that he is actually corrupt but he more or less admitted that there was a political element in his decision to close the investigation quickly. It's also true that he was aware of my unease about the accident and that could only have come from Manfred or Peter."

"What does Tom think about it."

"Like me, he doubts the Kommissar's report but advocates that we accept the inevitable findings of the Coroner."

"But you won't let it drop, will you?" Gaby sighed "I know you too well." I paused and poured more champagne into our glasses before continuing.

"There are two reasons why not. First, I feel we owe it to Bernard and his widow to pursue his killers if it was not an accident. Second, and perhaps more powerful, I don't believe this is the end of it anyway if, as we suspect, it was a consequence of the shipment to Campinas. If we're right, they've been trading in contraband of some sort for years and it's very likely that there will be a return shipment."

"In that case, will you do one thing for me before you plunge in any further?" Gaby asked. "Will you give Max a call on Monday and ask his advice? He did suggest you could be in touch if you were concerned about developments in Leuffen."

"Yes, he did and I'll do so. As always, my love, your slightest wish is my command."

I didn't spoil the moment by telling her that contact with Max Salinger was already on my list of things to do or that I had already equipped myself with the shipping documents to check out the cargo from Hartmann & Holst in Campinas if the opportunity presented itself.

Instead, I put my champagne glass down carefully on my night table and rolled over towards Gaby.

"And now, I'm ready for my treat."

"The things I do for England," she replied with the wicked grin that I adored and rolled over too.

---ooo0ooo---

On reaching the office Monday morning a few minutes before Tom I found the copy of a telex that Lloyd Parmentier had sent late Friday to Peter Hartmann announcing that he would be visiting Leuffen again for the week of 13 June to visit Hartmann & Holst's key customers and that he wished Peter to book meetings and accompany him on his tour. He had selected the buying offices of the five automotive manufacturers and the two component manufactures Robert Bosch and ZF featured at the top of the major parts customers that I had listed. A challenging schedule of meetings was demanded with heavy motoring involved between locations from Stuttgart, Ingoldstadt and Munich in the West, to Wolfsburg and Russelsheim in the North, Bamberg in the East, close to the border with East Germany, and South to Friederichshafen on the northern shoreline of Lake Konstanz. Peter was expected to confirm the schedule in the next few days before we all left for Rio.

"That's a tough task for Peter," commented Tom when he has scanned the telex. "I'd better call him to give encouragement."

"Will Lloyd ask you to accompany them?" I asked. "Lloyd speaks no German, but you have some."

"Unlikely that he will want a witness to the meetings. It's all an initiative by Lloyd to demonstrate his leadership. If he achieves price increases he will want to take all the credit, but if he fails the blame will fall on Peter."

"And curtains for Peter, I assume?"

"That's the way the land lies. You could put money on it, but look on the bright side. You won't be asked to join the baggage train either." I felt some relief; five days on the road with Lloyd and Peter would have been a daunting prospect.

---ooo0ooo---

Mid-morning I telephoned Max Salinger's direct line. He picked up his receiver on the fourth ring. "Good morning," he answered "Can I help you?" I recognized the voice. We exchanged pleasantries and I came to the point.

"When we met in Sussex recently you said that if I was uneasy about developments in Germany, I should get in touch. Does the offer still stand."

"Of course. Unless it's more urgent, would you be free to join me for lunch on Thursday?"

"Thank you, Max. Would you like a summary briefing on the telephone from me now?"

"Definitely not." He replied rather sharply "This is not a secure line. Thursday then at my club, the Athenaeum, if that suits you?" I confirmed the time with him and we rang off.

Next, I called the printer that I had selected for the DES catalogues and arranged a meeting for Wednesday morning, leaving me with the rest of the day to start preparing the two presentations that Bennett Pullman wanted me to make in Rio the following week.

---ooo0ooo---

Gaby had decided that I needed some lighter clothes to wear in Brazil where June temperatures in Rio were likely to exceed 80 degrees Fahrenheit. On Tuesday I met her for a pub lunch and we we trawled through men's clothing departments in Regent Street and Piccadilly. I finished up with two pairs of lightweight trousers, a seersucker jacket and an expensive Italian silk suit which Gaby assured me would not typecast me as "white trash" when worn in London. Mission accomplished, we spent the rest of the afternoon and evening at the flat where Gaby had calls to make setting up her next series of focus groups around London for research into a new brand of packet sauces.

The printer's offices were in Berwick Street in a shabby building on the top floor serviced by an ancient lift which laboured clunkily as it ascended. I started to wonder whether I was making the right choice as I approached a frosted glass door bearing the legend "Bradley Fowler & Sons". However, the interior inspired more confidence. The reception area was freshly painted and carpeted and the receptionist greeted me with a ready smile, telling me that "young Mr. Fowler was expecting me" and calling him from the switchboard. 'Young' Mr. Fowler with whom I had been communicating proved to be a spry, jovial man of medium height, probably in his late fifties, who greeted me warmly. He led me through to his office at the rear of a well-lit open-plan area in which three women and two men were sat at separate desks working on texts and layouts of various catalogues and magazines.

"As you can see," he said after sitting me down and telling me to call him Herbert "We do all of our design and preparation here for our publications before sending them down to the printshop at Sevenoaks where they are typeset. We edit the page proofs here before returning them back for correction and then go to press, assemble and staple or bind in the case of catalogues."

"That sounds very well organized. Who sets the deadlines for production runs?"

"The end deadlines are determined by the client's publication dates and the deadlines for each stage of production are set by my partner Derek Bradley who directs printshop operations at Sevenoaks in consultation with me." Herbert pointed to a flow chart which occupied a wall of his office on which the individual timing for each stage of operation for more than twenty publications was detailed. "Derek has an identical chart in his office and we consult on any adjustments together when there are delays or slippages. Are there any special requirements for your DES catalogues?"

I explained that ideally we would like all four language editions to be printed at the same time but that I realised that it would be probably be impossible to complete typesetting and editing simultaneously. Although the technical specifications would be the same throughout product descriptions and column headings would be in the individual languages. We discussed how best to coordinate the work and reduce timing delays to a minimum.

"Would it help if I brought the project managers responsible for the catalogue at each factory to London, one by one, to carry out the proof-reading with your editors here?" I asked. Herbert was enthusiastic.

"That will eliminate postal delays and miscommunication between our editors and your people, Julian. If you could bring the British project manager here first that will help my staff to become familiar with the page layouts and content before exposing them to the same texts in German, Dutch and Swedish."

Having agreed the procedure, we moved on to the likely timing of the project. I explained that I would be briefing the four companies in Rio the following week, agreeing the product categories with them for the catalogue and the time which each needed to prepare their versions. That would enable me to schedule the start time for catalogue production which I would convey to Herbert on my return together with formal confirmation of the order. Taking summer holiday periods into account, I doubted whether we would have final copy for the foreign language editions before the end of July. Our discussion seemed to have progressed as far as we could go and I returned to Buckingham Gate after excusing myself from Herbert's invitation to lunch.

Shortly after I reached the office, confident now that I had selected a reliable printer, a call came through for me from Viktor just after 9:00 a.m. Farmington time.

"Chester has read Tom's telex report of your meetings with Kommissar Vogel last week." He announced without preamble. "He would like to know if you are more comfortable with the inspector's report."

I marshalled my thoughts carefully before replying. "I have no evidence, let alone proof, that Bernard's death was anything other than an accident."

"Does that mean that I can tell Chester that you will not be investigating further in Leuffen?" "Viktor," I replied stretching the truth "I wouldn't know where to begin."

We chatted briefly about the coming week in Brazil and who would be coming. Then, always a man of few words, Viktor rang off.

----ooo0ooo----

CHAPTER 15

25 May, London

I LEFT THE OFFICE in good time on Thursday for my lunch with Max Salinger, cutting through from Buckingham Gate to Birdcage Walk, across St. James's Park, up Duke of York steps and so to the Athenaeum on the corner of Pall Mall. I registered as a guest with the porter and was directed to the member's Morning Room where I found Max finishing off the back page crossword of the Evening Standard. A distinguished figure and immaculate as ever, he was dressed today in a chalk stripe City suit, striped shirt with polka dot silk tie and highly polished black half brogues, the uniform of bankers or regimental officers out of uniform.

"Good to see you, Julian. You've caught me at my obsessive pastime. I try to polish off The Times crossword at breakfast, but seldom make it these days, and move on to the popular Press whenever the opportunity arises. We're not supposed to chatter at length in here and the bar is much too crowded; so, we'll move through to the coffee room, shall we?"

The coffee or dining room was a high ceilinged, conservatively decorated restaurant with well spaced tables, each set with linen napery, gleaming silver cutlery and its own unlit candelabra. We were led to a window table overlooking the garden; the immediately neighbouring tables were unoccupied.

"Let's get the ordering over first. Then we can talk without interruption," Max suggested handing me an unpriced menu. "You're in luck. Since it's Thursday we have the Club steak and kidney pie which I can recommend, but if you don't like that the Dover sole is always good."

We both chose the steak and kidney pie preceded by smoked trout and Max ordered a large carafe of the Club claret. With the trout served and our glasses charged, he encouraged me to start from the beginning of my experiences at Leuffen. I left out nothing relevant from the evening of my first visit with Bernard and Tom to the factory up to and including my last conversation with Kommissar Vogel. Finally, I mentioned the forthcoming visit to Brazil which had prompted my decision to call him. Max listened intently without interruption until I had finished. With the arrival of the steak and kidney pie and departure of the waiter, he finally commented:

"If I understand your concerns correctly, they stem, in summary, from the delivery at the warehouse on the night of your arrival and your suspicion that having stumbled into the unlocked blimp Bernard was struck down by Klinger or the man Glock. And your suspicions are fuelled by the chain of coincidences in what happened next and the day or so following."

"That's the nub of it and, if that is correct, I believe that whatever Bernard saw, and was not meant to see, was in the consignment to be shipped to Campinas on 12th May," I answered.

"I have little doubt but that you are correct. And that leads on to a bigger picture. What you have stumbled into is probably the most recent example of regular illegal trafficking between Leuffen and Campinas."

"And vice versa," I added. Max looked grave.

"That may be the more serious element of the trade. So, what are you looking for from me?" "Basically, your advice on what I should do next other than turn a blind eye and carry on regardless."

"I know you better than you may think and I'm sure you won't do that, whatever I say. Before I give you my advice and suggest any course of action which will probably put you at risk, I think I should come clean and declare my interest. Some of it you may have guessed already." He looked at me for affirmation.

"I wasn't really convinced that you had been pensioned off with a retirement job as part-time archivist of SOE with just a casual interest in the loose ends and leftovers of WWII in Germany."

"Quite right; the interest is rather more than casual. My brief extends to being a sort of glorified errand boy for MI6, our successor, on issues which resurface from those half-forgotten wartime adventures. Our main focus in Germany is on the activities of the Kamaradenwerke, ostensibly a charitable association for the support of German veterans who have fallen on hard times. Manfred Hartmann is a member although not a beneficiary. The Kamaradenwerke are well funded through bank accounts in Switzerland which we believe to be the repository of Nazi cash squirreled away at the end of the war. We have suspected for some time that they are engaged in the import and trafficking of drugs from Brazil but had no clue as to how they were brought in until we were alerted to Manfred Hartmann's acquisition of a factory in Campinas. You might be able to help us identify the supply chain and hopefully catch those involved red-landed."

"Does that mean that you are more interested in return shipments from Campinas to Leuffen rather than consignments from Hartmann & Holst. Presumably, they have no problem in transferring money from a numbered account in Switzerland to pay for whatever comes from Brazil?" I questioned.

"And so I thought, until you told me just now of Bernard Tompkins' death which suggests that advance payment is made in hard currency or some other medium of exchange. There must have been something physical that he saw or he wouldn't have been bumped off. It's also true that that any exporter, such as a drugs cartel, would have avoided showing any credits to their more identifiable bank accounts or related cash withdrawals."

"What more do you think I should do now? I have brought copies of the shipping documents and the invoice from Leuffen in the hope that I can find a way to compare them with the documentation in Campinas while I'm there."

"That makes sense and the next step is to find out when and how the return shipment from Campinas to Leuffen will be made. But you need to be careful; there will be an element of danger for you personally if our suspicions are correct and you are caught poking around. I'm afraid we have no one over there to watch your back. South America is outside our sphere of influence."

"What about the US Drug Enforcement Agency; presumably they would have an interest. Don't you have any friends there?"

"The DEA are very parochial," Max replied "They don't venture out of their backyard except for sources of narcotics supplying the USA. Of course, I could ask for help from the Cousins but that would mean your signing the Official Secrets Act and I doubt that you would want the CIA climbing all over you and Allied Autoparts like a cheap suit."

"To be avoided at all cost," I agreed. "Especially since my Chairman is planning to stand as State Governor this autumn."

"What I expected you to say. I can see that the only way I can help you is to be indiscreet. And if I'm going to be indiscreet I would prefer to carry on this conversation in the open air without risk of being overheard. Back to our lunch then. Can I offer you anything further?" "No thank you, Max. To eat more would be disrespectful to the memory of a superb steak and kidney pudding. But I will take a cup of coffee, if I may."

"Certainly, I shall do the same, but I think we'll have our coffee here at the table; and then I suggest a turn in the park to aid our digestion."

With the promise of our conversation continuing I willingly agreed. We drank our coffee with small talk about the Fentimans and how well they had adapted to Susses. Max paid the bill and collected his hat and beautifully furled umbrella from the cloakroom; we set forth together walking west along Pall Mall.

"You probably wonder how I know so much about you," Max resumed looking at me from under the brim of his soft black Homburg.

"It had crossed my mind."

"Your tutor at Oxford is an old acquaintance. Graham Stanfield was up at Balliol, although long after me; we didn't meet until he became a don and later a talent spotter for our lot. You were under consideration for a time as a potential recruit but you didn't quite make the selection board."

"I don't know whether to feel flattered or insulted," I countered.

"You were talented and had the right background but Graham felt that you were too flippant and self-willed to be suitable. Of course, that was before your military service which probably knocked corners off you. If you had gone up afterwards, the verdict might have been different."

"In that case, I feel relieved. I've never fancied being cast as a cloak and dagger man."

"But that is exactly what you may become now, albeit as an amateur. You've already decided to wear the cloak. Let's hope that there is no occasion for daggers."

We turned down at the corner between Clarence House and St. James's Palace, crossed The Mall and entered St. James's Park. In the Spring sunshine I could see now that Max was probably well into his seventies, and wondered what authority he still commanded in the murky world of the security service he was inviting me to enter. No doubt he was still well connected, but when he made a request I wondered how rapid a response he received.

We walked in the direction of the duck pond at the Buckingham Palace end of the Park until we found an unoccupied bench which Mac dusted with his handkerchief before sitting down. "The only help I can provide, on a strictly personal level, is to connect you with an old friend in Rio who owns a successful export and import agency trading in Brazilian coffee. Roderick can probably assist you in tracking consignments to and from Leuffen through the port." Max offered.

"That sounds like just the intelligence source I shall need if I am going to make any progress beyond document checking in Campinas. May I call him on arrival." I enquired.

"I'm not going to give you his telephone number, nor the name of his company until I have spoken to him., Max continued. "Roderick was a very dear colleague during the war, based in Spain. He returned to private life and emigrated to Brazil as soon as he could afterwards. His full name is Roderigo Morales and I need to ask him first if he is willing to do me a favour. Give me the name of the hotel where you will be staying and wait for him to contact you. It's entirely possible that he will prefer not to be involved."

"We're staying at the Hilton on the Copacabana beach front. I should be checking in about midday Sunday."

Neither of us had anything to add; so, I thanked Max again for lunch and promised him a full report on my return. He sauntered over to The Mall for a cab, an upright figure with a jaunty wave of his umbrella, and I returned to the office with more food for thought.

---ooo0ooo---

Leuffen, 27 May 1978

"Frederik, it's Manfred. I need to bring you up to date. There is good news and bad news." Manfred Hartmann in pyjamas and a brocade dressing gown was calling Amparo, Brazil, at midnight from Leuffen. He had debated with himself about making the call but had reasoned that the consignment would be reaching Rio soon and that he should

re-emphasise the necessity of suspending any return consignment.

"That's a very American expression, Manfred," responded Frederik von Falkenberg, disengaging from the strikingly beautiful girl who had been sitting on his lap. "You have become corrupted by your association with them and it must be long past your bedtime in Leuffen. I am sad, my friend, that you have nothing better to do than call me." He gave the strikingly beautiful girl an affectionate pat on the rump and motioned her towards the door.

"However," he resumed "It is always good to hear from you. Let me have the bad news first. No doubt that is why you have called me"

"There was a visit here last week with a group of the top US management including Chester Case," Manfred Hartmann reported. "The business review which they held with Peter and our managers did not go well – probably worse than Peter realises. And now I hear that ten days after the meeting of international managers in Brazil next week, which I am sure you will be attending, there will be a further visit to Germany by Lloyd Parmentier, their Vice President International, who has ordered Peter to visit our biggest customers with him. He has a very aggressive personality and I expect that the series of visits will be 'katostraphalen' both for Peter and for Hartmann & Holst. Inevitably, there will follow an invasion of more Allied Autoparts managers - what Americans call 'corporate firemen.' Therefore, you will understand that any further private consignments is 'ausser frage'."

Recognizing that Manfred's use of German phrases in their telephone conversations was a sign of stress, von Falkenberg changed the subject. "And now for the good news?" he asked.

"One good outcome is the Polizei final report on the Englishman Tompkins. They have classified his killing as death by misadventure. It was a stupid blunder by Klinger but at least the authorities are satisfied."

"That must be a weight off your mind, Manfred."

"Not really, Frederik," Hartmann replied wearily. "The Englishman Radclive, who was one of the last two to see him alive, is not satisfied that this is the truth. He visits Leuffen frequently and he may go on digging like a pig for truffles."

"I believe he is a participant in next week's meeting here. A visit to Campinas is on the agenda for the international managers. I will try to make a friend of him. Of course, I will be careful," he added in anticipation of the other's reaction.

"You will keep me informed, won't you, Frederik?" the older man asked.

"I always do, Manfred," said von Falkenberg reassuringly, neglecting to report that on receipt of Hartmann's telex he had immediately put in train arrangements for the next shipment to Germany. His shipping agents and collaborator, Transportico SA, had advised him that morning that the complete consignment would reach Valencia, their chosen European port of entry on 10 June.

"Alles gut. Gute nacht, Manfred." he said and put the receiver down.

"Klinger and our friends in the Kamaradenwerk can handle it well," he thought "The old man has lost his nerve. Better to leave him out of it from now on." He resolved to place two calls to Europe in the morning.

At the other end of the line, Manfred Hartmann replaced his receiver thoughtfully. He felt uneasy that von Falkenberg hadn't queried his instruction to stop shipping. "Was there something that Frederik had failed to tell him?"

----ooo0ooo----

Part Two

CHAPTER 16

THERE CAN BE no more spectacular view, I thought, of any city in the world than the panorama below greeting air passengers arriving at Rio de Janeiro. London, Paris and New York all have their merits, as do Hong Kong, Sydney and, today more than forty years later, Shanghai, which impress more. But none of these can match Rio. The wide sweep from Rio's port in the north down the coast with its unparalleled span of world-famous beaches and the monolithic statue of Christ the Redeemer atop Corcorado mountain, facing the Sugarloaf mountain across the Guanabara Bay, beats them all.

We landed mid-morning Sunday at Galeäo-Antonio Carlos Jobim airport after our long flight from Paris. Tom and I had met up with the two Tipton managers, Cyril Snell and Gerald Jarvis, at Charles de Gaulle. The passenger cabin was empty at the rear so that Tom and I, as seasoned travellers, were able to stretch out over three seats each and get some sleep lying down. The other two stayed in their allotted seats nearer the front. The bright sunlight and heat hit us as we alighted from the plane and we were grateful for the comparative cool of the terminal. Passport control was tedious and I was obliged to open my suitcase for inspection in the customs hall. It was too hot for the four of us to cram into a single taxi; Tom sent Cyril and Gerald ahead in one and waited for me to take a second cab to the Hilton on Copacabana beach front.

The drive to the hotel took about twenty minutes from the airport at the north end of the city to Copacabana in the South zone giving us a closer view of the sea and beaches as we swept down the broad coastal Avenida past massed ranks of rival hotels. The Hilton was among the tallest and newest; we checked in and were shown to our rooms on the tenth floor overlooking the sea with the hotel pool in the foreground. After tipping the bellhop and before unpacking I decided to telephone Gaby in London where it was now just before 8:00 p.m. "How was the flight?" she asked.

"Long and uneventful," I reported, "and I was able to sleep; so, bent but not broken. I'm looking forward to a dip in the pool."

"That's good and all is well here. Don't go walking on the beach with any girls from Iponema," she added, referring to the popular song of the '60s. "Miss you already."

"Unlikely, Iponema is the next beach several mile away. I miss you too and wish you were here," I replied closing the call.

As I put the receiver down, I noticed an envelope addressed to me on the bedside table. Inside was a note signed "Chester Case". It said "Cocktails at 6:00 p.m. in the penthouse top floor. Dress casual." With time to spare I unpacked, put on swimming shorts, a polo shirt and flip-flops, grabbed my sunglasses and a hotel towel and descended to the pool. A number of the Farmington office team were already there in the pool or on loungers. Floyd Parmentier, floating on a pink lilo with a glass in his hand, hailed me from the centre of the pool and invited me to join him. I dived in, swam two lengths fast to show a degree of independence and came up alongside him.

"You really must try one of these, Julian," he declared. "It's Brazil's national drink *'ciaparinha'*. I've a jug made up ready to pour at the bar," he added, signalling to the barman who filled a chilled glass and brought it to me at the edge of the pool. It consisted of squeezed limes over ice cubes with sugar added and a liberal dose of cachaca rum.

"That's delicious and thanks," I said rejoining Lloyd at his lilo.

"You're welcome. Many more to come while we're all here this week. Make the most of this opportunity to meet everyone and get to know the home team better. In case you hadn't realised," he added, "you're on the watch list for future promotion. You've made a good first impression and, if you support me, your career will be on the up and up."

I was saved the embarrassment of trying to reply by another call, this time from Bennett Pullman at the poolside, telling me that our first presentation was scheduled for the following day and suggesting that we dined together later. I agreed and, passing the sunbathers on the way back to my room, noticed the figure of Barry MacLennan on a lounger under a large sunshade, shrouded in a white towelling bathrobe behind outsize sunglasses. He waved to me languidly and I felt sure that he had watched closely my encounter with Lloyd. Back in my room I found a note from reception under the door; a Senhôr Roderigo Morales had telephoned in my absence and had left a return number which I called. On the fourth ring, the receiver was picked up. "Senhôr Morales, please," I asked.

"Morales here. May I help you?" Speaking perfect English in a warm voice with little trace of an accent. "It's Max's friend Julian from London. Thank you for your call," I said.

Roderigo put me at my ease by immediately expressing his willingness to help if he could and I explained that we were scheduled to fly up to Sao Paulo on the Tuesday morning returning Wednesday afternoon. We arranged to meet the next evening at 6:00 p.m. in the lobby bar of the Hilton so that I could brief Roderigo and he would decide how, if at all, to aid my investigations. "You'll recognize me," he said. "I always carry a cane."

---ooo0ooo---

Chester Case's spacious penthouse suite was luxuriously furnished for entertaining with twin sofas and comfortable chairs sufficient to seat the dozen who were bidden and had assembled there at the appointed hour. Aside from the AA head office team which included several whom I had not met before, only Tom, myself and our opposite numbers with Latin American responsibilities had been invited. A wet bar had been set up at one end of the room and guests were served drinks on arrival. Several followed Lloyd's example and accepted the proffered ciaparinha; others, like myself, preferred our normal tipples. When all of us were served, and with glass in hand, Chester raised his voice to gain our attention. "Welcome ladies and gentlemen," he said, "to the first Associated Autoparts conference for its international managers." The ladies referred to were the two staff members whom I had yet to meet: Shelley Frankel, Director of Procurement, and Donna Fairweather, Chester's PA.

"I wanted us to get together our first evening here in Rio," Chester resumed in his normal speaking voice "to explain what we hope to achieve during the week for the company and the managers of our overseas businesses. First, this is an opportunity for us to get to know and assess individual managers better and to give them confidence that we can be relied upon to support them. At the same time, through personal peer interaction during the group sessions and leisure time, it will encourage them to work together in harmony in joint projects on technology transfer or cross-border marketing of each factory's specialities into other territories. Finally, we have chosen Rio de Janeiro as our location because it is spectacular and will hopefully make the week truly memorable for us all as an enjoyable experience among colleagues and friends. And that's enough from me; the experience starts here right now."

Amid murmurs of appreciation we mingled in groups of two or three and started to engage in conversation. Tom and I moved towards our counterparts, Ronaldo Martini, Director of Latin American Operations, and Oswaldo Carioca, Marketing Services Manager, and introduced ourselves. Ronaldo was a suave middle-aged Argentinian with a world-weary expression and exquisite manners; perhaps surprisingly, he and Tom related immediately and moved away together, leaving me to spar conversationally with Oswaldo. In sharp contrast to Martini, Oswaldo was a skinny young olive-skinned Mexican, bubbling away with suppressed energy. Like me, he was a comparative newcomer to AA having served less than a year, and an enthusiastic supporter of Chester and the Farmington team. We exchanged information for some minutes on business conditions in Mexico, where AA had two plants and in Brazil where Oswaldo was still coming to terms with the Campinas operation and local inflation running in excess of nearly one hundred per cent.

"Actually," he said with an infectious grin, "inflation is only uncomfortable up to about fifty per cent while you have to negotiate a price increase every month or so. After that, everyone starts to give up and weekly price increases become automatic, adjusted according to the published inflation index."

"I can see that makes life easier for you and Grunwald Metallwerk," I commented, "but tell me something about the plant at Campinas that we are visiting on Tuesday."

"It's not just one factory, you know. There are two, about ten kilometres apart. The spring factory which does business with Hartmann & Holst is managed by Oskar Holst, son of Manfred Hartmann's partner. He's been here in Brazil for more than three years and is fully qualified by the German spring making institute. He's a good manager and very much respected by his workforce. However, he reports to Frederik von Falkenberg as director and Fred runs the press shop at the second factory."

"And how is Von Falkenberg to work with?" I asked.

"Well, he's a very tough manager, more feared by his workforce than respected," Oswaldo responded. "He gives Oskar a hard time too and treats me as a kind of servant. Frankly, the man's a bully and no-one likes working with him."

"Does that mean that Fred or Oskar organizes the shipments to and from Germany?" I inquired.

"Oskar says what he wants to receive from Hartmann & Holst for the spring factory and when he is ready to ship return cargos, but Fred authorizes all the shipments with the forwarding and delivery agents," Oswaldo replied.

"Hey, you guys, is this private shop talk or may I join in?" Shelley Frankel called in a deep Southern drawl as she joined us. She was an arresting figure in white linen slacks and an emerald green silk shirt and her short brunette bob and feisty manner signalled that she was at home with her male colleagues. I introduced myself and opened the conversation.

"Oswaldo was just telling me what treats are in store for us in Campinas but, of course, you've already been there," I conjectured.

"And how," Shelley responded with a gleam in her eye, "Oskar's a sweet guy with old school manners, but that Count von Falkenberg is a real piece of work. Don't leave me alone with him in the same room on any account when we're up there."

"Shelley, I shall make it my mission to be your protector," Oswaldo cried gallantly, bowing deeply; she responded in kind, exaggerating her accent. "Why, Oswaldo, I do declare that's the best offer I've had all month."

While Oswaldo retreated to the bar to freshen both their drinks Shelley laid a hand on my arm. "Seriously, Julian, I've been waiting to meet you and ask for your help on my trip to Europe. Loren says that I should talk to you."

"Of course, just go ahead and ask," I replied. "I must remember to thank Loren for the suggestion. I'm still the new kid on the block but I'll do my best. What is your mission in Europe?"

"I want to swing by some of the suppliers of spring wire located in Europe to discuss prices for supplying our factories in North America," Shelley explained. "You see our suppliers in the US cannot match the quality of the wire, particularly chrome vanadium, that Oskar Holst receives from Germany to manufacture valve springs."

"I'll be happy to help setting up appointments and planning your travelling arrangements when you let me know whom you want to meet," I told her.

Shelley looked at me up and down appraisingly. "Perhaps you'll be able to tour with me?" she suggested.

"A great idea but I may be too heavily occupied visiting the AA plants to get the European DES programme off the ground. But if you pass through London we'll be happy to look after you there," I replied returning the scrutiny.

"That sounds like the practised turn-off of a married man," Shelley challenged me.

"More like a married man's health warning to himself," I quipped ruefully as Oswaldo returned with their drinks. Leaving them together I ambled over to the bar, passing Erik Nielsen, who seemed less morose than in Leuffen, to have my glass refilled. After brief words with Erik and Loren Corley I took my scotch and soda across the room again and strolled out on to the penthouse terrace. The panorama of sandy beaches stretching in either direction and the vista across the sparkling bay to the Sugarloaf mountain was still breath- taking. Somehow the mountain seemed higher and greener than it had from the air.

"That's quite a view, Julian, isn't it?" said Chester Case who had joined me. "Knocks spots off Schloss Hohenleuffen, I'd say," I replied.

"Takes us back to reality and our last conversation on the way back to the Flughafen.The police report tidies things up but Viktor has the impression that you are not entirely comfortable with the outcome."

"That's right. In fact, I'm distinctly uncomfortable; it's all just too convenient," I replied.

"Sure, but it's convenient for us too. We can control strictly all future consignments from Leuffen to Campinas, which is your core area of concern, and keep AA's hands clean. Aside from trying to bring justice to the wrongdoers for Bernard Tompkins' death, that's not too bad a result." In other circumstances Chester's bland charm might have been persuasive.

"I'm afraid that may not be the real problem, Chester," I countered. "We don't know anything about the return shipments from Campinas: past consignments and what will be shipped now. If my suspicions have substance, there could be a history of contraband imported from Brazil and paid for through the return consignments from Leuffen."

"And that would take us into far more dangerous territory," Chester Case reflected. Then, after a pause for thought and in an altogether darker tone, he shared his conclusion. "The last thing I wish to do is to involve the CIA on the basis of suspicion rather than fact and I would prefer to avoid their involvement at all. Without exposing yourself to unnecessary risk, do you think that you could fish around the factories while you are in Campinas and see what you can find out?"

"I had that in mind anyway," I confessed, "but it would be good to have your blessing."

"Blessing, sure, but authorization no. If there are any questions or complaints about your actions, I shall deny all knowledge. You'll be on your own," Chester replied firmly.

"Not exactly comforting but no less than I would expect," I admitted.

"We'll catch up later in the week, then. At least you have my encouragement and best wishes to go with you," he replied bringing our conversation to a close.

----ooo0ooo----

CHAPTER 17

THE FULL GROUP of twenty-eight assembled for the first time the following morning in the conference room on the mezzanine floor of the Hilton. In addition to the twelve of us from the penthouse party there were two managers only from Leuffen and Tipton and three each from Amsterdam, Norkopping and the two Mexican subsidiaries at Monterrey and Guadalajara. Except for the British and German factories, both currently without sales managers, each plant was represented by its general manager, sales manager and accounts manager.

Grunwald Metallwerk were unrepresented but Frederik von Falkenberg and Oskar Holst would be joining the Group from Tuesday onwards when we arrived in Campinas.

After a few welcoming words from Chester Case and then Barry MacLennan - even shorter - the morning was devoted to presentations from each general manager, describing the product ranges and customer profiles of their companies, followed by the first part of a longer series of presentations from Bennett Pullman's marketing team detailing proposals for technology transfers of product specialities from one plant to another. I found the general managers' presentations of interest as an aid to broadening my knowledge of group activity. Most of them were informative, and delivered fluently but the two weakest were those of Cyril Snell who spent too much time talking about the history of the company before it became part of Allied Autoparts and Peter Hartmann who seemed to have forgotten Tom's careful coaching. His eulogy to the superior quality of German spring making impressed no-one and alienated several among his audience. Unwisely, he repeated his mantra from the recent business review to the effect that each factory worker treated his machine like 'one of his family.' When it came to his turn to present after the coffee break Jan van der Groot, the general manager of Ribenda, the Amsterdam subsidiary, provoked laughter by referring to the care and attention which his spring makers gave to the three machines for which they were responsible as 'their children.'

Oswaldo and I had worked hard with Bennett over dinner and afterwards the previous evening to rehearse our presentations, critiquing each other to prepare for questions from our audience. Now, Bennett kicked off explaining the strategy of transferring technology from one plant to another in order to gain market penetration. He argued the case lucidly and the constructive questioning that followed took us up to lunchtime.

The buffet lunch was served in an adjoining room set out with tables for six which ensured that some mixing between managers would take place. I joined a table at which two of the Dutch and two of the Swedish team had already chosen to sit. Looking round the room I could see that five of the account managers were sitting with Erik Nielsen at another table and four Mexicans were grouped with Lloyd Parmentier and Bennett. Barry MacLennan had chosen to sit with the two British managers, Peter Hartmann, Tom and Loren Corley at a third. The remaining plant managers and Oswaldo were clustered around Chester Case and Viktor Accona. Shelley Frankel, more soberly dressed today in a tan trouser suit, elected to join our table and immediately attracted the attentions of both Jan van der Groot and the Swedish general manager Óla Larsen.

It soon emerged that there was a generic antipathy by the Dutch towards the Germans, sparked by Jan's earlier brush with Peter Hartmann and fuelled further by Shelley's comment that Lloyd Parmentier was planning for visits by European plant management team to each other's factories.

"In 1940 the Germans came to Amsterdam and took away my bicycle," announced Bruin Brouwer, the sales manager for Ribenda. He was a tall, slim man with receding sandy hair and a permanently mournful expression. "Perhaps this time they will bring my bicycle back,"

Shelley and I exchanged amused glances across the table. "There's no answer to that," she said.

After lunch we returned to the conference room and the marketing team continued with its presentations. Oswaldo delivered a case history with flamboyant enthusiasm of how the technology for manufacturing seat belt retractor springs, a speciality of AA's Detroit factory, had been introduced to the Monterrey plant to serve the Mexican auto market. Bennett revealed that a similar transfer to Tipton Springs was under consideration and I gave a brief overview of market demand for seat belt retractors in the UK. We then referred to the arrangements for shipping European standard wire coils to Campinas and how Grunwald Metallwerk were manufacturing valve springs for sale to Volkswagen in both Brazil and Germany at a lower cost than in Germany. An open discussion followed with an exchange of views over other specialty product lines for which the technology and expertise were transferrable. The session concluded with a talk by Loren Corley on the complexities of injector nozzle spring manufacture and how he hoped to transfer that expertise from Leuffen to the AA plant in Greenville for the developing US fuel injection market.

Finally, after another coffee break, I delivered the set piece that I had prepared in London on the rationale for the DES range of standard springs and the opportunities in all European markets for repeating the success of the US programme. I distributed a handout for review and announced a further planning discussion later in the week to agree timing for catalogue production, stocking and start up of the programme. We finished with more questions at 4:30 p.m. leaving me time for a plunge in the pool before getting ready to meet Roderigo Morales.

---ooo0ooo---

I should have guessed that an old friend of Max would have a close affinity to him. Seated at the lobby bar of the Hilton in good time, I had no problem in recognizing Senhor Morales when he arrived promptly at 6:00 p.m. The ebony walking stick with silver handle confirmed his identity but I would have placed him anyway; the spotless white suit, two tone shoes and panama hat which he carried were the South American equivalent of Max's own sartorial elegance. I was glad that I was wearing a jacket and tie. We hailed each other across the room, then ordered our drinks and settled down at a table in the furthermost corner. "Please call be Roderic," Morales said. "It's nice to hear my name in English occasionally."

We started by exchanging basic information about ourselves: the context of my visit to Brazil and its duration; the range of his business interests, mainly the purchase and export of coffee beans for American and European clients and the selective import of fashion clothing for department stores in Rio and Sao Paulo. Roderigo mentioned that he was familiar with the Amparo area of Campinas in which both the Grunwald Metallwerk factories were located because this was the centre of a prime coffee growing region. Moving on to the matters which had bought us together, he confirmed that Max had given him an outline briefing.

"As I understand it, your concerns are over the exchange of goods between Leuffen and Amparo arising from the death of a colleague there in uncertain circumstances," he summarized.

"That's about all the background I can give you Roderic," I replied, "except to add that the trade has been going on for many years and that the corpse was found in the warehouse from which the last shipment was made a few days later."

"Is there anything more that you can tell me?"

"Only that I think the shipment may have just been delivered and that I hope to find out more when I am there tomorrow. I have brought with me copies of the shipping documents for you," I replied, passing the documents to him.

While Roderigo was examining them closely I ordered a further round of drinks and studied him across the table. He was of a similar age to Max I supposed but carried his years better. The tanned face with pencil line moustache, a glossy black head of hair and bright black eyes were those of a much younger man; he had clearly kept himself in good shape. At length he looked up and addressed me soberly.

"The most significant detail is the shipping and forward agent here in Rio, responsible for onward delivery to Amparo; it's Transportico Americana or 'TPA' as identified here in the documents."

"Are they a reputable company?" I asked.

"TPA are an efficient carrier, no question. But reputable?" Roderigo paused. "Let's just say that they have a certain reputation."

"I think you'll have to spell that out for me," I pressed him. "What exactly do you mean by 'a certain reputation'?"

"The largest shareholder in the Transportico Americana parent company is the Vincobar family, the second largest drug cartel operating out of Colombia," Roderigo revealed, "and that opens up disturbing possibilities. It suggests that the return shipments to Leuffen are the more interesting. Consignments to Leuffen of manufactured springs would be the perfect cover for drug running."

"And the consignments from Leuffen to Amparo contain payment in currency or kind for the drugs," I added, "in which case we need to find out all we can about the next shipment out of Amparo as well as the present delivery from Leuffen. What can you do to help?"

"While you are up country in Campinas I will check out any cargo reservations to Europe that TPA have made for the next few weeks and confirm that the cargo from Leuffen has cleared customs and is in their hands. When does it say that the collection was made from the factory?" Roderigo consulted the documents again. "Collected on 12th May by PanAlpina for shipment from Valencia – that's the fastest sea route to Rio from Europe; so it could have left from there on 15th and arrived here thirteen days later on 28th. With priority treatment by TPA through the port and rapid routing by road it's possible that the container reached Amparo today, in which case you may be able to view the consignment tomorrow or Wednesday morning."

"If our suspicions are correct, when do you think TPA will 'liberate' whatever it is the cartel are expecting from the container?" I questioned.

"Probably en route at some remote staging post, I imagine." Roderigo replied confidently, "Extracting it when the container is opened at the factory would be an unnecessary risk requiring accomplices on the spot, and these are people who are strongly risk averse."

"In that case, I shan't be able to spot anything unless the manifests don't match or there is a discrepancy between the goods unloaded and the invoice details," I concluded.

"And the same applies to return shipments. The drugs will be added en route and the container resealed before shipment. And at the Europe end PanAlpina, who are above suspicion as a leading carrier, will certainly not interfere with the cargo before they deliver at Leuffen," Roderigo completed his analysis.

There was nothing more to be said before my return from Amparo and we agreed to meet for dinner on the Thursday evening at Tijuca Tenis Clube, Roderigo's prestigious club in downtown central Rio. We finished our drinks while I explained how I knew Max and about his wartime connection woth my father, and Roderigo reminisced about his wartime life in London. We parted amicably and I watched his upright and elegant figure leave the hotel having ordered a taxi from the doorman.

---ooo0ooo---

In search of company I wandered on to the terrace leading to the pool and its surrounding circle of deckchairs and loungers. Loren Corley and Bennett Pullman invited me to join them at the poolside. It was cooling pleasantly but the sun was still hot and it was good to sit with them in the shade. We reviewed the day's proceedings, congratulating each other on our presentations and commenting on the audience reaction.

"I think the afternoon was more successful than the morning." Loren opined. "Two of the plant managers' presentations were poor and questioning was polite but sparse."

"Yes. The afternoon provoked more genuine interest and the questioning was more intelligent," Bennett agreed.

"The final session of open questioning was best of all." I suggested. "They nearly all seemed eager to take on new specialist product lines even if some of the ideas were a bit off the wall."

"What about the interchanges between the various country managers?" asked Loren.

"Some ice-breaking; but the four Mexicans seemed to cling together and there were some awkward moments between the Europeans," Bennett ventured.

"The Dutch and the Swedes seemed fine and the accounts managers mingled well, but there's much to do in creating the mood of corporate comfort in working together that Chester is looking for. Particularly the Dutch with the Germans," I said.

As if on cue, Jan van der Groot and Bruin Brouwer came up to our table and buttonholed me.

"Julian, we would like to talk to you about DES. There is a ready after-market for standard springs in the Netherlands. Perhaps we could talk about it over dinner," Jan suggested.

And so my day ended with dinner in the roof-top restaurant of the Hilton hotel with Bennett and some special pleading from Jan and Bruin for Ribenda to be assigned the role of master stockist in the European DES programme.

CHAPTER 18

IN CONTRAST TO the stunning vista on the approach to Rio, the skyline of Campinas appeared rather ordinary with tall modern office buildings and apartment blocks in the centre surrounded by one or two storey red roof-tiled buildings. and with clusters of factories in the industrial areas on the outskirts of the city. With a population of less than a million Campinas municipality dates back to the mid-eighteenth century when it was founded by searchers for precious metals; in the nineteenth century it became a commercial centre for coffee, cotton and sugarcane farmers and now thrived as a leading Brazilian location for industry including agricultural machinery, automotive, textiles and business machines. Chester Case and Barry McLennan had remained in Rio. The rest of us travelled on a domestic flight from Rio's Santos Dumont airport arriving at Vivacopra terminal, Campinas at around 9:30 a.m. on Tuesday. There was a bus waiting on arrival to take us to the first of the Grunwald Metallwerk plants outside Amparo, some fifty kilometres from the airport. We reached the pressworks before 10:30 a.m. to be greeted by our host, Frederik von Falkenberg.

Von Falkenberg was an impressive figure, with short grey hair, an aquiline nose and a military bearing. He was wearing riding breeches and knee-high leather boots with an open neck shirt, attire more suitable for the hunt or a pre-war Hollywood movie director. Had he been carrying a riding crop, it would not have seemed out of place. He greeted us with elaborate courtesy making little distinction between the corporate managers from Farmington and those of us from Europe or elsewhere in Latin America. The only exception was Peter Hartmann whom he greeted by name but without any particular enthusiasm. However, Lloyd Parmentier stepped forward, making it clear that he was the head of our party and expressing pleasure at the occasion of our visit. Our host led us into a large masonry building which I judged to have been built at least forty years ago and, after a short walk down a passage running off the reception area, flung open double doors to admit us to the factory itself. The clatter of machinery turning had been rising steadily as we approached and now became a cacophany of sound as we entered a cavernous workshop housing more than a hundred lathes, drills and presses, each attended by a worker hunched over his or her workbench. The noise level was appalling. All machines were belt driven from overhead shafts aligned in parallel across the roof of the workshop and connected in turn by wider belts to electric generators beyond the far end of the factory. Conversation was impossible over the oppressive din as we toured the shop floor.

The products manufactured were stamped metal components and extruded pressings; some were drilled components ready for assembly and others threaded parts turned on the lathes. None of these were springs by definition but qualified as custom metal parts manufactured to specification. A majority of the machine operators were female, working with automaton like intensity.

It was a relief to leave the workshop and retire along the passage to the general manager's office beyond the reception area. We re-assembled before von Falkenberg's vast desk standing like schoolboys in front of the headmaster in his study. The walls of his office were adorned with framed photographs of Frederik himself, all taken in Brazil, shaking hands with important looking civic officials, customers or staff. There was one photograph of him with Manfred Hartmann outside the factory and one of a much younger von Falkenberg with two rather sad looking older men whom I took to be the Grunwald brothers. The wall behind his desk carried a collection of primitive native weapons including several fearsome blowpipes and the woodblock floor was part covered with tiger skin rugs.

We were invited to ask questions on what we had seen. Predictably, the focus was on the product range, the origin of raw materials and the major customers that the factory served. The questioning extended to the machinery which we had seen in the workshop and was topped by a comment from Óla Larsen at the back of our group. "Fred," he said in that sing- song speech common to Swedes speaking English, "you have a very noisy factory. How do your workforce react to it ?"

"We keep the machines running in the lunch hour and they take their food at their benches," von Falkenberg replied with complete indifference. His conversation stopper brought the session to a close.

"And now," he continued "your bus will take you on to our spring factory where Oskar Holst is waiting to receive you. I shall look forward to seeing you all again in Rio tomorrow evening where I have organized a special entertainment for you."

We wandered back to the bus. As we climbed aboard von Falkenberg had a further word for Lloyd and myself. "Manfred Hartmann asked me to entertain you while you are here in Amparo. "Would the two of you care to join me for dinner at my house this evening?"

I could sense that Lloyd Parmentier had taken an instant dislike to him before he replied.

"Thank you but I must decline. I cannot abandon my colleagues but Julian is free to accept your invitation."

Frederik turned to me enquiringly: "Then I shall be delighted if you will accept my hospitality, Mr. Radclive. I will send my car to collect you from your hotel this evening at 7:30." The remark was delivered as a statement rather than a question not allowing for refusal. I confirmed my acceptance without enthusiasm.

The bus pulled away and Lloyd turned to me. "I don't know if that was your choice," he asked, "but someone has to maintain good relations and you're a better diplomat than I am." "More of a tethered goat," I commented, thinking of tiger skin rugs.

---ooo0ooo---

The second plant was located on the other side of Amparo furthest from Campinas. The bus travelled there around the periphery of the city and we arrived at lunchtime. This factory was a more modern single storey building than the pressworks with an adjoining small office block and the name "Grunwald Metallwerk" displayed prominently at roof level. Before we could disembark Oskar Holst joined us on the bus and instructed the driver to take us down the road to a nearby open air restaurant where a barbecue had been prepared for our lunch. We sat on benches at two large wooden tables under an awning; the food was served off the grill on wooden platters by smiling local girls under the supervision of the bistro owner who treated Oskar with the respect due to a regular customer.

Oskar in turn was a charming open-faced German of a similar age and build to Peter Hartmann; he treated Lloyd Parmentier with due deference and the rest of us with the easy courtesy of a good host. He told us that he would be completing four years' service as general manager in July, having moved there with his wife while his father was still alive. Oswaldo and he were clearly on the best of terms sharing jokes about their recent experiences.

Conversely, Oskar and Peter had only a slight acquaintance before he left Germany and their relationship was no more than cordial.

After a convivial lunch we returned to the factory for our guided tour. This time we split into two groups, one headed by Werner Reicher, the factory manager and the other by Oskar himself. Reicher, a small white-coated man with a toothbrush moustache, treated us all very formally including Oskar whom he addressed as "Herr Doktor" throughout our visit. On our arrival he had accepted his instructions for the tour with a stiff bow and a faint click of the heels.

"Werner is a strict disciplinarian, as you can see, and insists on keeping what I think you would call 'a tight ship'," remarked Oskar as he set off with our group in the wake of Werner's. After my repeated tours of the German factory I was familiar with the various processes and able to make comparisons as we passed through the workshops. I noted that there were more female staff here but less multi-machine operations. There was the same high standard of cleanliness and orderliness as the product was moved from one operation to the next. The machinery was well-maintained but the electronic quality assurance equipment was less sophisticated than in Leuffen. Passing through the various *Hallen* in sequence we finished our tour in the warehouse, organized in very much the same way as at its fellow factory although this time in an annexe rather than a separate building. The main doors of the warehouse were half open for the receipt and despatch of goods that day and I looked at the yard outside. Backed up to the doors but not yet unloaded was a truck with the logo "TPA" painted on its sides and rear doors. Roderigo's prediction had been borne out; the shipment from Leuffen had arrived.

Tom had noticed the truck too although he was unaware of its significance. "Is that a new delivery," he called, "or are you about to load a shipment?"

"No, Herr Hardy." Werner Reicher who was leading that group replied. "It is the latest shipment of wire and equipment from Hartmann & Holst. We shall be unloading this evening."

Tom and I exchanged glances. The tour was at an end and there was no way we could disengage from the party and hang around to watch the unloading and transfer to the warehouse. I decided to take Oswaldo, at least partly, into my confidence and took him on one side.

"Oswaldo, I wonder if I may ask you for your help?" I enquired. "Tom and I have an interest in the shipments here from Leuffen, particularly this one. We're coming up to the financial year-end stock check. Could you check for me with Oskar whether there is anything missing?" I passed him a copy of the invoice.

"Can't you ask Oskar yourself?" Oswaldo asked reasonably.

"Normally and if there was more time, yes. But I don't want to draw von Frankenberg's attention to me when Oskar reports to him."

"That I can understand." Oskar responded. "As it happens, I can do this for you without too much difficulty. I shall stay on here to review several of the customer issues with Werner while they are unloading and then drive in with him later to Amparo to join the group for dinner. Let's meet up in the hotel bar at the end of the evening and I'll give you my report."

"Sounds good," I thanked him "but you may have to wait some time for me. I don't know at what hour Count Fred will release me from our dinner *à deux.*"

Returning to the bus with Oskar's promise that he would join the group at the hotel later, we drove the short distance into Amparo, where AA had booked us overnight accommodation at the local Hilton as a part of its package deal with the chain. The small city, founded in 1829, a century after Campinas, had prospered with coffee farming after 1850. Its tree-lined streets and late nineteenth century architecture including several impressive civic buildings and museums suggested that it would be a pleasant enough location for Europeans to reside. On the way in Tom sat beside me in the bus and I relayed to him my conversation with Oswaldo. "Since the consignment from Leuffen has just arrived I want to explore while we are here whether there are any additions to or shortfalls from the contents that were sent," I explained.

"Do you think that you will find anything out at your dinner with von Falkenberg?" Tom asked.

"More likely, I would say, that he will be pumping me to find out what, if anything, I know or suspect."

"Be careful, Julian," Tom cautioned, "We're a long way from home and you could put yourself in harm's way."

We reached the hotel and checked into our rooms which were rather less well-appointed than those at the Rio Hilton but still had all the essential comforts. By 7:25 I had showered, dressed in clean clothes and was waiting in the lobby.

---ooo0ooo---

CHAPTER 19

Amparo Campinas, 30 May

AT 7:30 P.M. PRECISELY a grey Lincoln Town Car glided up to the hotel entrance. The duty doorman stepped forward to speak to the driver who lowered his window; then turned back into the lobby and, in a loud voice, announced "Car for Senhŏr Radclive." I tipped him appropriately as he handed me into the waiting limousine. The driver did not introduce himself by name and, after a perfunctory *"Boa noite"*, set off. We moved away from the city centre into an upmarket residential area of large, well-spaced houses set back from broad tree-lined avenues in their own grounds. Ten minutes after leaving the Hilton my chauffeur turned the nose of the Lincoln towards a pair of wrought iron gates set between stone pillars which opened automatically. Behind, up a short drive stood an imposing three storey villa clothed in terracotta stucco and built in a late-Victorian style of architecture.

I was dropped at the front door, already open and waiting for me was a stern-looking figure dressed in a black tail coat, matching trousers and white gloves. "Good evening, Senhŏr," it said, "I am Luiz Otavio, butler to Count von Falkenberg. The Count awaits you in the salon." We proceeded upstairs to a fine high-ceilinged reception room which appeared to occupy most of the first floor. My host came forward to greet me with a superficially disarming smile which didn't quite reach as far as his eyes.

"Minha casa é sua casa, as we say here in Amparo," Frederik von Falkenberg greeted me. This evening he was wearing a loose white shirt in fine lawn, embroidered and collarless, over loose black trousers and suede moccasins.

For once I felt overdressed in jacket and tie. And we were not alone.

"Allow me to introduce you to my companion Izabel Lopez; Izabel, this is Julian Radclive." He motioned towards the strikingly attractive young woman who came forward to shake hands. With lustrous black hair, olive skin and almond eyes she was dressed in a low-cut clinging black dress; a wicked smile playing about her full lips would have driven many men to distraction.

"*Como va socé*, Senhõr Radclive?" she intoned in a deep husky voice. "Julian, please," I replied bowing over her hand.

"Izabel speaks very little English," von Falkenberg explained "but she understands much of what you say. However, we may talk quite freely in front of her; Izabel is very discreet. And she has a very charming sister, Francesca, whom we can invite to join us if you feel he need of more female company – and would like to make a night of it."

The final phrase was accompanied by a quizzical lift of eyebrows. There was no mistaking its meaning and I responded with my first untruth of the evening. "You are a more than generous host but, sadly, I have someone expecting me at the hotel later."

"Ah, the alluring Miss Frankel, no doubt. Perhaps I should have invited her instead of Lloyd Parmentier."

"The present charming company will be quite sufficient," I said. Izabel appeared to understand and smiled at me directly.

"We were just about to open a bottle of champagne," my host resumed holding up for inspection and popping the cork of a bottle of Louis Roederer Cristal. "Now we can start our evening." He poured skilfully into three tulip glasses and handed them to us.

"I am able to indulge my taste in fine wine thanks to my friend Manfred who manages to include two or three cases in each consignment from Leuffen; but more of that while we dine. Long may it continue," he added.

While he was talking and pouring I looked around the room. The far end was clearly his study area with a vast mahogany partners' desk and swivel captain's chair but this part was the living area with comfortable twin sofas either side of an open fireplace and matching armchairs. What drew my attention were the pictures on the walls, each illuminated by its own light above. They all appeared to be French impressionist paintings or sketches in the style of well-known artists. Easily identifiable were a lily pond spanned by a bridge in glowing soft colours from the school of Monet, a distinctive wind-blown cornfield in brighter primary colours recognizably in the hand of Van Gogh, a charming sketch of a ballet dancer at the barre which I took to be from the school of Toulouse Lautrec and a lady lounging on a sofa *in flagrante* which had to be in the hand of Manet or a good imitator.

Von Falkenberg noted my interest with amusement. "What a wonderful collection of prints," I enthused.

"No. they're all originals, I can assure you," he replied. "When I left Germany in 1945 I was able to bring some of my favourite artworks with me. The Monet is mine; the rest were passed to me by friends who intended to follow after me. Unfortunately, only one of them made it to Paraguay and I am keeping the Lautrec sketch for him. For one reason or another, the others were detained or did not survive. And so, since possession is nine points of the law, I have become the owner."

"In that case you are a fortunate man; do you plan to offer them for sale by auction."

"No fear of that," von Falkenberg pouring us more champagne. "I am well aware that certain people in France and elsewhere in Europe might claim ownership; so, I sell only to private owners direct."

Luiz Otavio appeared at the doorway. "*Janto é servido*," he announced. Izabel and the Count drained their glasses.

The butler led the way into the adjacent dining room where we were seated comfortably at an oval table laid for three with linen napery and gleaming silverware. Von Falkenberg had placed himself opposite me with Izabel between us at the near end. A candelabra occupied the far end of the table with candles lit. Large pots of chilled caviar were served first with melba toast. To accompany the caviar a freezer chilled bottle of Swedish Absolut vodka was extracted from an ice bucket, uncorked at the table and poured into shot glasses which the Count instructed us to knock back in single gulps. Spreading caviar on to his toast, he reopened conversation.

"I invited Lloyd Parmentier to join us, not just as a courtesy but because there is something specific I wanted to ask from Allied Autoparts which only concerns Hartmann & Holst, Grunwald Metallwerk and myself and is therefore under his authority. On reflection, I sensed some hostility today on his part; so, I'm pleased that he chose not to accept. There is a simpler way to achieve my aim with a little friendly cooperation which I think you can provide. May I call you Julian and continue?"

"By all means, but I doubt that I shall be able to help you if it is an operational matter," I replied.

"Let me give a little background. Over the last five years Manfred Hartmann and I have been trading in products from Brazil which have profitable markets in Germany and European products which are difficult to buy here. The wine which we are drinking together tonight is an example. In some cases there would be difficulties with customs formalities and import taxes if we were to send them separately. And so, to avoid any complications we include our packages in the regular consignments between Leuffen and here. There is no extra cost or harm for either Hartmann & Holst or Grunwald Metallwerk."

"In principle, no, but surely there is the risk of discovery in transit by the customs authorities at either end. What happens if your packages are detected and there is a charge of smuggling?" I asked.

"That's very unlikely in Brazil. We use a most efficient shipping agent who collects from Amparo and permits us to add our product *en route* to Rio. At Leuffen the consignments are unopened until after delivery to the warehouse; so that has been easily managed by Manfred and his team until now. In any case, if a consignment was opened and there was a charge, we would pay the duty and the fine," the Count assured me.

"And so, you see," he continued "Manfred's retirement presents me with a problem. I need a reliable associate to take his place."

"Surely, you have Peter Hartmann to take on his father's role?"

"Do you really believe that Peter will remain as General Manager of Hartmann and Holst for long? I understand very well that when an American company takes over another the old general manager seldom lasts for more than a few months unless the business is highly successful and, even then, he is likely to be moved on within two years. Besides, to adopt the vocabulary of my former partners, Peter is not a *mensch* and I need someone of honour and integrity as a partner for my private business interests in Europe."

"But what about yourself?" I questioned "By your own reckoning, how long do you expect to remain here as General Manager?,"

Von Falkenberg gave a short laugh and appeared amused. "Certainly not long; I am a realist. I may last a little longer because recruiting management in Brazil is quite difficult, but they do have young Holst who could do the job perfectly well. It really doesn't matter anyway because I can work with the shipping and forward agents, as I do now, to insert my product in outward bound consignments after they leave Amparo."

His self-confidence was absolute. I was spared an instant reply by Luiz Otavio returning to remove our plates and serve the main course of tournedos Rossini with aubergines and lyonnaise potatoes. The accompanying wine was a fine Vosne Romanée which complemented the steak perfectly. "Another of my special imports," the Count commented good humouredly.

"You were right not to ask Lloyd Parmentier for his blessing," I remarked at length enjoying a mouthful of succulent steak. "There's no way that Farmington would sanction any concession for private dealing through its inter-company trade. What did you have in mind if I agreed to participate as your European correspondent?"

"Let me ask you a question first, Julian. How much do they pay you?"

This was the moment when I could have told him to mind his own business which might have ended his solicitation. Instead, I added fifty per cent to my actual salary and quoted him a figure.

"That's a respectable salary, but hardly sufficient for someone of your ability. What would you say if I told you that your share from the first shipment would be at least at least that amount?"

"And what would I be expected to do to earn my share?" I countered.

"Let's call it 'stage management'. Ensure,when you are advised of the delivery date for a consignment, that our accomplice Johann Klinger and our customers are alerted; that there are no visitors to the factory, and the warehouse in particular, during the evening after delivery and that arrangements are in place for the handover away from the factory."

"Surely Klinger could do all of that for you?"

"Some of it, yes. However, it needs you to control the movements of AA visitors and other outsiders and I prefer not to involve Klinger in the commercial arrangements. By the way, you do not seem surprised that Klinger is my inside man."

"No great deduction required. Klinger was in charge of the unloading on my first evening visit to the factory," I reminded him.

"Ah yes. Klinger was very clumsy. I blame Peter entirely for what happened; if he had been in control he would have kept you and your friends away from the factory that night. The death of your friend was completely unnecessary and a stupid mistake. So you will understand why I cannot rely on Peter." I had to agree with von Frankenberg's conclusion; his logic was indisputable.

Throughout this exchange Izabel had had been silent; however, she remained attentive and I had the impression that she had followed the drift of our conversation. Now, as Luiz Otavio wheeled in a trolley containing alternative desserts: profiteroles or fresh pineapple doused liberally in kirsch, she became more animated. As she indicated her preference for profiteroles, Frederik added his comment. "Senhorita Izabel's favourite dessert; ensures that she'll stay a nice girl all evening." I opted for the pineapple and he followed suit.

For the next few minutes I tried to include Izabel in the conversation but her English really was very limited. Von Falkenberg was amused at my efforts. Nevertheless, I established that she lived with her parents and sister on the outskirts of Amparo with a day job in a dress shop and that her regular visits to the Count were a kind of night job and the highlights of her week. We finished our meal and Frederik called for coffee suggesting that Izabel took hers in the salon and 'relaxed' while we remained at table. I stood up as she left the room with an enigmatic smile; von Falkenberg remained seated and waved her away. I was offered a cigar which I accepted and port or madeira which I turned down in favour of another glass of the excellent burgundy. Otavio left us and we sat opposite each other in the dimming light of the guttering candles.

"You may be right about Peter Hartmann," I said. "He didn't make a good first impression in Leuffen two weeks ago and he will have the best part of another week on the road with Lloyd Parmentier later this month. He could be on his way out soon after that."

"In that case there is some urgency. How do you view my offer?"

I had been preparing mentally for this question and decided that I needed to show interest if I wanted to extract further information.

"Your offer is certainly attractive financially but I would need to know more about the routines for delivery to clients in Germany before considering it seriously."

"Of course; you will have all the necessary details once I have your acceptance in principle. We shall need to trust each other," von Falkenberg continued "and I am prepared to offer you evidence of good faith. Obviously, there can be no written agreement between us; instead I will credit the sum of ten thousand dollars to any bank account in your name as a retainer once I have your firm verbal agreement."

"That will be more than satisfactory if we go ahead," I responded, "but there my be timing issues which we should discuss first."

"For my part there is no issue. I have a consignment which I wish to ship as soon as possible."

"That's precisely the point. Receiving any consignment at Leuffen for the time-being would be unwise and in the immediate future very dangerous. There will be far too many AA executives visiting the factory for the next two or three months. The financial year-end is 30th June and there will be a thorough stocktake in which they take part. Also, since Hartmann & Holst is making losses, there is sure to be an invasion of accountants and engineers seeking to improve manufacturing methods and reduce cost." Striving to show concern I drew on my Bolivar cigar and looked earnest.

"It is imperative that the next shipment is delivered to our customers as soon as possible. I am sure that you can overcome these little local difficulties." Von Falkenberg was adamant; for the first time in our dialogue von Falkenberg betrayed impatience.

"Is it not possible to extract your merchandise from the consignment before it reaches Leuffen?" I asked knowing in advance what his reply would be.

"Out of the question. The shipping agent in Europe is Pan Alpina, a very correct Swiss company which will not enter into side arrangements with third parties. They would not agree to the removal of anything from the shipment without written instructions from an authorized manager of Hartmann & Holst. Now, perhaps, you will understand why I need an internal partner."

"So, how are deliveries handled currently?"

"Klinger extracts the merchandise in the warehouse, reloads it into a company van and takes it to a private location outside Leuffen where he hands it over to the customer. You will need to find a secure location for handovers and instruct Klinger accordingly."

I couldn't expect to gain more information without confirming my intention to accept the Count's offer and needed to temporize.

"It is clear from what you are offering me that the merchandise has a high market value and that imports are probably illegal with heavy penalties for trafficking if detected. Therefore, the level of risk on my part is correspondingly high. You must give me time to decide," I said.

"If there was no risk, I wouldn't have invited you to join me. You must take it or leave it." The retort was sharp and his manner brusque.

"You'll have my answer before we leave Brazil at the end of the week."

"I'll give you until the day after tomorrow when we shall meet again in Rio. Think of the money and I'm sure you'll make the right decision. From three or four transactions a year your share could be half a million dollars." With that von Falkenberg rose to his feet, supremely confident that greed would prevail.

I followed him back to the salon where Izabel lounged languorously on a sofa.. She was barefoot now and appeared to be wearing nothing else under the black satin robe that she had exchanged for her dress. Her smile was blatantly suggestive rather than enigmatic.

"It's too late now to call for Francesca to join us. Let's hope that Miss Frankel awaits you while time and tide wait for no man," Frederick said smugly suggesting that he should call for the car to return me to the hotel. Accepting my dismissal with some relief I thanked him for his hospitality, waved farewell to Izabel and was wafted back to the hotel in the comfort of his limousine.

---ooo0ooo---

I found Shelley Frankel and Oswaldo Carioca seated together on high stools at the otherwise empty penthouse bar. Tonight Shelley was wearing a fuschia coloured silk shirt and black trousers. They seemed to have settled in with Oswaldo's hand on one of her satin-clad knees.

"How are you two tonight?" I asked, positioning myself on Shelley's other side and ordering drinks for the three of us.

"We're good." she replied "But how was your feast with Frederik?"

"Food and drink very classy. He lives in some style at his mansion with his butler and a glamourous part-time girlfriend."

"Is it true that the mansion is stuffed with art and antiques?" Oswaldo queried.

"Art certainly. If it's all as genuine as the girl friend and butler he must be loaded too." "And the conversation?" Shelley this time.

"Boring old robber baron stuff mainly. Not very exciting." I was certainly not going into any of that detail with them and changed the subject.

"Did you find out anything from Oskar about this afternoon's delivery, Oswaldo?"

"Yes. The shipment was short of two coils of chrome vanadium spring wire, would you believe it?"

"Well, that's not too much of a problem for Oskar. He can claim a credit from Leuffen and order replacement coils free of charge at the same time. No doubt he'll take it up with Peter Hartmann. The problem is Hartmann & Holst's who will have to pay freight on the replacement load."

"Oskar is travelling with us tomorrow on the flight back to Rio; so, he will get his chance then," Shelley added.

A thought struck me as she spoke. If the shipment was two coils of wire short that represented quite a weight loss as well as a waste of space in the container. Weight was the more significant and could provide a pointer towards what product had been substituted.

"Shelley," I asked "drawing on your expert knowledge and to satisfy my curiosity, how much does a coil of wire weigh?"

"That would depend on the specification, but chrome vanadium wire – I could find out if you like tomorrow," she offered.

I told her that would be very helpful and she agreed to telex her office in Farmington before we left for the airport. I drained my glass and withdrew tactfully leaving them to finish their drinks and head off to bed – either singly or jointly.

---oooOooo---

CHAPTER 20

Rio de Janeiro, May 31 and June 1

WE FLEW BACK TO RIO the following morning on a return flight in the same airplane which had carried us to Amparo the previous day. The mood was relaxed with much light-hearted banter. Travelling together seemed to have created a sense of group identity and more of the camaraderie that Chester Case was hoping to generate from the week. The Latin Americans and the Europeans were now chatting freely together, the fruits of the Farmington team's liaison work. Oskar Holst's addition to our party had contributed to the group dynamic. As general manager of the Amparo spring factory he was an accepted colleague of the Mexican managers and, as a German national, he was also treated as a fellow member of the European team. Having tackled Peter Hartmann on the topic of the missing coils of wire on the way to the airport, he was now seated towards the front of the plane between the Monterrey general manager and Óla Larsen. Across the aisle Cyril Snell had engaged with van der Groot and Bruin Brouwer while behind them Dieter Trautman and Gerald Jarvis were in animated discussion with one of the Mexican accountants. Lloyd Parmentier had buttonholed Peter Hartmann for a serious discussion about their forthcoming tour of Hartmann & Holst customers. The rest of us had seated ourselves randomly further back while Viktor Accona and Loren Corley mingled with the remaining line managers. I found myself in the back row with Tom Hardy giving us the opportunity to catch up on overnight developments. I gave him a summary of my conversation with von Falkenberg followed by Oswaldo's news of the missing wire from the Amparo factory.

"What are your conclusions?" Tom asked.

"By his own admission, Frederik von Falkenberg and Manfred Hartmann have been trafficking merchandise from Brazil to Germany and possibly vice versa for years – although it may be that the goods shipped from Leuffen are in exchange for the product shipped and are taken off as payment in transit from Rio."

"What do you think the merchandise can be?"

"Well, the return shipments are certainly more than cases of wine for Frederik's private consumption and the amount of commission which he offered me suggests that the merchandise trafficked from here is of considerable value," I replied. "The most likely high value product must be drugs," Tom commented.

"I agree; and the ownership of the forwarding agent by a drugs cartel makes it a near certainty".

"What shall you say to von Frankenberg in Rio and what happens next?"

"I've thought about that. Of course, the answer will be 'no' when he approaches me in the next day or so but I'll try to leave the door ajar, if not open. I shall say that I cannot accept his offer before the focus of AAs' attention shifts away from Leuffen and the number of visitors from Farmington has dwindled. Hopefully, that will cause him to delay the next shipment out of Rio."

"Do you think that strategy will work?"

"I've no idea," I responded. "It would be out of character for him to allow himself to be thwarted but he's not a fool and understands the risks. On the other hand, he may be under some pressure by his partner at this end. They're quite likely to have 'made him an offer he can't refuse'."

"Either way, we need to know what to expect," Tom concluded.

I explained my connection with Roderigo Morales and that he was investigating any forward bookings through his import-export contacts with the port authorities. We agreed that I should report fully to Chester Case while we were still here but that it would be best to wait until I heard from Roderigo what he had discovered when we met again on Thursday evening.

The rest of the flight passed pleasantly. I could see that even Viktor's normally dour expression had mellowed as he basked in the warmth of the group's ambience. We were treated again to the spectacular panorama of Rio de Janeiro's harbour and beaches as we descended through light cloud into the sunlight below and were returned to the Hilton in time for another buffet lunch.

For the afternoon's work programme we split up into smaller groups. One group under Erik Nielsen's leadership focused on budgets and monthly management accounting; a second group led by Shelley Frankel studied raw materials procurement and stock control; and a third group with Viktor Accona as moderator focused on wage negotiations by the role playing of trade union leaders and management in face to face discussions. The noisier third group was relegated to a side room so as to avoid disturbing the others. A fourth workshop led by Bennett Pullman and supported by me gave instruction on the use of action plans to organize and progress chase the details of key projects such as cross-border technology transfers. Mid-afternoon the sub-groups moved round for a second set of sessions with two further sessions scheduled for the following day. Members of the Farmington management team moved between the groups as observers assessing the performance of the participants.

---ooo0ooo---

For the evening's entertainment Count von Falkenberg had reserved dinner and cabaret at the Brazilian equivalent of a downtown club catering for well-heeled tourists. The main course of fiery chilli con carne with an unlimited flow of local beer was unremarkable. The cabaret was mainly cheerful local music provided by a colourful samba band with a glamorous trio of female lead singers, interspersed with juggling acts and a stand-up comedian whose ancient vaudeville jokes delivered in a mixture of Portuguese and broken English were sometimes unintentionally funny. However, the highlight of the cabaret was an extravagant parody of a Carmen Miranda routine performed by a singer-dancer proudly introduced by the bandleader as 'Lolita - Miss Brazil 1970'.

'I-Yi-Yi-Yi-Yi-I-like you very much', she carolled gyrating on platform heels under a towering head dress with extravagant twirls of hand and wrist. Time had been quite kind to Lolita. The figure may have thickened and her face become fuller but the sparkle was undimmed and she still swivelled her hips like a teenager. The audience responded enthusiastically. After a set of three songs she invited members of the audience to join her on stage and the first to jump up was Oswaldo Carioca who demonstrated his dancing skills as a stylish caballero accompanying her next song. To the surprise of all, the second to join Lolita was Dieter Trautman. Flushed of face and fortified by litres of beer he clambered clumsily on stage, grasped a pair of maracas from one of the band and capered about with the grace of a pantomime horse. What he lacked as a dancer he more than made up for in energy and general *joie de vivre*. The rest of us encouraged him with handclapping and shouts of *Olé*.

Peter Hartmann alone glared with disapproval at Dieter's antics.

After twenty minutes or so we managed to drag an exhausted but reluctant Dieter from the stage. By this time, Lolita who was also flagging had clutched him firmly to her and was trying to drag him offstage to continue the party in her dressing room or elsewhere. Any further entertainment could only have been an anti-climax and we returned to the Hilton in reasonably good order where Dieter was feted by the rest of the group in the rooftop bar. No-one remarked on the absence of Frederik von Falkenberg throughout the evening. We were told that he would be joining us the following day.

For Dieter Trautman the evening had been an unqualified success. Until then he had been steadily making friends but his exploits with Lolita raised him to the status of most popular team member. Unconscious of the social impact he had made at the restaurant he was now joking at ease with the Dutch managers who had decided that some Germans at least might be good chaps. Chester Case looked on approvingly.

---ooo0ooo---

No first time visit to Rio de Janeiro would be complete without an excursion up the Corcovado mountain to the Cristo Redentor statue, one of the seven wonders of the modern world. Our visit was arranged for Thursday morning leaving the Hilton by bus before the heat of the day after an early breakfast. We travelled west through affluent suburbs, soon replaced by a slum colony of favellas in the foothills of the mountain. Leaving the city the road spiralled ever more steeply, bounded on the right hand side by the lush green foliage of the Tijuca forest which clothes Corcovado.

The journey took about half an hour with the diesel engine of the bus labouring hard. As we neared the top a final series of corkscrew turns brought us to the parking area where we disembarked. On the way up the AA group were on more subdued form with some among them, notably Dieter, nursing hangovers from the previous night. Seated next to me on the back seat with Tom on her other side Shelley Frankel relayed to us the telex reply to her enquiry from Farmington. Wire to valve spring specifications was normally purchased in 1,000 kilogram coils meaning that the shortfall in weight of the consignment received in Amparo two days before was

2,000 kilograms equivalent to 900 pounds.. We would need to think through the implications in terms of value.

Printed notices in five languages informed us that in order to gain access to the observation deck at the very feet of the statue there were three alternative means of ascent: by escalator, by lift or by climbing stairs of 223 steps. Since the escalator was out of order most of us opted to take the lift; only a few hardy spirits led by Lloyd Parmentier elected to climb. We were met on the observation deck by a guide who told us that we were now more than 700 metres above sea level and that the head of the magnificent figure at whose feet we now stood towered a further 38 metres above us. Equally impressive was the 28 metres span of Christ the Redeemer's outstretched arms. Visitors to the platform were protected by a stout handrail enabling them to peer down into the abyss below in safety. At intervals telescopes were set enabling viewers to focus on to specific locations of the city and port; the Hilton hotel was readily identifiable. Turning my attention to the way we had come I observed a familiar long grey limousine sliding into the car park alongside our bus. Frederik von Falkenberg alighted and walked over to the lift; two minutes later he emerged onto the observation deck. After brief exchanges with Chester Case and Lloyd Parmentier he joined me at the rail.

"What have you decided?" he asked without preamble and smiling confidently. My response was equally blunt. "The reward doesn't justify the risk. While the present focus of attention on Hartmann & Holst remains, I can't help you."

The Count's smile faded and was replaced by a sneer. "So, you want more money, Herr Rdclive. I will pay you half a million dollars for each consignment safely delivered."

"That's even more tempting but you misunderstand me. In the coming few weeks there are sure to be a flood of visitors from Farmington climbing all over Leuffen and investigating every part of Hartmann & Holst's business.

Ask me again in two months' time and I may feel able to accept."

"You disappoint me, Julian Radclive. I took you for a man of spirit." Stone-faced, von Falkenberg glared at me down his beak of a nose. "My proposal is withdrawn and will not be repeated. But remember," he continued with icy calm as I turned away "a little knowledge can be dangerous. You must be careful not to interfere in matters that are none of your business."

---oooOooo---

We lingered on the observation platform for a time pointing out landmarks to each other before descending to the car park and re-embarking on the bus. The Count invited Barry MacLennan and Chester Case to take lifts back to the Hilton with him in the comfort of his Lincoln Town Car. They accepted and the limousine purred off down the mountain ahead of us. Half an hour later we were back at the hotel with time for a swim before another buffet lunch.

The afternoon was spent in two further rounds of the previous day's workshops in the same groups as before, by the end of which all line managers except for von Frankenberg had participated in each of the four sessions. The Count elected to attend the workshops on action planning and on procurement and stock control, eschewing the other two on wage negotiations and management accounting and budgeting. Throughout the action planning session which he attended I was conscious of his disdainful glare.

Afterwards I sought out Chester Case to take my leave of absence from dinner with the group in the hotel, explaining that I had an introduction through a family friend to a leading importer and exporter who might be able to enlighten me on the shipments and deliveries of consignments between Amparo and Leuffen. Chester suggested that we should meet the next day for a further catch-up on whatever I had discovered during the week.

---ooo0ooo---

CHAPTER 21

June 1, Rio de Janeiro

BY 7:30 P.M. I WAS READY to leave the Hilton for my
dinner with Roderigo Morales at the *Tijuca Tenis Clube*
having booked a taxi to transport me. Clad for the first time
in my expensive Italian suit, I was looking forward to an
evening in relaxed company. As its name suggested,
Roderigo's club was located on the edge of the Tijuca forest
and national park immediately behind the central district of
the city; the journey there gave me an opportunity to
observe with interest the many older municipal buildings
and large private dwellings along the way. The club itself
stood at the base of the Corcorado and was approached by a
narrow side street off the main thoroughfare between an
impressive pillared gateway where the taxi decanted me. In
the best tradition of London, Paris or Madrid clublands the
reception area was an imposing marble hall with a wide
double staircase at the rear. The kiosk at the entrance was
manned by a liveried concierge whose role as gatekeeper
was to admit only members and their guests. I announced
myself as Roderigo's guest and was directed to a terrace off
the members' bar where I was told that Senhor Morales
awaited me.

Roderigo rose from a wrought iron round table where he
had been enjoying the evening sunshine and the final set of
a men's doubles played on a magnificent grass court beyond
the terrace. "Julian, how nice to see you again," he greeted
me inviting me to join him in the bottle of chilled white
wine which rested in an ice bucket at the side of his table
"or anything else you may prefer." I assured him that the
wine would be perfect and we sat in companionable silence
for a few minutes while I adjusted to the relaxing plip-plop

of tennis balls exchanged across the net and the players battled on to the end of their game.

"How was your visit to Amparo?" Roderigo asked at length "I have news for you at this end, but first tell me first how you got on."

I gave him an unvarnished account of the dinner with von Falkenberg and our discovery of the missing coils of wire from the consignment delivered to the spring factory while we were there two days before. He listened attentively: with amusement through the first part of my tale; more thoughtfully after the revelation of shortfall in the cargo received. "Your Count sounds what Max would call 'a very nasty piece of work'," he said.

"Sadly, there are too many refugees of that type who fled to South America in 1945 at the end of the war: some to Paraguay, some to Chile and others to Argentina or here to Brazil." Roderigo poured the last of the wine into our glasses and recplaced the empty bottle upside down in the ice bucket.

"And now," he continued "for my news. I checked the past and forward freight bookings to Europe by Transportico Americana against the names of their consignor customers and the consignees. There's a long history of shipments from Amparo by Grunwald Metallwerk three or four times a year over the past five years, as we expected, but here is the surprise. The next consignment was checked on board yesterday and is due to sail tomorrow bound for Valencia. That means it is scheduled to arrive on 17th June. Allowing for unloading and port clearance the other end, we can expect that Pan Alpina will deliver at Leuffen on about 22nd June."

"It also means that TPA must have collected from Amparo some time last week, before we all arrived, with the contraband added en route to Rio. And so," I added, "von Frankenberg was trying to recruit me to supervise the delivery of a consignment that he had already shipped."

"Let's consider the implications and consequences over dinner, shall we?" Roderigo led me back into the club across the hall and into the members' dining room, an airy, softly lit chamber with photographs of tennis players, past and present, clutching silverware trophies adorning the light panelling of the walls. He ordered for both of us, a dish of antipasti, followed by *moqueca de peixa*, Brazil's noted fish stew, then a sorbet and finally a taste of Brazilian sheep cheese. We drank a Chilean sauvignon blanc throughout to accompany the food.

"It seems that your bird has flown," remarked Roderigo, reopening the conversation as the antipasto was served. "He may have been under some pressure from the cartel if our drug trafficking suspicions are correct."

"Also, the expectation that subsequent shipments would be curtailed following the AA acquisition was a good reason for haste. By the same token, the value of the contraband this time is probably greater than usual", I suggested.

"I think you're right, but how can we estimate what that value might be?"

"Let's start with the shipment from Leuffen which arrived this week. We know that the weight of the two wire coils that were missing is around is around 909 pounds. Let's suppose that the product substituted in the container was the most expensive form of bulk commodity readily tradeable as a medium of exchange. That has to be gold, doesn't it?"

"Again, I agree with you, Julian. Let's make some rough calculations." Roderigo called over the dining room manager and asked for that day's issue of the Rio Times, the English language newspaper with a financial section showing commodity prices. He was reminded politely that club rules forbade members and their guests to read in the dining room; so he left the table briefly to consult the Rio Times copy in the library before returning to the table as steaming plates of our fish stew was served. "$169.20 an ounce," he proclaimed "How's your mental arithmetic?"

His enthusiasm was infectious and I did my best. "As a first step, that makes about $2,715 a pound. Beyond that, I need a pencil and paper to work out the value of the consignment but plainly we're talking millions."

"We'll do our sums later when we take our coffee; meantime, let's discuss how you intend to use this information."

"I assume it's too late to cancel the shipment and take the container off the ship before she sails?" I asked.

"Even if you produced a signed instruction from Grunwald Metallwerk to TPA tonight with copies for the port authorities, I doubt that it would be possible. TPA would be unlikely to use their best efforts and, without their cooperation, it wouldn't be even worth trying."

"In that case, there's nothing more to be done in Brazil for the moment aside from keeping a close watch on the Count. The action moves back to Germany and there is time to make preparations with Max's assistance on how to receive the shipment when it arrives in Leuffen in about three weeks' time. I'll consult Max as soon as I'm back in London."

We finished our meal more rapidly than it deserved and returned to the terrace which was now illuminated by electric lamps in the gathering dusk. Roderigo ordered the club's port to accompany our coffee and produced notepaper for our calculations. There was a short silence while we each struggled separately with our arithmetic; neither of us had a calculator. We both arrived at approximately $25 million and looked at each other in awe. "How do we translate that into the quantity of drugs which could be on its way to Europe tomorrow?" I asked.

"I don't think that the quantity matters too much provided that there is sufficient space in the container," Rodrigo answered, "Focusing on worth, gold to that value, allowing for brokerage, would probably buy cocaine or heroin at source for no more than a third of its street value in Western markets. In that case, the street value in Europe could be seventy-five million dollars."

"Unless a part of the gold was intended for settlement of past debt," I suggested. "Unlikely. The cartel operates strictly on a cash with order basis."

We agreed that Max would be better able to confirm the market value and I promised to keep Roderigo informed. "It makes von Frankenberg's commission offer to you look pretty puny," was his only comment. Having taken a second glass of port and finished our coffee, it was time for me to return to the hotel. We ordered a taxi to pick me up at the gates and Roderigo insisted on accompanying me from the club. He collected his cane and we set out together down the narrow side street.

The only lights were from the club entrance and lamps on each pillar of the gateway. About half way down we became aware of two dark clothed figures approaching us at speed. The first held a large knife in his hand and the second was reaching into an inside pocket of his jacket. "The first one's mine," Roderigo said decisively twisting the silver handle of his cane and withdrawing a rapier. With that he lunged forward and ran the knifeman through his right shoulder. There was a short scream and the knife dropped to the ground.

Remembering the words of my unarmed combat instructor twenty years before, I ran at the second older man instead of waiting and clamped my left hand over his right wrist as he withdrew his gun. At the same time, I bunched the knuckles of my right fist and drove them as hard as I could into his windpipe. There was a satisfying gasp as he tottered back clutching his throat and gasping for air. I took the gun from him without any resistance. Both men turned and supporting each other staggered back to the gateway as a long grey saloon car slid to a halt. The back door was opened from inside and the two of them tumbled in.

Instinctively, I transferred the gun to my right hand and fired low at the rear of the car as it moved off. More by luck than judgment the bullet struck the nearside rear tyre; there was a whoosh of air as it started to deflate and the vehicle lumbered rather than glided away. The whole incident had taken little more than thirty seconds.

I turned back to Roderigo who was wiping his blade on a handkerchief before returning it to the swordstick. "Thank you for saving me," I said. "and for an entertaining evening."

---ooo0ooo---

Back in my room at the Hilton, I started to take stock of the situation. Roderigo had insisted that I retained the gun, an automatic Beretta, for the rest of my time in Rio in case there were further attempts to take me out. We agreed that I would leave it with reception for him to collect when I left on Saturday morning.

I needed to update Chester Case the next day and to agree with him my task at Leuffen over the coming weeks and whomever else I should involve. Meeting Max next week was a priority and I could start making arrangements now. It was shortly after midnight, six hours behind London on summertime; I put in a call to Gaby at the flat. A sleepy voice answered: "Still living it up in Rio are you. Have you mastered the lambada yet or are you ready to come home?"

"Definitely ready to come home," I assured her "but there's something you can do for me this morning. Would you invite Max and Miranda to supper, preferably Monday or Tuesday. I need his advice sooner rather than later."

"Sounds like you've got yourself into trouble. Do be careful, Julian."

"I have a guardian angel here in Rio and I shan't be leaving the hotel again before Saturday morning when we depart for the airport. Any trouble now is in Germany, no longer here."

"Then I shall be able to keep an eye on you. I've got some exciting news to share."

"Tell all, darling. I should have asked for your news first before laying Max and Miranda on you."

"You know the washing machine focus groups that I've been running this past few weeks. It seems that the German manufacturer is impressed and wants to run similar focus groups in all their European markets. They've invited me to discuss setting up the programme with them at their export marketing offices in – guess where - Stuttgart."

"You clever girl; that's terrific news." I replied "See if you can arrange it for next Friday or the Monday after. I have to be in Leuffen then and we could travel out together and spend the weekend there." I wanted to be at the factory on the Monday morning to greet Lloyd Parmentier before he sat out on his road trip with Peter Hartmann. "All my news when I get back on Sunday evening….." We concluded the conversation with our usual endearments and rang off.

---ooo0ooo---

CHAPTER 22

I SLEPT WELL after all the excitement and was still out to the world when the wake-up call roused me for Friday and the group's last day together in Rio. The morning was devoted to more workshops on the management of technology transfers between the Allied Autoparts factories picking up on the opportunities identified earlier in the week. I led a break-out workshop of the four European subsidiaries to plan the introduction and launch of the DES programme. We had to agree first which of the four would be assigned the role of master stockist, holding a larger inventory of all the spring parts from which the other three could draw replacement spring items on demand. There was little disagreement but that Ribenda was the preferred location. Only Peter Hartmann offered token resistance on the grounds of prestige and his perception of Hartmann & Holst's technical superiority.

There were three arguments in favour of Ribenda. First, it already had small order business with designers and the aftermarket in the Netherlands for the compression and extension springs which it supplied to IBM and Phillips, its major business machine and domestic appliance customers. Small orders were supplied by mail and the Netherlands had the benefit of a postal service offering same day local deliveries. Second, the greater part of the DES catalogue parts lay in a similar range of helical springs for which Ribenda was the logical manufacturing source. Finally, its location between the UK and Germany and a ready supply chain to Sweden gave Ribenda a logistical advantage. It was agreed next that larger compression springs would be best sourced from Leuffen and the larger extension springs from

AA Norrkoping. Opening stocks of the remaining DES range: torsion springs, spring washers and retractor springs would have to be be sourced from the Farmington plant.

The team spent the rest of the workshop in agreeing timed action plans, for manufacturing and stocking and for catalogue production; responsibility for steps within each action plan; and deadlines was assigned to individual managers. Managers, like Heinrich Hoffmeyer, who were not present would be briefed the following week. After two hours, including consultation with Bennett Pullman and Loren Corley on the supply of product from Farmington, we arrived at an overall action plan with a planned deadline of 15 September for the European launch of DES.

The highlight of the morning was the group photograph organized by Viktor Accona and timed for midday with a professional photographer. At a quarter to the hour he started to herd us past the pool to the back of the tennis court where benches had been set up in tiers by the hotel staff. The corporate office managers and staff, except for Viktor, were seated in the front row with Chester Case at the centre and Barry McLennan on his right hand. Standing behind them were the taller members of our group including Tom, Oswaldo and myself flanked by Ronaldo Martini on the left end and Viktor on the right with von Falkenberg sandwiched between him and Tom. The shorter members were stood on a row of benches behind us. There had seemed to be a marked reluctance on the Count's part to be included. It had taken Viktor to go back into the hotel and winkle him out before we were all present and correct. The photographer fiddled about with his equipment, then took several shots after the usual instruction to 'smile, please, now.'

That completed the morning's activities and the rest of the day was our own until a formal farewell dinner and wind-up session from 7:00 p.m. A water polo tournament was planned for the afternoon with four teams competing. The team leaders announced were Chester Case, Lloyd

Parmentier, Ronaldo and Tom; recruitment of team members took place over lunch.

Von Falkenberg was not staying at the Hilton and elected to return to his Rio apartment after we had lunched. Our paths crossed in the lobby as I returned to my room to change clothes and the familiar grey Lincoln town car drew up before the entrance to collect him. "It seems that I may have underestimated you." he greeted me. "I didn't know that you have friends in Rio. You may not be so fortunate next time."

"You know what to expect too," I replied, glancing pointedly at the tread of the replacement nearside rear tyre of the Lincoln. "If there is a next time, I can promise you an even bumpier ride." Bravado, of course, on my part, but I have an aversion to control freaks and saw no reason to give him any satisfaction.

---ooo0ooo---

The water polo was great fun involving considerable exertion from the players and much barracking from spectators. I was in Tom's team and we reached the final but were outclassed in the play-off by the Case team with Chester showing unexpected athleticism. As we towelled off afterwards he turned to me. "Any developments in Amparo this week?" he asked.

"Yes, and back here in Rio most recently. When should I give you my report?"

"At 6:00 p.m. in my room. Will one hour be enough?" I assured him that it would and we agreed to talk then.

When I entered the penthouse suite I found that there were two othrs present in addition to Chester Case: Barry MacLennan and Viktor Accona. "I want Barry to hear what you have to say in case this becomes an operational matter," Chester explained. "Go ahead when you're ready."

I gave them a full account of events in Amparo: from the discovery of the missing coils of wire from the shipment delivered to the spring factory and Shelley Frankel's estimate of their weight to von Falkenberg's attempt to recruit me as a participant in his smuggling activities. I included Roderigo Morales intelligence about the cartel connections of the carrier Transportico Americana and our belief that extraction of the cargo replacing the wire coils had been made somewhere between Rio and Amparo. At this stage Barry intervened to ask me about Roderigo and how I came to know him. I explained that I had been given an introduction by a friend of the family in England who thought that he might be useful.

While my listeners were digesting this information and before opening up the discussion I continued with a summary of the previous day's events back in Rio: my further encounter with Frederik von Falkenberg in the morning and dinner with Roderigo at the Tijuca tennis club. The revelation that a return consignment was already on its way to Europe and our calculation of what the value of an equivalent weight in gold bars might be to the missing coils were the bottom-line conclusions of my report. I decided not include an account of the attempt on my life for no particular reason except, perhaps, an uneasy feeling that Chester and Barry might have restrained me from taking any part in further proceedings.

There was a short silence while Viktor was asked to replenish our drinks, broken finally by Chester. "What's your assessment of the situation, Barry?" he asked.

"That's an impressive piece of detective work by Julian," Barry replied "but we need to be clear about what needs to be done now and by whom. My reading is that there's nothing more to be done here in Brazil until the end game is played out in Germany, except to decide how best to terminate von Falkenberg's employment by Allied Autoparts when the time comes."

"Let's focus on Germany then." Chester Case replied. "My concern is to separate Hartmann & Holst from any fall-out and the inevitable publicity from delivery of the contraband, whether it's drugs, which seems most likely, or anything else. Let me ask you, Julian, is there any possibility that it could be taken out of the consignment before delivery to Leuffen?"

"I don't think so. Pan Alpina is one of the most highly regarded carriers in Europe. Roderigo says that it would require joint written instructions from Grunwald Metallwerk and Hartmann & Holst for them to deviate from the contracted delivery."

"In that case," Chester continued "will Klinger, with Peter Hartmann's connivance, hand over the contraband to whomever is at that end of the smuggling ring beyond Leffen or allow them to collect from the factory?"

"My guess is that they won't risk a third party collection, that Klinger will separate the contraband from the rest of the cargo when unpacking and take it away to some place not too far away where he can hand it over."

"If that is the case, then there are no direct operational issues," Barry said. "We don't need to do anything more to avoid consequences for Allied Autoparts except to ensure that there is no further trafficking. Of course, we introduce tighter disciplines in Leuffen and Amparo and remove those who were involved."

Viktor spoke for the first time. "There is still a risk that the German Drug Enforcement Agency or Interpol intercepts a part of the drugs haul while it is being trafficked and traces the source back through Hartmann & Holst. If that were to happen we would find it difficult to claim ignorance. The penalties would be severe and the news media would make the most of it."

"There's another dimension to this:" Chester added gloomily, "the issue of civic responsibility. As a socially responsible corporation, AA can hardly ignore its obligation to prevent more than $25 million of drugs find their way into the market. The question is how to blow the whistle without exposing ourselves to media attention. We could take the whole thing to the CIA now who would alert the German authorities."

"They would be all over us like a cheap suit with publicity after a successful drugs bust on both sides of the Atlantic," Barry commented Barry.

"There is an alternative which you might like to consider," I countered "which involves some continuing engagement but hands the problem over to a lower profile authority who would exercise discretion."

"I'm open to any solution which keeps AA out of the spotlight but helps us to fulfil our obligations. Give us your suggestion, Julian."

"Several weeks ago I met by chance with the family friend who provided me with the introduction to Roderigo Morales. He signalled that he had a particular interest in Leuffen and Manfred Hartmann dating back to the end of the last war. His name is Max Salinger and he was an active agent in the British Special Operations Executive (SOE) which became MI6 after 1946. He still has a position as Adviser to the SOE, now an offshoot of MI6, with the apparent role of archivist and writer of its war history."

My audience showed a quickening interest as I continued. "However, Max has another unadvertised function. He holds a watching brief on loose ends – the missions that remained outstanding at the end of the war, in particular the ongoing activities of the former Nazis in Germany and their connections with those who escaped to South America. One of these neo-Nazi organizations is the Kamaradenwerke which poses as a welfare charity for servicemen who are disabled or have fallen on hard times, and Manfred Hartmann is on its board of Trustees. Therefore, any trafficking between Germany and Brazil in which Hartmann might be involved with von Falkenberg is of direct interest to him."

"How would the relationship between your friend Salinger and AA work?" asked Barry coming to the point.

"The only informal relationship would be between Max and me. I would be his informer and not required to sign the Official Secrets Act. He would work through MI6 and its German connections to arrest the traffickers and confiscate the drugs. An added incentive for them is that payment from Germany was probably in the form of gold and could lead them to the Nazi gold which is still missing twenty-three years later."

"And what happens if something goes wrong; if they fail to recover the drugs and have to trace their passage back through Hartmann & Holst," Barry persisted.

"You disclaim any knowledge and say that I acted without the company's authority," I replied "and I submit my resignation."

"That sounds like a plan;" Chester Case considered carefully. "Does anyone have an alternative proposal to Julian's or a preferred course of action?" After a short pause for thought both Barry and Viktor concurred. "In that case, Julian, you have our agreement to proceed as soon as you are back in London. As before, I want you to keep me up to speed by calling Viktor every other day, or immediately if anything unexpected happens. Is there any help you need from us at this point?"

"The only thing that springs to mind so far is that I might want to involve Tom Hardy if I need back-up when we're both in Leuffen"

"That's fine so long as his involvement is on a strictly personal rather than company basis," cautioned Barry MacLennan. "If he acts in an AA capacity he is bound to inform Floyd Parmentier as his line management superior and that entails company recognition of the problem which is what your plan helps us to avoid."

"Its all a bit tenuous but it seems the best way to go," Chester concluded. "Are there any loose ends that we should address right now?"

Viktor re-entered the discussion, looking worried "There are human relations issues which could drag Associated

Autoparts into the spotlight if we don't consider them in advance: the dismissal of Peter Hartmann and Gottfried Klinger from Hartmann & Holst, and how to sever all company connections with Count von Falkenberg."

"Remembering his performance at the business review last month, I doubt that Peter will satisfy Floyd during their week together visiting customers, in which case Floyd will probably want to replace him as General Manager," Barry answered. Having taken the strategic decision, he was gathering steam in addressing the consequences. "I don't see Klinger as much of a problem either," he continued. "He can be held responsible for the safety and maintenance failures on the night of the pneumatic warehouse collapse and dismissed accordingly."

"The trade union may object to the dismissal of Klinger, but I think I can handle that," Viktor agreed. "But neutralizing von Falkenberg will be more difficult. He can be removed as General Manager of the Amparo factories, but we cannot be sure that he would cease tampering with future consignments from Amparo to Leuffen in collaboration with the carrier."

"I agree that we need to take the Count out permanently. If we bring him to Farmington, is there any way to keep him out of Brazil for a period of time?" Chester asked, now pacing the room.

"Very difficult, I think. Although he is listed as a war criminal in Germany, he has a protected status in the United States,"

"How can that be? He escaped at the end of the war with his art treasures through the Vatican rat run. So, he counts as an illegal and could be deported from the USA back to Germany," Barry asked.

"Unfortunately not," Viktor explained. "When Wernher von Braun was taken by the Americans and brought back to work with NASA on its post-war space rocket program, the senior people who worked with him at Peenemünde including von Falkender were given dispensation; in some cases a right to US domicile. The Count was the senior SS security officer at Peenemünde until it was bombed by the Allies. He remained with von Braun, responsible for building the launch sites in France and the Netherlands using local slave labour, housed in concentration camp conditions and treated with extreme cruelty for which he was held accountable at the end of the war. Nevertheless, when he is in America he is immune from deportation."

"Is there no way in which he can be removed?"

"Criminal charges in Brazil for drug running is one possibility except that the cartel would almost certainly give him their protection and prevent his being arrested. However," Viktor continued on a more positive note "Frederik is vulnerable in one respect. The Israelis would like to put him on trial and he is on Mossad's snatch list. That is the reason why he tries to avoid being photographed in public and was reluctant to take part in our group photograph this morning."

"There's food for further thought in that," Chester Case suggested. He stopped pacing, glanced at his watch and resumed his seat to summarize our discussion. "I guess we've gone as far as we can this evening. We've decided what should be done in Germany but not yet how to contain securely the situation in Amparo. What we can do is to call Frederik von Falkenberg to Farmington for consultations in the context of future planning and time his visit for the week following delivery of the consignment to Leuffen. Now it's time to join the rest of our colleagues for the final company event of the week."

---oooOooo---

CHAPTER 23

THE DINNER WAS a more formal event than I had expected although the atmosphere was that of a school end-of-term supper. It was held in a private restaurant on the fifth floor of the hotel with its own kitchens and staff. The room was decorated in Louis XV style with painted panels, a multi-tiered chandelier, elaborate wall mounted sconces for additional lighting and gilt chairs for the diners. At the far end there was a raised platform for a discreet combo of musicians backed by a mural in the form of a *trompe l'oeil* painting of Rio harbour from the air, the view that we would carry with us when we flew out the following day.

On the way down I passed by my room, took the Beretta from my shirt drawer and tucked it into the waistband of my trousers under the back of my suit jacket where it was not noticeable under the Italian tailoring. It all felt rather cloak and dagger and probably quite unnecessary but I knew that von Falkenberg was attending and it was conceivable that he might have cooked up a surprise climax to my evening.

Our seating was arranged around four round tables each with name cards carefully placed, no doubt by Viktor, to ensure as much cross fertilisation between corporate office staff and managers from those subsidiaries with the least frequent contact. I found myself at the table hosted by Barry MacLennan with Oskar Holst on my right and one of the two Mexican General Managers to my left. Across the table, seated between Ronaldo Martini and Dieter Trautman, was Donna Fairweather, enjoying more than her normal share of attention. The two others at our table were the Finance Manager of the second Mexican factory and Bruin Brouwer.

As our first course of seafood cocktails was served I was able to glance around at the disposition of the other members of our group among the remaining three tables, hosted severally by Chester Case, Floyd Parmentier and Loren Corley. At Chester's table Viktor had placed von Falkenberg on his right and Cyril Snell on his left with Jan van der Groot to the right of the Count and himself to the left of Cyril and then Tom Hardy. This arrangement gave Viktor the opportunity to observe von Falkenberg closely from behind his pebble glasses without attracting attention. I paid passing attention to Floyd's table which he co- hosted with Bennett Pullman, noting only that Peter Hartmann was seated on his left, and to the fourth table headed by Loren Corley and Erik Nielsen. I noticed that Viktor had thoughtfully placed Shelley Frankel and Oswaldo Carioca together. Was there a hint of sentimantality lurking under Viktor's stern exterior, I wondered, or was he exploring how Erik Nielsen would react to any romantic relationship between members of the home team? Knowing Viktor, I thought the latter more likely.

At our table nothing of consequence transpired during dinner. The seafood cocktail was followed by fillet steak and a meringue and fruit concoction for dessert. The option of red or white wine was on offer throughout and, at our table, we drank sparingly in order to remain on our best behaviour in front of Barry. As the meal came to its close, Chester Case rose to his feet and tapped his glass to attract attention. He spoke simply, reviewing the week, thanking everyone for their attendance and hoping that we would all take away with us a better understanding of the corporation's activities. He would judge the success by the degree that the relationships developed during our time together as colleagues led to fruitful collaborations during the coming months. A standard Chairman's speech, delivered with a politician's facility and striking a chord with his captive audience; it was received with due applause.

However, this was not to be the end of the evening. Viktor announced that there would now be an Allied Autoparts "smoker" with an open invitation to all present to entertain the company with our party pieces. I had been warned that this form of cabaret was in the offing and so had others among us who were prepared to step onto the floor and give of their best. There was a succession of surprises. First up was a group of the Mexican managers who set the tone with a mariarchi band of assorted string instruments and a trumpet which they must have brought with them to Rio in their luggage. There was a surprise addition to the ensemble in the form of Dieter Trautman, who had been adopted as an honorary Latin American after his performance earlier in the week, and once again rattled a pair of maracas with enthusiasm.

More surprises followed. Erik Nielsen proved himself an accomplished jazz pianist with a laid back solo in the style of Count Basie and then by accompanying Shelley Frankel in smokey voiced renderings of *"The Lady is a Tramp"* and *"It had to be you"*. They say that everyone should have an alternative source of employment and there was a second career waiting for Shelley as a nightclub chanteuse. Next to perform were the three Swedish managers with a somewhat sombre military drinking song involving much formal quaffing and foot-stamping.

With urging from Tom to represent the London office, it was my turn to step forward. I decided to declain *"The Seven Ages of Man"* soliloquy from *As You Like it*. There was some familiarity with Shakespeare by all present and the recital was well received – more of a tribute to the Bard than my performance. The most applause was reserved for the act which followed. Having first sprinkled handfuls of sand on the dance floor and with Erik as his accompanist, Loren Corley gave us an elegant soft shoe shuffle to Cole Porter melodies, not quite Fred Astaire perhaps but to near-Hollywood standard. Anything after that Top of the Bill performance would have been an anti-climax; instead, we were invited to gather round the piano and join in singing to tunes which we nominated and were played by Eric.

---ooo0ooo---

The party broke up shortly after 10:30 when Chester Case and Barry MacLennan retired for the night. Having viewed the concert with disdain Von Falkenberg had departed earlier after proclaiming loudly that he would return in the morning to see the AA group off from the hotel. "I had no idea that you were a thespian, Julian," Bennett Pullman commented as we left the dining room.

"The product of a misspent youth; and I had no ides that Loren was an accomplished hoofer," I replied as Corley came alongside.

"Just a lifelong addiction to the movies," he responded modestly. Bennett suggested a nightcap but Loren preferred to turn in and we separated on the landing bidding each other goodnight.

I decided to take a breath of fresh air after the confined closeness of the restaurant and descended to the lobby. Strolling out on to the terrace I had intended to take a turn around the swimming pool to the tennis courts beyond, but found my way blocked as I reached the deep end. A burly figure stepped out from the shadows; I recognized the Count's driver. He was wearing a double-breasted grey suit and chauffeur's cap. "Buenos noces, Senhŏr Radclive," he said politely "you will please come with me. Count Frederik wishes to talk to you."

"I don't think that the Count and I have anything further to say to each other." There was nothing that could be gained from another conversation, even if no further assault was intended.

"I'm afraid that I must insist, Senhŏr," he continued evenly while his right hand crept slowly across his chest into his jacket.

Having anticipated his movement, I drew the Beretta fast from the back of my waistband and levelled it steadily at him. "I think not; on this occasion I must decline the Count's invitation. Step forward and face the pool." I directed. "Now, very carefully, using two fingers only please take the gun from your coat slowly and toss it into the pool."

Hesitating only briefly and, deciding that I was serious and determined, the driver did as he was told. I stepped behind him as his weapon splashed into the water and urged him forward with a nudge of the Beretta until he stood on the edge. "Time now for your midnight swim, amigo," I said in tough guy tones and pushed him hard in the small of his back.

Not waiting to see whether or not he could swim I turned on my heel and strode back into the hotel. The dregs of our party were still carousing in the lobby bar but I took the elevator and locked myself firmly in my room.

---ooo0ooo---

I had intended to leave the Beretta packaged up for collection by Roderigo from the concierge after we had all left but a better plan occurred to me when I rose the following morning and packed my belongings. I wrote a note for Roderigo on hotel stationery to explain what I was doing; then I unloaded the gun, wiped it for fingerprints and wrapped it tightly in a hand towel before dropping the package loosely into a hotel laundry bag. I placed the ammunition separately in a small box of tissues and deposited that in a housemaid's trolley of cleaning materials that I passed in the corridor before descending in the lift with suitcase in one hand and laundry bag in the other.

In the lobby most of the European team were already gathered with their luggage awaiting the airport, and the Farmington team who were flying later were there to see us off. As I arrived, Peter Hartmann appeared from a side room with Von Falkenberg who had no doubt been giving him final instructions. I left my room key and note for Roderigo Morales at the desk and wandered over casually to the Count who was now talking to Viktor Accona. "I don't suppose we shall be seeing each other again for some time," I said flashing my most charming smile and handing the laundry bag to him, "but, if you are ever in London, you must give me the opportunity to return your hospitality. In the meantime, I must return the article which you left with me two nights ago." In Viktor's presence he had no option but to take the bag from me. "I too shall look forward to our next meeting," he replied coolly with an accompanying smile as insincere as mine; there was ice in his piercing blue eyes.

There was no time to respond to Viktor's questioning glance as the bus had arrived and the hotel porters were loading bags into the hold. I said hurried goodbyes to Chester Case and Barry MacLennan and waved to the others before climbing aboard and taking my seat next to Tom Hardy.

"What was that all about?" he asked having watched the exchange with Von Falkenberg. "Plenty of time for that during the flight," I said. "It's a long and tangled tale."

---ooo0ooo---

CHAPTER 24

London, June 4 to 7

HOMECOMINGS ARE always a relief and this was no exception. The most tedious part of the journey was a two hour wait in Paris at Charles de Gaulle for our connection to Heathrow and it was almost 8:00 p.m. on Sunday evening before the taxi delivered me to Porchester Terrace. Gaby gave me a warm welcome. Judging correctly that I would be in need of more than a measure of TLC, she had prepared a sausage and bean casserole to be followed by plum and apple crumble and had laid out pyjamas and bathrobe. After a hot bath and fortified by a large J&B and soda I relaxed with her on our bed. Of course, her tender embrace was the best part of coming home with the promise of more later when revival was complete.

"I want to hear it all – every little bit: encounters and conversations," Gaby declared "but give me the headlines now."

"How about '*Brazilian cartel runs drugs from Amparo to Leuffen, Germany, in routine cargos. Payment in gold by former Nazi association in return shipments. Stop Press: next shipment due in Leuffen 22th June.*' Is that enough to earn me supper ?"

"More than enough. You can sing for it as you eat," Gaby conceded.

Later in the kitchen, replete with casserole and crumble, I poured us our third glasses of Rioja. Having delivered the full account of my week with few interruptions from Gaby, I was ready for her verdict.

"It's all turned out a bit James Bond-ish complete with Von Falkenberg in the role of Blofeld. I think all the sleuthing has taken you a bit out of your depth," she commented. "I can see that you had to follow it up but what do you expect to happen now?"

"Well, I'm hoping to cast Max in the role of M and hand the whole thing, or at least the German end of it, over to him. Presumably, I shall have to tell him when the shipment is delivered to the factory but after that it will be up to his people there to confiscate the drugs when they are detached from the consignment and detain those involved."

"I understand now why you want to see Max. He and Miranda are coming here to dinner on Tuesday evening. Will that be soon enough?"

"I don't think anything much will happen before then. Now, you've been very patient listening to my saga. What have you arranged for your client meeting in Stuttgart?"

Gaby looked pleased with herself. "I've booked a meeting for Friday morning in their offices, as you suggested, at 9:30. They seem pleased to be meeting sooner rather than later; apparently the stops are now out on their European research programme. They gave me the impression that a generous budget has been allocated."

"Good for you again," I responded. "We'll fly out on Thursday afternoon and stay somewhere in the Stuttgart area other than the horrid Flughafen hotel. Then, on Friday morning, I'll drive you to your meeting, spend the day down the road at the factory and collect you in the afternoon for the weekend. We'll stay at the Leuffen Gasthof and tour around a bit before returning home on Monday morning."

With our plans made for the coming week we finished our wine, retired upstairs again and fell into bed. "Do you have to be in the office tomorrow morning?" Gaby asked. "I'll go in at lunchtime for a couple of hours; so, don't put on the alarm." We were too tired to talk further; I turned over and fell immediately into a dreamless sleep.

---ooo0ooo---

We rose late the following morning after a langorous love-in and padded downstairs, still in our bedroom slippers. While Gaby put on the coffee and prepared scrambled eggs, I telephoned the office and asked Molly to book our travel arrangements. Tom was also expected in at lunchtime; so, there would be time to confer later. Then I called the printer for the DES catalogue to confirm AA orders for all four language editions and timing for the publishing part of the programme action plan. I promised to follow up with the written order later in the day.

Tom Hardy was already there when I reached the office. He was eager to discuss how best to manage the situation in Leuffen but was content to give me an hour in which to catch up with my paperwork. I sent a brief telex to Viktor to advise him that I would be meeting with Max Salinger the following evening and would call Wednesday to update him fully. I wrote out the print order to Bradley and Fowler for the catalogues which Molly typed up; then, I telexed Heinrich Hoffmeyer to arrange a meeting with him on Friday to review the DES action plans which the rest of us had made in Rio.

Mid-afternoon, Tom and I convened in his office. I had given him the gist of my meetings with Roderigo Moralez and subsequently with Chester, Barry and Viktor while we flew home but filled him in now on additional detail including the encounters with Von Frankenberg's hitmen and my interchanges with the Count himself at the hotel. At the end of my recital Tom gave me a baleful stare and delivered his response without any overtones of the Norfolk farmer.

"You do realise that you have put yourself in harm's way." The comment was delivered as a statement rather than a question. "What do you plan to do next?"

"In Brazil, yes, I was at risk but I don't mean to repeat the experience in Germany." "How do you intend to avoid that?" Tom asked.

"If Max Salinger has the authority and connections that I expect, we simply hand the whole thing over to him. I'm meeting him tomorrow evening. Hopefully, all that we will have to do is to inform his people when the shipment arrives at Leuffen."

Tom looked doubtful. "You know how this sort of situation usually develops," he said. "Badly. We may be required to do more. And don't imagine that you will be safe in Germany. If the Kamaradenwerke are involved and alerted by Von Falkenberg that you are a source of potential risk they may not hesitate to take you out. We must be prepared."

"There's no 'we' about it," I replied firmly. "I am under strict instructions not to let this become an operational issue and only to involve you as back-up if absolutely necessary.

Besides, if there is any danger it won't arise until the week after next when they get ready to collect the consignment. I'm taking Gaby there for the weekend on Thursday evening; she has a client meeting on Stuttgart on Friday. If I thought there was any risk we wouldn't be going."

Tom continued to look unconvinced but relaxed sufficiently to say "I shall make a point of being there from Wednesday 21st June in case it arrives early. And if it comes to direct action, be sure that I shall be there to take part."

We chatted a bit longer about work planned for the next fortnight: my roll-out of the DES programme and Lloyd Parmentier's forthcoming tour of Hartmann & Holst customers, which we agreed was unlikely to turn out well, and decided to call it a day.

Back at Porchester Terrace I found Gaby busy preparing for the meal on Tuesday evening: a roulade of salmon wrapped in smoked salmon for starters, boeuf bourguignon for the main course, a choice of lemon soufflé or tarte tatin for dessert and a cheeseboard. I selected wine from our modest cellar and made a mental note to pick up a decent bottle of dry sherry in the morning.

Max and Miranda arrived promptly by taxi at 7:30 on Tuesday evening and seemed pleased to have been invited. "So much nicer than dining out in restaurants," Miranda announced after kissing Gaby on both cheeks and handing her an expensive-looking box of Fortnum & Mason chocolates. She was dressed tonight in a plain plum-coloured wool dress with an enormous ruby, set as a brooch amid a cluster of diamonds, pinned to her left shoulder. I noted with relief that she was not shouting which gave hope that her hearing aid was working better than in Sussex when we last met her. Immaculate as always, Max wore a midnight blue velvet smoking jacket over evening trousers, a pleated dress shirt and plain silk bow tie. He greeted Gaby with a peck on the cheek and passed me a well-wrapped bottle as we shook hands.

I had not intended that our dinner should become a 'black tie' event and complained loudly. But Gaby had been insistent; she had telephoned Barbara Fentiman before inviting Miranda to ask for her advice on any preferences that the Salingers had when being entertained. She was told that they steadfastly retained their previous generation habits including that of dressing for dinner. Unless Gaby had specified 'kitchen supper' rather than 'dinner' we should expect them to arrive dressed as they were. And so, in spite of my grumbles, we were clothed accordingly: me in dinner jacket and Gaby in tailored black velvet trousers and a cream silk shirt with crimson cummerbund and her favourite gold jewellery. We seemed to have got it right as our guests relaxed immediately and we were soon seated in our living room sipping sherry companionably. The introductory small talk centred around our longstanding friendship with the Fentimans including Miranda's recollections of Barbara's childhood – "always such a jolly girl" – and moved on to Miranda's new hearing aid, now barely visible behind the ear, which she had acquired the week before. "I'm now able to converse normally even at quite large parties," she enthused "which is such a relief. It must have been so boring for everyone else before." Indeed, she had become quite animated and an altogether more congenial companion, although there was still a tendency to boom on occasion.

"You seem to have had quite an eventful time in Rio, Julian," Max remarked at length bringing the conversation round to the main topic of the evening. "Roderigo telephoned me yesterday to give me his account of your little adventure together."

"Do tell us the whole story right from the beginning. Max tells me you were frightfully brave," echoed Miranda.

I refilled our glasses and launched into my account of the week, giving due prominence to Roderigo Moralez's role as adviser and collaborator in my investigations while Gaby retired to the kitchen to check on the progress of boeuf bourgignon and vegetables. "But for Roderigo I wouldn't have reached any firm conclusions on the trafficking between Leuffen and Amparo," I concluded "and Roderigo certainly saved my life."

"It wasn't the end of the story for Roderigo either," Max added quietly. "He had uninvited visitors on Sunday night."

"Oh no. I didn't want him to be disturbed any further. I hope he hasn't come to any harm as a result of his involvement with me?"

"There were three of them this time, after midnight. However, Roderigo's house is well protected. Both the doors and ground floor windows are connected to the mains electricity when the alarm is set to repel intruders. The first man was electrocuted when gaining entry; then Roderigo in his pyjamas shot the second one dead on the stairs and held the third at gunpoint while Maria, his wife, called the police. It seems they were quite well-known local criminals but it's not established yet for whom they were working."

"Presumably Von Frankenberg," suggested Miranda as Gaby returned to her seat on the sofa.

"Quite so, but very unlikely that the police will be able to hang it on him. What it does show," Max resumed "is that our friend Von Falkenberg is a vicious opponent. Just as well that you left Rio, Julian, when you did."

"Is this a good moment to think about eating?" Gaby interjected and led us to the dining table which had been laid with slices of the roulade already in our places and where she now served warm toast. When we were seated and I had served a respectable Macon Villages to accompany the first course, she resumed the conversation.

"We are going to Germany for the weekend," she informed our guests. "I have a client meeting in Stuttgart on Friday and then Julian is taking me to Leuffen for Saturday and Sunday staying at the Gasthof. We thought we might do a bit of sight-seeing. Have you any suggestions, Max, where we might go during the day?"

"A client meeting in Stuttgart. That sounds very exciting," Miranda exclaimed. "How has that come about?"

Gaby explained how, having employed her for its market research in the UK, the German washing machine manufacturer was consulting her on carrying out similar research programmes for other European export markets.

"You clever girl. Be sure to charge them a handsome fee," Miranda ordered her firmly.

"To answer your question, Gaby," Max interjected. "there are plenty of stunning places to visit if you don't mind driving a bit. There's the 250 year old library at Wiblingen monastery just outside Ulm. Better still, if you take the Upper Swabian Baroque Road down towards Lake Constance there's the basilica and frescos at Steinhausen and, if you reach the lake, there's Mainau Island with its castle and church which is stunning at this time of year; flowers, shrubs and trees in profusion. Of course, on your doorstep you have Schloss Hohenleuffen if you fancy calling on Manfred Hartmann. On second thoughts, perhaps not, in view of what we expect to happen in two weeks' time"

"You sound like a tourist guide," warned Miranda.

"Then I shall behave like one and send you over some literature in the morning," Max persisted.

I decided it was time to bring the discussion back to the main topic of the evening. "More to the point, Max," I countered. "I'm hoping that you can take charge of the situation in Leuffen and organize a reception committee for the drugs consignment when it arrives. This is no longer a matter for the amateur investigator."

"And we don't want Julian playing games as an action hero anymore," Gaby added.

Max looked serious and paused in thought for several moments while we served the next course with an accompanying Chambertin. "This really is awfully good boeuf bourguignon, my dear," he said at length savouring his first mouthful.

"Quite excellent," agreed Miranda "and your roulade was delicious, Gaby. Now come on, Max, Julian is waiting for your response."

"It's not entirely straightforward. There are issues of protocol," Max admitted. "If this was simply a case of drug trafficking, it would be beyond my mandate and I could only put you in touch with the German drug enforcement authorities. However, there seems to be an additional element in the Leuffen to Amaro exchanges – Nazi gold – and that is very much within my remit. How certain are you, Julian, that the payments from Germany have been made in gold?"

"There's no proof positive, but given the weight of the unidentified part of the shipment from Leuffen and the space available in the container it's hard to think of anything else of similar value to fund the drug-trafficking."

"I agree with you. I think there's enough to convince MI6 who will have to sanction my involvement and give me a ringside seat in tracking the people collecting the consignment back to their base and the chance to interrogate them."

"If it really is Nazi gold where do you think it could have come from?"

"Yes. Do tell us more about Nazi gold, Max. Does it really exist anymore?" Gaby entreated.

"It certainly exists. There are three known locations and several other possible sources in Germany although billions were squirreled away in Swiss bank numbered accounts before and during the early part of the war. First, there is Lake Tirpitz in the middle of a forest in the Alps which was a naval testing site; it's said that $5.6 billion worth lie there. Then there is the gold train rumoured to be hidden deep in a tunnel under a castle at Welbrzych in Silesia, now Poland. For certain, there was a cache of Reichsbank gold, bonds, currency and stolen works of art discovered in an underground network of caves at Merkers by the U.S. army in 1945. In some respects, this third location is the most interesting."

I was curious. "Why is that? What did the U.S. army do with it?"

"A detachment from the transport section of the advance battalion was tasked to take it all by road in a fleet of trucks to Frankfurt but not all of it reached there. The currency and works of art did arrive but much of the gold and some of the bonds did not. The U.S are understandably cagey but it seems that several of the trucks peeled off from the convoy and offloaded their cargoes *en route*. There are conflicting accounts about what happened to the gold; the bearer bonds were cashed in after the war in Switzerland 'by person or persons unknown'. Among the theories about disposal of the gold are its possible shipment to the USA, storage elsewhere in Germany or even its deployment in Switzerland by the thieves to found a private bank. Whatever happened, the value of the gold stolen is probably more than $1 billion."

"What are the other possible locations in Germany where the Nazis may have stashed their loot?" I asked.

"Locations in East Germany which are, of course, out of bounds to us and, in the West, several places in the Black Forest and my own favourite, Lake Constance."

"Is that why you are encouraging us to visit Mainau Island?" Gaby asked.

"Well, it did occur to me that Julian might like to have some familiarity with the area in case he decides to join me in my search for the gold after the business in Leuffen is settled." Max's answer, delivered with an air of innocence, was followed by a mischievous grin.

We had moved on from the boeuf bourguignon to the dessert and Miranda was forking a helping of tarte tatin on her plate. "Don't let him lure Julian into his wretched treasure hunt. Nazi gold has been Max's obsession for as long as I've known him. More like fool's gold, I tell him," she cautioned.

"Why is it that a man's wife is his sternest critic?" Max complained.

For once I was ahead of Gaby. "You know very well, Max," I chided him "They know us better than anyone else – warts and all."

"Particularly the warts," added Gaby and Miranda in unison.

We finished our meal in good humour. I had decanted a bottle of Warre 1970 earlier and passed the port round with our cheese; a perfect accompaniment to the mature Stilton which contributed to our mellow mood. It was time for me to return the conversation to the problems at Leuffen.

"Back to cases, Max; what preparations should I make in Leuffen and who will be my contacts in Germany?"

"We're into need-to-know and Official Secrets Act territory now, I fear," Max replied." If you and I can leave the ladies to their coffee for a few minutes I'll tell you what I can."

---oooOooo---

And so, Max and I went upstairs to the spare bedroom which we had converted into a study for Gaby's use as an office during the week and the two of us at the weekends. We had brought our glasses and the port decanter to sustain us.

"The first thing I should explain to you," Max said, when we were comfortably settled with glasses recharged "is that, unlike the UK or the USA, Germany does not have a national enforcement agency. There is an investigation bureau attached to the police in each state; in the case of Baden-Württemberg, conveniently for us, the Landeskriminalamt, LKA for short, with narcotics responsibility is located at police headquarters in Stuttgart."

"Does that mean that I shall have to work with the bureau?" I asked.

"Hopefully not. If I am authorized, I intend to act as intermediary and will join you in Germany the day before the consignment is due. But one advantage of working with the LKA is that it has the equivalent of its own local SWAT team, the SEK or *Spetzaleinsatzkommando* which it can call upon when things get nasty. The bureau head in Stuttgart is Polizeihauptmeister Klaus Kramm, a stickler for the formalities but a good man in an emergency. Your problem, if I am not allowed to take part, is that Kramm may decide to storm the factory to seize the shipment on delivery which means that Hartmann & Holst will be exposed to a blast of publicity in Germany. Inevitably, by association, AA will receive the US media attention which your Chairman wants to avoid. If I can't be there, I will give you a direct telephone link to Kramm nearer the time. You'll have to persuade him that if you inform him when the consignment has arrived, he will wait to pounce until Klinger and his crew leave Leuffen with the offloaded drugs. He may not be easy to convince."

"It would help if you have your own man on the ground locally whom I can enlist for back- up, if I get into difficulty."

Max pondered for a moment before answering. "I may still have one asset around; he was a good man then but it is more than twenty years since he last worked with us and we are no longer in direct contact. He was a German prisoner of war whom I interrogated after he was captured and transferred to a POW camp in Lancashire. He was strongly anti-Nazi and, after the war, in 1945 and 1946, carried out several undercover missions for us in Germany. He married a local Lancashire lass when he came back for her after completing his university education - an engineering degree from Heidelberg. I lost touch with him after that but I believe that he may have moved to the Nurtingen area."

"What was he called? Maybe I can find him in the local telephone directory this weekend."

"Worth a try," Max agreed. "It's more than thirty years ago now since I last saw him; so, he must be in his late fifties now. His name is Heinrich Hoffmeyer."

"We may be in luck," I exclaimed. "The Technical Director at Hartmann & Holst is a Heinrich Hoffmeyer. He was with us in the factory the night of Bernard Tompkins' death; he wanted to be helpful afterwards and shared my suspicions. I like him but he has been on my list of alternative suspects. Now I can cross him off."

"There may be more Heinrich Hoffmeyers in the Stuttgart area. It's not an uncommon name," Max said.

"No doubt, but there can't be too many Heidelberg engineering graduates of that age and name around who spent the final years of the last War in an English prisoner of war camp. If he is the Heinrich Hoffmeyer you know, he's just the ally I need on the ground."

"By all means talk to him and if he is our Heinrich, give him my regards," Max concluded.

With that comfortable thought we went downstairs to join the ladies. We found Miranda and Gaby in animated conversation, comparing hairdressers and their shopping preferences among West End stores. They were nattering like old friends finding surprisingly similar tastes for quality in fashion despite the differences in age and lifestyle.

"Max," Gaby greeted us "Miranda tells me that your friend Roderigo is coming to London soon from Rio, with his wife Maria, for a holiday in Europe. You must give us the opportunity to return his hospitality to Julian while they are here."

We continued chatting for another half hour or so over a second pot of coffee until Miranda announced that it was time to leave. I volunteered to call a taxi but Max handed me a business card and asked me to call the number on it instead. "We have our own driver service," he explained "one of the perks of my retirement occupation."

Within a few minutes there was a discreet call on the entry voice phone and I released the door catch to let the driver in. He was a sober suited youngish man with wispy thinning hair and a face older than his years. I had no doubt that he was definitely not a regular black cab driver.

"Thank you so much for a splendid evening, my dears," said Miranda, kissing Gaby on both cheeks and with a peck on one of mine. "Do take care of yourselves in Germany, don't let Max lead you astray and give us a call when you are back next week." We promised to do so and Max added his thanks with a kiss for Gaby and a warm handshake for me.

I still had no misgivings about our weekend in Germany, more than ten days ahead of any consequences arising from reception of the shipment in Leuffen and, therefore, surely no imminent risk to our safety.

---ooo0ooo---

It was after midnight in Campinas as Count Frederik von Falkenberg dialled a private number in Munich, and about the same time as the Salingers and the Radclives were sitting down to dinner in London. He was seated at his study desk and not in the best of tempers. Izabel was already in bed in the next room but had turned over and fallen to sleep almost immediately before he joined her, which was not at all what he had planned. And so, alone with his thoughts, his mind had turned again to Leuffen and what problems the tiresome Englishman Radclive who had spurned his offer might cause.

The telephone in Munich was equipped with a scrambler which could be activated at the flick of a switch when an incoming caller gave an alert. Tonight someone picked up a receiver in the hall of a rather pleasant half-timbered house in a leafy suburb of the city.

"This is Siegfried calling Wotan," intoned von Falkenberg, giving the signal. There was a click as the scrambler engaged.

"What is your news, Siegfried. Wotan is entertaining guests and cannot take your call?" came the reply.

"Stop using these ridiculous, childish assumed names and pass the General to me. I do not communicate through messenger boys."

There was a pause, another click and a more mature, authoritative voice came on the line. "It's always a pleasure to hear from you, Frederik, but tonight we have friends to dinner to celebrate our silver wedding anniversary. Will this take long?"

"My congratulations to you and Gretchen, Wolfgang; I would not disturb you normally but there is something serious to discuss which should not wait."

"Very well, but please be brief. I can return your call tomorrow if necessary. How are things in Campinas?"

"First, I can report that your payment in kind arrived last week while the Americans were here. Vielen Dank. Also, the return shipment left Rio on June 5 and is scheduled for delivery in Leuffen on June 22. That is the good news." Von Falkenberg's report was delivered with satisfaction.

"So far, so good. But that is not why you called me, Frederik, nicht war?" the general responded silkily. "Give me the bad news now."

Von Falkenberg had rehearsed this part of the conversation carefully with himself. It would not be politic to confess that he had attempted, and failed, to recruit Radclive as his intermediary in Leuffen. "There are complications," he replied. "One of the American management team, an Englishman based in London, was very inquisitive about the transfers from Leuffen to Campinas and the return traffic. He visits Hartmann & Holst often and was there when Klinger foolishly disposed of that other Englishman a month ago."

"If you were so concerned, why could you not have detained him in Brazil?" the General asked impatiently.

"I tried to take him out when he returned to Rio, but the local hired help weren't up to it and failed. Worse still, the Englishman Radclive consulted an established local import-export trader who will certainly have researched the Rio port shipping records for him and briefed him fully on our current shipment."

"So, you have failed and are passing the problem over to me. What do you expect me to do?" "General, I offer my advice." Sensing his listener's displeasure, von Falkenberg reverted to formality. "I am sure that Radclive will plan to be in Leuffen before the cargo arrives. I recommend that he be neutralised on arrival."

"You know how much I dislike these untidy situations. My objective always is to keep the Kamaradenwerke out of the public eye. But you give me no alternative, von Falkenberg. We will take whatever action is necessary to entertain this Radclive. All that you have to do is to arrange that Manfred Hartmann informs us as soon as he reaches Leuffen."

"Of course, but the alert will come from Gottfried Klinger. I am not involving Manfred in our present plans; sadly, he has lost his nerve and we cannot rely on Peter

Hartmann in a situation such as this." Von Falkenberg managed to convey regret at abandoning his old associate.

"Very well," the General concluded "we shall expect to hear from Klinger. But he is not to ring here. Tell him that he must call my office as soon as Radclive arrives and ask for Willi. Now, Frederik, if you have finished with me I shall return to my guests."

"Jawohl, Wolfgang. Thank you for taking on the problem. I apologize again for disturbing your celebration." Not for the first time, the Count cursed himself for his futile attempt to recruit Julian Radclive, prompted by Manfred Hartmann's feebleness. He did not enjoy grovelling to any man, least of all the General.

General Wolfgang Kessler put down his receiver thoughtfully. He didn't trust von Falkenberg and the idea of communication with Gottfried Klinger was distasteful but if his old comrade Manfred Hartmann had lost his nerve he would do what had to be done.

---ooo0ooo---

CHAPTER 25

Germany, June 8 to 11

ON THURSDAY GABY and I travelled out to Stuttgart on the Lufthansa afternoon flight. I had telephoned Viktor Accona the day before to update him on my conversation with Max Salinger. I had told him that Max's involvement was definite and that he would ensure that any seizure of contraband by the police would take place after it had left Hartmann & Holst. There was no point in conveying doubt about Max's direct part in the proceedings. He seemed well satisfied with my report and welcomed the possible enrolment of Heinrich Hoffmeyer as our ally on the spot. Gaby's client had booked her into the Althoff Hotel in the Hauptbahnhof district of the city at their expense and we upgraded the reservation on arrival being careful to pay the additional charge. We enjoyed a relaxed evening in luxury, taking our drinks on the terrace and dining in the gourmet restaurant.

The following morning I delivered Gaby in good time to her client's office and watched her with affection as she strode confidently into the reception area in her Chanel business suit with a serious-looking briefcase. We had agreed that she would ask her hosts to arrange transport for her to the airport after the meeting and that I would collect her there mid- afternoon. Then I set out for Leuffen and arrived at Hartmann & Holst before 10:30. Parking in front of the offices I noted that Peter Hartmann was present but decided to go in search of Heinrich in the factory before talking to him – not very courteous, perhaps, but good manners were not in the forefront of my mind.

I found Heinrich in Halle 1 in his shirtsleeves, crouched over one of the coiling machines with a spanner and an audience of several machine setters and operators. He didn't notice me immediately and I hailed him across the factory floor. "*Guten Tag*, Herr Doktor," I shouted, extending my right arm in stiff salute.

"We are not permitted to make that gesture anymore, Herr Radclive," he shouted back in English. "I will not be long. Please make yourself at home in my office."

On my way down the passage from Halle 1 towards Heinrich's office I came across Gottfried Klinger emerging from his. He seemed surprised to see me but greeted me civilly enough before dodging back without engaging in conversation. I didn't think anything of the encounter at the time and settled in Heinrich's more comfortable visitors' chair. On the flight over from London Gaby and I had discussed how we could get to know Heinrich better and had decided that we would ask him and his wife to join us for a meal over the weekend.

When Heinrich joined me some fifteen minutes later, bustling into the office and wiping machine oil from his hands with cotton waste, I opened the conversation with our invitation. He responded enthusiastically, if a little formally: "Thank you, Herr Radclive – er, Julian. Of course, I must consult with Ethel but I am sure she will be very happy; she sees very few friends from England nowadays and it will be a great treat for her."

"Excellent;" I replied "shall we have dinner together tomorrow evening? One condition only: that you choose where we eat and reserve the table."

"Willingly. I will telephone Ethel in the lunch hour and then confirm to you."

After that, we got down to business; I brought him up to date on our DES discussions in Rio and was not surprised that Peter, who had been in attendance, had failed to brief him. He readily agreed that Ribenda was the optimal choice as European master stockist and as manufacturer of the lower part of the compression spring range in smaller diameter wire.

The remainder of the compression spring range could be produced without problem by Hartmann & Holst within the timing of the action plan. He would invite the Ribenda team to visit Leuffen in the next fortnight to discuss the details of the plan including the logistics for stock levels and transfers between the factories. Relationship building between the Dutch and German colleagues would be a useful by product of the visit, I thought.

I asked Heinrich how the factory had performed while we had all been away in Brazil and he was pleased to report that there had been no particular problems. Dieter Trautman's assistant accountant had managed the finance function efficiently and it was clear that Peter's absence had been barely noticed, although several decision-making issues had arisen which would normally have been a general management responsibility. For Heinrich, the most important event of the period was the arrival of the new tooling on which he had been working in the factory that morning. Manufactured in California and imported, he had attached it to a German-manufactured Wafios spring coiler in order to eliminate a secondary grinding operation. On our first meeting a month ago he had explained how the perpendicularity of fuel injector nozzle springs was critical to their quality and that hitherto this required a secondary grinding operation after coiling. The American tooling provided clean transverse cut-offs across each end of the spring during the coiling operation; although the coiling speeds were adversely affected, the cost-saving was significant delivering an overall gain in productivity. When I had arrived, he had been demonstrating to machine setters and operators how to fit the attachment. Heinrich was excited, his blue eyes twinkling behind rimless spectacles.

"*Sehr erfolgreich!*" he exclaimed adding for my benefit. "Very successful. Just what I was hoping for," in case I had not fully understood his jubilation.

"Congratulations, but aren't you reluctant to use American tooling on a quality German machine?" I asked.

"Not so, Julian. The Americans are the masters of mass production. How else could they possibly have won the war against German technology? No, this is an excellent example of how to combine US know-how with quality German engineering. Our friend Loren Corley will be pleased, I think."

"I think so too;" I assured him, "and everyone else at Farmington if next week confirms that price increases are impossible as you have suggested."

"Bah! These visits of Floyd and Peter are what you would call – mission idiotic." The thought of the forthcoming customer visits to Robert Bosch and others dampened Heinrich's mood.

"Mission impossible," I corrected him and we left it at that.

---ooo0ooo---

I wandered over to the main office building to see Peter Hartmann and came across Dieter Trautman on my way. "May I have your advice?" he asked earnestly, drawing me into his office where we remained standing. His normally cheerful expression was dulled and his brow furrowed.

"Julian," he said looking embarrassed, "I would like your opinion on a personal matter." "Go ahead, if you think that I can be helpful," I reassured him looking suitably grave.

"Peter tells me that I made a fool of myself in Rio and disgraced him and Hartmann & Holst. Everyone was so friendly and I enjoyed myself. Do you think I behaved badly? – and please tell me the truth."

"Dieter, you did not disgrace yourself or the company." I was relieved that something more serious had not disturbed him. "Yes, you were a bit over the top at the nightclub, but we all enjoyed your antics and your lack of inhibition helped you make many friends among your colleagues. You did not upset anyone – except Peter – and he will get over it."

I wanted to add that Peter's opinion didn't matter but that would have undermined his general manager's authority: not on my agenda and I said no more. Dieter's brow cleared and he resumed his sunny disposition, thanking me profusely for putting his mind at ease. I walked back through reception, greeting Frau Päsche as I passed, and knocked at Peter's door before entering; he was not alone. Peter was seated behind his desk but manifestly not in command of the situation. Leaning across the desk from the front stood Gottfried Klinger, both fists planted firmly on its surface. He straightened at my entrance, casting a malevolent glance in my direction. "*Danke schŏn,* Herr Direktor," he said and, for my benefit, unconvincingly, "I will do as you have instructed," before leaving the room. Peter remained seated, looking sheepish.

In order to relieve the tension, I took a seat in front of the desk and opened the conversation. "Do you have everything you need, Peter, for your tour with Lloyd next week?"

"I have a complete file on each customer we are visiting with a summary of our business during the past three years, but I don't think it will be much help," he replied gloomily. "I am concerned that he will upset them by demanding immediate price increases"

"Lloyd is not a stupid man," I replied. "He will probably be forceful and they may not like him, but he will remain polite. The time you spend with him between meetings on the road and in the evenings may be less comfortable."

Peter's confidence had been dented by his week in Brazil among other AA managers who were distinctly unimpressed by his habitual arrogance. Almost slumped behind his executive desk, he seemed even less confident now; he made no attempt to exert his authority.

"Julian," he said after an interval. "May I ask you for your advice – not as a friend, perhaps, but, as a colleague, who understands the situation here/"

"Of course," I replied, wondering how much von Falkenberg had told him in Brazil about his conversations with me and what Klinger had said to him a few moments ago. It seemed possible that the Count had merely told him what to do when the next shipment arrived but not given him a date. Perhaps, Klinger had surprised him by informing him of the delivery in ten days' time. I decided to give him the benefit of the doubt.

"I don't expect the week to go well," Peter resumed. "I expect to be blamed and to be given *der Sack* afterwards – it's the same word in English I think? My father says that I can manage the family properties instead, if I like – we have many in the Nurtingen area. Do you think I should resign first?"

I saw no point in giving false comfort. "After a company takeover, it is unusual for family management to last more than a year. In fact, Peter, my personal advice to you and your father would be to distance yourselves from Hartmann & Holst as soon as you are able."

Peter straightened his shoulders and passed a hand across his thinning hair; a trace of his former confidence returned. "Thank you." he said stiffly. "I shall consider your advice seriously."

There was no way of telling whether or not he knew that I knew about the contraband trading and the new shipment. Either way, my advice to Peter was as honest as that given to Dieter less than an hour before. I did not particularly like father or son, but if the Hartmanns chose to walk away from the forthcoming conflict there was no advantage in pursuing them.

---ooo0ooo---

I left Leuffen before 2:30 having checked with Dieter that he had issued a credit note to Grunwald Metallwerk for the missing coils of spring wire from the last shipment to Amparo; he would adjust his inventory accordingly on the assumption that the forthcoming end of year stock check would tally. I also asked him to check personally with PanAlpina when the next consignment from Grunwald was expected. Heinrich Hoffmeyer had sought me out in Dieter's office to say that he had called his wife and that regretfully they could not dine the following evening because their daughter, who worked in a lawyer's office in Dusseldorf, would be bringing her new boyfriend to visit them, arriving Saturday morning. "Would tonight be possible instead?" he asked. I confirmed that would be fine and we agreed that he and Ethel would collect us from the Gasthof at 7:30.

Gaby was waiting for me at the Flughafen in the arrivals hall and we motored back to Leuffen with Gaby doing most of the talking. Her client meeting had been a great success and she had been engaged to take part in their washing machine research programmes in France and the Netherlands, all three Scandinavian countries and Finland; her role would be as adviser to the local market research teams in the selection of respondents and in leading their focus groups.

"Congratulations," I said. "I'm sure you charmed the socks off them."

"More a matter of professional competence, although one of them did make a vague pass at me over lunch," Gaby replied smugly. "They're really a very serious bunch – some stilted attempts at jollity but not really much sense of humour. However, the fees that they are paying plus all expenses make the assignment unrefusable." Indeed, the amount offered was more than generous."

"In that case, I hope you won't mind that I have arranged for Heinrich and his wife Ethel to have dinner with us this evening. He does have quite a mischievous sense of humour and I hope that Ethel hasn't lost any of her native Lancashire wit."

"We can have our own private celebration tomorrow," Gaby replied. "What's more we can think about treating ourselves to an exotic holiday this year – something more than Cornwall without bucket and spade."

We contented ourselves for the rest of the journey as far as Nŭrtingen by discussing the merits of alternative holiday locations but without reaching a decision. Our short list ranged from Crete to Marrakech or further afield to Phuket or the Maldives and we left it that, after the weekend, Gaby would gather brochures from London tourist offices and I would explore when I could take my leave entitlement.

With these happy thoughts we arrived at Leuffen and I slowed the car so that Gaby could glance at the factory through the open gates. Peter Hartmann's Mercedes was still parked in front of the offices; so we did not enter and I drove on to the Gasthof where a more than friendly welcome awaited us. Brigitta was in the lobby as I entered ahead of Gaby; clad in customary red jumpsuit, she gave me a roguish smile.

"*Guten abend*, Herr Radclive," she drawled coyly but the smile faded as Gaby appeared behind me.

"Good evening, Brigitta," I replied evenly. "This is my wife Gaby who has been looking forward to staying in your Gasthof."

Advancing into the lobby, Gaby's greeting was friendly. "I have heard so much about you, Fraulein Krantz. I'm delighted to be here and I know we shall be very comfortable," she said holding out her hand.

Impressed by Gaby's ease of manner and, perhaps, the Chanel suit, Brigitta coloured slightly and, taking the proffered hand briefly, bobbed her head, grasped Gaby's luggage and galloped up the stairs. Over her shoulder, in normal tones, she called "I will show you to your room."

---ooo0ooo---

Our first floor room was probably the best room in the Gasthof. It was simply furnished, as with the other rooms, but more spacious with a larger bathroom and French windows giving on to a small balcony which faced West and overlooked the inn's beer garden. It had been an unusually warm day for early June and we were grateful to be able to throw open the windows and flop on the bed for half an hour before showering and changing into cooler clothes for the evening: a floaty dress for Gaby and for me the lightweight jacket and trousers from my Brazilian trip. We descended to the bar with half an hour to spare before Heinrich and Ethel were due to collect us. I had prepared Gaby for the shock of Otto Krantz's fearsome appearance and she managed not to show surprise when we encountered him behind the bar. He put down the napkin with which he was polishing glasses and came forward to greet us, beaming fearsomely. This evening, the livid scar on his cheek glowed more than I remembered in the warm weather.

"Willkommen, Frau Radclive. Your husband is already a good friend of our Gasthof and I hope you will feel at home." He bent over Gaby's hand which I feared, for a moment, that he might kiss gallantly rather than shake. Gaby murmured words of appreciation and thanked him for our "charming room". While continuing to look at her, Otto's right eye flickered in my direction.

"Shall you be eating here now, Herr Radclive?" he enquired.

"We're dining with Dr. Hoffmeyer this evening, but we shall certainly take dinner here tomorrow night, Herr Krantz," I explained. "We'd like to take a drink in your *biergarten* while we wait for him. A bottle of your best Mosel and four glasses, if you please. - Niersteiner Gutes Domtal, if you have it."

Otto Kratz approved my choice of wine; a few minutes later Brigitta served us at our table outside with a bottle of Niersteiner in an ice bucket and the appropriate long-stemmed Mosel glasses. She had regained her composure and seemed ready to chat. The evening sun was still hot and we had chosen to sit in the shade at the back of the small West facing garden. There were six tables of which one other at the front was occupied by two men with their backs turned to us: Gottfried Klinger and Johann Glock. Klinger was immediately recognizable by his square head and blonde hair cut *en brosse*, while Glock's exceptional height singled him out, even when seated. They had not noticed us until we started to talk with Brigitta; now, Klinger turned his head and, seeing me, spoke rapidly to his companion. The two of them drained their glasses and, scraping back their chairs, rose to their feet. As they passed us Gottfried Klinger gave me a curt nod but did not speak. Glock also remained mute, giving no sign of recognition and I could assess better his giant stature as he towered over Brigitta rendering her an almost petite figure; I reckoned that, side by side with Tom Hardy, he would stand some three inches the taller.

---ooo0ooo---

There was time only to identify them to Gaby before we were joined by Heinrich and Ethel Hoffmeyer. I poured them each a glass of wine and topped up our glasses with the rest of the bottle. Heinrich was on his best behaviour, greeting Gaby rather formally and introducing his wife with obvious pride.

"Ethel is British, but she has been a German citizen for many years," he said. "Natürlich, she is the commanding officer of our family."

Ethel looked at him with affection and Gaby hastened to dispel formality by addressing them both.

"Julian has told me so much about you, Heinrich, and your sense of humour," she said. "I can see already that he did not exaggerate. And, Ethel, it's lovely to meet you too."

Any ice that there might have been was broken immediately and Ethel responded while Heinrich twinkled behind his rimless spectacles.

"It's grand to meet English people here at home. My brother Jack comes over once a year to stay with us and used to bring his wife when she was alive, but that's about all."

There was still more than the trace of a Lancashire accent in her voice, but Ethel looked as much German as English. She was solidly built, but not fat, and it was easy to picture her as the farmer's daughter which she later identified herself to be. She had rather mousey ginger hair and an open, homely face with pleasant features; I could imagine that, in her youth, Ethel would have been a pretty girl. She was dressed this evening in a short sleeved patterned summer dress, not fashionable like Gaby's, with a cardigan over her arm in case of evening chills as it grew dark.

"You must tell us how you and Heinrich met," I asked.

"She can do that over dinner and I will tell my side of the story," Heinrich intervened. "It's a long tale and you must tell us how you both met."

"Our story is quite simple," Gaby said. "We met at a No. 74 bus stop in London six years ago and haven't looked back since."

"That's right romantic," Ethel said doubtfully.

"It's not quite the casual pick-up it sounds" I hastened to add. "We stepped off the same bus into the pouring rain. I had an umbrella and this attractive girl was without even a raincoat; since we were going in the same direction, I offered her the shelter of my brolly. We found that we were walking to the same office and one thing led to another."

"Ah, the perfect English gentleman. It could be the opening scene of a movie," Heinrich declared.

---ooo0ooo---

CHAPTER 26

WE FINISHED OUR WINE in good humour and Heinrich led the way to his car, calling out a cheerful greeting to Otto Krantz in the bar, with whom he was clearly on friendly terms.

"I have reserved us a table at the Gasthof in Hohenleuffen up the road. It has a restaurant which Ethel and I like and visit quite often when we want a meal out in the countryside," Heinrich informed us as we moved off. "I believe you will like it."

"I'm sure we shall," Gaby said and I did not spoil Heinrich's enjoyment by mentioning that Tom Hardy and I had dined there less than a month previously. The short drive up the mountainous hillside with its tortuous bends and precipitous drop to the right, down to the stream far below was becoming a familiar journey for me. There was more leaf now on the oak and beech trees so that the entrance to the Hartmann hunting lodge as we neared Hohenleuffen was barely noticeable; already the season was changing from late Spring into summer. In the evening sunlight the half-timbered Gasthof seemed even more welcoming than before; this time, the car park was almost full as Heinrich manoeuvred his green Audi carefully into a remaining space.

We entered the restaurant through the crowded bar and saw at once that making reservations at the weekend was essential. The manager greeted Heinrich and Ethel as old acquaintances confirming that they were familiar customers and led us to the corner table which he had kept for us. It was now the height of the asparagus season and almost every dish on the menu was offered *'mit spargel'*. I am not a fan of asparagus; unlike English asparagus which is generally green and succulent, the German variety is thicker and paler, almost white – "like vicars' fingers" Gaby remarked afterwards. Our companions ordered *spargel* as a starter and again with turbot for their main course. To be sociable, we chose *spargel* with melted butter as our first course and Gaby followed me in my selection of *kalbshaxen* veal shanks which I had enjoyed previously. Heinrich and Ethel continued to drink Mosel while I introduced Gaby to the delights of Lemberger.

Having ordered, I opened the conversation. "Before you tell us how you both met, we bring you greetings from an old friend, Max Salinger, who has lost touch with you," I said.

"Good heavens. We haven't seen the Colonel, have we Heinrich, since he came to our wedding? How is he?" Gaby asked. "and Mrs. Salinger? – a very strong lady."

"They're both very well. Max is expecting to come to Stuttgart in 10 days', time and hopes to see you then," I said.

She appeared to take my reply at its face value; while Heinrich looked quizzical, sensing that there was more to it. Ethel was ready to embark on the story of how she and Heinrich had met. "My father was a farmer up north of Bury," she began.

"In the war, Warth Mills, down the road at Redvales on the river Irwell, was requisitioned first as a camp for internees and then for low security prisoners of war. My dad was allocated two or three prisoners at a time, Germans or Italians, to help out on the farm. We were permitted to invite them to lunch on Sundays but very few of them seemed ready to socialize. Then, in the early spring of 1944, both of the farm's tractors broke down; all of the local garage mechanics were away at the war and, at first, my dad didn't know where to turn. My mum, who was always the practical one in our family, suggested that he asked the camp commandant if there were any POWs with engineering skills who could help. The next day they sent us Heinrich; he arrived mid-morning on a bicycle and by teatime he had the two tractors running. My dad was impressed and asked him to lunch the next Sunday and he turned up again on his bicycle, right neat and tidy this time – he even had had collar and tie with an old tweed jacket. It seemed that he had borrowed them from one of the internees still at the camp. What's more he had good manners which impressed my mum and, although his English was not very good, he fitted in with us immediately. I was a seventeen year old lass at the time and I fell for him immediately; although he was some years older than me and a bit big for his boots, he was a good-looking lad then." Ethel gazed at Heinrich fondly.

"For my part," said Heinrich taking up the story, "there was this beautiful girl, full of life, a *schnickiputzi* living in the English countryside, similar to my home in Saxony."
"He means that I was a sweetie-pie," Ethel explained.

"But, of course, she was too young to be my *schatz* – my sweetheart – and in any case POWs were not permitted to have girlfriends. So, we became good friends but we both knew that there was something more between us. Ethel's parents were very good people too and I looked forward all week to Sunday lunches at the farm."

"Life went on like this for almost a year and Heinrich became well-known among all the other farmers in the area as his skills in servicing farm machinery became known and he helped others out too," Ethel resumed her account. "But he came to lunch with us almost every Sunday and I was jealous when he went to others, particularly the parents of my school friends. Then, early in 1945 when we knew that the Allies were winning the war in Europe, a big car came up the track to the farm one weekend while Heinrich was with us. And when the army driver opened the rear door, out stepped a uniformed officer who introduced himself as Colonel Salinger; he asked to speak to Captain Hoffmeyer – the first time that we knew that Heinrich had been an officer himself. Heinrich was called and sat with the Colonel in the back of his staff car for more than an hour. I remember that the driver had to get out while they talked and stamped around in the cold smoking cigarettes. Heinrich looked thoughtful when he got out and the staff car drove off. He didn't tell us what they talked about and, of course, we didn't ask him – we realised that it was probably 'hush hush'. After that, he was more serious most of the time – except at Sunday lunch; and during the rest of the year he used to be away for two weeks or more at a time, never telling us where he had been – just saying, if pressed, that he had been 'doing something for the Colonel'." Ethel paused to consider what more she should say about Heinrich's activities.

"Yes," I intervened. "The Colonel explained to us that Heinrich had been carrying out occasional missions for him during that time and into 1946."

Ethel continued. "There came a day in 1946 when Heinrich told me that he would soon be free to go back to Germany. I was a year older then and he asked me if I would be his girlfriend and wait for me until he could come back. My dad wanted him to stay and his idea was to set up a sales and servicing business in farm machinery with Heinrich as his partner and manager. However, my brother, who had returned injured from the War, was not for it – understandable, I suppose, at the time. And so, Heinrich left us; I wasn't really sure that he would come back, although we agreed to write to each other regularly."

"I always intended to come back." Heinrich went on. "I had very little money although Colonel Max had arranged a form of regular retainer for me, enough for me to take up the place offered to me at Heidelberg University to complete my engineering degree but not enough to consider taking care of a wife. But we did write to each other and I was certain that I would return. Occasionally, during my three years at Heidelberg, I travelled to London during vacations to report to Colonel Max on my jobs for him but these were short visits only and I was always transported by military aircraft. Then, in 1949, I completed my studies and was able to return to Bury and revisit the farm. Ethel was now an even more beautiful young lady; we were able to 'walk out', as her mother called it. Within three weeks I proposed to her and she accepted with her father's approval. I had already found myself a good job at one of the big German companies which was rebuilding its post-war business. We were married that May in Bury, with Colonel Max and his wife as guests, just after Ethel's twenty-first birthday, and returned together to Germany as man and wife."

"And so, here we are as you can see nearly thirty years on with two grown-up children," Ethel concluded her tale.

While she had been talking with her back to the room opposite to me, I had been watching the other diners idly and had noticed that as one party of four left the restaurant they were replaced at the vacant table by a group of four men. Two of them were carrying glasses, indicating that they had been drinking at the bar; they were laughing loudly at a joke that another of the four, a completely bald middle-aged man of stocky build, had just finished telling. I remembered the bald man that Tom and I had seen at the same bar on our first visit and this one seemed similar. Seated next to me, Heinrich had noticed and commented on my interest.

"I recognize two of them. They're members of the *Nurtingen Fallschirmspringen Club*; they've probably come here for a meal after an evening's skydiving from the Schloss." "Is the bald-headed fellow one of them?" I asked.

"No, he's a stranger to me but people come from miles around for their skydiving here." I turned my attention back to Ethel while Gaby re-launched the general conversation.

"We want to tour around a bit tomorrow. Max gave us some ideas of where to visit but we'd like your advice."

"I'll give you a foreign resident's opinion first and then Heinrich can add his opinion," replied Ethel. "Where did Colonel Max suggest?"

"He gave us four locations and maybe we can visit more than one in the day or another on Sunday?" I reeled them off: "Alprisbach Monastery, the Wiblingen Monastery outside Ulm, down the Upper Swabian Baroque Road to the church at Steinhausen or all the way down to Lake Constance for a visit to Mainau Island – which would you recommend?"

"Well, they're all interesting," Ethel considered carefully "but the route to Alprisbach Monastery is not very nice, built up areas and no real countryside. The scenery down to Lake Constance is grand and it's an awful long way there – too long for a day trip. You'd like Mainau Island but if you're going that far you really ought to stay the night. The Steinhausen church is worth a visit but there's nothing else to stop for on the way. Wiblingen Monastery is better and the Baroque library there is champion. If you go on up the road from here to the top of the hill and on to the Swabian plateau you can drive all the way to Ulm over good farmland without using the autobahn and Ulm itself is a really beautiful city. So, my choice is Wiblingen." She turned to Heinrich for confirmation.

"I make a point of never arguing with my wife and, in this case, I agree with her completely. Wiblingen and Ulm for an excellent day out," said Heinrich with the familiar twinkle in his eye, adding mischievously "Of course, there is another good reason. Ulm was also the home of Field Marshall Erwin Rommel." I was never quite sure when he was joking.

"I wonder why the Colonel suggested Mainau Island. He must have known it would take too long to get there and drive back in the same day" Ethel intervened, deftly changing the subject.

"I think he had an ulterior motive for suggesting that Julian visits Lake Constance and Mainau," said Gaby.

Heinrich looked up. "And did Colonel Max have an ulterior motive in wanting to see me again; he generally did. Does he have a message for me, Julian?"

"Yes, there is something he wanted to ask you which would be helpful," I said being careful not to be explicit; I was unsure how much of his activities with Max he shared with Ethel.

"In that case, perhaps we should step outside for a few minutes so that you can tell me without troubling the ladies." Heinrich answered firmly.

Ethel looked anxious. "Do not involve Heinrich again in one of the Colonel's missions, please. He's no longer a young man and I won't let him put himself in harm's way again," she appealed.

"Max is an old man himself now and almost in retirement; he wouldn't want Heinrich to do anything dangerous. No more than a few 'phone calls, I expect," I sought to reassure her.

Gaby put a hand on her arm. "Julian's not a hero either," she said. "I won't let him do anything stupid."

Heinrich ordered apfelstrudel for Gaby and Ethel and led the way outside to the car park. We decided to walk instead of sitting in his car and strolled across the car park towards the entrance of the side road leading up to the schloss.

"What is the Colonel up to?" Heinrich asked. "It's thirty-three years since the war and the last time we spoke, he told me that his work in Germany was at an end."

"It's down to me, Heinrich. Because of his family connection to one of our closest friends, I asked his advice about Bernard's death in the factory last month and our suspicions about the delivery that night from Brazil," I explained. "He gave me a contact in the export-import business in Rio who investigated the traffic of containers between Leuffen and Amparo.

While I was at the Amparo spring factory, the last consignment from here arrived and and was found to be short of two coils of valve spring wire."

"Did your contact in Rio find out anything for you?"

"That's where it got really interesting. The weight of the container on arrival at the port tallied with the documents, but the import agency which transports all loads to and from Amparo is owned by a drugs cartel. We reckoned that they took whatever went missing *en route* and that it was probably advance payment for the next load of drugs to be exported back to Gemany. On an equivalent weight basis we think that the payment was probably made in gold with a value of, perhaps, $25 million. Then we translated that into the value the cocaine to be added by the shipping agency to the return shipment on its was back to Rio; the street value in Europe could be three times as much."

"If all this is true, when do you expect the return shipment to reach Leuffen?" Heinrich asked. "The week after next, 22ⁿᵈ June. In fact the consignment had already left Rio while we still there," I replied.

"I think you had better tell me who you think is involved and what Colonel Max wants us to do?"

I was pleased that Heinrich had jumped to the conclusion that he and I together were being asked to intervene and I told him the rest of the story including my dinner with von Falkenberg, his offer to pay me to take on the role played by Manfred Hartmann, my refusal and his intention to work through Klinger and Peter. I added our conclusion that the drug trafficking organisation in Germany was almost certainly the Kamaradenwerke. Finally, I explained that Max's main interest was in tracking down the source of any gold rather than the drugs operation and that AA's concern was that the drugs bust should take place outside the factory.

"Understood. Max has always had a bee in his helmet about Nazi gold," Heinrich remarked. "In his bonnet", I corrected him gently.

"As for the drug runners, without the protection of the Americans, von Falkenberg would have been treated as a war criminal and Klinger was always *eine Scheisse*. But

Manfred Hartmann – I'm disappointed; he was a good officer in the War. So, what is the plan for 22th June and what does the Colonel want me to do?"

"The plan is for Max to come over to Stuttgart on 21th; he has a chum in the SEK and he will go there and wait for us to call him when the consignment arrives. Then, they will send a team from the Spezaleinsatzkommando to wait outside the factory gates until Klinger leaves with drugs, follow him to his destination and arrest him and everyone else there. All we have to do is watch for the arrival of the shipment and make the telephone call", I explained.

Heinrich looked unconvinced. "It's too simple," he said. "In my experience, Julian, it's always the simple plans that go wrong. We should prepare for contingencies."

"Are there any weaknesses in the plan that you can see? The delivery agents are Pan Alpina who are completely reliable and a hijack between the port and Leuffen is hardly likely here in Europe."

"You are the weakness, my friend. Or to be exact, your meetings with von Falkenberg have made you a weakness. He will realise that you have discovered the delivery timing and expect you to interfere. I suspect that you will be a target. Did he make any moves against you in Rio?" Heinrich asked.

I confessed that there had been one definite attempt on my life and another on Roderigo Morales at his home after we all left. Heinrich looked concerned.

"In that case I think that you are already in danger. It was a risk for you to bring Gaby here this weekend; von Falkenberg's allies in Germany, the Kamaradenwerke - if you're right about them, may already be tracking you," he said gravely.

We turned back and retraced our steps towards the restaurant. Until then I hadn't really thought about any personal risk since leaving Brazil. Distance had instilled an unreality to everything that had happened to me there in the exotic atmosphere of Amparo and Rio. Now I started to think of those events in a different light. Heinrich had cast a shadow over the coming days.

"Surely, there's no immediate risk more than 10 days before the expected delivery. They wouldn't want to stimulate a murder investigation so close to home which might draw attention to their activities," I replied.

"I hope you're right, but be careful to watch for any signs that you are being followed tomorrow when you drive around or that you are being watched at the Gasthof," Heinrich cautioned.

As we passed by the car park again I recognized a dark red Porsche 911, the same model in which I had seen the bald-headed man inside drive off last time I had been here. Without remarking on the coincidence to Heinrich I made a mental note of the registration number.

We re-entered the restaurant to join Ethel and Gaby in the far corner; facing us at the skydivers' table as we passed was the bald-headed man, still joking with his companions. He looked across and gave me a baleful stare with no hint of humour. I noticed that his eyebrows were white and his pale eyes pink rimmed; he was the first bald albino I had ever come across.

---ooo0ooo---

CHAPTER 27

WE AWOKE ON Saturday morning to an already hot day. We had returned to our room the previous evening to find it uncomfortably close; flinging open the French doors on to our balcony had given little relief and we slept poorly even without the duvet. Before attempting to sleep we had compared notes on the evening with Heinrich and Ethel which we had both enjoyed. Gaby thought them a devoted couple; she was touched by the story of how they had met and married. She found Heinrich charming and good fun but detected in him a 'steely quality' beneath his rather ponderous humour. I agreed with her, adding that Ethel's down-to- earth personality seemed wholly compatible with the Swabian character and that it was delightful that she had retained so many Lancashire idioms.

While we showered and dressed, I recounted my conversation with Heinrich after we had left the table to walk outside, playing down his concerns for our safety and omitting my misgivings about the apparent coincidences of the bald albino. As an afterthought, I asked Gaby if she would prefer us to curtail our weekend and fly back to London on the afternoon flight.

"No way. We have a romantic weekend together as tourists abroad and I want to make the most of it," she replied robustly.

We took our breakfast downstairs served by Otto Krantz while Brigitta laboured in the background polishing and dusting the other tables and the bar.

"It will be hotter today," I remarked conversationally.

"Jawohl, we are in *ein hitzewelle*, Otto replied. "This is not the weather for driving too far."

We assured him that we would not go too far, requested bottled water to take with us and were on the road to Ulm before 9:30. Ethel had been right; the plateau at the top of the Swabian alp was well cultivated farmland on a grand scale. The uninterrupted vista was without the presence of any agricultural machinery and the farm buildings were of traditional rustic build; no trace of concrete or corrugated iron roofs. The few farmworkers labouring in the fields were mostly women in long skirts with wooden tools and woven baskets. Time seemed to have stood still here and I was reminded strongly of the Breughel paintings I had viewed in London and Amsterdam art gallery exhibitions over the years.

There was almost no traffic and although we drove at a leisurely pace and in comfort, thanks to the Golf's air conditioning, reached the outskirts of Ulm in under an hour and turned south to Wiblingen where we arrived less than 10 minutes later. Gaby had equipped herself before we left London with a Michelin guide to Southern Germany so that we had been able to brief ourselves over breakfast: "the monastery and church are the final masterpiece of baroque architecture in Swabia" we were informed. However, no guide book could have prepared us for the exuberant splendour of the monastery library.

At most great and ancient libraries, such as the Duke Humphrey part of the Bodleian at Oxford or the Fitzwilliam at Cambridge, the buildings, however magnificent, take second place as the setting and an accompaniment to the books; at Wiblingen monastery the reverse is the case. Like some flamboyant, overdressed hostess at a charity ball whose costume outshines her guests, the building and its interior decoration dominates the books and reduces their significance to little more than that of invited guests. From the oval painted ceiling to the ornate balustraded gallery and the ground floor furnished with ivory classical figures on their plinths and an abundance of *scagliola* marbled wood mounted on marble paving the building overwhelms the visitor. The walls are clothed with bookshelves but they make little impact and seem almost irrelevant. Overall, the library casts an overpowering impression of opulence on the grandest of scales.

After paying to enter we wandered around and finished up on the balcony for a closer view of the spectacular painted ceiling by craning our necks upwards. Then, surveying the hall below, we saw another couple who had arrived after us: a rather dumpy woman in a long denim skirt with mousey hair and a taller man with a black toothbrush moustache. They were still at ground level as we left the library but we paid little attention to each other. The hot air and humid atmosphere hit us as we stepped outside and made our way to the back to the Golf.

There was only one other vehicle in the car park, a hatchback Audi in a nondescript beige colour, presumably the other couple's car. The Golf, even with widows fully open, felt like a greenhouse and it was some minutes before the air conditioning had any effect as we motored across the Danube into the centre of Ulm. Neither of us had much appetite for more sightseeing; however, we consulted Gaby's Michelin Guide and decided to limit our attention to just one of the old city's attractions. The Ulm Munster, a church rather than cathedral dating from the 10th century with the world's tallest steeple, could not be ignored. We made a brief visit and admired the soaring vaulted ceiling of the nave but were not tempted to climb the 768 steps which Michelin identified for ascending the 530 feet tower and steeple.

Emerging into the stifling heat our first priority was to seek somewhere out of the sun for a cool drink.

We found a restaurant in the fishermen's quarter with a shaded terrace at the rear overlooking a stream where we parked ourselves gratefully. Long glasses of lemonade helped to quench thirst and refresh; since we were expected to eat we put aside the inevitable spargel menu and ordered matjesfilet herring salads with fresh fruit and ice cream to follow. Over coffee afterwards I glanced down the stream towards another restaurant terrace on the opposite bank in full sunlight. Without a parasol over their table, I recognized the same mousey-haired woman and man with a toothbrush moustache whom we had seen at the monastery library.

They were wearing sunglasses so that it was impossible to tell whether or not they were watching us. Surely just a coincidence, I thought, to find two fellow tourists lunching nearby.

Gaby had noticed them too. "Isn't that the couple we saw in the library?" she asked. "They must be very hot sitting over there. Why didn't they choose this side of the river?" Indeed, their terrace was otherwise empty whereas the half a dozen tables at ours were all occupied."

"What do you have in mind for this afternoon?" Gaby asked next, consulting her Michelin guide again. "In this temperature all one really wants to do is laze on a beach or in and around a swimming pool. I don't think I fancy wandering around more historical buildings today."

"Your slightest wish is my command," I replied. "The spa at Leuffen has an open-air swimming pool and I'm sure we can wheedle our way in. As for swimming costumes, I think we should be able to find a sports shop here somewhere in the new part of the city."

We returned to the car which I had managed to park in the shade. However, it was still stifling; so with windows open and air conditioning at full blast we re-crossed the Danube into Neu Ulm. The Danube marks the boundary between Baden Württemburg and Bavaria so that, dating from the early nineteenth century, the city and smaller town have been governed by separate administrations. Parking again in the main shopping square we soon found a sports clothing store where Gaby chose a one-piece fuchsia pink swim suit and I equipped myself with a more sober pair of baggy blue trunks. We returned to the car and I was about to drive off from the pavement when I saw a beige Audi hatchback in the driver's mirror pulling in several cars behind us. As I watched the man with a black toothbrush moustache crossed the road and entered the store where we had just shopped. I had the uneasy feeling that this was more than coincidence; were we being followed or was I becoming paranoiac?

It was now mid-afternoon and the heat was becoming less intense; it was, after all, late Spring and not high summer. We agreed to go direct to the Leuffen spa and set out on our journey in no particular hurry. We had nearly crossed the plateau when we were overtaken by a beige Audi Avant travelling too fast for us to have a close view of the occupants, or to be certain that it was the same car as before, but this time I asked Gaby to write down the registration number rather than commit a second number plate to memory.

"I'm sure that's the car we saw at the monastery," Gaby said as the Audi disappeared inti the distance.

"And for a second time in Neu Ulm, parked behind us as we were leaving," I replied. "I now believe that we've been followed all day by the man with the moustache and his companion."

"If that's so, it's probably quite harmless; just Klinger's chums keeping you under observation."

As we started downhill towards Hohenleuffen, Gaby suggested that we might turn off at the village and drive up to the schloss: "for a quick look without getting out of the car" to satisfy her curiosity.

"I think that's a bad idea. We might bump into Manfred or Peter Hartmann and we don't want any kind of encounter that could raise suspicions," I said.

Gaby accepted my reservations and we drove through the village, down the steep winding road to Leuffen, turning left to the lido before we reached the factory.

---ooo0ooo---

I had not visited the spa before but had heard much about it, both from Otto Krantz while staying at the Gasthof and from Tom who had been there to have a look around. Apparently, it had started life modestly when a local farmer discovered a spring on his land with clear, rather gaseous water which was analysed as having therapeutic properties. An entrepreneur by nature, he had erected a simple wooden building around the spring where people who wanted to "take the waters" could sample at a price. There was an outside area where visitors could sit in more clement weather to enjoy their "medicine". There were enough followers of alternative medicine and hypochondriacs locally who, attracted by word of mouth, became regular visitors and soon made the spa popular. Things moved on and professional investors moved in; a limited company was formed and a specialist developer of leisure centres drew up plans for an expanded spa, taking a major shareholding in the enterprise. The present complex included the original spa as its centrepiece with the addition of a swimming pool, saunas and an exercise gym together with changing rooms. Shrewdly, the farmer had hedged his bets by taking a shareholding in the company as well as granting it a lease. Not unexpectedly, Manfred Hartmann was an investor.

There was an extensive car park outside the white washed single storey building where we left the car with half a dozen or so others; at the entrance there was a large sign and map of the facility announcing *Leuffen Kurort*. Facing us as we entered was a reception counter manned by a rather flabby youth with acne who asked us to show our membership cards. I tried to buy single entry tickets explaining that we were visitors staying at the Gasthof and was told that this was not possible; I continued arguing but the youth was obdurate and seemed to enjoy my growing frustration. In the end, adopting a tone of almost military authority I called for the manager. Summoned from his office at the rear of the reception area, the manager emerged: a short harassed-looking middle-aged man with horn-rimmed spectacles and an irritable expression. Gaby flashed her most winning smile at him and I assumed a more conciliatory manner explaining that I was a manager of the US company that had recently acquired the factory and was interested in buying membership for our more senior staff. The irritation was replaced by a deferential air and the manager offered to show us around which was not at all what we had in mind; proudly, he told us that he had gained a licence to add a café to the spa and that the local authority had applied for the official designation which would enable them to add "Bad" to the name of the village. I assured him that we would welcome a guided tour but would like to sample the swimming bath first after our long hot day. He seemed disappointed and we agreed to call on him after our swim before departing. Having gained entry and the free use of towels we separated to our respective changing rooms and regrouped in the swimming pool area of the spa.

The layout was unusual in that the first part was a full-size swimming pool within the building and the remainder was open air approached through a hanging curtain of rubber strips – similar to those in a carwash. The deep end with diving boards came first and the shallow end was outside at the furthest end of the pool. One advantage of the arrangement was that there were no small children within the building to disturb adults; children were effectively banished from the spa, a prerequisite for "Bad" status, except during warmer weather.

We plunged into the pool, swam to the curtain where the depth was no more than chin height for Gaby and chest height for me; then, pushing the fronds aside, emerged into the sunlight. There were three families at the shallow end: small children, with much joyous splashing and shouting, supervised by their mothers. We stayed well away and floated on our backs enjoying the early evening air and debating how best to avoid the manager's tour when we decided to leave. I pointed out to Gaby the direction of

Schloss Hohenleuffen which the pool faced atop the alp in the far distance about a mile away. The pool gave on to several hundreds of yards of meadow extending to its lower slopes covered in trees which became denser as the ascent became steeper. A ridge of the alp formed our horizon and it was possible to see the towers of the castle above the trees just below the skyline.

As we watched, the first of the evening skydivers launched themselves from the platform of the right-hand tower which I had noted when visiting Manfred Hartmann. Clad in striking yellow and black wingsuits, a group of four divers floated in formation held aloft by the hotter air rising from the valley below. For a time, they hovered over the wooded slopes before part-closing their wings to dive towards Leuffen. As they neared us descending rapidly, they peeled off one by one to their left, spread out their wings again and landed gently in a field to the right of the spa.

"A bit like dive-bombing," I said in jest.

"I thought for a moment that they were going to come directly over us," Gaby remarked.

Several more divers in yellow and black wingsuits followed in pairs taking the same route and landing in the neighbouring field. Then, just as the novelty was starting to wear off and our attentions to wander, two more launched themselves from the platform. Descending in single file their flight path differed from those who had preceded them; their wingsuits were solid black and, instead of peeling off, they continued towards the spa. As the first in line swooped low above the shallow end of the pool he released something from his right hand, the size of a small pineapple; it fell among the family groups at the shallow end of the pool and – to my horror – exploded among them. Amid the consternation, screams of terror and pain that arose, my attention returned to the second skydiver travelling on the same path some ten seconds behind his companion. No time to hesitate. I gathered Gaby in my arms and hurled her through the curtain.

"Swim underwater to the deep end," I shouted and plunged after her. The second grenade exploded close behind me shredding the fronds of the rubber curtain. Shards of shrapnel seared my back as I submerged and swam towards shelter of the diving boards. I resurfaced next to Gaby and glanced back. The curtain, now in tatters, had taken the full force of the blast; the sides of the building to which it was attached were heavily damaged and lumps of concrete had fallen into the pool. The water at the entrance seethed where molten metal fragments were still sinking to the bottom. We were safe and relatively unscathed. My back was sore and no doubt bleeding; the full extent of the pain would come later.

We clung together treading water and could hear the sound of feet dragging across the flat roof above us. I realised that our assailant had cut it too fine and been unable to overshoot the building; he had landed heavily and was moving slowly in the direction of the car park. I hoisted myself out of the pool, snatched up my towel and hastened in bare feet towards the entrance.

"Take care. He may be armed," Gaby called after me.

In the entrance hall the spa manager had emerged, ashen-faced from his office. "Whatever has happened in the pool?" he cried, looking accusingly at me.

"Call for ambulance and doctor. There are people badly injured back there," I shouted back as I sped by. "And call the police. There's been a bomb."

I pushed aside the boy at the counter and rushed to the door hoping to engage with the bomber. I was too late; hampered by his wingsuit he was already shuffling across to the open door of a car parked across the entrance to the car park. He had cast aside his crash helmet exposing a familiar completely bald head and, as he tumbled into the waiting vehicle, I caught sight of his face; it was the same man

whom I had encountered twice at the Hohenleuffen Gasthof.
The car, a beige hatchback Audi, moved off at speed.

---ooo0ooo---

CHAPTER 28

WE WERE BACK in our room at the Gasthof nearly two hours later, both still shaken. By the time we reached there Otto Krantz had heard of the attack and had thoughtfully sent Brigitta up with two glasses of brandy.

At the spa we had tried to help and comfort the mothers and children that had suffered from the first grenade until the ambulance and a doctor arrived. One little girl had been killled outright; her mother had lost an arm and her older brother had shrapnel embedded in his chest. They were carried off by the ambulance crew to the hospital at Nurtingen while a local doctor attended to those with minor injuries including myself until a second ambulance could come. I had been lucky; the fragments lodged in my back from the second grenade were readily extracted without need for stitches and the wounds cleaned and dressed by the doctor. He also gave me a very welcome injection of painkiller with a packet of pills to take later.

The manager of the spa had kept his head but insisted rather officiously that everyone who had been in the building, mainly in the sauna or gymnasium including us, should wait in the lobby until the police had processed us. However, my old acquaintance Commissar Vogel appeared after the first hour. He looked tired, more harassed than I remembered and clearly not pleased to see me again. Learning that Gaby and I had been at the centre of the incident, he chose to banish us to the Gasthof on the understanding that he would be interviewing us later.

Perched side by side on the end of the bed I held Gaby's hand. "We need to prepare what we are going to say to the Kommissar before he arrives," I said. "I've been an overconfident fool. I should never have brought you here and exposed you to danger. I'm deeply ashamed, my love."

"Don't be an idiot. They can't have been bombing us in particular. It's not possible," she chided.

"I'm afraid it's all too possible, if you think about it. We were followed all day by the couple in the Audi hatchback: to Wiblingen monastery in the morning; then to Ulm where we lunched, to the sports shop in the afternoon; and then back towards Leuffen in the afternoon where they turned off up to the Schloss after passing us and joined the skydivers."

"Alright, I'll grant you that. But how could they possible have known that we were in the spa swimming pool at that time?"

"Not too difficult; let's follow the logic. Our moustached stalker went into the sports shop after us. No doubt he found out that we had purchased bathing suits; so, he knew that we were planning to swim. The Audi did not overtake us on the return journey until shortly before we reached Hohnleuffen; therefore, it was a fair guess we would continue down the alp to Leuffen. We can deduce that when he turned off up to the Schloss he joined the other windsurfers already there who included our friend with the bald head. He would have known that the spa swimming pool was the only one for miles around. All that they had to do then was to wait until we were actually in the pool."

"That's all very well but how could they possibly know, at that distance, that it was us in the pool?" Gaby asked.

"The perils of a fuchsia pink swimsuit. With strong field glasses they could have detected you as soon as you appeared in the open air."

"Serves me right for trying to be glamorous. From now on I'll only wear black on the beach," said Gaby with a return of her customary wit. "Do you really think the Commissar is going to believe us when we tell him all this?"

"Not for a moment, but we're not going to tell him. We stick to what actually happened at the spa?"

"Doesn't that amount to withholding police evidence?"

"Possibly," I conceded. "But the only facts we shan't disclose are the registration number of the Audi, which you took down in Ulm, and the appearance of the albino."

"Does that mean that you don't want the police to track them down?"

"I don't want to do anything to alert them before they pick up the drugs in ten days' time and Max Salinger arranges for them to be collared. And there's another reason," I added. "I don't entirely trust Kommissar Vogel. I don't think he's actually on the take, but he may be too close to Manfred Hartmann."

Gaby nodded her acceptance wearily as the full scale of the murder attempt hit her. There was no more to be said for the moment. We decided to eat something while we waited for Vogel and descended to the bar. The restaurant area was quite full but Otto Krantz had reserved a table for us well away from the crowd of locals at the bar. Conversation flagged; Otto was solicitous and Brigitta fluttered around Gaby like an oversized moth attracted to a light bulb; sidelong glances were cast in our direction from customers as we ordered.

Neither of us had much appetite; so we ordered the same meal as my first evening alone in the Gasthof: *Schwäbiche Spätzle* and a green salad.

The Kommissar and his sergeant arrived just as we were finishing. Our host unlocked the Gasthof television room and we arranged ourselves on uncomfortable upright chairs. As before, the sergeant sat at the back of the room with his notebook and took no part in the conversation.

"You've had a very unpleasant experience today," Vogel began by directing his attention to Gaby. "I hope you feel able to tell me what happened, Mrs. Radclive, - in your own words, please."

Ashen-faced and with dark smudges under her eyes, Gaby gave an unvarnished account of our last few minutes in the pool and the death and destruction visited upon us. "It was completely unexpected and, for a time, I was numbed by shock from the full horror," she concluded.

"Thank you, Mrs. Radclive. The families in the pool that you helped before the ambulance came are very grateful." He bowed his head formally and turned towards me.

"And now, Herr Radclive, I understand you ran out of the swimming bath and across the entrance hall to the car park. Very energetic, but why did you do that instead of looking after your wife?"

"That's quite simple, Kommissar. I heard the second bomber bumping across the roof where he landed. I thought I might catch him in the car park if I ran out."

"And what did you find when you reached the front door?"

"I was too late. I saw the back view of someone in a wingsuit shuffling across the car park and entering a car at the entrance."

"Did you recognize who it was? Was it a man or a woman?" "A man and definitely not someone I know."

"Can you give me a description – with the colour of his hair?"

"Medium height and a stocky build. The hood of his wingsuit was pulled up around the back of his head." I was doing my best to remain truthful.

"In that case, how do you know that the bomber was a man?"

"Kommissar, you can always tell a woman by the way she walks or runs." The painkiller was wearing off, my back was hurting again and I was beginning to feel bad-tempered.

"I agree, Herr Radclive," Vogel conceded. "Besides, we found a skydiver's helmet in the car park and it was of a large size."

"What kind of car took the bomber away and did you get the registration number?"

"It was a beige coloured hatchback – an Audi, I think – and I didn't see the number plate."

I decided to take the initiative with a tinge of sarcasm. "Have you any explanation who could have been responsible for the attack? Not the Bader Meinhoff gang this time, surely."

"No. We do realise that there are other violent criminals in Baden Württemburg," Vogel responded in kind. "There is one theory we are working on for the moment, but by no means a certainty."

"To satisfy our curiosity, would you share it with us, Kommissar?" Gaby asked sweetly, ignoring the growing antagonism which was infecting the conversation.

Kommissar Vogel seemed mollified. "Before coming here I visited Schloss Hohenleuffen. Two of the Nürtingen skydiving club were still there packing up their things. Their club wingsuits all have yellow stripes. The last two divers today were not members and the others were all down at the landing field when they jumped from the platform. Herr Manfred Hartmann corroborates their story. He was watching from his balcony and saw the whole thing. He suggested a motivation for the bombing which the other two thought possible. Are you aware the Leuffen spa is under consideration for upgrade as a Bad?"

We nodded our affirmative. "In that case," he went on. "You should know that there are people locally who are against the upgrade. Some of them fear that Leuffen will be overrun by too many visitors with new hotels, restaurants and shops springing up and destroying the village atmosphere. Others in the wider Nürtingen business community fear competition from more modern and better financed service providers. There is an Action Group which is already holding meetings and protest marches. There are hotheads among them who may have today resorted to violence."

"That's pretty far-fetched," I said.

"Have you an alternative explanation, Herr Radclive?"

"None that is any less far-fetched." At least, that was a truthful response.

Back in our bedroom, Gaby and I faced each other. "We'll take the first flight back tomorrow," I said.

"For the first time since we've been together, I'm frightened," Gaby admitted. "More for you than for me. Let's get back home as soon as we can."

"I've been a naïve idiot. I was carried away in Brazil by the exotic surroundings. From the moment I first met Roderigo Morales in his white suit, it became like some kind of a 1940's Hollywood spy movie with me as the central character. I allowed myself to be carried away by becoming involved and crossing swords with von Falkenberg; now, I'm out of my depth and, what is worse, I've got you involved too."

"Don't just feel penitent or sorry for yourself. Hand the whole thing over to Max and Henrich and don't come back here until it's all over."

"You're right. Let's hope that Max can perform. Otherwise, I'm stuck with the commitment I made to Chester Case to sort it all out."

"You'll do what you have to do. All I ask is that you remember this is no time for amateur heroes." I could see that Gaby was shivering. "Now, take your painkiller pill and let's go to bed," she said. "I'd like to be held very close tonight."

---ooo0ooo---

Surprisingly, we both slept well and it was past eight when we were roused by a discreet knock on our door. I struggled up stiffly in my pyjama trousers and found Brigitta there bearing a tray with our breakfast which she handed to me wishing us "*Guten morgen*" and reddening noticeably at the sight of my bare torso. Gaby called out thanks for her kindness from the bed. We found that we had appetites and consumed avidly the scrambled eggs, toast and jam which Brigitta and her father had thoughtfully provided with orange juice, hot water and tea bags.

Gaby opened the conversation as she swigged her first cup of tea. "Did you notice that the Kommissar's theory about the bombing was suggested by your friend Manfred Hartmann?"

"Yes. It suggests that he is back in the game. It also confirms his influence on Vogel's thought processes. Just as well that we did not give any indication of our suspicions," I replied.

I shaved and dressed quickly; then, leaving Gaby to shower and pack our bags, descended to the bar where Otto Krantz was helping Brigitta set the tables for Sunday lunch customers. He allowed me to make two local calls from his telephone behind the bar: the first to Lufthansa to change our home flight booking to that afternoon from Monday morning, the second to Heinrich. I apologized for disturbing his family Sunday at home.

"Have you heard of the bombing at Leuffen Spa yesterday evening?" I asked him. Gaby and I were in the swimming pool at the time."

"It was on the local radio news this morning; we never imagined that you were there. Are you both alright?"

"We're both fine. Gaby was unscathed and I have just a few scratches to show for it." "*Gruss Gott*," said Heinrich. "Do you know who did it?"

"I'll call you again this evening from London; we're flying back this afternoon. If anyone asks why I am not at the Flughafen tomorrow morning to meet Lloyd Parmentier, explain that I wanted to take Gaby home as soon as possible."

"I take that to mean you do know who the bombers were and that you were the target. Do you want an escort back to the airport?"

"We'll be fine, but thanks for the offer," I assured him.

I put down the receiver and, on an impulse, turned to Otto.

"Herr Krantz, I would like to ask your opinion about the bombing. Kommissar Vogel has a theory that it may have been an Action Group who don't want the spa and village to be upgraded as a Bad. Do you think that is likely?"

"That is an insulting suggestion," he replied angrily. "Yes, there are many of us who are conservationists and do not want our village to become some kind of holiday suburb and we do have an *Aktionscomitee* of which I am the Secretary. But it is a peaceful *Burgeritiative*, not a terrorist organisation. We have made a formal protest against the application in writing and will continue to campaign in public – maybe a demonstration – but nothing further."

"Perhaps there are a few fringe die-hards who have taken it upon themselves to resort to violence?" I suggested.

"*Absolut nichts.* There are no die-hards here in our group. We are civilised people in Leuffen, Herr Radclive. You know that from staying here."

"Have you any idea who might be responsible?"

"We read about neo-Nazi cells in Mŭnchen and sometimes there are reports of criminal activities. Perhaps they came here for the publicity."

Now there were two red herrings for Kommissar Vogel to pursue, I thought. Enough to keep him occupied for the next ten days.

---ooo0ooo---

Our journey back to London was uneventful. No red Porsche 911 or beige Audi on our tail. The check-in clerk at the Flughafen seemed Sunday afternoon sleepy. We languished in the departure lounge when the incoming flight from London disgorged a trickle of passengers while the aircraft was refuelled. Embarking on time with customary Lufthansa efficiency there was still a sense of relief when we took off and soared steeply into a cloudless sky.

Four hours later we were back at Porchester Terrace having dropped into A&E at St. Mary's hospital, Paddington on our way home. My back had become more painful on the flight back and needed attention. The efficient young Pakistani doctor on duty gave me an anti-tetanus jab, treated the cuts with antiseptic and waterproof dressings and gave me a packet of painkillers. Thankfully, the temperature outside had fallen to a comfortable level as the heat of the day had abated.

"You seem to have been in the wars," he said.

"Just an evening swim in a German sports centre," I replied.

"German sports training very violent, I can see." He did not question further.

It was now just after six and a good time to ring Heinrich at home. He picked up his 'phone on the third ring. "The whole incident is on the evening television news with pictures of the damage and an account by the spa manager of what happened," he told me.

"Was I mentioned by name?"

"No names but a reference to an Englander tourist and his wife who helped after the explosion. Now tell me how it occurred."

I gave Heinrich the full story of our visit to Wiblingen monastery and Ulm and how we were shadowed from the moment we arrived until the beige Audi overtook us shortly before we reached Hohenleuffen on the return journey. He agreed that our stalker had probably tuned off up to the schloss and watched out for us until we appeared in the swimming pool. I completed the tale with my attempted pursuit and recognition of the bomber from his back view as he scuttled across the park to the waiting car.

Heinrich who had kept silent during my resume gave his verdict. "*Alles ist klar*. You and Gaby were the target from the moment you left the Gasthof. If it had not been bombs at the pool, it would have been something else *schreklich* during the weekend. So, you have become a liability if we are to complete this adventure successfully."

"What do you suggest?"

"As I told you on Friday evening, you are in danger all the time in Germany. Therefore, you should leave the battlefield and not return. If Colonel Max will provide the contact details, I can raise the alarm when the shipment arrives and the consignment leaves the factory and the two of us will take care of everything as we did many times in the past. You can trust me, Julian."

"I have every confidence in you, Heinrich, but I am involved and don't want to run away."

"You English and your stupid heroics. You have a saying – 'distraction is the better part of courage'. Take that advice now," he urged.

"I know you're right," I replied, ignoring the misquotation. "I'll call you again during the week when I have Max's movements and contact details for the week following."

My next call was to Max Salinger in Sussex before he and Miranda settled down for the evening. This time I telephoned from the kitchen where Gaby was preparing a casserole for dinner and I had poured us drinks. Miranda answered and, after I had declared myself, asked how our weekend had been.

"Did you have a marvellous time?"

"It had its moments but more exciting than we had expected."

"In that case you will want to speak to Max on the other line. I'll hang on and you can pass me to Gaby when you've finished."

I repeated the complete story to Max, adding that we had met with Heinrich and Ethel and that he was keen to do whatever he could to help on the day. There was a squawk from Miranda who was still listening on an extension when I described the swimming pool bombing but Max seemed unconcerned.

"It's helpful that they have shown their hand," he commented at the end with some satisfaction. "But I'm having difficulty in convincing my people that your affair is something in which we should be involved. Not enough hard facts, you know."

"They're hard enough for us at the receiving end," I said showing some annoyance at his indifference. "If you want something more to go on, we have the numbers of the two cars involved. Perhaps Interpol can give you the names and rundown on the registered owners." I quoted the to him.

"That's something for me to get my teeth into. I'll call you during the week when there's something to report. Oh, and give my regards to Gaby; I'm sorry she was involved."

He put the receiver down at his end. I passed our telephone to Gaby so that she could continue the call with Miranda while I took my whisky into the living room to reflect. It seemed that Max's influence with MI6 might be less than he had made out. His special adviser status might be little more than the humouring of a former security legend put out to pasture. I hoped that I was wrong.

We ate Gaby's spicy casserole in the kitchen with a robust rioja to help it down and compared notes. I repeated my conversation with Max and she nodded.

"What did Miranda have to say?" I asked.

"She says that I must expect Max to find a way to keep you involved on the ground. She says that he is expert at delegating any risk to other people and that I should stay with her in their flat or go down to Bill and Barbara while you are in Germany."

"I'm having difficulty too in believing that Max will be able to perform. In which case we shall have to think again."

"Let's cross that bridge when we come to it," Gaby said wearily.

---ooo0ooo---

259

Part Three

CHAPTER 29

EARLIER THAT DAY General Wolfgang Kessler received another unwelcome telephone call at home, this time from Manfred Hartmann. They talked in English to reduce the chances of the conversation being intercepted locally and understood.

"Have you any idea of the after effects of your bungling assassins' attack on the Leuffen swimming pool yesterday?" Hartmann demanded without preamble. "Aside from the personal embarrassment of their skydiving from the schloss, the death and injury to local Leuffen residents has brought the police around our ears like a swarm of bees."

"You have reason to be angry, Manfred," the General admitted. "Willi exceeded his orders and used his initiative unwisely."

"Don't be dismissive about this, Wolfgang. The delivery next week of the shipment which I warned Frederik not to make was already risky. Now it has become highly dangerous with the spotlight on Leuffen and an American management presence in the factory."

"Frederik told me that you were not going to take part in this affair any more and that the Englishman had discovered about the shipment. He asked me to take care of Radclive when he reached Leuffen and before he could interfere. If I had thought you were still involved, of course I would have called you." The General remained conciliatory.

"Yes, I wanted the shipment to be delayed and to walk away from this business altogether but now that is impossible. In any case, having failed to enlist Radclive – a foolish endeavour in any case – Frederik has now recruited

Peter to work with Klinger and that involves me again as his father."

"Must I remind you, Manfred, that you are still a trustee of the Kamaradenwerke and that your loyalties remain to the organisation and me personally," General Kessler replied reasserting his authority.

"So, how did this excessive initiative of Willi occur?"

"On Friday afternoon Klinger informed us that Radclive was in Leuffen; that evening Willi saw him at the Hohenleuffen Gasthof having dinner with his wife and two others. This presented him with an unforeseen opportunity; yesterday morning he sent someone to follow them all the way to Ulm, where they bought swimming costumes, and back again as far as Hohenleuffen. Skydiving is a hobby which Willi enjoys. Without consulting me, he planned and led the attack, knowing that Radclive and his wife would probably be in the spa pool; you know the rest. He was over-enthusiastic but, at least, he has probably deterred Radclive from coming back next week and after that our trade with Brazil can become history."

"I think you may be optimistic, Wolfgang," Hartmann cautioned. "Having met this Julian Radclive, I would say that he is not easily deflected from his purpose and his wife is even more inquisitive."

"Very well, we will ensure that he does not leave London next week. We will ask our distributor there to take care of him until our business is over when we know that he is coming." "How will you find out?"

"I have access to the Lufthansa passenger bookings. If his name shows up from 19th June onwards, our friends in the East End of London will give us a very professional service – nothing that will cause an international incident."

"And if anything should still go wrong on the day here in Leuffen?" Hartmann asked, only partially reassured.

The General decided to acknowledge the risk, if not its extent. "Of course, there's a degree of risk. We've known each other, Manfred, for nearly forty years and faced risks *together as comrades. Under your command I am confident that our cargo will be received and delivered safely next week. But, of course, we should each have a personal contingency plan in case of failure and there is time next week to make those plans."*

"I take on this responsibility with misgivings, Wolfgang, because I have no choice but you know that I will exercise every effort to achieve a successful outcome," Hartmann replied.

"I know that I can count on you. Viel Glück und Gute Nacht," the General said, reverting to German.

General Wolfgang Kessler sat for some time afterwards, fortified by a glass of his favourite schnapps, and weighed up the situation. With Manfred back in the saddle he knew that the operation at his end would be conducted with intelligence and in meticulous detail. However, that might not be enough if the Englishman Radclive and any ally he had enlisted were to interfere actively. And interference could result in disaster – not just the confiscation of the consignment but the arrest of those involved in handling the drugs by the Polizei. Worse still, the trafficking would almost certainly be traced back to the Kamaradenwerke involving him personally. There were three conclusions: first, he must instruct the distributor in London to prevent Radclive from leaving London by kidnap or termination – it did not matter which – and he would call them tomorrow; second, if the balloon went up Manfred was unlikely to escape arrest; third, and most important, the trail would lead inevitably to him and he should make his preparations accordingly.

He already had his contingency plan. After von Falkenberg had called him at the beginning of the month he had opened an account with Hong Kong and Shanghai Bank and transferred a substantial sum; he had put most of his investments into bearer bonds, now sitting in the wall safe behind him; finally he had bought open air tickets to Bangkok for Gretchen and himself and travellers cheques to the value of twenty thousand dollars. A shame about Manfred, he thought; professionally a good field officer but a poor strategist. He'd always liked him since they were first at the military academy together in happier times so many years ago.

---oooOooo---

12 to 18 June, London

After the drama of the weekend the week following was uneventful. When I reached the office on Monday morning, Tom was already there, struggling with the May month-end financials and 'Where do I stand' reports. Surprised to see me back early, his reaction to the story of our Saturday escapade was predictable. "You're in the frame, Julian, as I warned you. One thing is quite clear: you're not going to Leuffen next week."

"I've already promised Gaby that if Max Salinger is authorised to run the operation I'll leave it all to him and Heinrich. After all, they've worked together as a team in the past and we'd only be in the way," I assured him, being careful to confirm that there was no place for Tom either in the proceedings. He looked unconvinced but there was nothing more he could say.

Later, as soon as the Farmington office was open, I called Viktor Accona and repeated my account of the weekend's events once again. He made appropriate noises of shock and concern but they sounded mechanical. His only question was whether or not Heinrich Hoffmeyer had agreed to participate in the action at Leuffen on 22nd June. Satisfied that Henrich was onside, he told me that he would report immediately to Chester Case and call back. Within the hour Chester himself ws on the line.

"Julian, I'm horrified that you and your wife were almost killed on Saturday. Are you both OK? There's no way I would have wished you to expose yourself to physical

264

danger," he said, sounding genuinely solicitous. "From now on in, you will keep out of the firing line and away from Germany until this is safely over. Viktor tells me that you have it all set up with your secret service friend and Heinrich to catch the drug dealers with their haul away from the factory. You've delivered on your promise to me; just sit back and monitor what happens at a distance."

"Thank you, Chester," I replied. "It should be alright next week but I shan't begin to relax until the logistics are confirmed."

"Understood. Call again when you're confident that you have all the bases covered," he directed. "Oh and, Julian, give my regards to your wife."

---ooo0ooo---

On Tuesday and Wednesday my days at the office were mainly occupied with the DES catalogue programme. The Ribenda team had sent me their specification for the spring product range to be stocked and offered for sale. They had included the complete range of compression and extension springs from the US catalogue and identified what they could manufacture themselves for stock. The remainder would be sourced from Hartmann & Holst and AA Norrköping as we had agreed in Rio. The spring washer range from the US catalogue had also been included and I was asked to suggest opening inventory levels both for Ribenda as master stockist and for the three other European plants. I had no idea of how much stock should be held and consulted with Bennett Pullman; he undertook to find out by part number what usage the various US plants had experienced in the early years of their trading since launching DES. Ribenda had retained the English language text alongside the specification while they prepared their Dutch edition of the catalogue; so I circulated copies by airmail to AA Norrköping and to Heinrich at Hartmann & Holst and by letter post to Cyril Snell at Tipton Springs asking the first two to prepare Swedish and German language editions and all three to declare whether they wanted to include any other items from the American version.

Cyril had invited me to attend the interviews of shortlisted candidates to replace Bernard Tompkins on Thursday and by the time I left for Tipton early that morning I had still not heard from Max Salinger which gave me growing cause for unease. I resolved to call him the following morning if there was no news by then.

Unlike my last visit to Tipton for Bernard's funeral the weather was fine, an early summer's day with only light traffic on the roads after leaving London. I reached the factory shortly before 10:00 and found Cyril in his rather untidy office. Strewn across his desk was a file of papers, not relating to Tipton Springs as I would have expected, but to a complex case of burglaries which were due to come before him as a local Justice of the Peace the following day. I wondered how compatible his part-time role as Chairman of the Bench was with his job as General Manager and whether Farmington was aware of his extra curricula activity.

There were three candidates for Sales Manager whom we interviewed in the Board Room, an ill-lit oppressive chamber with dark oak panelling and matching heavy table and chairs. From Cyril's notes and their written applications, I found that two of them were external candidates and the third was a Tipton employee who had worked as Bernard Tompkins' assistant and customer service manager; he was carrying on as interim manager currently. The first to be interviewed was the sales manager of a smaller springmaker from Redditch, a colourless man who had been with his employer for more than ten years and had achieved less than little for his company. The second interviewee was superficially more attractive; he was the senior representative for a major Midlands manufacturer of automotive components responsible for key accounts with car and truck OEMs throughout the UK. Confident, rather brash and in early middle age, he displayed some of Bernard's bounce and made a good impression. However, he was looking for a higher salary than the Tipton job description and a big expenses allowance for the entertainment of customers way beyond AA guidelines. Also, there was no track record of achievement in developing new customers which is what Tipton Springs was looking for to achieve AA targets. That left Bernard's deputy as a serious contender. At least existing customers knew him by telephone contact, but how would he fare face to face? Appearances were against him; tall and gangling with a beard and an irritating nervous laugh, it was difficult to imagine customers taking to him however detailed his knowledge of their business. Today for his interview he was wearing tan suede desert boots with an electric blue suit which aroused my prejudice although I tried not to let it colour my judgement.

So far Cyril Snell had relied on regional Press advertising to attract candidates and it was clear that something more was required. The position wasn't really senior enough to justify the expense of employing a recruitment consultant or 'head hunter' but that might be the only way to make a good appointment. It would require Tom Hardy's approval and I undertook to discuss with Tom the next day.

Mulling it over on the drive back to London and applying some lateral thinking I was struck by another possibility. Bernard Tompkins' son Arthur, whom Tom and I had met at the funeral, had expressed an interest in moving from his job in Canada to join Associated Autoparts and Viktor Accona had offered to put him in contact with Erik Nielson. Although Arthur was a qualified accountant he might like the idea of moving back to England and working in the same town as his family. The merit, from the AA point of view, would be that he would inherit some of the goodwill that his father had generated with Tipton Springs customers. He was personable and intelligent; although he had no experience of the spring industry he would be able to acquire the product knowledge in the same way as I was doing myself. I would put the idea to Tom as an alternative to head-hunting.

I reached Porchester Terrace well before 6:00 p.m. and found Gaby busy planning her tour around the European markets of her German client to help set up their washing machine research programme. The plan was to complete staff briefings on the ground during the first half of July before the main summer holiday period. During the afternoon there had been a telephone message at the office from Max Salinger asking me to call him which Molly had passed on.

---ooo0ooo---

When I reached Max at home half an hour later I found him in positive mood.

"I've had difficulty in convincing my masters that the Leuffen drugs delivery requires my attention; they said that I should hand it over to Interpol and not to interfere," he said.

"So why are you so cheerful, Max?" I enquired.

"Your car registration numbers have made the difference. The Porsche is registered to one Willi Schmidt and the Audi to the Kamaradenwerke in Munich. Schmidt is a known associate of General Wolfgang Kessler, the Kamaradenwerke president. We have been after that organization for more than thirty years and its involvement makes our theory of payment in gold for the drugs the more plausible. And so, 'the game's afoot' and I am authorized to proceed."

I stifled an image of Max in a deerstalker with magnifying glass and meerschaum pipe. I was beginning to doubt whether the incident was anything more than a game for Max.

"Have you made all your arrangements for next week?" I asked.

"Not yet. I have to be in contact with Stuttgart tomorrow morning and the deployment of their special squad will have to be authorized too," he admitted. "However, I should have everything in place by Monday; I plan to fly out there on Wednesday, a day ahead of the shipment delivery. Will you meet me on Tuesday for the details and final briefing – this time at the SOE club in Hans Crescent at lunchtime?"

I readily agreed and, mindful of Miranda's caution to Gaby, decided not to tell Max that I had been ordered not to be there in Leuffen with him the following week. Time enough to tell him on Tuesday; for now, I would do nothing to deflect him from his purpose.

The following morning I reported to Tom Hardy on the interviewing at Tipton and we discussed the recruitment alternatives for Bernard Tompkins' successor. Tom liked my suggestion of appointing Arthur Tompkins as sales manager and agreed to call Erik Nielsen on his availability.

During the day word came from Floyd Parmentier on the last leg of his tour of Hartmann & Holst major customers summoning Tom and myself to meet with him at the London office first thing on Monday morning. We speculated about the outcome of Floyd's tour and reached no conclusion except that it must have gone badly.

And so the week ended. Gaby and I spent an evening at the theatre on Saturday and on Sunday paid a visit to the Royal Horticultural Society gardens at Wisley for lunch and a relaxed stroll around the grounds, enjoying the display of rhododendrons and camelias now past their best. A lull before the storm of the week to follow.

---ooo0ooo---

CHAPTER 30

19 and 20 June, London

LLOYD PARMENTIER, Tom Hardy and I were grouped around Tom's desk in his cramped office at 8:00 on Monday morning. The office was empty except for the three of us and I had put on the percolator for coffee. Lloyd was in his AA travelling uniform of blazer, grey worsted trousers and loafers; he had left his luggage in the lobby and would be on a midday flight back to Boston. We settled down rather uncomfortably with our coffee and Lloyd started the meeting; he was deceptively casual about his week with Peter Hartmann.

"I made notes on each visit. If your secretary will type them up before I leave for Heathrow, you may take copies; for now, let's cut to the chase," he said, placing his hands flat on the desk and flexing his fingers. "The bottom line is that Hartmann & Holst is not the preferred supplier at any of its major customers except for Robert Bosch and there only for injector nozzle springs. It may have been once for Volkswagen valve springs but only Grunwald in Brazil has that status now. Gentlemen, AA has a big problem which we have to address immediately."

"Does ownership by Allied Autoparts carry weight?" Tom asked.

"Yes, but not at all to our advantage in the short term. Heinrich Hoffmeyer was right when he told us that the customers expect us to invest more in capital equipment in order to contain prices."

"In that case, immediate price increases are out of the question?" I hazarded.

"We have a choice: wait until the next annual round of price negotiations this fall or cut off those parts which are heavy losers. We have three months to get our act together.

Cutting off now will damage relationships and make it unlikely that Hartmann & Holst is offered the opportunity to quote for new parts."

"What do you intend?" Tom asked again.

Floyd clenched his fists, placed them on the desk and gave us an unblinking stare. "The corporate office has accepted my recommendations. So, I'll lay it out for you now. We're sending a task force to Leuffen for a month to restructure, cut overhead costs and streamline manufacturing methods. There will be a limited capital expenditure budget. I will direct the task force myself; it will arrive in Leuffen a week today."

We heard Molly Fellows arrive in the outer office and Tom called her in to type up Lloyd's handwritten notes and order a taxi to take him to the airport in an hour's time.

"We come now to the line management on which I have Farmington's agreement," Floyd resumed. "Peter Hartmann will leave the company this week. He brings nothing to the party and I don't want him around when the task force arrives. It's your job, Tom, to arrange his departure without hassle and to start the recruitment process for a new general manager. If you want advice about separation terms, ask Viktor. We also need an experienced sales manager. I want you to start the executive searches today; telex me your draft job descriptions for approval by the end of your day."

"Tell us more about how the task force will operate," Tom prompted. He was doing his best to hide his pique that he had not been included in the decision- making.

"The first wave coming with me will be Loren Corley to work on manufacturing methods with Heinrich, Shelley Frankel to review the procurement and purchasing function and one of Erik Nielsen's senior bean counters to install the AA management accounting system working with Dieter Trautman. I shall focus on cutting fixed costs. You will need to book accommodation at the local inn for the first few nights and then a local house or flat for the team which they can rent to self-cater for the duration." Lloyd had finished what he came to say and looked at each of us in turn. "Any questions?" he asked.

"You're very clear," Tom replied. "No doubt there will be questions later; plenty for us to do now. I'll fly out this afternoon and Julian can follow later in the week if required."

Then, demonstrating his resolve, he called out to Molly to book his flight when she had finished typing Lloyd's notes and to make a reserve booking for me to follow him on Wednesday morning. We despatched Lloyd with his notes and luggage to the airport half an hour later and re-grouped in Tom's office.

"Well, you have to say that he's decisive and convinced of what he is doing," I said.

"All a bit military for me," Tom replied. "He's seen too many American war movies. I expected him to say 'Now listen up' at any moment. However, we have our marching orders and had better get on with it."

"What can I do to help while you're tied up in Leuffen?"

"When I have arranged the logistics for the task force this week and, hopefully your business is done, we should keep away until summoned. This is Lloyd's party and he's positioned himself politically to his career advantage. Whatever the outcome, he'll came out smelling of roses. From next week you and I, Julian, will start working with the other three companies on preparing their business plans for next year. The Learjet group will be back in September to review them."

"Tell me how you think that Lloyd is playing the Hartmann & Holst situation tactically to his own advantage," I asked.

"He wins either way. If his task force succeeds in restoring the company to profitability Lloyd becomes the corporate hero. If they fail in their combined effort and it continues to run at a loss, he will have shown that buying Hartmann & Holst was a bad decision for which Barry

MacLennan – and Chester Case too – are responsible. One step nearer to supplanting Barry."

I could follow Tom's logic: devious rather than naked ambition, not at odds with my impressions to date of Lloyd Parmentier. Together, Tom and I drafted the job descriptions for General Manager and Sales Manager and telexed them to Farmington to await Lloyd's return. Tom's Lufthansa air ticket was delivered around midday and he left the office for home to pack a bag before driving to Heathrow.

Early afternoon I received a telephone call from Viktor. This time he made no reference to the previous weekend's events in Leuffen. "Are all the arrangements for Thursday in place?" he asked.

"I shall be given the contact details and telephone numbers tomorrow which I will pass on to Heinrich; my SOE friend Max has confirmed that he will be there in Stuttgart waiting for the alert," I replied.

"That's good, Julian. It needs to be all out of the way before Floyd and his task force arrive. Chester has asked me to say that he and Barry rely on you for a successful outcome." He had nothing more to say except that he was ready to advise Tom on the terms of Peter Hartmann's dismissal.

Driving home across Hyde Park at the end of the day I turned on the car radio to a pop music channel. The studio disk jockey was playing the current Abba hit; "*Take a chance on me*" they sang. How true, I thought, and switched channels to the news.

---ooo0ooo---

Gaby voiced some of my misgivings that evening as we spent a companionable evening in the flat. "Do you really think that Max can pull it off?" she asked.

"And how will Lloyd Parmentier react when he finds out afterwards that he wasn't informed?"

"Both good questions. I shall have a better idea of whether or not it will go well after I've met with Max tomorrow. As to Lloyd, there's not much he can say if all goes well. I was acting under Chester Case's orders," I replied.

"And if it doesn't go according to plan?"

"Let's keep our glasses more than half full, my love," I said, reaching for the bottle of Chilean Cabernet Sauvignon.

---ooo0ooo---

There was a telex waiting addressed to Tom Hardy when I reached the office on Tuesday morning. Lloyd Parmentier had made several unnecessary tweaks to the job descriptions we had drafted and told him to instruct AA's favoured executive search consultants in Europe to start their hunt for both Hartmann & Holst positions. I called Tom in Leuffen and read the telex to him. The head hunters, based in London, were the same firm that had recruited me and Tom asked me to contact them on his behalf. Of more interest was his news that Peter Hartmann had resigned of his own accord and had left the company with an agreement to pay his salary up to the month-end. That was a quick win for Tom but I wondered how involved Peter would be in the receipt and onward delivery of the drugs consignment in two days' time.

Shortly after 12:30 I took a taxi to the Knightsbridge end of Sloane Street and walked the last few hundred yards up Basil Street, bearing left at the top opposite Harrods towards Hans Crescent. The row of Edwardian redbrick houses facing me, more of an arc than a crescent linking Basil Street to Pavilion Road, were tall and narrow with steps up to each front door. Front room bay windows in the single frontages were well above street level providing observation posts for inmates. I found the house number that Max had given me and mounted the steps. There was no distinguishing plate on the front door; only a voice entry pad which I pressed and identified myself as "Julian

Radclive for Colonel Salinger". An answering bleep enabled me to push the door open. The entrance hall was dingy with a coat rack to the left and a steep staircase facing visitors. There was an underlying scent of cabbage and floor polish. To the right a narrow passage led to the nether regions and a single door to the front room at which Max appeared.

"There you are, Julian. Come in," he said. Today, he was less formally dressed than usual in a tweed jacket and cavalry twill trousers with regimental tie. "I came up to Town this morning to see you," he explained. He led me to a round table in the bay. The rest of the room was furnished with three more tables and chairs with a well-stocked bar at the back. The only other occupant was an elderly man with a military moustache behind the bar picking runners from a copy of last weekend's *Green'un.*

"We're quite secure here. Fred's rather deaf and is trained not to remember anything he hears," Max continued nodding towards the bar. "Let's get down to the basics before we order something to eat. Have there been any developments on your side since we spoke last Thursday?" he asked.

"Nothing in Leuffen except that Peter Hartmann has resigned as general manager – he would have been sacked otherwise. We assume that he's still involved in the trafficking although obviously of less use. At this end, after attempt on Gaby's and my life, I've been instructed by our chairman to keep away from Leuffen until after the drug bust. That means that Heinrich Hoffmeyer will be your contact there after today. I'm sorry but there's nothing I can do about it," I answered.

Max did not seem particularly perturbed. "You poor chap," he said. "You'll miss the fun. Of course, we'll manage without you and you can join in afterwards when we get to tracking down the Kamaradenwerke gold."

At that moment it came to me that the drug trafficking was no more than a curtain raiser for Max: the hors d'oeuvres to his main course of a gold hunt. I hoped that he was not taking it too lightly. The conversation that followed gave me limited reassurance. Before resuming he gave a shout to Fred at the bar and ordered us shepherd's pie with cheese and biscuits to follow, accompanied by pints of draught bitter drawn from the bar.

"We shall use codenames for this exercise, of course. Heinrich shall be Horatio, Klaus Kramm is Claudius and I shall be Hamlet. In case we have to call you from Claudius's car radio, you had better be Polonius," Max decreed.

"What about the opposition?"

"No need to give them cover. It's our communications that matter. We'll refer to their leader on the ground, Klinger, as Yorick. Now, these are the telephone numbers that Heinrich needs to call when the shipment arrives at the factory and then when the drug consignment is taken away by Klinger." He handed me a card with the two numbers and I added to it the codenames which I was to pass on to Henrich later. Gaby described it later as 'cloak and dagger' but I supposed it was necessary. In return, I gave Max Heinrich's telephone numbers at home and the factory,

Arrangements for the day were straightforward. The first number was Polizeihauptmeister Kramm's direct office line to which Heinrich was to report arrival of the container at the factory. On receipt, Klaus Kramm and Max would drive to Nurtingen where Kramm's SEK team would be installed since early Thursday morning in an undercover outpost opposite the Hartmann & Holst gates. The second telephone number was the outpost's radio line which Heinrich was to call when he could see that the consignment was about to leave. There was no obvious flaw in the plan but I still felt uneasy, perhaps because I had no direct part to play.

The shepherd's pie – with cabbage – delivered from the nether regions was surprisingly good. As we were finishing our meal two pairs of newcomers entered the bar: three men and one woman of late middle-age. They all seemed to know Max, smiling or nodding to him with varying degrees of friendliness as they arrived; nondescript in their appearance, only the flat glazing of eyes behind their smiles set them apart from normal acquaintances. What was the collective noun for spooks, I wondered? A 'simulation of spies' perhaps?

When I left, Max saw me to the front door; I wished him good luck and meant it. I needed time to think through everything that had happened since Bernard Tompkins' death in case we had missed some critical angle; so, I decided to leave the Volvo at the office overnight and walk home across the Park. I retraced my steps down Basil Street to the bottom of Sloane Street and crossed Brompton Road to the corner of Knightsbridge. As always at this time of year the pavement was crowded with foreign tourists but I was dimly aware of a burly figure behind me in a pork pie hat, the only pedestrian with a head covering. Having traversed Knightsbridge, I entered Hyde Park at the side of Bowater House and crossed South Carriage Drive intending to walk round the Serpentine and exit by Victoria Gate on the north side. It was then that I realised I was being followed; the man in the pork pie hat was thirty yards behind me and closing steadily. Instead, I turned left and quickened my pace with the idea of walking up to West Carriage Drive and flagging down a taxi on its way across the park from Kensington to Bayswater. However, there was a second figure in motorcycle leathers advancing on me from that direction and so I reverted to my original plan of circumnavigating the Serpentine anti-clockwise. It seemed clear that my followers were intent on interception rather than shadowing at a distance.

Two horses and their riders from Knightsbridge Barracks, harnesses jingling, were trotting down Rotten Row; I scampered across in front of them and set off half walking and half running. Why, I asked myself, was I being attacked again, this time in London, when I had decided to stay put for the rest of the week?

The answer came to me as I rounded the east end of the Serpentine: I had forgotten to cancel the reservation for my flight to Stuttgart the next morning and this was an attempt to prevent me from flying. No doubt someone in the Kamaradenwerke had access to Lufthansa booking lists. Looking back I was pleased to find that pork pie's pace was flagging and the distance between us had lengthened; as a heavier and probably older man he was unable to keep up. There was no sign of the second man and I assumed that he had turned back in order cut me off as I completed my circuit.

Unable to maintain my gruelling pace, I modified it to alternate walking and running as I struggled up the north side of the lake. The park was almost empty, aside from a group of hardy swimmers from the swimming club on the far side; the sight of a man in a business suit puffing and panting along in obvious discomfort attracted little attention from the one or two passers-by. There were only four vehicles in the car park at the edge of the water as I neared the bridge over which the West Carriage Drive passed on its way across the Serpentine.

Three of the cars were empty; in the backseat of the fourth a couple were occupied in their own intense social activity. No hope of attracting attention there. Ahead of me on the bridge I could see a parked motorcycle with the rider leaning on the railings: my second pursuer waiting for me. There was only one way to avoid him. I jogged on under the bridge and followed the pathway alongside the continuing stretch of water into Kensington Gardens. The Long Water end of the lake finished just short of the elevated water garden with its cluster of fountains. I climbed the few steps, dodged between the playing jets of water and exited on the footpath through the pedestrian Marlborough Gate. As I dashed across the Bayswater Road between passing traffic, I half-expected to see a motorbike bearing down on me; in my pursuer's absence I feared that he had the address of the flat and was heading for Porchester Terrace to wait for me there. I needed to warn Gaby urgently.

I took a few deep breaths, straightened my tie and, walking normally, strode up the entrance ramp to the Royal Lancaster Hotel. There was a bank of telephone booths at the rear of the foyer under the overhang of its balustraded first floor; I selected one which offered an uninterrupted view of comings and goings. With my telephone credit card I called the flat and was relieved when Gaby picked up on the fourth ring.

"I'm under attack and you're possibly in danger as we speak," I said. "Listen carefully and don't say anything until I've finished. I'm calling from the Royal Lancaster Hotel down the road. I want you to take my briefcase from the study with my passport and travellers' cheques; then pack a bag for me and an overnight case for yourself – enough clothes for two days. After that, take them down to the garage in the lift, load them into the Capri and drive here as quickly as you can. Whatever else you do, on no account open the door or allow anyone into the building."

"Julian, I won't ask questions now but there's someone on the entry phone with a delivery. What should I do?" Gaby asked.

"Nothing. Ignore it and start packing. I'll call you back in ten minutes." I disconnected and called the office.

"Molly, I'm not coming back today and I shan't be in tomorrow. Have there been any messages for me?" I was speaking too quickly and she sensed that there was something amiss.

"A despatch rider called at the desk with a bouquet for Gaby. When I told him that you weren't here, he asked where he could deliver to her in person and I gave him the flat address. I shouldn't have done that, should I?" Molly asked, sounding worried.

"That's alright. Now, book seats for Gaby and me on the first BA flight to Frankfurt tomorrow morning, but leave the Lufthansa flight reservation to Stuttgart on hold overnight. I'll deal with that later. And if anyone else calls, say that you expect me back in the morning."

"Julian, I don't understand what's happening but please take care."

I rang Gaby again. "Slight change of plan. Bring your passport too. You're coming with me to Frankfurt. All will be revealed when you pick me up. I'll be waiting for you at the hotel entrance. Drive normally so as not to attract attention. Oh, one more thing – I love you."

"Me too. I hear and I obey," she said.

There was enough time before Gaby arrived to book somewhere for us to spend the night. I wanted to avoid the airport hotels where attackers would surely look for us; so, I telephoned The Compleat Angler at Marlow and was pleased to find that they had one double room left in the main building which they would hold for us until six o'clock. I was on the forecourt of the hotel when Gaby drove up the ramp and brought the Capri to a halt just fifteen minutes later.

"Were you followed?" I asked as I sat down in the passenger seat.

"I don't think so. I drove out of the garage slowly and looked left and right carefully before turning on to the road. There was a motorcyclist at the entryphone looking up at our flat but he didn't seem to take much notice."

Gaby was wearing a polka dot scarf tucked into the neck of her navy blue jumpsuit with her hair bundled up under one of my tweed flatcaps. At a distance and through the windscreen of a motor car I thought that she could have been taken for a man.

"Carry on spying," I commented.

"All in a day's work. After all, what else is market research?" Gaby joked.

----oooOooo----

CHAPTER 31

20 and 21 June, London and Leuffen

WE TURNED ONTO the Bayswater Road heading west and I brought Gaby up to date. "So, what's the plan?" she asked. As we came up to Notting Hill, I directed her to turn left down Kensington Church Street.

"The idea is that we fly by BA to Frankfurt from Terminal 1 while they look for us at the Lufthansa check-in at Terminal 2."

"And what happens when we get to Frankfurt?"

"We hire a car from Hertz and drive down the Autobahn past Stuttgart to Leuffen. If we drive fast, we should reach there early afternoon," I explained.

As we passed by the entrance to Kensington Palace Gaby peered in the rear view mirror, cursed and exclaimed that she thought we were being followed. I turned in my seat and looked back; sure enough there was a motorcycle on our tail. I couldn't be certain but the bike and helmet of the rider seemed familiar. At the bottom of the hill the traffic lights turned orange and then red bringing the traffic to a halt behind us as we slowed.

"What do we do now?" Gaby asked.

"Turn right when the lights change, and pretend we haven't noticed him," I advised. "We'll find some way of shaking him off before we reach Hammersmith."

"I've got a better idea. I'm fed up with being a sitting duck," she said.

Gaby indicated that we were turning right, waited until the lights turned green and stayed put. The traffic behind hooted and when the lights turned orange she moved off slowly before engaging in low gear and accelerating. The motorcyclist moved up on our inside and attempted to turn with us as the lights went to red. With a flick of her wrist

Gaby turned the steering wheel left and the Capri struck the rider sharply on his right leg; the bike skittered off onto the pavement kerb outside Derry and Toms department store unseating its rider. I looked back as we sped off and viewed the commotion behind us among pedestrians with all traffic halted.

"Atta girl. That was neatly done," I said with satisfaction.

"Bang goes my no claim bonus if someone took our numberplate," Gaby replied.

---ooo0ooo---

The rest of our journey to Marlow passed without incident. Gaby took us to the Cromwell Road with a series of back doubles and we sailed over the Hammersmith flyover within the speed limit. Once on the M4 she opened up a bit and we slid into the car park of the Compleat Angler at 17:45. From our comfortable room overlooking the river I made two further calls: the first to Heinrich Hoffmeyer at home to tell him we were coming tomorrow; the second to Max Salinger who was now back in Sussex. Heinrich was concerned by the afternoon's events and the new threat to our safety; he insisted that we should stay with him and Ethel where we would be less exposed rather than at the Gasthof. Predictably, Max was less concerned than pleased at the additional support on the ground. "Good to have you on board. You must be delighted to be joining the party," was how he put it. I gave him a description of our two pursuers who would probably be waiting for us to check-in at Terminal 2 and he assured me that he would have them picked up by an MI5 snatch team in the morning before flying out himself.

I decided not to telephone Farmington; plenty of time to call Viktor Accona from Leuffen when there was progress to report. I tried unsuccessfully to reach Tom Hardy at the Gasthof and had to leave a message with Otto Krantz for him to call Heinrich. I thought it unwise to tell Otto that we were coming back. We took an early dinner in the room, ordering from the limited room service menu - overpriced and delivered by a ham-fisted and unsmiling middle-aged waitress. She had brought the wrong wine but, at least, it was red and I didn't have the heart to send it back. After dinner we strolled along the river bank in the twilight enjoying the sound of the river running over the weir and wondering what challenges the next two days would bring. On the way back to the room I paid our bill in preparation for an early start.

In the morning, we flew in to Frankfurt Flughafen at about midday local time. At the Hertz desk they had a wide range of motorcars for hire; using my AA Hertz credit card I picked out a Mercedes of the same model and colour as Peter Hartmann's. Beyond my pay grade and no doubt cause for criticism by the Farmington bean counters at the end of the month, but we wanted to travel fast and I thought it might be a good idea when parking at the Leuffen factory to be mistaken for Peter. From the Flughafen we drove directly on to the autobahn and I put my foot down, travelling at just below the speed limit of 150 km per hour for much of the time. We pulled into the Hartmann & Holst car park well before 16:00 and hastened to the General Managers office where we found Tom and Heinrich, both looking disturbed with Heinrich on the telephone; from the tone I could tell that he was talking insistently and with urgency in rapid German.

"What's the problem?" I asked after Tom greeted us perfunctorily. For once, the calm surface of his Norfolk farmer's mien had shattered.

"More than a problem. We have a crisis," he said. "Trans Alpina delivered the container two hours ago and Heinrich can't reach your friend Salinger."

"That's not surprising. He's on the afternoon Lufthansa flight arriving about now. But how on earth did the shipment get to be delivered a day early?"

"My first thought too. I had Dieter Trautman call them on the pretext of an invoice query. It seems that Manfred Hartmann telephoned them last Friday and asked them to accelerate delivery as a favour. They didn't question the request because Manfred had been a regular contact over the years."

"So, the Prince of Darkness is involved again," Gaby said. "What difference does that make?"

"It means that we are up against a superior opponent locally. Not just Peter with Gottfried Klinger and Glock. He's already moved the goalposts," Tom answered.

Heinrich had put down the telephone in frustration. "I can't connect with the Polizeihauptmeister. He's not in his office," he reported.

"He's probably in his car being driven to the Flughafen to meet Max," I hazarded. "Can't they patch you through to his car radio?"

"Not can't – won't. They will contact him and ask him to call back here on this line."

"In that case we must face up to the possibility that they will transport the drugs away from here when the factory closes and before the Polizei can get here." Tom was regaining an air of authority.

"Agreed. Let's put ourselves in Manfred Hartmann's shoes and think how he is likely to organize things when Klinger and Glock have taken them away in whatever packaging they have," I said. "I don't see them in the warehouse now when they could be interrupted breaking the drugs consignment down into smaller packages for delivery to individual distributors. They could do that this evening after the factory closes for the weekend, but more likely that they will take the goods away in bulk as they were packed originally in Brazil."

"Then they will have to take the consignment as it is all the way in a company van to Munich or to some sorting venue along the way."

"Since Herr Hartmann is directing the operation for the Kamaradenwerke personally, he will want to discharge his duties as near to home as he dares," Henrich suggested.

"And where do you think that might be?" Tom asked.

The four of us looked at each other. "The Hohenleuffen hunting lodge!" we exclaimed together.

---ooo0ooo---

In the next half hour we fleshed out our contingency plan. If there was still no word from Max or the Polizeihauptmeister's office before Klinger and Glock left with their consignment, Tom and I would give them a head start, drive up close to the hunting lodge, conceal the car and monitor what was happening. If they weren't there we would come back and admit failure. Heinrich and Gaby would hang on for the call and direct the police to the hunting lodge if we were still absent.

Promptly at 17:00 the factory workers began to leave, walking or bicycling if they lived nearby; others left by car or on motorcycles. Within twenty minutes only the van remained outside the blimp, presumably with Klinger and Glock inside. Fifteen minutes later they emerged and loaded the van with eight heavy- looking wooden boxes before driving off and turning right outside the gate. Still no call from Stuttgart. We gave them five minutes; then Tom and I drove our cars up to the Gasthof, left the more noticeable Mercedes there and proceeded in Tom's modest Golf. Before leaving the Mercedes Tom asked me to open the boot and extracted a heavy tyre lever from the toolkit.

"We don't know what we shall be up against; best to be prepared," he said.

Driving up the hill to Hohenleuffen we found a turn-off where we could leave the Golf not too far below the track leading to the hunting lodge and parked with the bonnet of the Golf in undergrowth. Tom took his raincoat from the back seat so that he could hold the tyre lever against his left leg through the pocket of the coat and we clambered up through the trees for several minutes, aiming to approach the lodge from the rear. 'Hunting lodge' was too grandiose a description for the building we came upon. It was constructed from weather beaten timber with the sides fashioned from logs, double doors under a porch overhang with a stovepipe chimney poking from the fibre covered roof: really no more than a large log cabin. Three vehicles were parked in the clearing in front of the porch: the factory van, Peter Hoffman's white Mercedes and a familiar beige Audi Avant.

We edged our way along the one side of the cabin which had windows set high in the wall and peered cautiously, on tiptoe in my case, at the scene inside.

Across the far end of the single room there was a long trestle table upon which Klinger and Glock were placing plastic packs from the boxes brought up from the Hartmann & Holst warehouse. On the opposite side of the table, furthest from us, were the man with the toothbrush moustache who had followed Gaby and me around Ulm and the hairless Willi Schmitt. They were occupied in repacking smaller batches of packets containing white powder into canvas holdalls. Halfway up the cabin and across from us a cast iron stove was set against the wall and close by Manfred Hartmann was seated in a wing chair. He was smoking a cigar and seemed bored by the proceedings. Under the window on our side, with his back to the room, Peter Hartmann was restless, sometimes prowling restlessly in front of the table and waving his hands, apparently issuing orders to which no-one paid attention.

We watched for about twenty minutes while Klinger and Glock finished their unpacking, and loaded the empty boxes back into the company van. Klinger returned to the cabin to join in the repacking and we heard Glock starting up and turning the van round before driving off, presumably back down to the factory. The repacking of cocaine packets into holdalls continued.

I tugged Tom's sleeve and motioned him to kneel down so that we could talk. "How much longer do you think they'll be here?" I whispered.

"Less than an hour, I'd say," he whispered back.

"In that case, unless the cavalry has already set out from Stuttgart, they'll be gone before relief arrives. We'll have to do something."

"Give it another half hour or so in the hope that Salinger and his forces arrive. If not, let's move in and hope to delay them a bit longer." I nodded agreement.

Forty minutes later we heard another vehicle draw up in front the lodge. Peering round the side of the lodge we saw Glock emerge from Klinger's Opel Rekord and go inside. We crept back to our window and looked in again; the repacking task was almost complete with only a small pile of packets remaining on the table. If we were going to achieve anything, now was the time to intervene; I led the way with Tom close behind.

Strolling in I tried to appear casual. "Peter, you said I must visit your hunting lodge some time. We saw your car as we were passing – and here we are." Then, looking around the room:

"Good evening everybody. I hope we haven't interrupted anything?"

They all stopped what they were doing and Peter Hartmann's mouth fell open. Manfred Hartmann was the first to recover, matching my attempt at nonchalance.

"Good evening, Mr. Radclive. What a pleasant surprise." Suave and sardonic as usual, he was relaxed in his wing chair, legs crossed as if waiting to be amused. "And Mr. Hardy too; we're honoured."

"I found the invitation which was almost delivered to me in London yesterday quite irresistible," I said.

"On the contrary; that was meant to be a pressing invitation to stay in London. But I'm sure you know that very well."

"So hard to find good messenger boys these days."

"Before we get down to more serious business – 'brass tacks' as I think you British like to call it," Hartmann continued "I do want to apologize to you and your wife for the crude and quite unnecessary attack on you at the swimming pool the Saturday before last. I assure you that was not at my direction – an overenthusiastic initiative by a member of staff. I really do not bear any malice towards you personally, believe me Mr. Radclive."

I almost believed him. "Not your style I agree. Apology accepted but not, I think, by the family of the little boy who was killed. I'd like to have a word with Willi while we are all here this evening." I glanced in Willi Schmitt's direction across the trestle table.

"I see that you have been investigating the organisation whose work I am reluctantly supervising and I conclude that you will have other forces unfriendly to us following behind you." Hartmann's tone hardened as he replied.

I realised that mentioning Schmitt's name had been a mistake, stifling any thought he might have had that we were amateurs and no real threat. I could only play the cards I had now dealt myself.

"Of course. Polizeihauptmeister Kramm and his boys are on their way," I declared.

"Perhaps, but not soon. If they were coming you wouldn't have brought Tom Hardy with you."

"Not so, Manfred," Tom came to my rescue. "I never could resist a good party. When Julian said he was going to join you, I decided to gatecrash."

"Enough of the pleasantries. I had hoped that my acceleration of the schedule would allow me to complete this business before you or the polizei could interrupt. Once again, I underestimated you. Time for me to leave you in the capable hands of Klinger and his friends." Addressing his remarks to us both, Hartmann stood up, called Klinger over and gave him rapid instructions in German.

"I have told him to tie you up securely when Peter and I have gone and leave you bound when he departs himself."

As if to confirm his orders Gottfried Klinger picked up a machine pistol with magazine attached from the table and waved it languidly in our direction.

Unexpectedly, Peter Hartmann, who had remained silent up to now, picked a handsome-looking hunting rifle from a pair on the wall behind him and pointed at me, determined to show that he too was a man to be reckoned with or, perhaps, to demonstrate that he was earning his cut of the future cocaine sale proceeds.

"We should tie them up now, father, in case they give trouble as soon as we go," he said.

"Don't be silly, Peter, you know that you're not going to shoot me; anyway, your rifle is unloaded," I told him and knocked the barrel aside.

I was wrong. He pulled the trigger before I could wrest the gun away from him; the sharp crack was followed by a ping as the shot hit the metal frame of the window and ricocheted round the room, off the cast-iron stove and into the padding of the wing chair which his father had vacated. I punched Peter squarely on the nose and snatched the rifle from him as he staggered back against the wall. The weapon was now unloaded; I flung it under the table out of reach.

"*Dummer Junge,*" Manfred Hatmann snapped back at his son. "Stop fooling about. We leave now." He nodded to us summarily, turned on his heel and left the cabin without further word. Holding a blood-stained handkerchief to his nose, Peter followed in his wake. Car doors slammed and we heard the Mercedes drive off.

As the sound of the car engine died away Klinger motioned to Johann Glock who moved forward, taking plastic handcuffs from a pocket in his boiler suit to secure us. As he approached Tom whipped out the tyre lever from his raincoat with his right hand and slashed the iron bar viciously across the bigger man's shins. The speed of the attack caught Glock unawares and the blow felled him; he grunted in pain and clutched his lower legs as he sank to the ground. We were now both facing Gottfried Klinger with his machine pistol raised. Tom flung the tyre lever at him and lunged forward; Klinger sidestepped and pulled the trigger. The single bullet at close range spun Tom around; he staggered back and fell into the wingchair.

Klinger swung the barrel of his pistol towards me. "Surely you could not have thought we would leave witnesses behind us?" he sneered. "I would have preferred to march you both out into forest and execute you but this seems as good a time as any." The black eyes in his square head were slitted; there was no doubting his intention.

They say that your whole life flashes before you at the moment of death. Not so; that's no more than a novelist's or film maker's dramatic flourish. In my case, I had time only to curse myself for over-confidence as Klinger squeezed the trigger again. There was a click as the firing pin fell on an empty chamber. I should have jumped him then but I was too slow in my reactions. Klinger stepped back, cast off the dud magazine, grabbed another from the pocket of his coat and deftly slotted it in place. He levelled the pistol at me again and his finger tightened on the trigger a second time.

---oooOooo---

CHAPTER 32

"YOU WON'T DO ANY BETTER this time." Heinrich's voice came from behind me as he bustled through the door in his usual manner. He was flanked by Otto Krantz in a voluminous grey despatch rider's mackintosh with his most fearsome expression, carrying an ancient double-barrelled shotgun.

"You people never did learn to take care of your weapons," said Heinrich, blue eyes twinkling behind his rimless spectacles.

Gottfried Klinger pulled the trigger of the machine pistol, now set to automatic, intending to spray the three of us from left to right. Again, the firing pin fell on an empty chamber. Feverishly, he tried to crank a first bullet into the chamber.

"*Verdammt du, Hoffmeyer*," he shouted.

"My turn now, Klinger." Raising the Luger in his right hand slowly and with studied precision, Dr. Heinrich Hoffmeyer shot him neatly between the eyes.

"Keep them covered, Otto, while we look after Mr. Hardy," he called out. At the other end of the room Willi Schmitt thought better of sliding his right hand towards an inside breast pocket as Otto cocked both hammers of his shotgun.

He and his Kamradenwerke colleague placed their hand palms downwards on the table in front of them.

Tom Hardy lay back in the wing chair; he was ashen faced and blood stained his shirt where it had pumped from the wound in his chest. His breath rasped painfully and there was a trickle of blood from the corner his mouth. Heinrich examined him carefully and looked grave. He took a clean white handkerchief from his trousers and pressed it gently but firmly against Tom's chest wound.

"Keep holding it there until the ambulance comes," he instructed me. "How bad is it?" I asked.

"I think he's taken the shot in his right lung. Without turning him over I can't tell whether or not the bullet exited but it's probably still in there. We need to get him to hospital as soon as we can."

"There's no telephone here. One of us could drive up to Hohnleuffen and call from the Gasthof," I suggested.

"That may not be necessary. I think they have a radio telephone in that Audi Avant outside. Since it's their delivery vehicle they need to keep in touch with their command post in Munich."

"The one with the moustache is the driver," I called after Heinrich as he strode down the cabin and levelled his Luger, calling for car keys and the entry code and call sign to the radio. The Avant driver remained mute; so, Heinrich struck him across the cheek with the barrel of the Luger. I couldn't understand what he said next except for the word 'schnell' repeated urgently but the meaning was clear. The driver did not delay further; he wrote down the codes on the sheet of paper handed to him with a pencil and handed over his keys. Turning to Schmitt Heinrich extracted an automatic pistol from inside his jacket with practised military efficiency; Willi offered no resistance.

"Shoot them both if either of them moves," Heinrich instructed Otto and hastened outside while I maintained the pressure on Tom's chest. He was back within five minutes to announce that an ambulance was on its way from the Hospital at Nürtingen. "How is he?" Heinrich asked and answered his own question by inspecting the wounded man a second time. "His pulse is quite strong but his breathing is worse. I think he's conscious."

Tom seemed to be trying to speak. "Don't talk, Tom. The ambulance is on its way. Just hold on," I urged him.

There was nothing to do but wait for the ambulance and Polizeihauptmeister Kramm with Max. I wondered which would arrive first. Sensing my thoughts, Heinrich brought me up to date. "We finally connected with Kramm half an hour after you left. He thought that it would take about ninety minutes to gather his team together and drive here; they should arrive anytime now. We hung on at the factory for about another half hour until Glock came back with the van and drove off again in the Opel. We judged then that they were about to finish the packing and you would need *verstärkugen* - reinforcements; so, I drove Gaby up to the Gasthof and picked up Otto who volunteered to help."

"You missed the Hartmanns," I said. "Manfred was directing operations; they drove off before you arrived. They must have got away."

"No, we were here before they left. I parked my car behind yours further down in the woods; then we watched outside until the right moment. They won't have gone far."

"Do you mean……," I started to say but was interrupted by a mounting wail of approaching police sirens. Questions would wait until later. We heard the sound of vehicles drawing up outside the cabin and car doors slamming as the sirens were switched off and orders were issued. Polizeihauptmeister Kramm and his SEK team stormed in; clad in a lightweight Barbour over his immaculate Prince of Wales check suit, Max Salinger was amongst the six-man team in Kevlar vests over their uniforms; except for Klaus Kramm, they were heavily armed with submachine guns and equipped with steel helmets and heavy boots. They fanned out either side of the entrance, their backs against the wall - an impressive supporting cast but too late to play any significant part in the drama.

Standing foursquare in front of us with Max at his side, the Polizeihauptmeister was a commanding figure. Of average height and grizzled aspect, his deeply lined face bore evidence of many years' service in front line action as a soldier or policeman. His expression was world weary but he emanated suppressed energy; his piercing gaze demanded the complete attention of all upon whom it fell. For Max's and my benefit he addressed us in English.

"That man is seriously wounded," he said pointing at Tom. "He needs an ambulance."

I explained that Heinrich had used the radio in the Audi Avant to call for one and it was on the way.

"Has anyone else used that radio?" he asked sharply. "No-one since we have been here," I replied.

"Good. Now please introduce yourselves," he continued including Heinrich, Tom and Otto in a sweeping glance. Max, who had seemed ill at ease, decided it was time for him to join in the proceedings.

"This is Julian Radclive, who brought all this to my attention. That is Dr. Heinrich Hoffmeyer, a former colleague, and I take the wounded man to be Tom Hardy," he said.

"And this is Otto Krantz, the owner of the Leuffener Gasthof," Heinrich added, pointing at Otto who had eased down the hammers of his shotgun.

"And the others?" Kramm again.

"Of the two on the ground, the big man is Johann Glock, warehouseman from Hartmann & Holst and the dead man is his manager, Gottfried Klinger," I said.

"Ah, Yorick," Max commented remembering the codenames he had set for the operation. It's a pity you killed him. We wanted to interrogate him."

"Alas, poor Yorick. It was difficult to play Hamlet without the Prince. If Heinrich and Otto had not arrived, Tom and I would both be dead," I snapped back.

"And the two the other side of the table are from the Kamaradenwerke I assume?" Kramm questioned, regaining his authority.

"Yes, the bald-headed one is Willi Schmitt and the one with the moustache his colleague. And so, Max," I addressed him sarcastically "your Rosenkrantz and Guildenstern are still available for questioning."

"We'll do just that. But first please, cut the Shakespeare; was there anyone else here?" the Polizeihauptmeister asked me.

"Both Manfred and Peter Hartmann. They left in haste before Dr. Hoffmeyer and Herr Krantz arrived. Will they get away?"

Our interchange was interrupted by the sing-song sound of another siren as the ambulance arrived with flashing lights.

---ooo0ooo---

The paramedics wheeled Tom out gently on a gurney to the ambulance and sped off without delay to the hospital in Nürtingen. I offered to go with him in the ambulance, but he was unconscious and Kramm was insistent that I remained at the hunting lodge to answer questions. With a few concise orders he organised the transfer of the cocaine filled holdalls to the first of the police vans parked outside and the removal of Klinger's corpse to the second van which would act as *fleischwagen* – meat wagon - for the day. Willi Schmitt and his assistant were brought to the front of the cabin; cuffed and placed on hard chairs two metres apart to which they were tied securely. Johann Glock remained on the floor against a wall covered by Otto's shotgun. Four of the SEK team were sent outside to remain with the vans, leaving only the squad leader Leutnant with us in the room.

"Now, take me through the sequence of events since your arrival at Hartmann & Holst this afternoon," the Hauptmeister demanded.

I gave him a succinct account up to the point when the Hartmanns left, explaining that Klinger had intended to tie us up and how Tom had been shot by Kilinger after striking Gantz down with the tyre lever.

"I would have been shot too if Dr. Hoffmeyer had not arrived when he did," I concluded.

"You were fortunate, Herr Radclive. The Schmeisser machine pistol is a unreliable weapon but failure to fire a single shot from a new magazine is unusual," Kramm commented; then turning to Heinrich "A fine shot, Herr Doktor, but Colonel Salinger tells me you are not exactly an amateur."

"That was a long time ago, Hauptmeister," Heinrich replied. Holding the Luger by its barrel he offered the pistol to him. Kramm waved it away.

"I have no interest in your target shooting this evening and will assume that you have a licence," he said.

Then, turning to me, he added "I will now answer your question, Mr. Radclive, about the Hartmanns, father and son. Do I think they will get away? No. I can assure you they will not. If they turned left up the hill, we will arrest them before they reach Munich; that route is already patrolled. If they turned right down the Alp, their journey may already be over. On our way here we saw that some vehicle had recently crashed through the barrier on a sharp bend into the valley below."

While we were paying close attention to the Hauptmeister, Max Salinger called out. Johann Glock had struggled. to his feet behind us and was inching his way towards the door. With four members of the SEK squad outside he could not have possibly escaped, but Otto Krantz was taking no chances. He swung the barrels of his shotgun around, re-cocked the hammers and fired the first barrel.

Glock screamed and fell to the floor again, the knee and lower part of his right leg a shattered mess of blood and bone. An acrid smell of cordite filled the air.

"Remove this creature and place him in the *fleischwagen*. You can drop him at the hospital under guard on your way to the mortuary," Kramm instructed his Leutnant.

With that task accomplished, the Leutnant was ordered to have the first van with the cocaine haul driven away at the same time and delivered to the drug squad headquarters in Stuttgart.

"Colonel Salinger and I will carry out a preliminary interrogation of these two; then you can drive us all back to Stuttgart in their Audi," the Hauptmeister directed, completing his instructions.

"In that case you'll need the car keys," Heinrich remarked tossing them to the Leutnant.

"Now you three, Doktor Hoffmeyer and Herren Radclive and Krantz, you may leave," Kramm continued. "Thank you for your assistance. We have more questioning to do here which does not involve you." He drew a pair of black leather gloves from a pocket and eyed the two prisoners thoughtfully.

We were being summarily dismissed but I decided to have a last word. "In case Colonel Salinger has not told you, you may find it helpful to know they both face charges of murder and attempted murder for the attack on the Leuffen swimming pool ten days ago."

"And by the way, Hauptmeister Kramm, you will find that the one with a moustache is quite talkative if you ask him nicely," Heinrich added turning at the door.

Kramm nodded his acknowledgment curtly and returned to his task. Max, who had not spoken since his earlier intervention, looked uncomfortable but remained silent.

---ooo0ooo---

It was getting dark and drizzling as the three of us returned to the cars parked further down the hill. We stumbled through the trees in the gloom and, at times, slithered down the slope; it took much longer to get down than my earlier ascent with Tom several hours before. Impeded by his heavy despatch rider's mackintosh and tripping over tree roots, Otto found the going particularly hard and I was glad that he had removed the second cartridge from his shotgun as we left the hunting lodge. I didn't have the keys to the

Hertz Golf - they had gone with Tom in the ambulance – so we seated ourselves in Heinrich's green Audi.

"You've lost two customers in an hour this evening, Otto," Heinrich joked as he reversed slowly towards the road.

"*Das macht nichts*," Otto Krantz shrugged his shoulders. "They weren't popular and never bought more than one drink each."

We set off and at the first hairpin bend we found the road blocked with traffic cones and police cars with roof lights flashing. Heinrich halted in front of the cones and we got out to peer over the edge into the ravine where the steel barrier had been breached. We could see wisps of smoke rising from the smouldering wreckage of a vehicle which had plunged down to the bottom of the gorge; it had come to rest upside down on the near bank of the stream running through. It could have been a large car or a small van; make and model were indistinguishable. Looking more closely at the trail of broken branches and undergrowth, it must have bounced down from about half way but it seemed impossible that anyone could have survived unless, by a miracle, thrown clear.

A voice that I knew all too well came from behind me. "How is it, Herr Radclive, that I always find you at the scene of every violent incident around Leuffen?" I turned to find Kommissar Kurt Vogel hovering like my personal nemesis.

"Good evening, Kommissar. Another coincidence," I said. "What happened here - someone driving too fast, I suppose?"

"So it would seem. We shall know more when we have identified the remains of the vehicle and its occupants. If you are interested, I will let you know what we find," he said.

We returned to the Audi and the police moved enough cones for us to proceed. As Heinrich prepared to move off, there was a tap on his window; Vogel's face appeared as he lowered it. "Shall you be in Leuffen for the next few days, Herr Radclive?" he asked.

"Until the weekend," I replied.

"I may need to speak with you over the next two days. By the way, where were the three of you coming from?"

"We were attending an event up the hill." As always, I was careful not to tell a direct untruth to the Kommissar; we would have to think of a more detailed answer , I thought, before he questioned any of us again.

Heinrich drove off slowly and I reflected aloud that we had seen no tyre marks on the tarmac of any vehicle braking hard or skidding as it veered off road.

Heinrich read my expression and looked bland. I no longer wanted to hear his explanation of why the Hartmanns wouldn't 'get far' when they left the cabin. Instead, I opened a related subject.

"I was very lucky back there. Why didn't you come into the hunting lodge sooner? I was nearly killed by Klinger."

"You were not lucky, Julian. Tom was unlucky," Heinrich replied. "You were never at risk. I took the Schmeisser machine pistol from the bottom drawer of Klinger' desk while he was in the warehouse and reloaded the magazines so that they would jam. I used the MP40 for my unit and myself but we always checked and rechecked the magazines before any operation."

"So, how did Tom get shot?" I asked.

"I didn't give Klinger credit for loading a single bullet into the breech. That was my mistake."

"Tom could have let us be tied up but he suspected that Klinger was planning to shoot us both anyway; he didn't know that you were in waiting outside. We must hope that he recovers."

The rest of our journey back to Leuffen was taken in silence until we were approaching the Gasthof.

"Let us keep our account of what happened to a summary of the events," Heinrich requested. "Ethel will be here and she would not approve of my shooting people these days." At least he has some kind of a conscience I told myself.

We found Gaby and Ethel seated together with a half empty bottle of Lemberger between them. There were only three other customers in the bar so that Brigitta was able to join us when Heinrich, Otto Krantz and I arrived. Relief and hugs all round. Otto substituted an apron for his mackintosh and resumed his normal place behind the bar.

"But where is Tom?" Gaby asked.

"He's in hospital in Nürtingen. He was shot," I said bluntly.

There was a shocked silence and I asked Otto to telephone the hospital for news while I explained briefly what had happened, confining my account to the sequence of events and outcomes. Ethel and Brigitta were relieved but I could sense that Gaby guessed there was more to tell. For the moment she held her counsel. Otto completed his call, looking serious, and reported his hospital conversation.

"He's out of surgery. They say that the bullet is removed but his condition is critical. We may telephone again in the morning."

Brigitta had prepared a stew for us which we sat down to eat together; none of us had much appetite or more to say but a second bottle of Lemberger eased gaps in the conversation. Ethel invited Gaby and me to stay the night with them; Gaby was grateful but declined, saying meaningfully that she felt they each had much to discuss with their husbands. We broke up and bid each other goodnight, Ethel and Gaby affectionately and Heinrich rather stiffly with us both. Gaby and I retired to the same bedroom in the Gasthof that we had occupied before less than two weeks ago.

---ooo0ooo---

"C'mon; I want the full story now," Gaby said firmly as soon as I had closed the bedroom door. She sat on the bed leaving me to sit on the only upright chair.

"You won't like it," I replied and told it all again in detail, leaving nothing out.

Gaby was uncharacteristically quiet and there was a pause before she commented. "Thank heaven, at least you are alive and unharmed," she said finally without much conviction. "But, otherwise, it was a pretty horrible mess. Nobody emerges with much credit."

"The biggest factor was Max's contingency planning and his communications failure. If he'd taken the first flight to Stuttgart this morning he would still have arrived in time to arrange for the SEK team to be deployed locally. However, thanks to our intervention the cocaine haul was recovered well away from the factory and without involving Hartmann & Holst." My justification did little to assuage her.

"Yes, but at a miserable human cost. If I understand correctly, Tom got himself shot for being unnecessarily heroic; Heinrich delayed his entry because he was arranging for the Hartmann's fatal accident and then shot Klinger in cold blood. As for Otto, he behaved like a Northern Ireland terrorist," Gaby continued.

"That's not entirely fair," I remonstrated. "You must realise that they both reverted to their previous occupation as soldiers. Once they took off up the hill they behaved as if they were on a war footing. Aside from Polizeihauptmeister Kramm and the SEK, Heinrich was the only professional there. I agree that Otto need not have shot Glock; he was over excited."

"I shall still feel uncomfortable around them: in my book an assassin and a sadist. I'm not sure that I want to visit Leuffen ever again."

---ooo0ooo---

CHAPTER 33

WE HAD WISHED each other goodnight but with minimal endearments and there was still an atmosphere between us when we arose on Thursday morning.

Descending for breakfast, I asked Otto Krantz to call the hospital for me; the ward sister spoke good English and reported that Tom Hardy had passed a quiet night and was now plugged into a ventilator. They hoped to reflate his collapsed right lung in the next few days. When could we visit him? The sister said his doctor might allow us a few minutes in the evening – but not to talk. I said that we would be there at around 6:00 p.m.

Over breakfast we discussed plans for the rest of the week. In Tom's absence, I would have to stay in Leuffen to complete arrangements for Lloyd Parmentier's task force and to meet them on Sunday when they flew in. Gaby said that she couldn't stand another four days in Germany with me; she would meet with her washing-machine client in Stuttgart for further planning if they were available, visit Tom with me in the evening and return to England by herself on Friday.

The client confirmed that they were available when she telephoned and I sent her off in the Mercedes by herself, agreeing to meet up at the hospital later. I could have offered to drive her there and collect her but there was too much to be done; I also thought she was being unsympathetic and unreasonable in not staying to help me clear up loose ends. Gaby dropped me off at the factory gate and I walked over to Dieter Trautman's office asking him to join me in the boardroom. I called Heinrich to attend and the three of us sat down.

"Gottfried Klinger and Johann Glock won't be coming back to Hartmann & Holst," I announced for Dieter's benefit. "We need to inform the workforce today and to replace them. Is there anyone who can take over as warehouse manager?"

"I can offer Klinger's job on trial to my production planning manager and promote his number two," suggested Heinrich.

"Replacing Glock is no problem. I will advertise for a warehouse labourer in the Nürtingen weekly paper, if Heinrich agrees," said Dieter taking the news in his stride. Heinrich nodded approval.

"But what shall we tell the workforce?" I asked.

"Always better to tell the bare facts but no more. Let's just say that they were found red-handed with stolen items from the warehouse last night and fired." said Heinrich innocently. I marvelled at his bare-faced gall while Dieter raised an eyebrow.

"You need to know, Dieter, that Tom Hardy was injured last night when we arrested them and handed them over to the police. Heinrich and I were there too. We won't be seeing Tom back here for a few weeks. Lloyd Parmentier and his team will be arriving at the weekend and until then I'll carry on with the arrangements for them that Tom was making." My embroidery of Heinrich's story carried conviction but it wouldn't do for Kommissar Vogel when he reappeared.

"Is there anything more that I should know?" Dieter asked.

"Better not now. I'll tell you more in confidence when the dust has settled," I promised.

I spent the rest of the morning with Frau Päsche reviewing what she and Tom had arranged for the task force. We visited the apartment that they had leased for the team which was frugal but seemed reasonably comfortable as a base for some weeks. We reviewed the arrangements she had made for daily cleaning and the regular delivery of basic foods. Finally, I instructed her to hire a television set which I knew any red bloodied American would consider an essential. The apartment was midway between the factory and the spa - an easy ten minutes walk from either; I congratulated Frau Päsche on the choice. She was curious about Tom's condition and I promised to give her a report the next day after a first hospital visit.

At lunch time I took the usual cheese and salami rolls in the boardroom with Dieter and we discussed the areas of his work where he needed guidance from the accountant whom Erik Nielsen was sending as his member of the task force. It sounded as if the Hartmann & Holst finance function was already in pretty good shape. When the Farmington office had opened I called Viktor Accona on his direct line and I told him I was in the factory with an update for him.

"Is it all happening? Have Pan Alpina delivered yet?" he asked.

"It's done and dusted," I told him. "The container arrived yesterday while I was on my way. There were glitches in police communications; so we let them take the shipment away up the Alp to the Hartmanns' hunting lodge. Then Tom and I, with Heinrich joining us later, followed them; we held them up until the drug squad arrived and took over."

"So, you have completed your mission. Congratulations. May I tell Chester that it was a compete success?" For once, Viktor sounded impressed.

"Not quite. Now for the bad news; Tom was shot in the chest and is in Nürtingen hospital on life support. And the Hartmanns, father and son, escaped. We think they died in a car crash during their getaway." I didn't need to tell him more over the telephone.

"That is bad. Is there anything the company can do for Tom? Chester will be very concerned."

"Probably. I'll know more when I visit him in the hospital this evening. I'll call again later if you wish," I offered.

"Please do. Chester will want to speak to you himself. Oh, and you will be submitting a written report, I assume." The assumption was delivered as a statement rather than a question.

"Definitely not," I replied. "No written reports by me or the authorities. I'll brief Chester fully and yourself verbally in person when we next meet"

I expected a firmer demand for a written account, but he backed off.

---oooOooo---

As I put the telephone down, Frau Päsche poked her head round the door. "There's a Mr. Salinger in reception. He wants to speak with you and Dr. Hoffmeyer. Shall I show him in?"

I asked her to do so but, on no account to call Heinrich. I wanted to have what they refer to in press releases as a "full and frank discussion." I seated myself behind the general manager's desk, giving Max no option but to take a visitor's chair. I rose when he entered to shake hands and motioned him to sit down.

Frau Päsche was asked to bring us coffee.

If I had expected any sign of contrition I would have been disappointed. Jaunty and dapper as ever, Max made himself comfortable and crossed one well- tailored, grey flannelled trouser leg over the other. He had recovered his composure from the evening before and exuded confidence.

"Well, Julian," he began "I think we can say that was a successful operation. Shame about Tom Hardy, of course, but I'm sure he'll be up on his feet again in no time. We captured your cocaine haul well away from the factory and I have a confirmed lead on the location of the Nazi gold."

"No, Max, it was a shambles. You arrived late and your lines of communication through the Hauptmeister's office didn't work. Tom was shot because we had to go up there to prevent the drugs being taken away. He's in the local hospital now on a ventilator in intensive care. We don't know that he will survive," I said.

"Your fault too," he answered. "Your intelligence was wrong; the shipment arrived a day early."

"We were outwitted on the delivery by Manfred Hartmann," I agreed "but haven't you people ever heard of contingency planning? If you had taken an earlier flight yesterday morning, you might still have been here in time. As it was, Kramm and his SEK team were stood down; but for Heinrich both Tom and I would be dead now." I had held back the extent of my anger but it was now on display.

Max's response was disarming. He assumed his most charming smile as if he were a tutor addressing a subversive student. "Good to get that off your chest, but no point in recriminations; it's time to look forwards. You can always depend on Heinrich to come through."

I smothered my urge to reply with even greater asperity as Frau Päsche re- entered with our coffee. She must have heard my raised voice. "Is there anything more you require, Herr Radclive?" she asked.

"Perhaps this is a good moment to invite Doktor Hoffmeyer to join us so that we can plan our next steps?" Max intervened addressing me, casting an enquiring glance in her direction.

"Not for the moment, thank you Frau Päsche," I replied firmly; then, when she had left the room "Not now and not ever; neither of us are available for the foreseeable future."

"But I need your help in following the trail. Your friend Willi Schmitt was very informative by the time Hauptmeister Klaus Kramm had finished with him. We know now that the Nazi gold is definitely on Mainau Island at Lake Constance in one of three places. We can go down there and recover the hoard within the week. Surely, you can both take a few days holiday?"

"Out of the question. We have a group of visiting firemen from the US office arriving Sunday and I shall have to take Tom's place in meeting and settling them in. One of them is their Vice-President Engineering who will want to work with Heinrich all of the time while he is here." I didn't want to tell him outright that I wouldn't work with him again on any account; no point in offending someone I was sure to meet again socially. He looked crestfallen but face-saving inspiration came to my aid.

"Max, you said that Roderigo Morales and his wife were coming to Europe on holiday at the end of this month. Surely he would be a better partner in your quest?"

"Yes! They leave Rio this weekend. I will telex him today and invite him to join me." Any disappointment had abated and his ebullience was restored. "Of course, I would have preferred to have you with us," he added politely.

I offered him the use of the office telex and he wrote down his message in capital letters for Frau Päsche to transcribe. While she was performing her task in the outer office, Max briefed me on the fall-out from the night before. When the Munich Polizei raided the Kamaradenwerke offices they had found no records of drug trafficking; when they went with a search warrant to General Kessler's home the bird had flown. Wolfgang Kessler and his wife had already left for a long tour of the Far East, flying first to Dubai as a staging post. He must have activated his contingency plans as soon as he heard of the failure to detain me in London. Willi Schmitt and his moustached sidekick were under close arrest in Stuttgart, "awaiting the State Prosecutor's pleasure" as Max put it. Johann Glock was in the prison hospital.

Having checked his telex Max prepared to leave. "Before you go," I asked "can you tell me whether it is safe now for Gaby and me to return to London?"

"Certainly. The two men who were trying to kidnap you were identified and arrested on suspicion at Heathrow Terminal 2. We couldn't hold them and they were sent back to their boss with instructions to leave you both alone on pain of a visit from the Metropolitan drug squad."

"And will they take any notice of the warning?"

"They usually do," Max said heading to the door. "We must do lunch when we're all back in London."

---ooo0ooo---

A perfunctory tour of the factory reassured me that the level of activity was normal: the steady clatter of machinery in the main workshops, batches of parts being moved between spring coilers and heat set furnaces, a relentless throb from the injector spring test bed and a more strident tumbling from the shot-peening drum in Halle 8 confirmed that business was operating as usual at Hartmann & Holst. I found Heinrich in his office instructing the new production planning team in their routines; there was no other sign that Klinger or Glock were much missed.

After the siren sounded for the end of the working day, we watched the workforce depart at their usual pace; Dieter and Frau Päsche were among the last to leave. Heinrich had agreed to drive me to the hospital on his way home and we set off in the Audi soon afterwards.

"How are you doing after yesterday evening?" he asked.

"Bent, not broken," I said "but still mad at Max for his failure to perform. I should warn you that Gaby is mad at us too for letting Tom get shot; you may not find her too friendly when you see her at the hospital."

"Ethel has been giving me a bad time also. She says I'm too old to play these kinds of games and that we could both have got ourselves killed; you're in her black book too as a bad influence," he replied.

I told him about Max's visit not two hours ago, his obsession with recovering gold from Mainau Island and how he had expected us both to accompany him down there. Heinrich thought that the story of gold in or around Lake Constance was probably a myth and had been trotted out by Willi Schmitt in an attempt to save his own skin. We agreed that Max was little more than an old man in a hurry; Heinrich was pleased that I had headed him off.

"Ethel would have left me if had got myself involved in another *missgesicht*," he said.

---ooo0ooo---

The hospital was on the outskirts of Nŭrtingen close by the run-off from the autobahn; a large cube of white cement and glass, it projected a cultivated impression of clinical efficiency. The ground floor receptionist directed us to the third floor, Ward C, where we found the ward sister in hushed conversation with an earnest looking young doctor in scrubs, 'D. Finkelstein' as his name tag proclaimed. He took us to the outside of a side ward where we could see Tom through the glass lying propped up with a face mask and connected by a network of tubes to a series of machines and screens.

Dr. Finkelstein looked us up and down and asked whether either of us was a relation of his patient. I explained that we were colleagues in the European division of an international corporation and had been with him when he was shot.

"In that case, I will give you a very clear report on his condition," the doctor began. "He was shot at close range. The bullet passed through his right lung and lodged close to his spine between two ribs. I was able to extract the bullet and to sew up the lung. If the bullet had struck 2 millimetres to the right, he might have been paralysed. Fortunately, his general condition is good for a man of his age: a little overweight but no heart problems."

Gaby had arrived behind us, looking less relaxed than usual, in time to hear the last of the diagnosis.

"What will happen next, Doctor?" I asked.

"Tomorrow, we will try to reinflate the lung. If we are successful, we can remove the ventilator but he will find breathing painful for some weeks. If we fail and the ventilator is removed he will have to learn to live with one lung."

"And the prognosis, looking further ahead?"

"If he can breathe on both lungs, there is no reason why he should not return to his normal life within three months. On one lung his activity will be reduced, but he could have many years ahead in the absence of infection. If you come back tomorrow evening at the same time, you may have my further opinion."

"May we visit him now?" Gaby asked after I explained who she was.

"One of you, for two minutes only, with the sister," Dr. Finkelstein ruled.

I entered the side ward and stood at the side of the bed looking at my fallen friend: no longer any likeness to a bucolic Norfolk farmer. His eyes were closed and breathing shallow; his pallor was deathly. There was a background thrumming from the ventilator. "We're all here for you, Tom. You're in good hands," I said trying to sound more cheerful than I felt. After a pause his eyes flickered open and I could se that he recognised me. His lips moved.

"Don't try to talk now. I'll be back tomorrow and we can catch up then," I promised. Taking his hand I gave it a firm squeeze which he returned. I backed away and gave him a wave as I left the room.

Gaby and Heinrich stood outside engaged in stilted conversation and looking uncomfortable. I felt too tired to play the peace broker; there was nothing further to be done that evening. So, we descended to the car park and parted there, Gaby and me in the Hertz Mercedes back to Leuffen and Heinrich home to Ethel. I had retrieved the keys for the Golf from the ward sister and Gaby drove me up the hill beyond the village to the off-road place where Tom had parked less than twenty-four hours before. We drove back slowly to the Gasthof in convoy pausing on the way down to note the broken barrier where Peter Hartmann's Mercedes had crashed through to its destruction.

Over dinner, the atmosphere between us was less chilly than at breakfast; Gaby seemed more resigned to what had happened and no longer cast me in the role of public enemy. Instead, she now treated me as a victim of circumstances, a status with which I was prepared to go along. Sensing her displeasure, Otto Krantz was more subdued than usual and wisely left Brigitta to serve us; even she was less bouncy than normal.

"How did you get on with the client," I asked munching on the bratwurst and sauerkraut which was the Gasthof's dish of the day.

"They've planned the schedule for the briefing sessions in their Northern European markets. We start next week with a visit to Amsterdam on Thursday and then, after the weekend, a tour of the Scandinavian capitals. I don't suppose you will be able to synchronise with any of your visits?" She didn't sound too disappointed.

"I'm stuck here until Monday morning. In Tom's absence I have to stay around to welcome Lloyd on Sunday and settle in his merry men. After that, I shall have to fill in for Tom unless they send a replacement. You might as well go back tomorrow."

"I've already booked a flight for the morning. Will I be safe in London?"

"Max says that the gang that set upon us has been warned off but I no longer believe entirely in any arrangement he claims to have made. You'll be safer staying with Bill and Barbara Fentiman in Sussex over the weekend until I get back."

I gave her an account of Max's visit that afternoon detailing his plans for chasing down the missing gold on Mainau Island and how I opted out. Retelling the story made it seem even more outlandish and we finished up with a fit of the giggles as we imagined the sedate pursuit by Max and Roderigo, a partnership of two stylish but elderly gentlemen elegantly hellbent on a quest for their grail.

"And slowly answered Arthur from the barge…," said Gaby, quoting Tennyson's *Morte d'Arthur*. We fell about again and I refilled our glasses.

"Miranda will murder him when Max tells her what he's about. Seriously though, do you think that we are in danger in London?" she asked.

"Not really," I said "but I'd feel more comfortable with you in Sussex for the next few days. I can keep tabs on you there with Barbara and Bill."

Gaby nodded appreciatively and went off to telephone the Fentimans immediately; the frost between us had melted. There was even a smile for Otto when she returned to say that all was arranged and that Barbara sent me her love. We retired to bed early in harmony and slept the sleep of the just; I was tempted to go for more than a cuddle, but didn't push my luck. In the morning, I drove Gaby to the Flughafen where I dropped her off; we parted amicably but her closing remark reflected reality:

"Probably a good thing to spend a few days apart," she said and I couldn't disagree.

---ooo0ooo---

CHAPTER 34

THE REST OF THAT FRIDAY was routine. I spent much of the time on the telephone calling Molly Fellows in London to arrange a preliminary timetable for visits to Nŏrkopping, Amsterdam and Tipton with the general managers and then Viktor again in Farmington to report on Tom's condition. He passed me quickly to Chester Case who enquired first about Tom.

"The hospital seems confident that he'll live but unsure whether he will have the use of both lungs. They're trying to reflate the collapsed lung today," I reported.

"Give Viktor another call as soon as you know. I want the company to arrange and pay for his transfer to a London hospital at its expense as soon as he's fit enough to be moved. Now, how about yourself?" he continued. "Do you want to tell me the complete story of what happened?"

"Yes, but I prefer to do that face to face; not over the telephone and certainly not in writing. The bottom line is that it's all over in Leuffen without involving Hartmann & Holst by name or Allied Autoparts. There are no witnesses who will talk although it's possible that Manfred Hartmann will be connected to any story personally by reason of his death. The local police want to interview me but I don't expect them to push me for detail."

"That's great, Julian. I'll brief Lloyd before he leaves for Germany and Barry may want to talk to you next week about your role in the operations of the London office. Meantime, I'm planning to visit London in two or three weeks if there's no further fall-out from this week's events. We can sit down together then." Chester gave no information about why he would be coming to Europe. No doubt all would be revealed in his own good time.

I checked with Heinrich whether he wanted to come to the hospital with me and he said that he and Ethel planned to visit Tom over the weekend instead. At six o'clock I was back in the ward waiting for Dr. Finkelstein. This time the blind was pulled on the window to Tom's private room and a different ward sister was on duty. When he arrived, still in his gown and cap from the operating theatre, he apologised for keeping me waiting.

"Another emergency; the third today on my shift," he announced. Pulling off his cap he invited me to sit down with him in the ward office. "The news is not bad but not yet good. We reflated your friend's lung but his breathing is very painful; so we have to continue giving him some oxygen. The best part is that he is no longer on a ventilator. You can see him in a moment but don't encourage him to speak."

"That sounds like satisfactory progress. What happens next?" I asked.

"Herr Hardy has a strong constitution and if all continues to go well, we would expect to move him into the general ward after the weekend. After that it could be several weeks before we can think of discharging him. Of course, if the lung collapses again, he might have to go back on the ventilator until he learns to breathe and move about with just the good lung."

I told the doctor that the company wanted to move Tom to a private hospital in London - entirely at its own expense I assured him when he looked worried; and asked when that might be. "If all goes well, perhaps Wednesday next week, but no promises," Dr. Finkelstein said. Thanking him again for his care and attention, I entered the private ward. Sitting up against his pillows, Tom still had a drip into his left arm but there were no other tubes or connections to screen monitors; there was some colour in his shrunken cheeks. His breathing was laboured and he held an oxygen mask in his right hand to which he resorted at intervals. He raised his left hand in greeting and tried to croak a welcome; I marvelled at his powers of recuperation.

"Don't overdo it by talking just yet, Tom," I cautioned. "You had us all worried but it's great to see you on the road to recovery today. Gaby sends her love, Chester is waiting to hear how you are and Viktor is ready to start arranging for you to be airlifted back to England when the hospital says that you're fit to travel. You may ask me three questions which I will answer but that's your lot for today."

"How did it all …. end up?" he gasped painfully.

I gave him a summary report including the information that Max had provided the day before but avoided telling him that Heinrich had spent time tampering with Peter Hartmann's car outside the hunting lodge before coming to our rescue. There was no point in putting the finger on Heinrich's delay as a cause of Tom's shooting; if Heinrich decided to apologise, that was up to him. Tom looked pleased.

"So, we won," he managed to say.

"I won't count that as a question. Yes, but I wish we could give von Falkenberg his comeuppance. Anyway, Heinrich and Ethel are coming to see you tomorrow. Is there anything you'd like them to bring?"

"Something to read …in English. Can't listen to radio …..all day."

"I'll call her this evening and be back again myself tomorrow evening," I promised. "Is there anything else you want this evening?"

"Have you told Sybil and when do Lloyd and his …. gang arrive?"

"That's two questions. Viktor is keeping Sybil informed as your wife; if you're not back midweek, she'll fly out to be with you. And the war party arrives on Sunday; I'll settle them in and then return to London on Monday."

I could see that Tom was tiring and called time on my visit. As I left he reached for the oxygen mask; it was clear to me that he would probably be out of action for months rather than weeks. I returned to the factory to make my telephone calls, using the entry pad to gain access; there was only one car parked in front of the office but no sign of Heinrich who was usually the last to leave. I telephoned Ethel first who said that she still read English language novels and would look out some thrillers for Tom; she invited me to supper the next evening but I suggested that we wait until Gaby next visited Stuttgart and declined. Viktor welcomed the positive news from the hospital and declared that he would start immediately to make arrangements for Tom's transfer. I left my call to Sussex until last and Barbara answered.

"Julian," she cried. "How are you doing? Gaby's told us what you've been up to – playing at heroes again."

"Languishing. I'm looking forward to seeing you all soon, perhaps on Monday if she's still with you," I replied.

"There's someone languishing here too. I'll put her on."

Background voices and then Gaby. "Is everything alright and how is Tom?" she asked in a rush and, before I could answer. "Any chance that you'll come down on Monday. It's good to get back to normal with Barbara and Bill here. You need a break too after this week's horrors."

"Tom's much improved today and can even speak a bit. They're talking about flying him back to London next week."

"That's good. But I'm worried about you too; I wasn't very understanding or supportive. Bill tells me that you acted honourably and that I should be ashamed of myself. I want to put things right between us."

"We're fine," I assured her. "We were both under strain; sitting and waiting is as bad as being in the hot seat. And you were the one who got us out of London. I'll come down on Monday if I possibly can for the night. I look forward to the 'putting it right' bit."

"I love you too," she said and, as an afterthought "Say hello to Heinrich. I've almost forgiven him."

---oooOooo---

I rose late on Saturday having nothing specific to do and anticipating a boring day until it was time to visit Tom again in the early evening. After a leisurely breakfast I drifted down to the factory to check any incoming telexes from Farmington. A single telex from Lloyd Parmentier's secretary informed me that the task force would be arriving by local flight at Sunday midday having taken the TWA overnight 'red eye' to Frankfurt. There was an addition to the team that Lloyd had mentioned in London: Loren Corley, Shelley Frankel and Erik Nielsen's deputy, Fred Simpson; they would be joined by Viktor Accona – presumably to complete arrangements for Tom's transfer. I decided to give up my room in the Gasthof to Lloyd for Sunday night and book into the Flughafen hotel instead for an early start on the first flight to London Monday morning.

Using the company airline travel card I booked my flight and then made the hotel reservation.

Wandering out of the office I found Dieter Trautman emerging from the warehouse with a bundle of papers and looking puzzled:

"Good morning, Julian. I've been checking the consignment from Campinas against the paperwork; they weighed the crate yesterday before they unpacked it. It's very strange," he said. I looked interested and waited for him to explain.

"The items, their quantities and value are the same on the manifest as on the invoice but the combined weight of the products recorded here yesterday by Klinger's replacement is much less. How can this be?"

"I'm sure you can work that out for yourself, Dieter. I can think of only one explanation," I replied.

"You mean that part of the shipment has been taken out of the crate – by Klinger I suppose?"

"Keep going. You're nearly there."

"So, there was some kind of unauthorised import activity from Campinas to Leuffen not for the benefit of the company." Dieter thought for a moment before asking "Is that how Tom was injured – chasing after them?"

"That's just about what happened," I agreed. "We did catch up with Klinger and Glock and, what's more, the police recovered everything they had taken. That's why you won't see either of them again in Leuffen." I sensed that he would keep on probing for more of the story than I was prepared to share; so, I continued in a way that would close off any discussion, although it would probably not satisfy Dieter's curiosity.

"The important thing is that everything took place away from the factory so that Hartmann & Holst is not involved with the police. The goods are now in police custody; we can all get on with the company's business and forget about it." I was aware that I was being disingenuous, but he seemed to accept the logic.

"And none of this will be considered during the audit. The weight of cargoes received cannot be reconciled with stock records," he said echoing my conclusion.

"May I come with you if you are visiting Tom later?" Dieter asked as I returned to my car.

"Of course. Tom will be pleased to see you. Let's meet here at about 5:30," I replied.

---ooo0ooo---

CHAPTER 35

June 24, Leuffen

WANTING TO MEET Lloyd and his group on Sunday looking clean and tidy I had intended to drive into Nürtingen for lunch and to buy a new shirt, but the conversation with Dieter had rekindled my appetite for pinning responsibility on Frederik von Falkenberg. The thought came to me that if I could gain entry to Schloss Hohenleuffen I might find evidence of his connection to the drugs trading in the form of telexes to and from Brazil or other documentary evidence; so I turned right out of the factory gates and drove once again up the Schwäbische alp passing the familiar landmarks of the accident site, the turn-off on the left where Tom and Heinrich had parked cars and the entrance to the hunting lodge. It was another fine Spring day without the sweltering heat which Gaby and I had experienced on our ill-fated expedition to Ulm only a fortnight before. The forest foliage was even heavier than then; when I crossed the village square and started to ascend the narrow road to the Schloss the canopy of trees overhead blotted out any sunlight until shortly before reaching the castle gates. I passed through the cool of the tunnel between the twin towers on to the gravel sweep of the sunlit inner courtyard. It seemed a shame that Manfred Hartmann's plans for putting on Chichester productions there the following year would come to nought.

Parked in front of the entrance to Manfred's quarters in the keep was a new- looking Opel Commodore coupe; it seemed that there was already at least one visitor giving me increased hope of access. I tugged on the bell pull and a deep clanging reverberated inside the building. While waiting I concocted a story about wanting to recover files that were the property of the factory 'following Herr Hartmann's tragic accident' but subterfuge proved unnecessary. After a long delay and a second yank on the bell pull, a familiar face appeared at the half-open door; Kommissar Vogel in civilian clothes stood on the threshold, looking as surprised as I was.

"Herr Radclive, I was coming to see you this evening. This will save us both the trouble. Let us go upstairs where we shall be undisturbed," he said.

We took the elevator up to the floor where Manfred Hartmann had entertained me to lunch in April. In an olive-green linen suit and floral tie with his dark good looks Kurt Vogel cut quite a dashing figure. We settled ourselves in comfortable chairs in the sitting area of the large room, a file of papers on the coffee table in front of us.

"What brings you here today?" Vogel asked conversationally, hitching his trousers carefully as he sat down.

"Great minds think alike, perhaps?" I suggested.

"And fools seldom differ?" he countered, completing the proverb. "Let me make this easier for you; I have been briefed fully by Polizeihauptmeister Kramm and I am instructed not to interview you formally. I am here off duty today, at his request, to search for any evidence of recent communications between Herr Hartmann and General Wolfgang Kessler, President of the Kamaradenwerke."

"My mission is similar. I want to search for any telexes between Hartmann and Count Frederik von Falkenberg in Brazil over the last few months relating to shipments and return shipments between Leuffen and Amparo. I'm looking for evidence against him personally as the prime mover in the drug trafficking."

"Then it seems we are on the same side," Vogel concluded. "I have already studied the past telexes before you arrive, Herr Radclive, and ....."

"Julian, please – now that we are allies," I interrupted.

"….and, in my case, there are no telexes on file. However, there were several telephone calls between them logged in the past three weeks. Perhaps you would like to see the telex file?" He handed it to me.

There were a series of intermittent telexes relating to shipments between the two locations, Leuffen and Amparo, stretching back over the past three months increasing to a flurry of more urgent communications in April and early May immediately before and after the sale of the two companies to Associated Autoparts. Hartmann's attempts to defer further exchanges and von Falkenberg's overriding insistence on continued shipment were immediately apparent.

"That's exactly what I was hoping to find," I exclaimed. "May I take copies, Kommissar?"

"Of course, Julian." He pointed to the photocopier at the side of the telex machine. "And you may call me Kurt, when I am off duty."

While the copier was doing its work, Vogel called across the room to me.

"Would you say that all these incidents around Leuffen involving deaths were connected and that there will be no more now?"

"Yes, they are connected and yes, there will be no more. With both Hartmanns gone, I see no risk of anyone else locally reviving the drugs trade with Brazil."

"There is one slight complication, Julian, which I should tell you in confidence. There was only one dead body in the crashed Mercedes and no sign of anyone else in the ravine," he. said flatly.

I stopped watching the photocopier and returned to my chair. "How could anyone survive that crash? I suppose Peter could have jumped out on the way down, in which case he will be on the run and you'll catch up with him."

"We've matched Peter's dental records with the corpse; he is accounted for. So, Manfred was not in the car; however, we have partly traced his movements. We think that Peter drove him here up the hill from the cabin to the schloss where there was another car waiting with or without a driver. Then Peter turned back and drove himself downhill at speed to his death. It seems that the steering and the brakes of the Mercedes had been loosened so that after a short time the car would run out of control. By the way, Julian, I think we can both guess who tampered with the Mercedes – that is of no consequence." Kurt glanced at me with a deadpan expression.

"But what happened to Manfred next? Are you on his trail?" I asked impatiently. A resilient Hartmann senior alive and active was potentially more dangerous than any number of Peters.

"That's where it becomes interesting and why I am telling you all this. We tracked him to Stuttgart Flughafen where there was a private aircraft waiting for him. A Piper M600 was fully fuelled up and the charter pilot had already filed a flight plan to England. Someone has suggested that you might be willing to help us locate him."

"Why me?" I protested. "Surely Hauptmeister Kramm can call upon Colonel Salinger for his services. He is owed a return favour."

"That may be but the Hauptmeister has advised his superior that you would be more reliable for the delicate mission that they have in mind. Will you listen to what I have been asked to tell you?"

"I'll hear you out, Kurt, on a personal level but I promise nothing in advance. Let's start with your telling me who is Kramm's superior and what authority he has."

"I'm really only the messenger boy in all this and out of my depth too. I'm asking on behalf of the State Prosecutor who is in league with his opposite number in Bavaria. Together, they want to use the captured drug haul as a reason for disbanding the Kamaradenwerke, but to put it out of business permanently they need more information on its inner workings. For that reason they are prepared to offer Manfred Hartmann immunity from prosecution in return for information and for being the chief witness against Wolfgang Kessler, when they finally arrest him, and any of the other managers. If Hartmann won't accept the offer they will indict him for drug trafficking and apply for an extradition warrant from the UK for his arrest."

I was impressed and intrigued; it would be good to have Manfred finally neutralised but how on earth could I help? It sounded like another time- consuming adventure as nebulous as Max's crusade to Mainau island.

"What makes the State Prosecutor and you think that I could possibly find him ? You need the British police or a detective agency," I replied.

"We don't want to use official channels to deliver an offer that we would deny making if he turns it down. For the same reason, the matter is too sensitive to entrust to unknown private detectives. And we do have a starting point in England for investigation, confirmed by the pilot who flew him. The airfield where he landed is the United States Air Force base at Ford in Sussex which is now available for private use. That's not too far from London is it?"

Several thoughts flashed through my mind in quick succession. First, the USAF airfield opposite Ford Open Prison was midway between Arundel and Chichester, Bill Fentiman's professional bailiwick as a solicitor. Second, we had encountered Manfred Hartmann at Chichester Festival Theatre no more than a month ago as the house guest of Baron von Richthaven, a local land owner. Finally, Bill had a previous connection to the Baron and could be confident of attracting his serious attention. It all added up to a sporting chance that Hartmann could be found with von Richthaven.

"As it happens, I might be able to help you," I replied cautiously. "I know the area quite well and, by coincidence, have the means to contact friends of Manfred Hartmann who live locally."

"Does that mean you're willing to act as a personal emissary for the State Prosecutor?" Vogel asked.

"I think so – subject to three conditions: that I can confirm access to him or his friends who will pass on to him any written offer; second that you will agree not to interview Doktor Hoffmeyer or Herr Krantz about what happened on Wednesday evening; and third that you will provide me with a copy of Hartmann's telephone call data for the past three months. I want to check on his calls with Brazil over the period."

"The second condition is already satisfied by order of the Polizeihauptmeister and the third condition is not a problem. How long will it take you to find out if you can make contact?"

"Possibly by tomorrow. If you give me a telephone number where I can reach you tonight or tomorrow morning, I'll call you. How quickly can you get me the signed offer of indemnity?"

"The letter is already drafted. I can have it signed tomorrow and delivered to you before you leave if you confirm. I'll await your call, Julian; this is my home number – there is an answer machine if I am not there."

We shook hands, descended in the elevator together and left the building. This time, the same aged retainer who had served at table was waiting for us in the entrance hall to let us out. Back in the sunshine, Vogel paused as he opened the door of his car.

"I'm meeting a friend for lunch down at the Gasthof; you would be very welcome, Julian, to join us," he said, politely rather than enthusiastically.

"That's very kind of you, Kurt, but I won't impose anymore on your free time. Besides, I have a busy afternoon ahead before I can call you."

I followed Vogel down to the village where he parked his Opel in the Gasthof car park and waved as I passed. At the same moment a scarlet open top Mercedes slid in alongside him. The driver was a long-haired brunette with outsize sunglasses who greeted him warmly as it drew to a halt. Good for you Kurt, I thought. The Kommissar had hidden depths.

---ooo0ooo---

I returned to the factory after completing my shopping expedition in Nürtingen. This time, the car park was empty and I had the offices to myself; I stared at the telephone before lifting the receiver. Was it really wise to take on the State Prosecutor's assignment, I asked myself? If I refused and Hartmann remained in England, presumably they would find a way to have him deported without too much fuss but back in Germany there would be a show trial and inevitably Hartmann & Holst and Allied Autoparts would find themselves in the public eye. That was something to be avoided and I would be failing in my assignment if I allowed it to happen by default. The truth, of course, was that I was being propelled by the same curiosity that had driven me to investigate in the first place.

It was teatime in Sussex as I dialled the Fentiman's number. I was pleased when Bill picked up the receiver himself. He offered to pass me to Gaby but I said that it was him I wanted to talk to. I repeated the conversation with Kurt Vogel almost verbatim and asked for his opinion on my deductions.

"I think you're right and I agree that you have to respond positively," he said at length "but we need to strike the right note when approaching von Richthaven." I noted Bill's use of "we" and was pleased that he had already cast himself as a player.

"What do you suggest?" I asked.

"I could say that I am acting as lawyer for the representative of the Baden Württemberg State Prosecutor who has an offer to make to Manfred Hartmann whom we believe to be in England and would the Baron be able to put us in touch with him. I can add that the emissary will be

325

coming to this country on Monday carrying the written offer. What do you think?"

"It might work provided that you don't tell him that I'm the representative, but he might suggest delivering the amnesty offer himself. What do you say then?"

"If that's what the Baron says we can be pretty sure that Hartmann is staying with him and my response would be that I'm unsure whether or not the State Prosecutor's representative will be authorised to leave the offer with a third party, but that I could bring the representative to visit him on Monday afternoon if he thinks he can help. What time can you get down here?" he asked.

"I'm on the first flight back and should be able to take the train down to Pulborough by early afternoon. If you collect me, we can be with the Baron at teatime. The only problem could be that to secure a signed written offer before I leave I need to call Kurt Vogel tonight or first thing tomorrow morning."

"Consider it done," Bill said. "I'll call the Baron in the next hour to set it up. Call me back later. Shall I pass Gaby to you now?"

"No. We can talk when I telephone again; I leave it up to you to tell her and Barbara some of what we are planning. On second thoughts you'd better tell all; the pair of them will winkle it out of you anyway."

On that happy thought we rang off and I gathered up Dieter for our visit to the hospital. We found Tom Hardy in good spirits reading an Agatha Christie novel, one of several which Ethel Hoffmeyer had supplied when she and Heinrich had visited that morning. His breathing was better but still ragged; he still needed recourse to the oxygen mask after speaking more then a few words at a time. I produced a bunch of grapes which I had purchased in the town earlier and Dieter had brought a cake which his wife had baked; he seemed pleased by the attention. I was able to tell Tom that Viktor Accona would be arriving with Lloyd's task force to make arrangements for his transfer to a London hospital. I did not add that I thought an ulterior motive for his trip would be to assess how long he might be out of action or whether he would be able to return to his duties in the long-term; I guessed that Tom would reach that conclusion for himself.

With Dieter present, there was no opportunity to tell Tom of Manfred Hartmann's escape, nor of the mission on behalf of the State Prosecutor that I had undertaken to accept. I doubted that I would have told him in any case; his reaction would almost certainly have been that I was out of my mind and should walk away. Perhaps I would tell him in London when it was all over.

We stayed with Tom for about half an hour chatting cheerfully until the ward sister told us firmly that it was time to leave before we overtired her patient. On the way out I asked her how Tom was doing and was told that it was still uncertain that he would fully recover the use of his right lung.

In the car park Dieter asked me rather diffidently if I would join him and his wife Gretel for their evening meal, assuring me that she was a very good cook. I would have preferred to spend the evening by myself before telephoning Bill again, but it would have been churlish to refuse and I accepted. The Trautmans lived in an old house in a side street off the Leuffen village square; so, I parked outside the Gasthof and made the excuse of needing a quick tidy up to dodge into the inn before joining them. At the bar I bought a bottle of Otto's Niersteiner Domtal to take as a gift, made a quick visit to my room and ten minutes later rang their doorbell. Gretel Trautman was a jolly, rosy-cheeked and flaxen haired young woman; she and Dieter made me immediately welcome in their simply furnished but spotlessly clean home. We ate in their immaculate kitchen at a stout wooden table with place mats depicting scenes of traditional boar-hunting. Dieter was right; Gretel was an excellent plain cook serving us *schweinsaxe* with home-cured sauerkraut. The ham hock, she explained in halting

English, came from her father's shop; he was the village butcher. To begin with, our conversation was stilted but any ice was soon broken when I started to recall for Gretel's benefit the recent AA managers meeting in Brazil. Although her English was limited, she enjoyed my account if Dieter's social success in Rio, delivered with animated hand movements and received with much amusement by her and some embarrassment by Dieter. I was careful to spare him the complete story of his drunken capering at the floorshow; by the end of the meal I could see that Gretel was delighted that her husband now had standing and had gained respect within a wider community of multi-national business associates. They were a well-matched couple in a small community; I wondered how they would both adapt to wider horizons as Dieter's career progressed.

Returning to the factory office shortly after 10:00 p.m. or 9:00 p.m. in Sussex. I called Bill Fentiman again.

"How did it go with the Baron?" I asked.

"We're on," Bill replied. "Konrad von Richthaven was a bit cautious to start with but quickly responded to the request to assist the State Prosecutor's office. He said that he was confident he could 'find a way to deliver any offer to his friend Manfred'. If he was in England, he was sure that Manfred would be in touch with him. The upshot is that I am welcome to bring 'The State Prosecutor's emissary' to meet with him on Monday afternoon."

"Fantastic, Bill. Are you sure that you are comfortable doing this professionally?"

"I've become too comfortable here. I may regret it later but I'm looking forward to our little adventure. Now, there's someone else expecting to speak with you."

Gaby came on the line. "Here we go again. At least you've got Bill to look after you this time," she said resignedly.

"Think of it this way. Compared to West Sussex, Leuffen is the Wild West; the only action you have locally is at the Goodwood race meetings or car rally."

"Think of it another way. To finish off Manfred you may have to drive a stake through his heart."

"You're making a sharp point," I punned appallingly. "There's no answer to that. See you Monday evening."

My final call of the day was to Kurt Vogel at home. The voice that came on the line was sleepy and I could hear the sound of soft music and feminine laughter in the background.

"My apologies for disturbing your domestic bliss," I said "but I'm just ringing to say that I am confident that I can reach Manfred Hartmann when I am back in England on Monday."

"That's good, Julian. Where can I deliver the offer tomorrow evening?"

"I shall be staying at the Flughafen hotel but may not get there until quite late. You can leave it for me on the desk."

"I will deliver it in person. Gute nacht."

"Goodnight Kurt," I said, but he had already rung off.

---oooOooo---

CHAPTER 36

WE NEEDED TWO CARS on Sunday morning to meet the incoming task force; by prior arrangement I met Heinrich at the Flughafen in good time. While waiting for the flight from Frankfurt to arrive I took the opportunity to brief him on the part of my agreement with the Kommissar which concerned him.

"Vogel has been instructed by Hauptmeister Kramm not to interview you or Otto about what happened on Wednesday evening. As far as he is concerned Leuffen has returned to normal and Hartmann & Holst are in the clear."

"No more questions then. That's good, but how does he explain what happened to Tom or the others?" he asked.

"That's not our problem," I answered "Just put Heinrich the hero back in the box, hide your unlicensed Luger at home and tell Otto Krantz the same thing, although I suppose that antique shotgun is licensed."

Heinrich nodded but looked rather regretful. A few minutes later the flight landed and shortly afterwards Lloyd Parmentier and his team straggled through with their baggage, Viktor Accona bringing up the rear. They all looked tired and relieved that there was a welcoming committee. By common consent, Loren Corley and Shelley Frankel gravitated to Heinrich and Lloyd directed Fred Simpson, the new boy on the task force, to join them. He and Viktor walked with me to the Mercedes and I dropped in on the Hertz counter for Lloyd to register as the named driver in my place; while Heinrich whisked his passengers away at speed in his Audi A8 turbo, I drove off more sedately taking the non- autobahn route back to Leuffen.

"Well, Julian. I hear you've had a busy week since we were together last Monday," Lloyd said settling back in the front passenger seat. "I ask no questions; it would have been good to be in the know but I understand that you were under direct instructions from Chester. Bring me up to speed on the situation here; that is my responsibility."

"Before you do that, Julian, tell us how Tom is doing," asked Viktor leaning over from the back seat, the heavy lenses of his black-framed, tinted spectacles glinting and, for once, sounding solicitous.

"Much better when I saw him yesterday evening, sitting up in bed and reading. He's able to talk a bit but they're not sure whether he will recover the full use of his right lung."

"You'll be able to judge for your self tomorrow, Viktor, when you visit him and talk to the hospital. Sounds like he's out of action for some time," Lloyd intervened wanting to return the conversation to his agenda.

"The factory is running normally," I reported. "No-one misses Peter Hartmann and Heinrich has assigned one of his team to take on Klinger's job. Dieter has the accounting and inventory records in good order; the two of them are holding the fort until you get there."

"OK, sounds like things are under control. What's the reaction to the disappearance of Klinger and his sidekick?"

"The cover story is that they were stealing from the warehouse and that Tom and I followed them and caught up with them. Tom was wounded but the police arrested them; end of story. No mention of Heinrich's involvement."

"That's much the same scenario that has been fed to the guys in the other car. Did it take here?" Lloyd asked.

"So far as I know, yes. Dieter suspects that there's more to tell but he won't make waves."

"In that case, wake me up before we reach Leuffen." Lloyd cranked down the backrest of his seat, put on an eye mask extracted from his pocket and fell promptly asleep. On the back seat of the Mercedes, inscrutable as ever, Viktor had already stretched out and was snoring gently.

I woke them up as we approached the village. "What's the plan?" Lloyd asked.

"We check you all in at the Gasthof; your rooms are booked for as long as you wish; the other three move tomorrow into the apartment that Tom rented for them within 10 minutes' walk from the factory. When you're all rested up, I thought we would inspect it later this afternoon," I replied.

"And what are your movements?"

"I'm staying at the Flughafen hotel tonight and flying back to London in the morning."

"Then you and I will talk at the Gasthof while the others are resting. I slept most of the flight over." He made no pretence of including Viktor in the conversation.

Heinrich and the others were waiting for us at the inn car park with Otto Krantz and Brigitta on hand to show their visitors to their rooms. Toting their luggage they clambered after Brigitta up the narrow stairs; I offered to carry Shelley Frankel's heavy suitcase for her.

"Not unless you're planning to crash out with me when we get there," she replied with a flash of her Rio repartee.

I simulated deep disappointment. "Sadly, I'm otherwise engaged," I said, casting a glance in Lloyd's direction.

And so the afternoon passed with little of consequence beyond my personal meeting with Lloyd Parmentier. He reviewed with me my schedule for visiting the other European subsidiaries over the coming fortnight to discuss their business planning exercise and asked for a telex with details of all my flights and where I would be staying to be telexed to him from the London office. I told him that I would be taking the next day off to take care of personal business in the UK; he acknowledged grudgingly that I had "earned it." The only remark of real interest came at the end of our conversation.

"You'll be doing Tom's job in the rest of Europe while I'm here at Hartmann & Holst. Are you comfortable with that?" he asked. I assured him that I was fine.

"If Tom is likely to be out of action for an extended period, AA will probably want to restructure the London office. Chester and Barry may decide to send over someone to take up the position of European Director, but I could suggest that they offer it to you. Would you take the job if invited?"

"I'd be happy to consider it," I replied. I was careful to be cautious - not just to avoid sounding eager to take Tom's job, but also because the reference to restructuring suggested that the job description might change.

The group reassembled early evening to inspect the apartment which gained approval from the three managers who would be staying there, including the sleeping arrangements: a single bedroom for Shelley and a double for the other two; the addition of a television was noted with satisfaction. We returned to the Gasthof for an early dinner together; the group were suffering jet lag and feeling the effects of the change in time zone. and the conversation was subdued. I set off again back to Stuttgart in the Golf as soon as I decently could and shortly after 9:00 p.m. I walked into the unlovely Flughafen hotel with my overnight bag, having returned the car to Hertz to save time in the morning. I found Kurt Vogel in the *Fliegerin Bar* sitting under the wooden propellor, nursing a cup of coffee and waiting for me. He was dressed in casual clothes again: a roll neck pullover under a tweed jacket this time with grey flannel trousers and loafers.

"I have the letter here" he said pulling a crested envelope from an inside pocket and laying it on the table in front of him. His manner seemed less friendly than the day before but I affected not to notice.

"That's nice of you to deliver it in person, Kurt. I hope you've not been waiting too long."

"Sit down, Julian. Before I give it to you, the State Prosecutor wants me to ask you how you will proceed."

"I'm working on a need-to-know basis," I replied. "I believe I've located where he is and hope to meet him tomorrow afternoon or evening."

"And where is that? Who is your point of contact?" he demanded.

"As I told you: strictly need-to-know. There are other people, quite innocent, who won't want to be involved. Either the Prosecutor can trust me or I withdraw my offer of help." I maintained a poker face, while we stared at each other for a good seven seconds.

"Very well," Vogel said finally "I trust you and I'll put my name on the line too. When will you let me know what happens? He stood up and handed the envelope to me.

"Either tomorrow night on your home number or Tuesday morning at your office. If I have to leave a message, it will be 'letter delivered' or if I have failed 'the bird has flown.'" We shook hands and parted.

---ooo0ooo---

CHAPTER 37

BILL FENTIMAN WAS waiting for me in his sedate Rover at Pulborough when I emerged from the station mid-afternoon. There had been time to return to the flat, change my clothes and repack the overnight bag before taking a taxi to Victoria where I telephoned Bill to tell him the arrival time of my train. I also called Molly Fellows to tell her to telex my forward schedule to Lloyd in Leuffen as he had requested and advise her that she could expect me in the office by midday Tuesday. The journey after Leatherhead through the lush green Sussex countryside was a pleasant relief from harsher scenery of Baden Württemburg where I had spent such an eventful past week. By the time the train reached Pulborough I was relaxed and ready for the next episode in my undertaking.

We greeted each other cheerfully with the easy confidence of old friends who know that they can rely on each other in any adventure on which they embark together. Driving west towards Petworth, Bill asked for the complete story of my past week to supplement what Gaby had already told him.

"I can understand now why you feel compelled to go after Manfred Hartmann. But for the arrival of your chum Heinrich, who seems a real professional in despatching his enemies - if not the cold blooded killer which Gaby claims him to be – you wouldn't have survived the experience," Bill said after hearing me out.

We skirted the Goodwood estate and turned right on to the Petworth to Midhurst main road. After about five minutes Bill slowed down and turned left between open wrought iron gates flanked by a pair of stone lodges.

"Tell me, Bill, what do you think are the chances of finding Manfred Hartmann here – based on your conversation with the Baron?" I asked. He thought for a moment.

"I'd say odds-on that he has been here and about 70 per cent that he's still here. He may have moved on, but odds-on again that he's still in the country."

The private road on which we were now driving was tarmacked and wide enough for two cars travelling in opposite directions; it stretched ahead out of sight beyond a curve to the right some quarter of a mile ahead. Post and rail fencing separated the grass verges either side: on the left, a park where roe deer grazed; on the right extensive grass paddocks where more than a dozen horses stood in twos or threes sheltering from the sun under sturdy oaks or clumps of flowering chestnut trees. Beyond the paddocks we could see the tiled roof of a singe storey block of stables. This was the estate of a seriously rich man.

Rounding the bend the house came into view: an early Georgian mansion in ironstone of fine proportions in three storeys with tall sash windows on the ground floor, less ornate than I had expected and more comfortable to live in, I judged, than the florid Palladian mansions of a later period on similar estates in Sussex or Hampshire.

The drive ended in a circular expanse of raked gravel in front of the house. In the centre was an enormous jardiniere full of scarlet geraniums and on the paddock side a row of well weeded rose beds. Bill parked the Rover beyond the front entrance and we walked back to ring the doorbell; the chimes echoed pleasantly through the interior. I expected to be greeted by a butler or some other retainer but the front door was opened after less than half a minute by our host himself. Baron Konrad von Richthaven was a tall, handsome man in middle age with the presence of a FTSE 100 company chairman, equally at home in the Boardroom or watching his racehorses gallop home at Goodwood or

Ascot. Today, his informality seemed studied and I sensed that he was less relaxed than he was seeking to appear.

The Baron greeted Bill by name and gave me a searching glance. "Haven't I seen you somewhere before?" he asked.

"At the Chichester Memorial Theatre a few weeks ago," Bill replied for me "across the lobby in the interval when we we're talking with Manfred Hartmann. He's called Julian Radclive and he's carrying the letter from the State Prosecutor which we spoke about on the telephone."

"In that case, come in both of you and explain yourselves."

The welcome was hardly warm, but at least we were in. The Baron led us across a spacious, stone flagged hall. An imposing double staircase rose either side of the oval-shaped hall to the first-floor landing under which we passed to a pair of half open doors. We entered a salon or large drawing room decorated in the style of Robert Adam with what were probably the genuine original fireplaces and surrounds; the furnishings and furniture were less formal but of the period. The walls were painted celadon green and covered with a variety of gold- framed portraits of ancestors – probably not von Richthaven's, I thought - and 18th or 19th century landscapes. At the far end, more comfortably furnished than the rest of the room, wide-open French windows gave on to an expanse of immaculately manicured lawn. Seated in the middle of a low four-seat sofa sat Baroness Magda von Richthaven with a tray on the table before her bearing all the implements and china for a traditional English tea.

"You're still in time for tea. Won't you join us?" she said motioning us to armchairs and patting the vacant end of her sofa.

The Baron introduced us to his wife and sat alongside her leaving the alternative of the chairs or a companion sofa on the opposite side of the room; we chose the chairs wondering why our visit of an intrusive nature had been turned into a social occasion. Only when we had been served with tea in delicate porcelain cups and saucers, poured through a strainer from a Georgian silver teapot with a plate of cucumber sandwiches between us, was the Baron ready to open the conversation.

The elaborate and unnecessary tea ceremony had given me an opportunity to appraise our hosts. I decided that they were too well prepared, as if waiting to play some kind of charade. The Baron was dressed casually but too carefully to convince from his open-necked cream silk shirt with French cuffs and heavy gold links to his cashmere navy blue trousers and Gucci loafers, while Magda's printed silk dress, more fashion boutique than country life, contrasted strangely with her hair; her blonde mane was plaited and piled on top of her head in a severe Teutonic style which Gaby would have described as 'bagel-like'. It seemed unlikely that she had prepared and set out the tea things herself; it occurred to me then that we were on a stage and that the servants – the stage hands in this production – having set the scene, had been given the evening off.

"We understand, Mr. Fentiman, that you believe our friend Manfred Hartmann may be here in England and could be in touch with us. Perhaps you would explain to us, Mr. - ah – Radclive, why you are representing the Baden Wŭrttemberg State Prosecutor, what message you have for him and what you intend?"

There was no point in prevaricating, so I told it straight. "I work for the American company that bought Mr. Hartmann's company and the Brazilian company with which it is linked. I uncovered their drug smuggling activity which he tried and failed to close down after the acquisition. Last Wednesday evening I was there just before the latest drugs haul was busted by the police at the Hartmann hunting lodge; Manfred Hartmann was present but he and his son left before the drugs squad arrived."

"That's an incredible story. It explains who you are and how you became involved, but not why you are here as the State Prosecutor's emissary."

"After the drugs bust Peter Hartmann's Mercedes was found crashed and burnt out at the bottom of a ravine on the way down to Leuffen. At first, they assumed that both Hartmanns were killed; the next day they discovered that there was only one body in the car and that the body was Peter's. They investigated further and found that Manfred had chartered an aircraft at Stuttgart airport and flown out on Wednesday night; the flight plan gave England as the destination. Because I had set up the operation for them, the head of the drugs squad recommended me to the State Prosecutor to help them find him. You see, the plan had been to deliver the drugs to the Kamaradenwerke in Munich and the Prosecutor and his counterpart in Bavaria want to close down the Kamaradenwerke permanently; they thought that they could use Manfred as an informer." So far so good, but I had to play my cards in the right order. I wanted to relax him before backing him into a corner.

"But you agreed to do what you could to help?" the Baron asked, helped himself to a cucumber sandwich and passing his cup to be refilled.

"Not at first. I was flattered of course but thought that they should enlist the British police to search for him; besides the only possible contact that I could think of was yourselves; I knew that he had been your house guest recently but he could have landed anywhere in England. Then they told me that they didn't want to contact Manfred Hartmann through official channels; they wanted to make a personal offer of immunity from prosecution for drug trafficking which they could deny if he turned them down. If that happened they would apply to the British government for an extradition order and prosecute him. And so, reluctantly, I agreed to try without much hope of success and asked Mr. Fentiman to call you."

339

"Yes, I quite see that you felt obliged to assist. A public trial of Manfred for dealing in drugs would throw a spotlight on Hartmann & Holst and, in turn, on your company as the new owner – unwelcome publicity, I should think. Will you have a second cup of tea?" the Baron asked. He was playing it cool but had grasped the point for himself of my motive for becoming involved. I took my and Bill's cups and saucers over to the tea tray for Baroness Magda to refill, the same formal procedure as before: tea poured first through the strainer from the solid silver teapot; then milk from the creamer.

"But rather a longshot surely, Mr. Radclive?" she queried.

"Not so long, Baroness, as it happened," I said. I could feel the tension in the room growing as I returned to my chair. "When the letter of offer was delivered to me, I was told that they had confirmation from the USAF that Manfred Hartmann's plane landed at their base in Sussex at Ford."

In the pin-dropping silence that followed, the Baron was the first to recover.

"Do the German authorities know that you intended to contact us?" he drawled, attempting to sound casual.

"Not at all. it would serve no useful purpose. Of course, if an extradition order is granted, I suppose the police here may very well have questions for you."

Husband and wife: their eyes met in acknowledgment. It was Magda who broke the silence by losing her patience. "Don't play games with them, Konrad. You know that an arrest of Manfred would cause us social embarrassment locally," she snapped.

"Very well, Manfred did call us in the early hours of Thursday morning asking for help," the Baron confessed. "I took my wife's car and collected him from the Ford airfield. He stayed with us for several nights while he tried to book passage on a freighter to South America. If you give me the letter of offer, I will see that he receives it before he leaves."

I knew then that I had him cornered and pushed my advantage. It was time to call his bluff.

"Not good enough, Baron. I am required to deliver the offer to him in person." I paused briefly. "He's still here, isn't he?" I asked abruptly.

Konrad von Richthaven smiled ruefully and seemed to have made up his mind.

"Manfred was right; you are very persistent. You may see him shortly, not just because you may be bringing the best solution for us all but because I want to do the best I can for a very old friend in trouble. You should know something of the history first to put what he did in perspective."

There was no longer any need to keep up the pressure and I was happy to let him continue; I nodded my encouragement.

---ooo0ooo---

"I've known Manfred since the age of eight," the Baron resumed. "I was the second son in our family. My elder brother Erwin by my father's first wife was ten years older than me and, at the age of eighteen he went to Paris where he studied at the same university as the young Manfred. They struck up a firm friendship, sharing rooms at the university; Manfred was a regular visitor to our home. When both his parents were killed in an air crash, he stayed with us throughout the vacations and became a kind of second brother to me. We were an old family and my great grandfather had founded our family business as steelmakers. By 1937 it came eclear to us in Germany – not me, of course, as a child – that Hitler was taking us into war; Erwin and Manfred decided that they would enlist in the army. This was a career decision for Manfred who came from a military family and had not inherited money; for Erwin the decision was motivated by a sense of adventure and, I think, a desire to get away from my dominating father. It was a great disappointment to my father because our factories were booming; they produced more and more steel for armaments and we were becoming wealthier by the day; he had looked to Erwin to take on some of the management workload. I'm telling you all this because it helps to explain what happened to Manfred after the war." He paused again to take another sip from his almost cold tea.

"They both proved themselves as soldiers although neither of them joined the Nazi party. Erwin served with Rommel in North Africa as a tank commander and was promoted to a Panzer squadron major when he returned to France.

Manfred became an infantry staff officer on the Russian front under General Wolfgang Kessler until he was wounded and then promoted to Colonel as Commandant of the POW camp at Leuffen. My brother was not so fortunate; he was killed in January 1945 in the Ardennes. By then I was a teenager and working for my father in the Ruhr factories where I learnt the basic business of making steel. He was a hard taskmaster but a good teacher and I like to think I was a ready pupil. Of course, our factories were bombed by the Allies and by the end of the war the business was in ruins. Manfred kept in touch and visited us as often as he could. When the Armistice was declared my father offered Manfred a job as general manager with a small share in the business on the understanding that I would eventually inherit control and take over. At the time, Manfred thought that our business might not recover and he decided to go into business himself by converting the Leuffen camp into a spring factory. I think you already know some of the story how he did that from 1945 onwards."

"Yes," I agreed "not all the detail, of course, but how he built it up and entered into a joint venture with Count von Falkenburg in Amparo. What I don't understand is why he agreed to engage in drug smuggling and became involved with the Kamaradenwerke. Can you explain. Was it just greed?"

"Greed, but not in the way you imagine. He was motivated by ambition and a sense of rivalry. Let me explain." The Baron broke off again and asked for more tea. The pot was empty, so he took the rest of the milk before continuing.

"You see things had not turned out as he expected. By 1947 steel making had started to revive. The new German government, backed by the Allies, had identified steel as a pillar of industrial recovery and was pouring investment into the factories of the Ruhr including ours. And the steel barons, such as my father, started to make handsome profits again; as you know, our prosperity continues to the present day thanks to the European Iron and Steel Community which has now become the European Economic Community. Our success was not matched by spring making or by Manfred personally. He had judged that the German automotive industry, of which springs are a key component, would recover too and he was right, but he was unable to carve a leadership role for Hartmann & Holst. His discontent was also probably fuelled by my success. In 1947 my father paid for me to read Engineering at Cambridge where I graduated in 1950. A few weeks later my father suffered a severe stroke; I was catapulted back into the business to run it as managing director. My father was incapacitated physically but not mentally; so he was able to give me a crash course in the financial controls and managing the accounting functions. It could have gone badly with a severe loss of investor confidence but I inherited an excellent team of managers and we continued to thrive. Manfred and I resumed contact as friends and as the years rolled by our relationship reversed. He has never shown me resentment over more than twenty-five years but he is no longer my mentor and occasionally seeks my advice; the change in circumstances must rankle sometimes." Von Richthaven completed his explanation.

"And is that why you think he was tempted to partner von Falkenburg in drug- trafficking?" I asked.

"Frustration too, I'm sure. The truth is that Manfred is an excellent administrator and a good tactician but he lacks the essential ingredient of successful entrepreneurs - the Midas touch. For some people, every project which they engage in makes money; others never hit the jackpot. However clever the concept, however careful the planning, however well executed, the venture never makes big money. And that's how it has been for Manfred."

"And you have the Midas touch?"

"As you can see, it seems to be a gift I've inherited from my father," von Richthaven admitted modestly, waving a hand at the room and the estate beyond. "I'm not just making excuses for Manfred. I want you to know he's not a bad man."

I was beginning to warm to the Baron as he went on:

"Last year, at about the end of May, he finally asked me outright for my advice. This time, he told me all that he was doing, that he felt trapped and knew that the drug trafficking was bound to be revealed in the end. He asked me what he should do; I said that he should sell Hartmann & Holst and ban von Falkenburg from sending any more consignments as soon as he had a firm buyer and before completion. As you know, he found his buyer in your company and was clever enough to suggest that Allied Autoparts take over the Brazilian business at the same time. He thought that would cause Frederik von Falkenburg to stop the trade anyway. We know now that he failed."

"Yes, and I know that he tried. I have copies of his telex correspondence with the Count and there were telephone calls too. Ultimately, it was Peter who let him down by wanting to continue on his own account; in addition, Manfred was pressured by General Kessler to oversee the delivery operation last week."

"Peter, bah!" Baroness Magda snorted. Throughout my sparring with Konrad she had kept silent but could no longer contain herself. "Always, he let his father down. When he was sent to England to a boarding school in Wiltshire, we took him out on visiting days and he spent his holidays with us here. Always, he was a conceited boy; the private school made him arrogant. He was encouraged to believe he was intelligent, but he had no common sense; also, he was completely without charm. We did our best to teach him some social graces, but it was a waste of time."

It was a devastating character reference but tallied with my experience of Peter. So, I asked her what she thought of Peter's stillborn alliance with von Falkenburg.

"Flattery and greed. Peter was easily flattered and Frederik would have played him like a fish with a mixture of respect and financial reward. I knew him quite well when he was a young man; the 'count' title was phoney but he could be very charming. He is self-serving, what you call a 'chancer' here in England, and completely unreliable. Frederik was among the first to join the Nazi Party and attached himself to Himmler," she added for good measure.

"I met him in Brazil last month. Age has not improved him, He is over- confident and ruthless," I said echoing her dismissive style.

The three of us seemed to have reached a consensus on the back story to Manfred Hartmann's present plight. I declared that it was time for me to deliver the letter to him. Bill, who had followed the conversation closely, asked if I would like him to accompany me; I told him that it was something I had to do on my own. The Baron concurred.

"I will show you where you will find him, but I shall not come with you; better not to allow Manfred to imagine that I had a hand in arranging the amnesty for him," he said. "Besides, I want to consult Mr. Fentiman on a property transaction."

He led me back to the hall and through a green baize door to our left under the staircase and down a long corridor. To the right, were half closed doors to a series of kitchens through which I glimpsed expensive ranges of gleaming stainless steel appliances and equipment as we passed. At the far end sunlight filtered in through a glass-panelled door and, to its right, a closed door with a key in the lock through which the Baron invited me to pass, gave access to his gun room. On the nearside wall fishing rods, creels, gaffs and waders were stored with wet weather clothing in racks; on the far wall, glass-fronted cabinets held a row of shotguns and sporting rifles with boots and cleaning equipment underneath. There was a pervasive but not unpleasant scent of gun oil.

"You'll need boots in the woods where you're going; it's quite wet underfoot. What size do you take?" he asked. We found a pair of wellingtons which fitted well and I borrowed one of von Richthaven's lightweight shooting coats.

"I see that Manfred has taken one of my Holland & Holland shotguns," he said pointing to a gap in the first cabinet and an open box of cartridges. He likes to have a crack at the pigeons in early evening. Now, you'll probably find him in Gameless Grove, the larch wood to the right of the long valley facing you when you walk through beyond the stable yard."

The Baron led me through the outside door into the yard. As an afterthought he asked me if I would like to take a gun so that I could "have a shot at a pigeon or two." I declined saying that I would feel safer without a weapon.

"Manfred would never shoot an unarmed man," he agreed. Not personally, I thought, but kept the thought to myself.

---ooo0ooo---

CHAPTER 38

FACING ME ACROSS the Baron's stable yard was a stone arch with a five-barred gate giving on to a rough track across an expanse of green fields. To the right of the yard was a similar arch through which cars could be driven to and from the gravel sweep in front of the house. The left side of the yard was flanked by a block of coach houses, now used as garages for the family's fleet of motor cars with flats above. Stone cottages stood at each of the outer corners of the yard with views over the meadows and woods beyond offering pleasant accommodation for staff members with families. I walked across the yard towards the gate and observed two men around the Rolls Royce in the centre garage, the same black limousine which we had seen at the Chichester Memorial Theatre less than two months before. One in shirtsleeves and jeans was giving an occasional loving polish to the gleaming coachwork of the Rolls; the other, cigarette in hand, wore striped trousers and a black waistcoat and was chatting to his companion – the missing butler I supposed. Neither of them paid me the slightest attention as I passed.

I opened the five-barred gate and entered another, more rustic world. In contrast to the manicured splendour of the von Richthaven's gardens there lay before me a sun-drenched vista of grass and woodland. I was at the open end of a long re-entrant valley stretching back more than half a mile into wooded hillside beyond. The valley was about one hundred yards wide at this end tapering as it advanced towards the far hillside. On the right-hand side of the re-entrant was the large wood, mainly of larch trees, which the Baron had mentioned as Hartmann's likely location. The track petered out quickly but the going underfoot remained good with the meadow close-cropped by the flock of sheep dotted around in the middle distance. I kept close to the edge of the wood as I proceeded and after about two hundred yards came upon a shallow stream which traversed the valley. Splashing across I was confronted by a figure emerging from the wood; he must have been waiting for me.

Manfred Hartmann stood his ground twenty paces ahead of me, legs astride with the Baron's shot gun, breech open, over his right forearm; he wore a light gilet with a cartridge belt about his waist and a green Tyrolean-style felt hat.

"When I heard they had tracked me down here, I guessed that you had made the connection for them," he greeted me. "However, I did not expect them to send you as their envoy."

"That's easily explained. If you don't accept the offer, they can deny that it was ever made," I replied.

"And why have you agreed to act as their agent, Mr. Radclive?"

"To avoid the publicity if you were extradited and put on trial in Germany which would reflect badly on Hartmann & Holst and in turn on Allied Autoparts."

"So, it would have been better for your company if I had been in Peter's car when it crashed," he smiled sardonically.

"That would have been a tidier outcome," I admitted. Manfred Hartmann reflected for a moment.

"Do you really think that I would prefer the relative dishonour of appearing as a witness and betraying my friends in Munich to personal prosecution?" he asked contemptuously.

"Your loyalty would be misplaced, Herr Hartmann. General Kessler left Germany last Wednesday morning for an unknown destination in the Far East with no return flight booked."

For the first time Manfred Hartmann's mask of composure slipped and he appeared a tired and saddened old man.

"In that case, I had better read this amnesty document you have brought with you," he conceded.

I stepped forward and handed the letter to him.

"You will understand that I need to read this by myself," he said. "I will not keep you long, if you will return to the house." With an oddly formal half bow he turned on his heel and prepared to walk back in to the wood.

"Just one question," I called after him. "When you left me in your hunting lodge with Klinger, did you expect him to shoot me or leave me tied up?"

"I will answer you with the same honesty that you showed me. Quite frankly, Mr. Radclive, I could not have cared either way at the time. I see now that was a mistake." With a final nod to me, he strode back between the trees. Re-crossing the stream, I returned the way I had come. As I reached the track, a gunshot rang out from the wood behind me and reverberated around the valley. I turned round and there was the cackle of a cock pheasant; a single bird rose steeply from Gameless Grove and powered its way across the valley from right to left.

---ooo0ooo---

The door to the kitchen corridor opened as I started to cross the stable yard. The Baron and Bill emerged in haste, both looking worried.

"We heard a shot. Are you alright?" cried Bill, although it was apparent that I was.

Where is Manfred; did you find him?" the Baron asked. "I left him in the wood beyond the stream," I replied.

"What has he decided to do?"

"I think we just heard. He found a third way of his own."

The three of us traipsed back up the valley without conversation. I led the way into the wood after we had crossed the stream. We found him just a few yards in, seated with his back against the trunk of a tree and his feet in the water.

From a distance he looked relaxed and comfortable with the brim of his hat over his eyes; only as we drew near could we see that the back of his head was missing. The shotgun rested between his knees with the barrels pointed upwards; in his right hand was a stick with forked end pointing downwards. It seemed that he had placed the mouths of the barrels under his chin and used the stick to depress the trigger. An efficient method of despatch – typical of the man, I thought. The State Prosecutor's letter in its envelope rested at his side; I picked it up and saw that Manfred had written on it four words – *zuruck an den Absender*. No-one could deny that Manfred Hartmann had style.

Von Richthaven stood for a time with his head bowed. "The end of an era," he said at length and then, more briskly, addressing Bill as much as me:

"We must deal with this as well as we can."

"I hope that you're not intending to disturb things before the police get here," Bill cautioned.

"Of course not. The body must not be disturbed; but two small things. The document is recovered and I will make how he did it a little less obvious." With this statement the Baron took the forked stick from the corpse's right hand, holding it with a handkerchief, and flung it into the bushes. It was too late for Bill to protest; and he could hardly replace it.

We trudged back to the house side by side in near silence. Partly to dispel the gloom and partly out of curiosity I asked one question:

"Why do you call this wood Gameless Grove?"

"Because until today guests found it surprisingly difficult to shoot anything there," the Baron replied grimly.

When we reached the house we discarded coats and boots in the gun room and regrouped in the hall where we agreed the action to be taken. Von Richthaven took the lead:

"We need to manage this with as little drama as possible. I shall telephone the Chief Constable who is a regular guest here instead of the local police and ask him to give instructions. Before I do that we should decide whether you will be here when the police arrive and who found Manfred's body."

"If Julian remains, he will have to explain why he is here and the same applies to me although that is easier to explain," said Bill.

"Let's keep it simple," I suggested. "I was never here and Bill came at your request to advise you on your property deal."

"In which case we found the body, I suppose. I would prefer not to be in the position of withholding evidence," Bill said.

"In that case I know what to say; neither of you were here. If they want me to make a statement at the police station, I can always call you to attend as my solicitor," the Baron decided and lifting the receiver from the telephone on the hall dialled a six figure number. After only a few rings it was answered.

"Helen. It's Konrad here; we're looking forward to seeing you for lunch next Sunday but there's something rather urgent I have to ask Derek about now," he began. There was a twitter at the other end and a pause before a male voice came on the line.

"Derek," he continued. "I apologise for disturbing you at home but something rather awful has happened here – that's very good of you – I've just found our house guest dead in the woods .... it'someone you've met with us, Manfred Hartmann....... yes, he was here in April .... no, he's been shot .... it could have been an accident ...... I'm afraid that's possible ..... yes, he was very depressed; he came over from Germany last week immediately after his only son was killed in a car crash and stayed here over the weekend……. no, of course, I won't let the body be moved before they get here ……… should I call your people in Chichester or the local station in Petworth? ……… Chichester, then …….. thank you, I'd be more than grateful if you would   you'll turn out yourself – that's even better

I'll expect you here then, Derek, in half an hour or so." The Baron replaced the receiver with assurance and gave us our instructions.

"You understood what's happening? It will take the police team coming from Chichester the best part of an hour to get here. Derek Houldsworth lives the other side of Petworth and you have time to get away unnoticed if you cut through the Goodwood estate. Before you leave, Mr. Radclive, tell me what you intend to do with the State Prosecutor's letter?" he asked.

"I've thought about that. I could return it, but I have a better idea; I propose handing it to Bill as a lawyer for his safekeeping. That way, if they are tempted to make Manfred a public scapegoat for the drug traffic they will know that they risk their offer of indemnity also becoming public knowledge," I stated. Bill and the Baron looked at each other and nodded their acceptance.

"Splendid, Mr. Radclive. You have the same devious mind as Konrad," exclaimed Magda von Richthaven sashaying down a wing of the great staircase.

She had changed from her staid silk dress into white jeans, a Gucci shirt printed with poppy design and gold sandals; she now wore her hair loose down to her shoulders, transforming her appearance for the better.

"I shall write to Mrs. Fentiman tomorrow and invite her to bring you and your wife to dinner the next time you are here. Thank you for your consideration this afternoon," she added crossing the floor and extending her hand.

"We shall look forward to that with great pleasure," I responded bending over her hand with continental courtesy.

We left the house and drove off with the Baron's promise that he would have papers sent to Bill's office in the morning for him to consider and his assurance that he and I would no doubt be in touch.

"You old smoothie !" were Bill's first words as he turned the Rover on to the main road. "Baroness Magda is notoriously prickly and you've stormed the ice queen's castle at the first assault. We're now on the Sussex social register."

"You've not done too badly yourself," I replied. "Can I congratulate you on gaining a new client?"

"That remains to be seen. Konrad's property assets are held in tax havens in the West Indies and he's trying to complete a complicated series of transactions here in the UK. He thinks that his financial advisers are ripping him off and that his lawyers are unable to handle them. He's offered me a mouth-watering monthly retainer to advise him. I've told him I need to look at the file before I decide whether I can handle it."

"Why you, and do you think he is being ripped off?"

Bill turned left off the Petworth road and into the Goodwood estate before answering.

"He knows several of my old City clients and they must have put in a good word. As for his concerns, he's very likely right on both counts. The law firm is old and respectable but more used to family affairs and straightforward conveyancing; so, the financial advisers are probably taking advantage of their ignorance."

"Does that mean that you'll take on his work?" I asked.

"Probably. I'll need to catch up on international tax law and spend more time in London than Barbara and I would wish; so, I'll have to talk to her first. Also, of course, the Baron will be a very demanding client, but I've had some of those before."

I kept quiet while Bill negotiated the back doubles sweeping wide of Chichester to get us on to the Arundel road before returning to the afternoon's events.

"You didn't much like it when Konrad removed the stick from Manfred's hand and threw it away. It seemed pretty pointless to me," I commented.

"Do not deceive yourself. I very much doubt of he ever does anything pointless," Bill answered.

"But in this case ....?"

"....... he was thinking ahead to the inquest. If the police can't show how the trigger was pulled and the Coroner knows his stuff, he can't really bring in a clean verdict of suicide. The Baron seeks to obfuscate in the hope that a more open verdict of 'death by misadventure' is given. Underestimate Konrad at your peril."

"It seems that we're on the same side in wanting to kick the whole matter of Manfred's death into the long grass."

"Now you've got it," said Bill complacently.

---ooo0ooo---

When we reached Badgers I let Bill relate the story and answer most of the many questions that Barbara and Gaby asked. Since he and Barbara would have to live with any of the local outcomes, I wanted him to tell the tale in terms which he found comfortable and were repeatable in respect of how we discovered Manfred's body. Gaby sensed this and waited to quiz me further until after dinner when we were upstairs in bed together.

"I suppose Manfred comes out of this having behaved rather better than we gave him credit for. In a way, shooting himself was the honourable thing to do," she mused.

"He certainly wasn't the villain of the piece as we thought originally. But don't let's overdo it."

" 'His honour rooted in dishonour stood, and faith unfaithful kept him falsely true'," Gaby replied quoting Tennyson once again and I thought of General Kessler.

---ooo0ooo---

CHAPTER 39

THE NEXT FORTNIGHT was an anti-climax in some respects but active otherwise; the final act in the drama was yet to come. We drove back to London together on Tuesday morning and Gaby dropped me off at the office where I had left the Volvo seven days before. Molly was relieved to see me and I had to give her the same account of Tom Hardy's shooting that I had circulated at Leuffen and the news that she should not expect to see him back for several months.

There were messages from Lloyd Parmentier and Viktor Accona to call them and a telex from Barry MacLennan's secretary instructing me to telephone him on Friday.

The first thing I needed to do was to telephone Commissar Vogel's office and leave a message before he called me. As I had hoped he wasn't there; I left my coded message along the lines we had agreed:

"Letter delivered but the bird has expired," I told his office speaking very slowly and had it read back to me. I had no doubt he would call back and had agreed with Bill what I should say.

I called Lloyd next. He approved my schedule for the coming ten days and told me that his task force had settled in and started to make progress. His main concern was finding a new general manager quickly. The head hunters had told him that it would be difficult; in Germany, there were 'no competition' clauses in the contracts of most senior managers which employers usually enforced when a senior employee wanted to leave and join a rival company. Recruitment opportunities, therefore, were limited to managers who had worked in other industries, the implication being that anyone released from another spring maker was likely to be a dud. I asked him if he had thought of making a promotion from within Hartmann & Holst. He replied that Heinrich was too busy in his technical and production role and that Loren might need his help on the US where the AA plants were having difficulty in adjusting to fuel injection specifications. I suggested that he considered Dieter for general manager; Lloyd thought that he was too young and would not command the respect of the workforce.

"Pass it by Heinrich," I said. "You might be surprised by his reaction." Lloyd didn't much like being told what to do.

The rest of the afternoon passed quickly in conversation with the general managers at Tipton, Amsterdam and Norrköping confirming arrangements for my visits with them in the coming days. I told each of them in turn of Tom's 'accident' and that I would be filling in for him until he was better. The Dutch and Swedish managers were concerned and sympathetic; Cyril Snell in Tipton showed little interest.

I left Viktor to last knowing that it was only mid-morning in Farmington and having little to tell him. I had resolved to make no mention of my commitment as envoy for the State Prosecutor and of events in Sussex the previous day; I would give the full story to Chester Case when I next met with him and he would decide whether or not to share it within the corporate office. Viktor was curious about how things were going in Leuffen when and since I left; I relayed the gist of my conversation with Floyd that afternoon including my suggestion of Dieter for the general manager appointment which he thought "interesting". Viktor's news was that Tom Hardy would be transported by charter aircraft to London at the end of the week where he would be placed in a private clinic in St. John's Wood run by nursing sisters of a Catholic order.

I sent Molly home early and was half way through the outer door when the telephone rang in Tom's office; it was, of course, Kurt Vogel.

"I do not understand your message. What is this 'bird has expired'?" he demanded without any preliminaries.

"It means that Manfred Hartmann shot himself after I gave him the letter," I told him. There was a long silence and I thought I heard him talking to someone else on another line.

"What has happened to the letter? Do you have it with you?" he asked finally. "The letter is in the hands of Hartmann's lawyer in Sussex."

"Then you must collect it from this lawyer and return it to me."

"Not possible, Kurt," I responded, trying and failing to sound regretful. "From the moment Manfred took the letter from me it became his property under English law and a part of his estate when he died. His lawyer will decide if and when he can release it; you and I can do nothing. The State Prosecutor's office can call him tomorrow morning," I added helpfully and gave him Bill's name and his firm's telephone number and address.

There was an exasperated sigh from the other end. "Why is it, Julian, you always cause me so much trouble?"

---ooo0ooo---

For the following ten days Gaby and I saw little of each other. On the Thursday morning we both left Porchester Terrace early: Gaby by taxi to Heathrow for her flight to Amsterdam and me to drive up to Tipton where I wanted to pin down the appointment of Bernard Tompkins' successor. As always at Tipton Springs I felt uneasy with the performance of its management. Gerald Snell, the Accounts Manager, seemed solid enough and confirmed that the monthly numbers for June would be with me by the fifth of July but there was no sense of urgency in preparing for the annual stock take. Bernard's young assistant whom I had interviewed previously made a better impression this time. He had realised that there was an opportunity for advancement; he had cleaned up his appearance with a haircut and discarded the suede boots for black shoes. More importantly, he had developed specific sales targets and plans how to achieve them for each of Tipton's top ten customers. I was happy to confirm his appointment as sales manager for review after six months. There had been no response from Erik Nielsen as to Arthur Tompkins' availability; perhaps it wasn't such a good idea anyway.

The main source of my unease, I realised was Cyril Snell. It was not just the distraction of his time and attention on his duties as a JP; there was an absence of enthusiasm and energy, as well as understanding that his company should be doing better, which I thought had probably infected his work force generally. I spent time telling him how to prepare the elements of next year's business plan but came away feeling that he regarded the process as little more than a tiresome chore. That evening, soon after I reached home and was soaking in a hot bath, there was a call from Gaby; she had successfully completed the Amsterdam market research briefing and her client had decided that they could add a further briefing to the schedule in Brussels the next day. Therefore, she would not be back until early Friday evening; I said that I would collect her from Heathrow – "My turn this time," I told her.

Friday at the office was of interest only for the call with Barry MacLennan.

"Now that your crime-busting adventures are over, you can stop playing private eye and get back to business," he directed. "I want you to do two things: carry on with doing Tom's job and start thinking about changes you would make in European operations if you were to take over permanently. Viktor tells me there's no certainty that Tom will make it back. We're going to focus on improvements to all the plants and heavy up on the management effort by adding a financial controller to the European office team. Send me a telex on Monday with your recommendations as a memo of not more than four bullet points. We can discuss fully at the next review when I'm over in three weeks' time."

"Should I copy Lloyd?" I asked.

"Lloyd has enough on his plate at the moment. Telex me first, for my attention. If I like what you say, we can share it with him later. Oh, by the way Julian, if no-one else has said it, thank you for a good job done."

Asking me to telex him direct and cutting out Lloyd Parmentier was not according to the book; was this Barry's way of testing my leadership skills, or was he playing politics? I had changed my Monday flight to Sweden from morning to afternoon, giving me a night in Stockholm before flying down to Norrköping next Tuesday morning.

It was good to have Gaby back on Friday evening and we spent a relaxed weekend with plenty of quality time in bed as we wound down together from the last three unsettling weeks. On Monday, we were both off again: Gaby to Oslo where she was to meet up with her washing machine client and me to the office to send my memo to Barry before setting off to Heathrow once more. I had thought carefully over the weekend about what to write and had decided to be bold. The text I drafted was short and to the point as Barry had instructed:

- Move European office from central to outer London en route to Heathrow: benefits in reduced rent, travel times, and accommodation costs for visitors.
- Appoint AA manager with international experienced as replacement Director of European Sales and Marketing to focus on cross-border specialty markets.
- Monthly reviews by European Director of Operations and Financial Controller at each plant.
- Replace Tipton Springs general manager.

I read it back to myself and decided that the last bullet point was too specific without lengthy explanation; so, I amended it to "Strengthen Tipton Springs management" and sent the telex myself.

On Tuesday I flew down to Norrköpping from Bromma, Stockholm's domestic airport, several hours before Gaby and her crew landed at the international airport Arlanda. After satisfactory meetings there, I flew south again the following morning on another internal flight to Malmo and from there took the ferry to Copenhagen and a second flight to Amsterdam. There had to be a better way to travel to travel to and from the Swedish plant, I thought, and made a note to ask Molly to explore alternatives.

Having checked in at the Amstel hotel I was in good time for dinner with Jan van der Groot. Jan was unique among the European Managers; he had been part educated in Connecticut and spent his vacation as an intern on the shop floor at Farmington. He was the only senior European manager, aside from Heinrich Hoffmeyer, who could claim genuine spring-making experience. We had a pleasant evening gossiping mostly about head office people rather than discussing Ribenda business; on Thursday morning he collected me from the hotel for our review and discussion with his management team in the factory and from there to Schipol late afternoon for a KLM flight to London. Reflecting on my two visits, I decided that the Dutch subsidiary was the more tightly managed with some imaginative management. The Norrköpping factory was also well-managed but Ola Larsen's team were less inspired and I thought they would have difficulty in taking on board the seat belt retractor specialty which had been assigned to them in Rio.

I reached Porchester Terrace quite late having eaten on the plane – KLM food was a distinct improvement on BA fare – and I was deciding over a whisky whether I wanted to eat more when Gaby telephoned from Copenhagen. They had only just arrived at the Admiral hotel after another brief unscheduled visit to Helsinki which the client had added on after Stockholm. In all, they had criss- crossed Scandinavia for briefings of market research teams in four capital cities. Not surprisingly, she sounded weary – a punishing itinerary for even a seasoned traveller which Gaby was not. She gave me the new flight number for her return next day and, for the second week running, I volunteered to collect her from Heathrow.

And so to Friday and the end of the working week. At the office the month-end financial reports from Norrköping and Tipton awaited attention and there were two short telexes from Farmington: the first an invitation or, more accurately, summons from Chester Case to dine with him at his London hotel on Monday; and the second an acknowledgment from Barry MacLennan's office: PREPARE ONE PAGE REPORT ON EACH OF FOUR RECOMMENDATIONS AND SEND BY DHL NEXT WEEK. At least he wanted a considered rather than an instant response.

---ooo0ooo---

Gaby greeted me with weary relief when I met her at Terminal 2; she kept up a chatty account of her adventures on the way back but was flagging by the time we arrived home. It was an evening for a hot bath, a nap in bathrobes and scrambled egg on smoked salmon in the bedroom with a glass of wine. The prelude to a well-earned lazy weekend.

We breakfasted late and the telephone rang in the kitchen while I was putting bread in the toaster. From the moment that Gaby picked up the receiver I could tell that it was Miranda from the megaphone voice – too early in the day for her hearing aid.

"My dears," she trumpeted "I'm calling you while Max and Roderigo are playing golf. He won't want to tell you himself but the crusade to Lake Constance was a complete fiasco. No holy grail on his wretched island."

Gaby made suitably sympathetic noises and Miranda continued. "They found an ancient verger or gravedigger or someone at the church who was there at the end of the war. He remembers that at the beginning of 1945 the Wehrmacht

361

brought loads of heavy boxes across from the shore over two days which he helped bury in the churchyard. Then in 1947 American soldiers came and took it all away."

"So, the US army recovered it and we'll never know how much it was worth?" Gaby said.

"Worse than that," Miranda said. "The gravedigger remembers clearly that there were two officers present in 1947: an American major and a British captain. It was an Allied operation and yet there is nothing which Max could find in the London archives."

"What do Max and Roderigo think now?" Gaby asked.

"Max is very depressed. He thinks that the information was withheld from him deliberately and that MI6 were happy for him to set out on a fool's errand. I really don't know how to cheer him up," Miranda said.

Gaby asked her if she would like to bring Max with Roderigo and his wife to dinner in the coming week as a distraction to brighten him up and Miranda said she would call back after she had consulted them.

We watched Bjorn Borg win his third Wimbledon singles title on television that afternoon and early evening there was another call, this time from Barbara Fentiman in great excitement to tell us that a hand-delivered formal invitation had arrived from Magda von Richthaven summoning her and Bill "with your friends the Radclives" to a concert of chamber music and dinner on the last Saturday of the month. I nodded approval and Gaby asked her to accept for us.

"Of course, I don't have a thing to wear," Barbara said and Gaby agreed with enthusiasm that she too needed something new for this formal occasion.

"Bill has an evening meeting with the Baron's advisers on Monday; if I come up with him could you put us up for the night and then you and I can shop together on Tuesday morning?" Barbara suggested. The arrangement was made and I knew that Bill's and my credit cards would be in for punishment in their Knightsbridge shopping expedition.

On Sunday, after another long lie-in, we decided that it was time to visit Tom in hospital and rang to say that we would be in early afternoon. The nursing home was an anonymous building in a leafy St. John's Wood street with a parking area in front. At first sight it seemed like an expensive block of flats; there was no board outside to inform otherwise. We checked in at the reception desk bearing gifts: a large bunch of flowers from Gaby and a six-pack of champagne splits for Tom's personal sustenance. We were introduced to a smiling Sister Cecilia in her working uniform who wafted us to the third floor in a near noiseless lift and led the way down a wide sunlit corridor. Like the other nursing Sisters in their long skirts whom we passed, she seemed to glide as if on castors rather than walk. Cecilia took us to the last door on the left and admitted us to Tom Hardy's single ward, a pleasant airy room with a balcony overlooking the rear garden. We found Tom sitting in a comfortable chair with all the windows open; he was wearing a maroon silk dressing gown over plain blue pyjamas and slippers; he looked much recovered since I saw him ten days before but unnaturally thin and gaunt. He seemed genuinely pleased to see us and even more when he had examined the champagne.

"It must be my day for visitors," Tom said. "Chester Case was in here this morning and much concerned for my health." He was croaking but his breathing was unassisted albeit still laboured. I hadn't realised that Chester was already in London.

"That's good; everyone's worried about you. You'll probably have Molly in here tomorrow," I said.

We chatted inconsequentially for a time and I told him how things were in the plants I had visited.

"Tomorrow, you have the monthly chore of putting the general managers' reports together and telexing them through. Rather you than I," Tom joked.

"When you expect to get out of here?" Gaby asked.

"The doctor is deciding tomorrow when he has inspected me on his rounds; hopefully not more than three or four days. They're marvellous people here, but I'm getting thoroughly bored," Tom told her.

"Any thoughts yet about when you expect to be back at work?" I asked casually.

"Plenty of thoughts but no plans," he replied. "The family want me to stop working but I can't really afford to. I'll be alright coming back except for the flying. I'm not sure that I can manage regular flights around Europe as you did this past week."

Neither of us wanted to explore the subject further; so we left it at that.

---ooo0ooo---

CHAPTER 40

THE TWO FURTHER monthly reports were on my desk when I reached the office on Monday morning. No issues with the accounting data in either; the Ribenda report was immaculate, and the report from Hartmann & Holst included general manager's 'Where do I stand' comments from Lloyd Parmentier which were a model of succinct information. They could have served, and may well have done later, as a training prototype for aspiring general managers.

We managed to put the consolidated report on telex tape by midday and Molly punched it through to Farmington before lunch. After treating her to a quick snack at the pizzeria, I sent her off to visit Tom in the nursing home and spent the afternoon researching comparative office rents and hotel costs in areas of West London beyond the North Circular for the first part of my report to Barry MacLennan. It occurred to me that Chester Case might question me at dinner on comparative costs if Barry had shared my bullet points telex with him.

When I returned to Porchester Terrace to shower and change Barbara Fentiman was already there; she and Gaby were crouched over the kitchen table with back copies of *Vogue* and *Harper Queen* studying the fashion plate advertisements.

"You've met her in her own home. What do you think Magda will wear?" she asked.

"Oh, any old thing," I said, hoping to steer them away from the more expensive fashion labels.

I dressed carefully in a dark suit with sober tie and joined them briefly before leaving to meet Chester at Duke's hotel where he was staying.

"Shall you be late?" Gaby asked.

"I shouldn't think so. Are you staying in?"

"I'm taking Barbara to the taverna round the corner. You'll find us there, maybe with Bill if you get back early."

"Don't let Stelios seduce you with his bazouki," I said aiming the remark at Barbara.

"More likely Bill than Barbara," Gaby giggled.

---ooo0ooo---

Dukes is a comfortable, conservative hotel in Mayfair, much favoured by East Coast Americans with a taste for Edwardian England. Tucked away in a private close off St. James's, Dukes is less than five minutes walk from the Ritz and Piccadilly. I found Chester waiting for me in the smoking room to the right of reception seated at a corner table with an empty glass in front of him. He looked tanned and relaxed in a blue pin-striped City suit and rose to greet me.

"Good to see you, Julian. I think we can sit here in peace before dining and without being overheard." He waved a hand around the oak-panelled room with its subdued lighting from wall brackets; there was only one other table occupied by two couples at the far end of the room. He called over a waiter who was hovering in the background. "A very dry Martini for me, Dawson, with a twist if lemon – no olive," he said "and for my guest a large Scotch on the rocks with a club soda, if memory serves me right."

"I'm impressed at your mastery of essential information. J & B, if you have it. or Ballantyne's and in a tall glass, please," I said.

"It's an old trick my Dad taught me to put one's guests at ease. 'Remember what a man drinks and you have a pal for life'."

"When did you come over?" I asked to keep the casual conversation going.

"Betsy and I flew in Friday evening for Wimbledon where we were guests on Saturday. Betsy's at the theatre with friends this evening or you would have met her."

Dawson returned with our drinks looking suitably grave. He seemed to have modelled himself on the archetypal English butler of Hollywood movies; he was either an out of work actor, I thought, or just part of the cultivated Dukes atmosphere. He set down our glasses together with bowls of cashew nuts and gherkins.

"We met a friend of yours in the debenture holders bar at the back of Centre Court on Saturday before the final," Chester resumed. "He was singing your praises; name of von Richthaven. Said he owes you a favour."

"Did he tell you why?" I asked.

"He said he was sure you'd tell me if I was interested."

"You'll be interested. In fact, it's the final part of the story that I promised to tell you." I took a first drink of my whisky.

"That's one reason why I asked you here. Tell me your tale. I won't interrupt," Chester Case said, spearing a gherkin with a cocktail stick and taking a measured sip of his martini.

He was as good as his word. I gave him the full story, sparing no detail. The recital took a full twenty minutes including my deal with Kommissar Vogel and the final events in Sussex on the Baron's estate. Chester showed particular interest in parts of the tale; Heinrich Hoffmeyer's intervention at the shooting lodge and the revelation that Peter Hartmann was the only occupant of the crashed Mercedes provoked a raised eyebrow. The final encounter with Manfred Hartmann and Bill Fentiman's custody of the State Prosecutor's letter were met with appreciative nods. When I had finished and taken another draught:

"That's quite a saga. I think we'll keep the last part to ourselves for the moment. Only one question, really: how watertight are we against bad publicity now in Germany?" Chester asked.

"Water resistant, I'd say, but not hermetically sealed. Better off than if Manfred had died in the car crash; they can't connect him directly with the drugs bust."

"How reliable is your friend Fentiman?"

"He's my oldest friend, Chester, and I trust him completely. He'll find reasons not to hand back the letter for a year or so until the dust settles. Without that in their possession the State Prosecutor won't make a meal of the episode," I said looking at him squarely in the eye.

"If I've offended you, Julian, I apologize. My reason for pressing the point is that I am here in London, not just for the tennis but to discuss a listing for Allied Autoparts on the Stock Exchange. We are already listed on the Big Board in New York and we can list here without too much cost or hassle. Bad publicity would be fatal; so, it's important we have closure."

"Understood. Closure here, yes but there's still one weak link: Brazil and von Falkenberg," I said.

"I have news for you on that front," Chester said patting a slim leather document case at the side of his chair and glancing at his even slimmer gold wristwatch, "but I'll keep it as a surprise for your dessert. Time now for us to eat."

Dukes dining room was in keeping with its smoking room: faded rose-painted walls, velvet green curtains, electric candlelight from brass wall sconces and oil paintings of serious Edwardian gentlemen and elegant ladies who might have been descendants of those on the walls of the von Richthaven salon. We sat side by side on a long banquette, our backs to a wall, and studied the menu.

"I always eat lamb when I'm here in England; the lamb in America is poor, like your steaks compared to ours," Chester Case said. He was half right but I didn't argue with him.

We both ordered saddle of lamb from the trolley, carved at the table, with smoked trout as our first course; Chester ordered a bottle of Volnay from the wine list, a tame choice but more than adequate.

"You have a talent as a detective. Have you thought of taking it up as a career? We could create a position of AA Corporate Compliance Officer for you," he said reopening the conversation.

"I doubt that I would be more than a one-trick pony as a corporate dick. Anyway, it doesn't sound like much of a career," I said treating the thought as a joke and not, I hoped, a serious suggestion.

"You're quite right. Let's talk about what we have in mind for you." He cut off a piece of fish and dipped it in horseradish sauce before eating.

"As you've probably guessed, we want to appoint you Director of European Operations. You have the backing of Lloyd and Barry," he continued.

"What about Tom? I'm happy to keep his seat warm until he comes back, but I don't want to displace him."

"Tom won't be coming back. Having visited him in hospital, it's good to see that he's recovering but he's never going to manage the increased air travel which you've identified in your telex to Barry. We'll award him full pension rights to retirement; Viktor will put it to him later in the week." The verdict still seemed harsh although logical.

"I feel responsible for getting him shot," I said.

"He knew what he was doing; so, no feelings of guilt at profiting from his injury. The job you've outlined needs a younger man anyway," Chester Case said flatly.

The waiter removed our fish plates. The cover to the meat trolley was rolled back and slices of lamb from the sizzling joint were carved and placed before us accompanied by redcurrant jelly and vegetables. Chester tasted the wine as a formality and our glasses were charged.

"Alright. Let's talk about the job as you and Barry see it," I said.

"The Allied Autoparts subsidiaries in Europe need a shot in the arm. Aside from Ribenda, they don't give a decent return on our investment; the Board are coming under pressure from investors and the financial analysts. With the ideas you are giving to Barry you are preaching to the converted," Chester said raising his glass to me. I returned the gesture.

"And the addition of a CPA to the London office team is a part of the new focus?"

"You've got it. How do you feel about having a bean counter on board under your direction but reporting to Erik Nielsen?"

"That depends on who Erik dumps on me. Some of my best friends are qualified accountants," I answered, enjoying my first taste of succulent lamb.

"The leading candidate is Fred Simpson, currently in Leuffen as a member of Lloyd Parmentier's task force."

"I've met him but I haven't spent time with him yet. At least, he's getting European experience at the deep end," I commented.

"Tell me about the economic advantage of moving the London office, as you've suggested," Chester said, spearing a sprout and changing the subject.

"I haven't completed my research, but I estimate that we could find one in a modern block with fifty per cent more space at about half the current rental."

"If we can do that, the cost saving will cover the expense of adding a Financial Controller to the team."

"Do you want to talk about my other suggestions?" I said.

"No. That's for you to discuss with Barry including the terms of your appointment. You'll be reporting to him until Lloyd is through with his Leuffen exploits. Time now for the surprise I promised you with dessert."

Chester Case unzipped his document case and passed me the June edition of the Alled Autoparts house magazine with the familiar AA logo in blue on the masthead. The front page story was the recent international managers' meeting in Rio with an account of the proceedings and quotes from Chester, Barry and several delegates under the open air group photograph taken at the hotel. In the right hand column, boxed heavily, was a regular feature headed *'Manager of the Month'*. Staring at me was a head and shoulders blow-up from the main photograph over the caption 'Frederik von Falkenburg, General Manager Grunwald Metallwerk, Allied Autoparts new subsidiary in Brazil' and the beginning of an article '(contd. p3)' which read 'Formerly the wartime associate of NASA's Dr. Wehrner von Braun, Frederik brings with him a long experience in developing facilities and original equipment manufacture'

The page 3 follow-on contained a description of the two Amparo plants and a passing reference to 'rocket technology in Germany'. The meat of the story was the front page identification of Frederik's past.

While I was reading and admiring Viktor Accona's editorial handiwork we finished our main course and the dessert menus arrived. I chose a blackcurrant sorbet while my host went for lemon meringue pie.

"Won't you take something more? Chester asked.

"No thank you. There's enough here in the magazine to satisfy my appetite. Viktor's done a good job of character assassination but how can it be deployed to neutralise von Falkenberg," I said.

"Viktor's excelled himself with a little help from Barry. He normally sends copies to the Commercial Counsellors in Washington at the embassies of the countries where we do business. This time he extended circulation to include our ally at the Eastern end of the Mediterranean. Frederik was invited to Farmington for a discussion with Barry on development opportunities in other markets of Latin America. The meeting broke up today and he's on his way right now to Kennedy with a company driver to catch a flight home. Arrangements have been made, I'm told, to meet him at the airport." "How will we hear what happens?" I asked.

"I'm expecting a telex from Viktor within the hour. Shall we take our coffee and a cigar, perhaps, while we wait?" Chester Case suggested.

---ooo0ooo---

CHAPTER 41

COUNT FREDERIK VON FALKENBERG relaxed in the back seat of the Buick Electra sedan which the Farmington office had supplied to ferry him in air-conditioned comfort to Kennedy where he was booked on the evening PanAm flight back to Rio de Janeiro. His driver, a retired Allied Autoparts employee supplemented his pension by driving senior AA managers to and from John F. Kennedy or Boston's Logan airport; he was dressed informally in slacks, a windbreaker and open-neck shirt. He drove smoothly at a constant 49 mph, just below the freeway speed limit. Often his passengers, usually arrivals, chose to travel in the front passenger seat and chat. Today, his taciturn and arrogant-looking passenger had swept into the back as if being chauffeured was a matter of right. He had spoken barely a word since they left and any polite questions had been rebuffed curtly or even ignored.

There was something comforting about passing under the succession of bridges over the freeway through lower Connecticut as they drew steadily nearer to his destination. He would have preferred not to suffer the scent of the air freshener which permeated the car and added that to his mental list of things he hated about Americans. He realised, of course, that bringing him here all the way from Brazil for a half day discussion had been a charade: the first move in a plan to remove him from office without paying compensation for terminating his employment contract. However, von Falkenburg had gone along with his reassignment to a role of roving 'corporate development consultant' because it suited him. Sooner or later that ridiculous group photograph into which he had been coerced would attract attention from his enemies and there were places in South America safer than Brazil where wealthy exiles like himself could live comfortably and undisturbed. Already he had rented an apartment in a fashionable part of Asuncion in a new name as the prelude to a change of identity and Luiz Otavio, his steward , was engaged in shipping his paintings there from the house in Amparo. Many of his old friends and comrades had already made the transfer. Even the long arm of Mossad found it almost impossible to extract their prey from Paraguay's capital city.

He had decided to take Izabel with him for two reasons: it would be easier to enter Asuncion society with a glamorous companion as his mistress than alone; also, she was a very compliant companion and would continue to satisfy his needs for some years yet. Brazilian women tended to lose their looks and figures before they reached the age of thirty and it was important to assess how well their mothers had adapted to advancing years; Izabel's mother was still a handsome woman at forty; so she passed the test. He could be confident of ten years or more with Izabel before needing to trade her in for a younger model.

Planning for the future continued to occupy von Falkenburg's mind until the Buick drew up at the airport PanAm terminal for international flights.

The driver found a baggage trolley for him and helped unload his luggage: only one suitcase for this short trip and a flight bag. He proffered a twenty dollar bill, but the driver looked offended and drove off without wishing him a good flight. There was a short queue of two middle-aged and one young couple ahead of him at the check-in desk; he stood in line and became aware that two men had joined him, one on either side. The one on his left was young with a crew cut and tanned face wearing a leather bomber jacket and jeans. The one on his right was a taller older man with a sallow connection and greying hair; he was wearing a cheap blue twill suit and thick-sole shoes.

"Mr. Falkenburg," the older man addressed him politely. "I need to speak to you for a moment. My colleague will look after your bags. Please step this way." His accent was not quite American and he couldn't quite place it.

The man took his right elbow in a surprisingly strong grip and steered him towards the centre of the concourse. Von Falkenburg noticed the top of a folded magazine in the pocket of the man's suit with the letters 'AA' on the header.

"What is this all about? I don't know you, and I have no business with you," he said.

"I'm afraid you do," the man replied firmly and he felt a sharp sting in the back of his thigh.

Then everything happened quickly with rehearsed precision. Von Falkenburg felt the urge to sit down and suddenly the edge of a wheelchair was thrust behind his knees. He sat. Handling the chair was a youngish woman in nurse's uniform who pressed his shoulders down so that he couldn't rise. And he felt increasingly unable to do anything. His legs and arms clenching the arms of the chair were becoming rapidly numb and extreme weariness overtook him. Soon he was unable to move at all and found that when he tried to shout for help no one could hear him speak; his mouth opened and shut like a goldfish.

"We'll take good care of you, Count von Falkenburg," the nurse said and placed a pair of sunglasses on his nose so that the distress in his eyes remained unnoticed. The man in the suit bent down and placed his feet on the footrest of the wheelchair, then covered his knees with a rug. He found that his hearing and sight were unimpaired so that he could understand what was happening to him as they wheeled him away from the PanAm line in full sight of anyone passing. Out of the corner of his left eye he noticed that the younger man was pushing the trolley with his bags alongside.

The man in the suit took his passport from his breast pocket and the air ticket which he tore up and dumped in a litter bin as the three of them crossed the concourse. Where were they taking him; Some safe house in downturn Manhattan or perhaps away from New York City? The reality was worse. The little group moved briskly into the next terminal for non-American airlines and fetched up in front of another check-in desk. The leader of his kidnappers took three air tickets from his pocket and handed one to the baggage handler and two to the nurse.

"My friends will take care of you on your journey. Have a pleasant flight, Count," he said and then to the others. "You'll be met at the other end. Give him another jab every six hours. I'm leaving you now; I have a telephone report to make."

Von Falkenburg looked up. The airline was EL AL and his destination Tel Aviv.

---ooo0ooo---

At Dukes hotel we had retreated from the restaurant to the residents smoking room with our coffee and the rest of the wine. Chester Case selected a Monte Cristo No 1 from the cigar humidor offered by Dawson with reverence and clipped with due ceremony. We did not have long to wait. Soon after ten o'clock Dawson reappeared with a silver salver bearing an envelope addressed to 'Chester Case Esq.' Chester told him that there would be no reply and extracted a telex. As he slit the envelope Chester nodded towards the retreating Dawson.

"He does rather overdo it, doesn't he?" he said.

"Yes, but we all enjoy the performance, don't we," I replied.

The telex was short. Chester Case read for a few seconds and passed it to me; the message was cryptic:

ATTN: CHESTER CASE. PACKAGE DELIVERED JOHN F. KENNEDY. RECEIPT CONNFIRMED. LIFT-OFF 17:20 EST.

RGDS VA

"Does that mean we have closure?" I asked.

Chester poured the last of the wine and we raised our glasses. He gave me his Ivy League campus grin.

"They never come back, you know," he said.

---ooo0ooo---

THE END

Lightning Source UK Ltd.
Milton Keynes UK
UKHW012141231221
396150UK00001B/81